ANNA'S MAKE

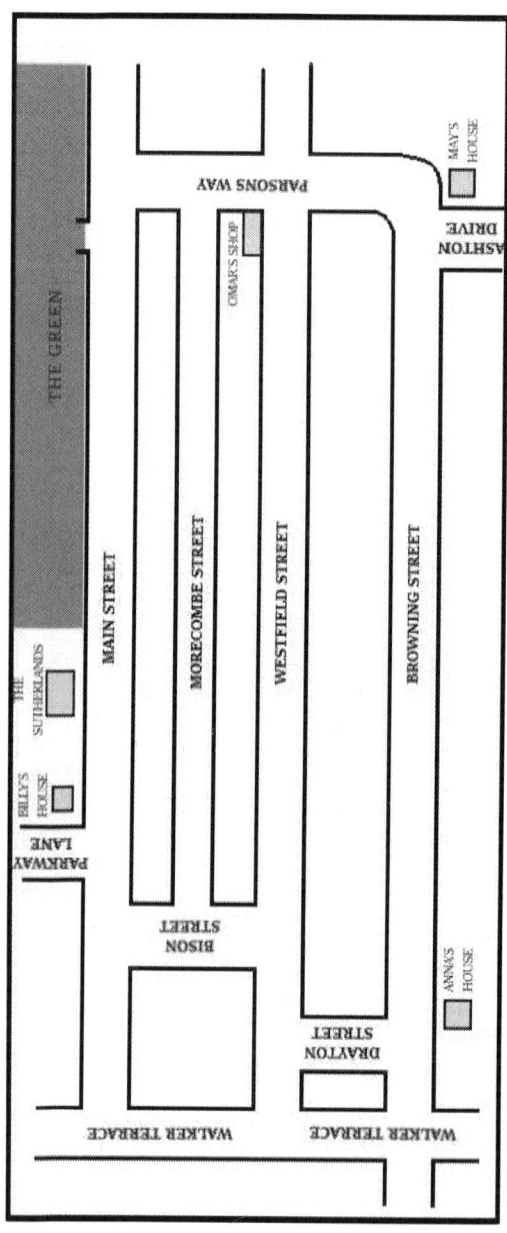

1

Anna Ross opened her eyes and fear squeezed her throat as if a boa constrictor had her firmly in its grasp. She jerked her head around from one side then the other, taking in her surroundings with wide eyes. She was lying on a black padded bed and was wearing what looked like a robe, but not made of any kind of fabric she had ever seen. It was silky or velvety, she could not decide, it was grey in colour, it seemed to shimmer weirdly. The room she was in was light and bright. The walls, ceiling and floor were all white, so much so that she could hardly tell where the floor finished and the wall started. She put her hand to the back of her head; she found it strange that she felt nothing out of the ordinary. The last thing she remembered was being hit very hard.

Where the hell am I? Tom must be wondering where I am. I wonder how long I have been here. It's got to be the person who hit me on the head; they must be keeping me here. I wonder if this is one of the cults you hear about, people being held against their will until they finally get brainwashed enough to join the nutters. I am so scared and confused. At least this room is clean... how can I think of something like that at a time like this, it is true though people get held in more filthy places than this. Rex got hurt I heard him yelp, I hope he is ok and made it home, if he did then surely alarm bells will be ringing with Tom. I'm dreaming. That's got to be it, I'm unconscious from the hit on my head, or maybe the blow to my head is part of the dream as well. I just don't know.

She knew she didn't have her watch on, but looked at her wrist to be sure, no not there. Anna looked up to the ceiling, the light in the room was small and round, it seemed to let off more light than it should. There was no evidence of a door; everything seemed to blend together because it was all the same colour. Slipping off the bed she held out a hand and moved towards the wall, she was steadier on her feet than she anticipated. The room was bigger than it appeared to be, she was deceived into thinking that she would be at the wall in four steps, in reality it took eight.

There must be a door here somewhere. Why the robe? I need to get out of here Tom will be going out of his mind that I'm not back. I saw someone, just before I was hit, I saw that young woman, the one that's been missing for months, it didn't say on the local news that she was pregnant. I must be out of my mind if I think this could be real, I need to wake up from this nightmare.

A door appeared in the wall opposite, a man stepped in. The door closed behind him. He stood there just looking at her. He was at least six foot eight inches tall, with dark skin and dark eyes. Anna thought he was handsome in a pretty sort of way. He looked quite young; maybe about twenty-five, she thought that he would be popular in the modelling world as he had a unique look about him. He too was wearing a robe of the same fabric as the one Anna wore; the only difference was that his was whiter than snow.

'Where am I?' Anna asked with anger in her voice.

'Anna all your questions will be answered, I promise you that. First lay back down on the bed, there is something important I must tell you,' the tall man said calmly.

'How do you know my name? I don't know you.'

The tall man ignored her question.

'My name is Ravi and I am going to make you understand all that has happened to you. Lay down on the bed then we can begin.'

Ravi moved towards her, took her by the arm and guided her to the bed. Anna walked slowly, looking up at the stranger as she allowed him to lead her. She was so confused by this whole situation, fear made her do as she was told, she didn't want to anger or upset him as she didn't know him or what he could be capable of.

'I am going to tell you things that you will not believe at first, but I will make you understand and accept what is happening to you,' Ravi said in an even tone as he stood by the bedside.

'Please just let me go home, I won't tell anyone any of this, you don't need to do whatever it is you're planning to do. I am a good person, I don't deserve this. I have a husband who will be very worried about me. He will call the police if I'm not home soon. Exactly how long have I been here? My little dog needs me, he's been hurt.' Anna couldn't stop herself, she was angry. 'Why are you doing this? I won't say anything about the girl I saw in that shed.'

Ravi held up his hand and waved it in front of her face slowly and calmly in one motion. Anna didn't know why or how, she just knew that she had to stop talking long enough to let this man speak. It was if he had put some kind of a spell on her.

'Now I going to tell you everything you need to know, all I ask of you is to let me finish, then I am sure you will have lots of questions which I will answer for you,' Ravi looked at her as she nodded her agreement as if a little defeated.

'Anna you were murdered,' he blurted.

'No I can't be that would mean that I am dead are you insane,' she spat just before she remembered she had promised to listen.

Murdered, does he really expect me to believe all this bullshit? So what is he trying to tell me that I'm in heaven or hell, if there is a heaven or hell? I'm sure he's not planning on letting me go home that's for sure.

'I am going to have to convince you of this' Ravi said as he waved his hand in front of her again.

'I have just given you some understanding by doing that with my hand. It is not a trick. It is a gift given to me by The Supreme,' Ravi waited for a moment to let this all sink in.

'Now you know you are dead Anna and I will only use my gift again if you have trouble understanding or dealing with what I am about to tell you.'

'I don't know how you did that, but I do believe now I am dead. I know I was murdered. I saw too much in that shed, that girl, I can't even remember her name. I saw her on the local news, she's been missing for so long. She has been right there all this time,' Anna said with resignation.

I'm really dead, I know that now, I am willing to accept it as much as I don't want to. Who is The Supreme? I wonder what happens next. I guess that's what Ravi is going to tell me.

'Anna you are in what you would call heaven, but the true name is The Realm. Well you are not truly in The Realm just yet; no one goes straight into The Realm unless their make is pure white. A make is what we call the robe you have on, the darker the make, the darker your soul. Once your make is white you are allowed to enter The Realm. Children sometimes go straight in because they haven't had any bad thoughts or did any bad actions, usually anyone under three years old will have a white make and will be allowed straight in. At the moment you are in The Before, which is kind of like a waiting room and work area where you have to work to get your make white. Do you understand so far?'

Anna nodded her head as the tears softly rolled down her ashen face. She did understand, she was gutted that she was no longer alive.

'Now there is only one Supreme, That is the one who is called many different things by many different people, I believe you call The Supreme God. Many other people use many different names like Jehovah, Allah and Brahman. There is only one Supreme, the same one for all religions. 'Ravi paused there for a second before continuing.

'The Supreme is the only one to allow access to The Realm, and only when your make is white.'

'How exactly do you get your make white?'

'There is a programme here that makes you go through all your bad thoughts and actions, if you totally realise why the thought or action was wrong then your make will get whiter. Not every wrong thought you have will add a shade of grey to your make, over time it builds up shade on shade. A single bad action can add a shade. Some actions will add many shades. Some single actions will turn your make black, but that's a conversation for another day, 'Ravi spoke softly he had said these words many times to souls. This was his destiny.

'How many shades do I have, and how long until I'm allowed in The Realm?'

'You have twenty-three shades and how long it takes will depend on you. I have a proposition for you; you are in a very special position. When someone comes here and they already have a pure soul, they are known as an Innocent. The Supreme requests you to save an Innocent, if you choose to accept you will have ten shades lifted from your make. If you refuse the request twenty shades will be added,' Ravi said.

I don't think I have an option here. I might as well try. The punishment for refusal seems a little harsh. I can only give it my best effort.

'I will do it, I will help save the Innocent, just tell me how and who. This is all a bit crazy; I don't even know if I will be able to do this, although I want to try.' More tears made their way down her face as she said the words, resigned to the fact that her life was over and was now in the afterlife.

'That's a good decision Anna,' Ravi answered with a slight smile on his face. 'We should get started right away. You will be put back down on Earth as soon as you are told the rules and the consequences for breaking them, then I will answer any questions you may have. The young lady you saw in the shed, her name is Jasmine Brown and her baby is the Innocent you will try to save.'

'Why is she being held there?'

'The people that have her want The Innocent to bring up as their own.'

2
Thursday 14th November 2019

Tom Ross awoke to the sound of some sort of scratching. He rubbed his eyes and stretched, then sat up on the couch where he had fallen asleep. He heard the noise again, with a puzzled expression he walked out to the hall where he stopped and strained to listen. There it was again, it was coming from the back door. He walked to the door in the dimly lit kitchen; the only light in here was coming from the hall. He opened the door; Rex walked in limping and whimpering and went straight under the kitchen table. Tom immediately switched on the light and went over and sat on the floor next to him.

'What's wrong boy, what's happened to you?' Over his shoulder and in the direction of the hall he shouted. 'Anna there's something wrong with Rex,' he thought that Anna was upstairs, so he shouted again.

Then he wondered how Rex got out. If they let Rex out in the garden they usually leave the back door open and make sure the gate is closed.

Tom gave Rex a pat on the head. He couldn't see any blood which was reassuring, but the dog wasn't limping and crying for nothing.

'I'm going to go and get your mummy then we

will get you seen to.'

He went to the bottom of the stairs and shouted again, upon receiving no answer he went up. There was no sign of her anywhere. When he got back down the stairs he looked for Rex's lead, it always hung over the back of the chair closest to the back door. It was gone. Rex gave another cry from under the table.

'It's ok boy. Did she let you off your lead again when she had you out for a walk? Were you a bad boy and run away from her? She will probably be looking for you.'

Tom walked back into the living room and lifted his mobile from the floor next to the couch where he had been sleeping and called Anna. He hung up when he could hear her ringtone coming from the kitchen. He walked back through and saw the phone on the counter top and sat back down on the floor next to his dog. They had got him from The Dog's Trust two years ago. Rex was a small brown dog, a mixed breed, scruffy, totally adorable; it was love at first sight. They didn't know his exact age; the vet at Dog's Trust reckoned he would be around three years old when they got him. Tom looked at his mobile, he would need to call the vet, Rex was in pain that was obvious. He also had to go and find Anna to let her know Rex was home. He made another call first.

'Hello.'

'Hello, George I know it's late; however, I really need you to come over, Anna has taken Rex for a walk and he must have got away from her, you know how she likes to let him walk home without the lead on when there is no one around . I have warned her about it, you know what she's like,' Tom explained to Anna's dad. 'I need to go look for her so maybe you could take the dog to the vet if I can get hold of them.'

'Anna not got her phone with her? Why the vet, has he been injured?'

'Yes George he has, I don't know how. He is limping and crying and no her mobile is here.'

'I will phone the Village Vet before I leave, you just find Anna, I'm sure Rex will be fine till I get there.' George said just before Rex gave another cry.

'I can hear him, poor thing. Tell you what you take him, I will look for Anna, she can't be far away. I will go round the long way past The Green, I'm sure she will be home before I get there.' George had a husky voice which had always calmed and reassured Tom.

'Sounds like plan, see you soon George, bye.'

'I'm sure the dog will be fine, try not to worry, bye.'

The town of Hallington where they lived is just on the outskirts of Edinburgh. The Andersons had lived here all their lives and are well known in the town. George had been a bus driver since he was twenty one and had just recently retired. Ruby works in Smith's Chemist and had been there since Anna was five years old. They were a pretty normal couple, they both played bowls at their local club, where they have been members for twelve years now. Ruby had the most amazing red hair when she was younger, with the grey shining through she opted to dye it dark brown. She thought grey hair looked a bit better on men, which was just as well, because what hair George had left was totally grey. With green eyes and high cheek bones, George always tells her it was her eyes that had struck the first chord in his heart. Ruby was always slim and even lost her baby weight no problem after both her pregnancies. They were both the same height at five foot ten, George insists he is taller at every opportunity; Ruby humours him, lets him have it, thinks it's good for his ego. Swimming was Ruby's sport of choice and always tried to encourage her husband to join her as he could do with losing a few pounds especially round the middle, he never takes her up on the offer. He says walking is his thing and he will stick to that.

George filled Ruby in on what was happening before he left the house, she wanted to go with him, but he told her he would give her a call as soon as he found Anna. He looked at his phone after he put on his clothes, quicker than he had done for a long time. It was 11.05 pm.

Tom called the vet as soon as he hung up from George, he was told to bring the dog in right away; there is always a vet at the surgery to look after the overnighters. He was also told it would be an out of hours appointment therefore would cost more, Tom didn't care about that, he just wanted his little dog out of pain, he just wished that Anna was going with him. The vet took his details, said her name was Katie and she would see him soon. Tom had a pair of grey jogging bottoms and a grey t-shirt on. He didn't want to waste time so he pulled his trainers onto his bare feet, grabbed his car key and wallet from the table, opened the back door, moved the key from the inside lock to the outside lock then bent down to his poorly dog.

'Come on boy time to go in the car for a trip to the vet, need to get you sorted.'

He leaned forward and carefully put his arms around his beloved pet and shuffled Rex towards him gently. Rex let out another whimper, but he let Tom lift him up from the floor. Keeping a loving hold on his dog Tom managed to lean over, get the door locked and get him in the car.

'I will take it easy on the bumps pal. I know

you're in pain. I wish I knew what happened and where your Mummy is,' Tom spoke softly and sullenly, he wanted Rex to understand him in that moment.

The drive to vet took about a quarter of an hour, it seemed longer to Tom as he listened heartbroken to his companion whimpering. Upon arriving he noticed a light in the front window and the door slightly ajar, Katie was ready and waiting for him. He parked in the closest spot, hurriedly went around the car and gingerly lifted Rex out and took him in.

'You must be Tom and this must be Rex,' Katie said to them both as they came through the door. She was standing behind the counter in front of a computer with a pale blue top and trousers on. Her light brown hair was tied up in a bun on the top of her head; green eyes sparkled behind her dark framed glasses. She stood at five-foot-six and had a muscular, medium build.

'Yes and thanks so much for seeing him at this time of night.'

He realised that he didn't exactly know what time it was. He didn't know where Anna was and he didn't know what happened to Rex. He felt helpless.

'It's a pleasure and of course it's my job. Bring him through,' she said as she led the way into one of the three rooms leading from the reception area.

Everything about the surgery was plain. Light grey walls with a row of plastic chairs lined up along the window and a separate three chair area in the far corner by the side window with a sign on the wall saying it was the Cats' Corner. Tom followed Katie into the room and very softly laid Rex down on the table. The examination room was painted the same colour as the waiting room with the usual stuff you would find here, scales, a laptop on a small table in front a few shelves that housed medications.

'Well what happened to you?' Katie asked directing her question to Rex as she always did with her furry patients.

'I've not got a clue what has happened to him. He was scratching at the door, when I opened it I found him like this, I believe my wife Anna took him for a walk. He must have got off the lead somehow,' Tom replied for Rex missing out the part that Anna always let him off the lead.

'You believe your wife took him for a walk?' Katie asked a little curious that he wasn't sure.'

'I was sleeping and woke up with Rex scratching at the door. It's the only explanation. Anna must still be looking for him. I hope her dad has found her by now to let her know that Rex is here with me. Do you think he could have been hit with a car?'

'It is possible. Let's have look, see if we can find any obvious injuries,' Katie said as she gave Rex a little rub on the head.

Katie came round the long side of the rectangular table and placed her hands gently under the dog to get a feel about and a good look. Rex yelped as she pressed his right side. She continued on, looking through his fur for any sign of blood, feeling and pressing as Rex yelped when she touched a tender spot.

'It could be possible that he has a couple of cracked ribs. I can't say for sure without an x-ray. He certainly has a bit of tenderness to his right back leg. If he has broken or cracked ribs on that side it would affect that leg. Is he limping?'

'Yes he is.'

She lifted him off the table to have a look at the limp for herself. He was reluctant to walk. Tom encouraged him into doing a few steps, afterward Katie lifted him back up onto the table.

'I would like to keep him over night and do an x-ray in the morning if that's ok.'

'Yes of course that's fine.'

'I will give him some pain killers tonight, will need to sedate him in the morning for the x-ray, try not to worry. Give us a call maybe around eleven o'clock tomorrow morning and we will fill you in on what we find.' Katie said as she gave Rex another pat on the head.

'That's great thank-you,' and to Rex he said, 'I will see you in the morning, be a good boy for Katie.'

Tom bent down and gave his pet a kiss on the head like he always did, Rex gave him a big lick on the face just like *he* always did.

'Right I will speak to you tomorrow Katie.'

'Yes you will, don't worry, he is in excellent hands.'

3

After another wave of his magic hand Anna now sat at a table across from Ravi in the same room where she had lain on the bed. The table and chairs were red in colour and reminded her of the dining set in her sister Clara's kitchen, they were the same colour. Not made from the same material though. Clara's were a hard plastic; she wasn't sure which type of material these were. Probably something that is unique to the afterlife.

Ravi broke her train of thought. 'Anna along with the rules I have a few other things to tell you before you go. As you may or may not know by now you cannot feel anything physical, like pain or cold, you do have emotional feelings like empathy, joy, sadness and fear.'

'Will I still need to sleep? Will I still feel hungry?' Anna asked curiously.

'You will not feel hunger. You will need to sleep, not as much as a living person does. I will warn you that loneliness and boredom will make you want to sleep more, three hours a day will be sufficient for you.'

'What do you mean loneliness and boredom?'

'Let me explain. There is going to be only three people that you will be able to make a certain amount of contact with, this is your power. I can't tell you who these people are, that is something you will need to figure out on your own I'm afraid. You will not be able to do this in the normal manner of just speaking to them and them hearing you. The best way to make contact is to do this when they are sleeping, through their subconscious. You must say Anna Anderson, the full name you were given at birth. If they hear you, you will get some sort of response, they may mumble or move about or wake up. Once you achieve this then through time and effort you can start to plant the truth in their minds, then if it is possible they can start to help. No one alive will be able to see you.'

'Wait a minute you said no one alive will be able to see me, what does that mean?'

'It means Anna that you may come into contact with other souls down there. They will be able to hear and see you as if you were both alive.' Ravi paused for a moment then continued.

'These other souls are on missions of their own and some may have been down there for a while.'

'Am I to interact with these souls if I come across any?'

'I will get to that soon as one of the rules I spoke about does concern them.'

Anna sat in silence for a few moments to let everything she had just heard sink in. Ravi let her.

How am I to find these three people? What other souls that maybe around me? This is going to be a lot harder than I first anticipated. Will the loneliness get the better of me? What will I do all day if it is better to try to make contact when people are asleep? I just can't lift a book or flick through my Facebook when I want. Maybe I could watch TV if someone else is watching it. I still have so many questions.

'Ravi how do I get about, do I walk through walls like you see in the movies?'

'You could do it that way. You just need to close your eyes and think of where you want to go or who you want to be with. This could mean moving from one side of your town to another or just going from one room to another. Walking through walls will take a lot longer to do than what you would see in the movies. It would take about an hour for you to pull your soul through a wall and will drain you causing you to need much more sleep. Think of moving from place to place like teleportation. You have seen that in the movies haven't you?'

'Yes I have and that sounds cool. What is worrying me most is what I am to do all day? When everyone is awake and I can't contact them. Am I allowed to sit with my family?'

'Anna your main purpose here is to save the Innocent. You will need to spend a lot of your time with Jasmine Brown. Her kidnappers will be there too, so this may help you gather important information, little, subtle things that may not seem important might help you save the Innocent. You can go visit your loved ones from time to time; you have to pick your moments carefully. You don't want to miss anything that might help with your purpose.'

'I don't know if I can do this.'

'All that we are asking is that you try Anna. This baby needs your help and we are asking you to do this because of the connection, you have seen where Jasmine is. You now know her situation.'

'No pressure then.' Anna responded a little sarcastically.

'I am not going to say it will be easy or that you will succeed, I know that you will give this your best effort.'

'How long do I get once I'm back down on earth' Ravi pondered for a moment. 'Three to four months.'

'That's when the baby will be due isn't it?'

'Give or take, yes.'

'So when do I go?' Anna said positively as if she had found new determination within herself.'

I need to save that baby no matter what it takes. Just saying the words about the baby being due has made me realise just how important this is, failing is not an option for me.

'First Anna I must tell you the rules.'
'Oh I forgot for a moment there was going to be rules.'
'The first rule is about the other souls, you will see and hear them; however, you must not take yourself away from your task to help them with theirs, no matter how much they ask you. They may not be saving an Innocent, but have important business to do of their own that is why you can't ask them to help you with your mission. Along with each rule comes a consequence. If you break this rule two shades will be added to your make.'
'Can I talk to them? Will I see the colour of their make?' Anna asked
'You may acknowledge these other souls, again do not forget what you are being put down there to do. Yes you will see the colour of their make.'
'Will I see the colour of the souls of the living?'
Ravi had answered these questions many times so responded as he always did. 'No Anna you will not, you will see them just as you did when you were alive. The next rule is most important that you do not break it for it carries a huge price for you to pay. Do not, I repeat, do not enter into a graveyard. If people are buried alive their souls cannot escape and come here

because the earth's soil is on top of them and a soul cannot travel through this. The soul will eventually be released after fifty years; this is a long, lonely time for a soul to spend. If you go into a graveyard and one such soul happens to be buried there they can sense you and they will hold you there like a magnet to them. Don't forget they may have been there for a long time on their own and will keep you there for the company, you will only be released from the graveyard when they are.'

'Are you telling me that people get buried alive at their funeral?' Anna asked incredulously.

'Anna this is very, very rare, I am not trying to scare you. I am only warning you because in the very long time we have been sending souls back down there, two have been trapped in this manner. If you enter into one, along with the sentence you will pay by being held there two shades will be added to your make for breaking the rule.'

'What if someone is buried alive by someone else in another place and I happen to go near them?' Anna asked.

'They will still be able to draw you in and keep you there until they are released, this has never happened. The people that bury someone in this manner are usually murderers. They like to make sure their victim is dead,' Ravi explained in a sort of reassuring tone.

'Stay away from graveyards then, got it,' Anna confirmed

'The third rule will wreck your mission if you break it so be very aware of this. You must not communicate anything you have seen or heard up here to any of the three people that you may be able to make contact with. Everyone will have to learn all of this on their own. If you break this rule you will be straight back here with five shades added to your make.' Ravi said this sternly to make his point.

'I understand. If I break this rule the Innocent will not be saved.'

'Do you have any more questions Anna?'

'What about psychics or spiritualists?'

'If you come across one, good luck with that.'

'What do you mean by that?'

There are only three true connectors as we call them down there, the chances you come across one will be very slim,' Ravi went on. 'Now have you any more questions?'

'No I think I've got what I need though I don't know if I'm ready.'

'You need to be Anna because you will be going soon. I need to warn you, you will go back to the place you died first so be prepared to see your dead body, they may not have got rid of it right away.'

'Oh I have thought of another question. What if I need you for something?'

'All you have to do is say my name. I have a few other souls to look after. I will get to you as soon as I can.'

4

Tom hurried to his car when he left the vet. He had only one thing on his mind now and that was Anna. As soon as he closed the car door he took the mobile from his pocket and called Anna's number.

'Come on, come on, come on,' he said to himself while impatiently tapping the steering wheel.

It went to voicemail, he was sure she was going to pick up; she should have been home by now he thought. He looked at the time. 11.55. He didn't know what to think. He felt utterly lost.

George pulled his car over when he heard his phone ringing, just a normal ring tone none of the fancy tunes as he would put it. Just something that you would know it was a phone and not a music device. He was old fashioned that way, didn't go in much for the latest technology.

'Tom I haven't found her yet. I went right around and around the circuit she would go, there's no sign of her anywhere. I'm getting a little worried and so is Ruby. She's called me three times since I left the house. Do you think we should try The Green?'

The Green was the name the local people of the town call Hallington Park.

'She would never go in the park after dark, no way,' Tom said adamantly. 'I'm beside myself here George. I just tried to ring her. I was sure she would be back by now and would answer her phone. Just meet me at my house and we will take it from there.'

Tom and George pulled up to the house at nearly the same time from different directions. Both got out of their cars and met at the gate.
'I didn't even see anyone out and about that I could ask if they had seen her Tom.'
'Do you think we should call the police? If she went looking for Rex I'm sure she would have checked back here long before this. I don't even know what time she went out, I was sleeping on the couch.'
'Let's go inside. I want to call Ruby and maybe go pick her up; she's definitely going to want to come over here,' George said trying to sound strong and reassuring, he was fretting just as much as his son in-law.
Tom went through the motions of sorting two mugs for coffee for him and George, while George went into the hall to call Ruby.
'Hi honey, I know you want to come over here, we will give it another half hour and see if she turns up. Tom wants to call the police; I don't want to jump the gun just yet. I'm sure she's going to walk through that door any minute.'
'Well I hope so George. 'Ruby answered sounding tired and a little anxious. 'If she isn't home

soon I think we should call the police as Tom said.'

'Of course we will, I'm still hoping it doesn't come to that.'

'How did Rex get on?'

'You know I forgot to ask, I've only been thinking about Anna. I will call you back in half an hour and if she's not back I promise I will come get you. I'm sure she will be, she's got to be, she can't keep looking for Rex all night.'

'Ok speak to you then, love you.'

'Love you too, bye.'

George went into the kitchen just as Tom was finishing making the coffee. He placed them on the coasters on the oak dining table, pulled out a chair and sat down immediately putting his head in his hands.

'What are we going to do George?'

'We give it another half hour, if there is still no sign we will call the police. I don't know if you need to wait twenty four hours to report someone missing, we will call and find out anyway. Under the circumstances I think they will need to do something,' he said sitting down on the chair next to Tom.

'What do you mean under the circumstances?'

'Well I just mean the dog came back injured and she hasn't came back to see if he's here or not. It's late and dark and I've been out looking to no avail,' George stopped talking, he knew by the look on Tom's face this was not helping.

'It doesn't look good does it?' Tom asked

'Let's just give it a while longer and we will see. I forgot to ask until Ruby reminded me, how did Rex get on?'

The vet thinks that he might have broken or cracked ribs on the side that he was limping on. He is getting x-rays in the morning; I've to call her tomorrow to find out and go get him hopefully.'

Both men checked the time it was now 12.20 am

They sat in silence and drank their coffee until George's phone rang and tore them from their individual thoughts.

'Hello Darling, I told you I would call you in half an hour,' George checked the time again before continuing. 'It's only been twenty five minutes.'

'I don't care just come get me I'm going crazy sitting here. I take it she's not back?'

'No she's not. Right I'm on my way bye.'

'I need to go get Ruby I think it's time you called the police.'

Tom dialled the number for Hallington Police Station, as this was only open for the public between 7 am and 7 pm, although the station was used by police officers twenty-four-seven; he was put through to Goldfield Square Police Station in Edinburgh. After he explained the situation to Sergeant Jackson Gardiner he was assured that someone would be with him soon.

5

'Right Anna it is time to go.'
'I'm scared Ravi. Scared of a lot of things, what if I can't cope?'
'I am sure you will do great. Now just close your eyes and think of Jasmine Brown and you will be there before her.'

I don't know if I'm ready for this, now is not the time to have doubts I suppose. What if my body is still there, will I fall to pieces? This is the scariest moment of my life, I'm an eejit I can't say in my life, I suppose I mean my death.

'Ok here goes nothing, bye Ravi hope to see you real soon.'
Anna closed her eyes slower than she had probably ever done before, she did not want this moment to come. She kept them closed for a good while before opening them as she was convinced she was not totally prepared for what was in front of her.
When she did open them she could hardly digest everything in the scene before her. Indeed her body was still on the floor where she had died. She felt a rush of fear and anger. More anger than anything else. It was her life that was over at the hands of a monster that she did not know. Just for seeing something she was not meant to see and being in the wrong place

at the wrong time. The blood from the wound on her head had seeped to a large pool, nearly half a metre wide, it looked very dark and was starting to congeal a little; her eyes were open and staring. She was absolutely repulsed by the sight, but could not draw her eyes away from it. Not until she heard a croaked voice,

It was Jasmine Brown.

She was lying on a single camp bed with a thin mattress which was concreted to the floor by the legs. Her wrist was chained to the top metal rail under the mattress. The duvet cover was a dark brown, flowery thing; the duvet inside it seemed to be thick and warm. An observation Anna took comfort from as the weather was getting cold. Jasmine; however, was not under the duvet she was laying on top of it; all Anna could think of was how cold she must be.

'Don't panic, everything will be all right.' She was not talking to herself, but to her unborn child. She was looking down at her bump, rubbing it as she spoke.

'The lady will be fine when they call an ambulance. I'm sure they will call. They wouldn't let anything terrible happen to the lady.'

Jasmine was saying these words to her baby, although she knew they wouldn't call anyone. She knew the woman on the floor was dead; there was just too much blood. She knew it had been a couple of hours since it happened, the woman had not moved since. She was trying not to look at her, looking instead at her unborn child, she felt she needed to just in case the lady moved. She had tried to wake her with her voice as soon as her captors had left the shed and locked the door. Jasmine must have tried about a hundred times, saying 'hello' and 'wake up' time after time. She tried to get over to her; the chain on her wrist was short, just too short to get to her. There was nothing she could do to help her or herself and her baby, she felt totally useless.

Anna noticed how pretty this young woman was. She had blue eyes and dirty blonde hair tied back, a fair complexion, quite a thin face and full lips. The clothes she wore; however, were not so pretty. She wore a pair of black jogging bottoms and an oversized white t-shirt; well it was meant to be white, it looked like it had been washed hundreds of times so was more grey than white. It put Anna in mind of a make in a way.

She glanced around at the girl's home. The shed was of medium size and made from brick on the outside, she remembered this as she had seen it when she had came round here to look for Rex. The inside walls were maroon in colour, some sort of panelling. Anna was no expert, but she thought she knew what they were.

That must be sound proofing. It's got to be. This abduction must have been planned out. If not Jasmine then it would have been someone else.

She looked up and saw a ceiling that would not be out of place in a living room except there was no light fitting in the middle of it. Anna turned to see where the light was coming from. There was a table lamp on the floor next to what she presumed was the door which had strips of rubber around it. A small halogen heater sat on the floor at the other side of the presumed door. The floor had beige vinyl on it, the sight of the bucket next to the miserable bed really put into perspective what this young woman was going through. Jasmine was going through hell. Anna could only imagine how all this felt for the poor girl, doing the toilet right next to where she slept and ate, how degrading for her. How did this girl keep going? Anna then noticed a book on the bed. A John Grisham novel if she was not mistaken. So the monster did have a bit of a heart after all. She thought about that for a moment then changed her mind.

Of course this monster has no heart if they did none of this would be happening. Yes they have given her a thick duvet and a heater to keep her warm, yes they have given her a book to ease the boredom. That does not make them any less evil.

'Maybe someone will come looking for the lady,' Jasmine was talking to her baby again. 'Someone will miss her sooner or later,' she rubbed her belly again and said something that stirred Anna's emotions. 'Someone loves her, they will call the police and come looking for her.'

Tom, my mum and dad, all my friends and family, they all love me and I love them all so much. They will be calling the police. They will be looking for me. I'm not so sure they will find me here in this shed. I'm dead now anyway. I need to start my work here; the Innocent is what is important now.

Anna said her full name out loud in the outside chance that Jasmine would respond in some way.
Nothing triggered. She kind of knew it was futile, Jasmine was awake; Ravi had told her it was best to try when people were sleeping. She really didn't know where to start with all this. What good would it be for Jasmine to acknowledge her anyway; she was the one that was trapped.

Maybe I should be going around trying to communicate with someone. I don't want to leave her here all alone in this terrible situation. I will need to do something to get her out of it. Where to start is the question.

Jasmine slipped off the men's tartan slippers she had on her feet and slid under the duvet, plumped up the pillow as much as she could and tried to sleep. She knew it wouldn't happen; she gave it a go anyway.

Anna walked slowly towards her. She realised she wasn't really touching the floor, she was about an inch above it, as if she was just kind of floating, going through the motions of taking the steps. All she wanted to do was to give this girl a cuddle and tell her everything was going to be all right. She reached down to touch the hand Jasmine had outside the duvet then hesitated.

What will happen if I try to touch her? I didn't ask Ravi this question and he never told me.

Anna took a chance and put her hand to Jasmine's. It went straight through it and she pulled it back rapidly.

Did I just feel something just then? I think I did.

She did it again; this time she let it linger for a few seconds. She did feel something, she felt a strange warmth, starting in her fingers then growing up towards her wrist. She pulled back again. Ravi told her she would not feel anything physical, she was not imagining this. She would need to ask him about this.

I know what I will do. I will stay here until I get a good look at my murderer. They will need to come in here to move my body, maybe before morning. The one thing I have is time; the only problem is the Innocent doesn't. I need to know the name of the person that killed me, Ravi told me to get as much information as possible so that's where I will start.

Anna sat on the bottom of the bed; well not completely she was doing the floaty thing again so she was an inch above it. She could hear nothing from outside. That was the whole point of this place she thought to herself. Anna kept looking at herself on the floor, the longer she sat there the more the anger bubbled up inside her.

I just don't understand how someone could do all this to other human beings. The world has turned into one crazy place or has it always been like this? It probably has. Murders have been going on since day one.

Jasmine gave a slight snore and shifted slightly on the narrow bed.
'At least you got to sleep,' Anna said out loud with no one to hear her.
'It's a good thing you can, better than looking at a dead body any day.'
After a long time of waiting the door eventually

opened and closed again after two people came in as quickly as she could imagine possible. They tried to avoid her body, but the blood pool was disturbed by their feet. The shed seemed a little cramped now that the monsters were here. It was a man and a woman. She knew the woman from somewhere, she could not think of where right away. She was mid forties Anna thought, dyed black hair, medium build and height with quite a pale complexion. Her eyes were light grey and she had sharp facial features, she had a pointed chin that totally reminded Anna of a typical witch from a children's story. The man was tall and well built especially round the middle. He had dark brown hair, brown eyes, a knobbly nose that looked like it had been broken a few times and his cheeks were red with what looked like broken veins. If Anna didn't know any better she would say he was or still is a heavy drinker. Both of them were wearing the white paper suits that people wear in clean rooms or forensic people examining a scene wear. They didn't have the shoe covers on, although they did sport some rubber gloves, both were carrying what looked like plastic tarps.

They are here to get rid of my body. She looks like she couldn't care less, he looks worried and stressed. Maybe he will snap under the pressure of all this and do the right thing? Who am I trying to kid? Myself? I take it was him that hit me. I hate them both. Hate at first sight. There's nothing I can do to stop them taking my body away. Maybe I can go with them and see where they take it.

They started opening up their white plastic sheets and the noise woke Jasmine. She sat up quickly and Anna knew then the fear that she must be feeling. She sat against the wall and drew her knees up as far as her bump would allow.

'You go back to sleep Jasmine it's been a long night for us all,' the woman said with authority in her voice.

Jasmine started crying and this seemed to annoy the woman.

'Do I need to sedate you again; you know you don't like that.'

'No, you don't need to,' said Jasmine as she did what she was told. She lay back down this time facing the wall away from them and pulled the duvet over her head.

She is terrified of them and no wonder. These people need to be caught; they need to pay for all that they are doing.

The couple got to work wrapping the body which was not that easy given the lack of space they had, they managed. Their white suits were covered in blood, the blood on the floor was smeared everywhere.

'Right come on get it in the van. I will get the top you get the legs,' the man said impatiently.

They opened the door, picked up the body and locked the door behind them with speed and efficiency. Anna stood up, closed her eyes and thought of being outside the shed. A second later she was outside with the murderous couple. The outside light at the back door was on to give them some illumination. They had a tub of industrial wipes and got to work right away cleaning the outside of the plastic shroud. Anna was sure they had done this before; they just looked comfortable doing it. A white transit van had been reversed around the back of the house, as close to the shed as possible with the back doors lying open. There was a garage at the side of the house with a mono blocked drive leading down to the gate. After they did their cleaning they took off their suits and stashed them then in a bin bag along with the wipes they had used to clean the outside of the tarp, their rubber gloves, the poo bag Anna had used for Rex and Rex's lead. They hoisted the corpse into the open van that was waiting for them and threw the bin bag in after it, then closed the door.

'Right, you go and get started cleaning up that shed. I will be back as soon as I can,' the man said.

'Remember put on another white suit, then burn anything you need to in the wood stove, and Candice be thorough.'

Candice! I know who she is. Candice is quite an unusual name I remember now. She's the receptionist at Brownhill Doctors' Surgery. She's meant to be a pillar of the community, yet here she is kidnapping a pregnant woman.

Anna's blood was boiling with anger. She just stood there, her usual inch above the grass and stared at her in disbelief until Candice turned and walked towards the house probably to get her cleaning supplies.

Right I need to decide if I'm staying here or going with him.

She opted to go with him, just to see where her body was going, she knew she should stay with Jasmine, but she needed to know.

If I don't go with him then I will never know where he puts me and that's something I could maybe pass on to someone if I make contact. I don't know how, it might be possible; it will be more evidence against these poor excuses for humans.

6

PC Paul Jones and PC Graham McCartney pulled up outside the Ross house. Anna's red Ford Fiesta was parked in the driveway; while Tom's blue VW Golf and George's black Suzuki Swift were parked at the gate. The house itself was semi detached as were most of the houses in Browning Street. It had a small front garden with a square of grass with a border around it where small bushes and shrubs were planted. A three foot high dyke ran the length of their front garden and the garden next door, with a dark brown fence separating them. Behind Anna's car was a fence with a gate at the side next to the house which led to their back garden. They put down a generous deposit for their mortgage when they got married six years ago with a generous donation from Tom's parents. His parents spend most of their time abroad; they rarely visit their son which he doesn't seem to mind. He was brought up by a Nanny while his parents chased their careers. He was an only child.

'Right Graham lets go find out if there is anything here to be worried about.'
'I don't know if I should be here. I know these people, I used to date Anna many moons ago. I don't know Tom that well though.'
'The serge said he sounded really worried on

the phone so we will get the facts first,' Paul said then added. 'I will do the talking; you look around and take everything in.'

'No probs.'

They knocked on the door at seventy-three Browning Street, the white PVC door was answer by Ruby.

'Oh please come in, so sorry to have to call you out at this time of night, we are worried sick.'

'That's quite alright. Let's just hope it turns out there is nothing to worry about,' Paul answered in his most calming voice.

'Graham I didn't notice you there, how are you doing?' Ruby asked the young policeman.

'I'm fine. Wish this could be under better circumstances Mrs Anderson.'

'Come into the living room please.'

The policemen followed Ruby in and closed the door. Tom and George were seated on a dark brown, leather couch which had two matching chairs. The floor was wooden and had a light brown rug covering the middle of it, with a mahogany coffee table on top. There was a matching mahogany side board in the corner; the curtains matched the colour of the rug. The white vertical blinds were closed to the dark, rainy night outside.

'I'm PC Jones; this is PC McCartney whom I believe you all already know'

'Yes we do,' Tom said. 'How are you doing

Graham?'

'I'm doing good Tom thanks for asking,' Graham responded not knowing what else to say.

Graham realised it was Anna's birthday last week. He remembered because she was three days older than him. Years ago when he dated her for a short time she used to say he was her toy-boy. His birthday is the eleventh of November, hers is the eighth. It was now the early hours of the fifteenth.

'Right so what can you tell me about Anna's movements in the hours leading up to her going missing?' Paul said taking the bull by the horns.

'She came home from work at 5. I got home at half-past'.

'Where do you two work?'

'I'm a plasterer and work for Taylor's Decor. Anna has her own business, well her and her friend Sam Thomas run it together. They do dry cleaning, ironing and clothing repairs; they have a shop on Barnes Road just next to the precinct in the Town Centre.'

'And is this the normal times you both would be home?' PC Jones continued.

'Yes normally unless Anna has something she really needs for a customer, then she would stay behind and finish it.'

'Then what did you do?'

'Anna already had dinner on the go, so it was ready about ten minutes after I came in. I then had a shower and went to play five a side football with a few of the lads at the Leisure Centre at around 6.45, Anna went to her parents' house at the same time. She was back by the time I got back and was watching that show about the young autistic doctor on catch up. I took another shower and lay down on the couch; I was watching the show with her, but must have dozed off after a while. I was woken up by scratching which turned out to be my dog at the back door. He's at the vets just now, he was injured. The vet thinks he may have cracked or broken ribs can't be sure,' Tom explained

'So when you woke Anna was gone?'

'Yes I believe she took the dog for a walk and he got away from her. I thought she was just out looking for Rex, George, that's her dad,' Tom said while motioning to the other man on the couch. 'He went around the streets, but couldn't find her.'

PC Jones pressed on with his questions. 'I believe you said on the phone she hasn't got her mobile or her bag or any of her belongings with her.'

'That's right,' Tom said with a sigh.

'When she takes the dog out what is her usual route?'

'It all depends on how long a walk she or I want to take him on a certain night. If it's bad weather we tend to go down our street into Parson's Way then down Westfield Street or Morcombe Street then down Drayton Street and we are home. Anna likes to take him longer walks sometimes, goes past Morcombe Street right down to Main Street past The Green. From there we go into Bison Street then Drayton Street.'

While PC Jones was busy talking PC McCartney was taking notes.

'That's a lot of Streets, I'm sure PC McCartney will help me out and show me on a street map,' PC Jones said looking towards his fellow policeman.

'Yes I've got one in the car, brought it just in case, I will go fetch it.'

Graham went to get the map and was back in a few minutes.

'While you guys are doing the map thing I'm going to make some tea would anyone like something?' Ruby asked and nodded her head for George to follow her to the kitchen.

'Coffee for me please, Ruby,' Tom answered 'Officers can I get you some?'

Both officers thanked her, but declined the offer. They were spreading the map on the table as Anna's parents went to the kitchen.

'You don't think Tom would have anything to do with Anna going missing do you?'

'Ruby don't be so stupid, he would never do anything to hurt Anna.'

'Oh don't be too sure of that. She told me tonight that she thinks he's having an affair.'

'You are joking; I thought they were trying for a baby.'

'They are. Some men take it wherever they can get it.'

'Just wait till I see him alone,' George said through gritted teeth.

'You can't say anything George, she doesn't know for sure, maybe her imagination is just running riot. Anyway she confided in me, I swore I wouldn't even tell you.'

'Well I won't say anything just yet. But if I find out he has been cheating I will wring his fucking neck.'

George helped his wife with the coffee then they returned to the living room. Tom and the officers were still looking at the map.

'Have you tried to contact any of her friends?' PC Jones asked them.

'Yes while we were waiting on you lot coming we tried her business partner and a couple of her close friends, no joy there,' George replied.

'Has she got any medical conditions or mental health issues we should be aware of?' PC McCartney questioned this time.

'No nothing she's in perfect health,' Tom said.

'Tom we need a description and if you can remember what she was wearing,' PC McCartney asked.

'You know what she looks like Graham.'

PC Jones said abruptly, 'Tom I know your upset, for the record we need this information. I don't know what she looks like just humour me please.'

I'm sorry I shouldn't be taking this out on you. Well she was twenty-nine last week: 08/11/1990 is her date DOB, she has brown, shoulder length hair and beautiful, hazel eyes. She's five foot six and has a slim build.'

'She's nine and a half stone if that helps you picture her size,' Ruby interrupted.

'Sure anything helps.'

'She has a pale complexion and a mole on her right temple,' Tom went on with tears in his eyes, his voice trembling. 'Anna has the most amazing white, straight teeth and thin lips.'

'Here's a recent picture of her,' Ruby said going into her bag and pulling out her purse.' It's not very large. It's clear enough though.'

'Thank you Mrs Anderson.' PC McCartney took it from her hand. 'What was she wearing?'

It was George who answered this time. 'When she was at our house earlier she had on a pair of dark blue jeans, black trainers, a red jumper and a dark blue jacket.'

'The trainers are Sketchers and the jacket is from Rab,' Tom added.

'Is she in any clubs or groups?'

She goes to the gym once a week on a Tuesday night and a spin class on a Saturday morning both at the Leisure Centre,' Tom informed them.

'So what happens now?' George inquired eagerly.

'I've got to admit it does sound a bit strange, we will go and report all this back to our superiors and go around all these streets. Tom said there is no chance that Anna would go into Hallington Park at night, we will go and check it out anyway. Normally with an adult we would advise people to wait twenty-four hours before they report them missing, but as I said it does seem a bit weird. In the meantime if you think of anything else that might help please let us know.' PC Jones said.

'Is that it? Ruby said a little angrily. 'My daughter is missing and I want her found.'

'Mrs Anderson we will do all we can, she's only been missing for a few hours, she will probably turn up safe and sound. As a matter of procedure we will check with the Hospitals in Edinburgh just to make sure she hasn't been taken in there. If you need to go out and look for her feel free just make sure one of you stay here in case she comes back,'

We have your number Tom; we will call as soon as we have any news,' PC McCartney said as they went for the door.

George seen them out then went back to the

others.

'Right Tom you and I will go out looking, Ruby you can stay here and call us if she appears or should I say when she appears.'

'Sounds good to me,' Tom said as he went for his car keys and jacket.

Back in the car the policemen reported back to their sergeant, who agreed with them that it did seem strange. He told them to do a search of the streets she frequented with her dog and to have a look in Hallington Park as they themselves had suggested. The park would be dark; there are a few lights in it. Their torches would help them.

'Do you think the husband could have something to do with this, you know them?' Paul asked Graham

'I knew Anna years ago. I don't really know Tom that well. He grew up miles away from here. I don't think I'm qualified to answer that.

'Well if she doesn't show by morning I think we might be looking at him.'

'Of course we will. If just to rule him out. Hey it's too early for that I'm hoping she will turn up.

7
Five hours earlier

Anna looked over at Tom and saw he was asleep. His black hair was still a little damp from his earlier shower. To Anna he was one of the most handsome men she had ever met. He had sallow skin, the most amazing brown eyes, long eye lashes and a chiselled jaw. He had not a muscular body, more an athletic one which his work and playing football kept in shape.

I hope you're not seeing someone else. I don't know how I would react to that if confronted with it. Maybe I would be cool and collected as if it didn't bother me? No I would be one of the women that would fall apart because I love you so much. I hope you know how much.

Anna went into the kitchen, saw Rex sitting at the back door so went over and opened it.
'You go into the garden just now I will get my shoes and jacket on pal and take you for a walk. Hope you appreciate it considering how cold and wet it is tonight.'
She went into the hall; got her Rab jacket from the peg and the trainers that were sitting underneath then took them into the kitchen to put them on. She took the lead from the back of the chair then went out to get Rex.
'Come on baby let's get your lead on you.'

Rex came running over all happy that he was going walkies. Anna clipped on the lead, opened the gate and off they went.

'You know Daddy and I are going on holiday in a few weeks, well I don't like leaving you buddy, but don't worry Granny and Grandpa will be watching you. You have to promise me you won't annoy Fluff too much, it is her house after all,' Anna spoke to Rex knowing fine well he did not understand her. 'If only you could understand me baby it would make it all so much easier.'

I can't wait to get to Lanzarote. Get away from this weather and if Tom is seeing someone it will get him away from whoever it is as well. Maybe I'm just imagining it. Maybe the honeymoon period is well and truly over. Maybe this is what it is going to be like now. We don't spend as much time together, doing as many things together as we used to. Then I look at Mum and Dad, they look as if the spark has never left. Maybe this holiday will pull us back together.

Anna walked out her gate on Browning Street and turned right, walked to the end of it, past Ashton Drive into Parson's way. The rain was the small kind that soaks you through in no time, there was a cold breeze blowing in her face. She pulled her hood and jacket zip up as far as they would go and tucked her chin down.

She was wishing she had put on a scarf and gloves now. The leaves that had fallen on the pavement from the few trees that were dotted here and there in people's gardens felt slimy and slippy underfoot, some of them looked like snails; she was trying to avoid the pavement where clumps of them had formed.

'I know it's not nice out here tonight baby, not that it bothers you of course. I will take you the long way round. Don't let it be said that I don't spoil you.'

She walked up Parson's Way past the entrance at the cross road to Westfield Street, past the entrance to Morcombe Street, then on to Main Street. The Green was across the road from here, but she wouldn't dream of going in there at this time of night alone. Maybe if it was summer and the light nights were here she would, not tonight. She walked on.

'Well, look who it is Rex, it's your wee pal Buster.'

Buster was straining on his lead to get to Rex and Rex was doing the same to get to his friend.

'Hello Anna, hell of a night for it,' Billy Barclay declared to Anna as he reached her.

'Hi Billy, how are you doing?'

'I'm ok darling, had buster at the vet yesterday though. He has an ear infection, don't worry it's not contagious, Rex is quite safe.'

'Oh that's not so good is it Buster,' she said as

she bent down to give Buster a pat on the head. Then she rubbed her hand down the front of her jeans as he was all wet.

'The vet gave him drops, be good as new in no time.'

The two dogs were excited to see each other; they were wagging their tails and sniffing each other like crazy.

'It's been a few weeks since they saw each other, you would think it was months the way they are carrying on,' Billy said laughing.

Rex and Buster knew each other because they had the same walk route. Anna and Tom are always in The Green with Rex in the better weather as is Billy with Buster. Billy had known Anna for years; he worked with her father before her father retired. Billy was only five foot four and had a skinny build which her father said he couldn't understand because he ate like a horse. He was going bald, but chose just to shave what little hair he did have making him look younger than his forty-seven years.

'Are you going right round the long circuit tonight?' Billy asked Anna.

'You got it, feeling guilty about going on holiday and leaving him with my mum and dad, their cat is not too keen on him being there. I just can't put him in a kennel. I mean I know there are really good places, I prefer to leave him with people he knows.'

'Well Buster and Rex are pretty friendly if you ever need a dog sitter I'm your man.'
'Thank you Billy I will certainly keep it in mind. How far are you going tonight?'
'Same walk as you, just in the opposite direction.'
'How is Kate?'
'Oh you know Kate, never changes, she's fine.'
'Well I better get moving Billy. It was really nice to see you.'
'Tell your dad I was asking for him.'
'Will do, see you later.'
Anna and Billy had to practically pull the dogs away from each other as they went their separate ways. Anna never got far before she had to pull out a poo bag from her pocket. She waited for him to finish his deed then she picked it up. There was a bin at the next corner where she could dump it.

'Do you want off your lead boy? Just don't tell Daddy ok.'
She bent down and unclipped his lead. He never went far in front of her; he just liked to sniff around on his own terms. A car pulled out of Bison Street, turned in her direction and sped up the road.

'Rex, stay where you are boy,' she said, again knowing he didn't understand her. He stopped anyway surprising her.

Maybe he does understand what I'm saying to him after all.

After the car passed a scruffy, ginger cat jumped out of nowhere onto the fence next to her letting out a loud meow. She stopped suddenly and put her hand to her chest.

'For fuck sake cat you scared me half to death.'

Rex turned and came back the half a dozen steps he was in front of her, seen the cat and gave it a couple of barks. The cat jumped off the fence and ran across the road with Rex running straight after it.

'Rex, come back here now,' she called after him impatiently.

Rex did not stop. The cat ran into the driveway of the big bungalow at the side of The Green with Rex behind it. Anna ran across the road, stood at the end of the driveway and shouted on her dog. She was reluctant to go round the back of the house to find him, but when he didn't return after her calling on him for a few minutes she decided she had to.

There was a white transit van on the drive in front of the garage that said JJ Sutherland Construction on the side in green lettering, behind it stood a white Ford Focus car. There was a few metres between the vehicles and the house all paved nicely with monoblock.

'Rex,' Anna called again a little quieter this

time; she didn't want to disturb the people in the house.

Rex was still a no show so she continued round the back of the house into a large garden. The only light she could see round here was the lights at the edge of The Green. There was enough light to see the basic outlay. She knew she was standing on grass, it was soft underfoot. The door to the shed that sat at the bottom of the garden blew open a little in the wind; she saw a light coming out of it. It was then she heard her dog give an almighty yelp, it was coming from that shed. The door blew closed again and the light vanished. Anna ran towards where the light had been, she needed to see what was happening to Rex. She opened the door and stepped into a sight she never intended in her life to see. Rex was stunned and whimpering on the floor. Then she saw a young, pregnant woman chained to the bed by the wrist, Anna stood there for a few seconds with her mouth agape not knowing what to say or do. There was another woman in the room with her back to her; she seemed as if she didn't want to turn round to face her for some reason.

'What the fuck is going on here,' Anna shouted at the top of her voice.'

The door behind her creaked a little as it was being opened, Anna saw her dog limp towards it as fast as he could whimpering, but before Anna had a chance to turn round and follow him she was hit on the back of head, hard. She never had a chance to see stars or feel dizzy or anything else. The blow was that harsh she was dead before she hit the floor.

'Candice what the hell were you thinking?'

'I'm so sorry Jack, this is the first time I've left it open I swear. I always come in and put the bolt on the inside on straight away, I was just nipping back in here with the hot water bottle for her,' she said through tears pointing at Jasmine Brown chained to the camp bed.

'Well, look what you made me do now you stupid bitch, this is getting way out of hand.'

'I know, it will be worth it when we have our baby.'

'You obviously want this baby a whole lot more than me Candice.'

Jasmine Brown was on the bed crying her eyes out, just when she thought things couldn't get any worse.

Jack reached down to the woman he had just struck to feel for a pulse and check her pockets for a phone. He found neither. Even if he found a pulse he couldn't let her live now anyway after what she just saw.

'Do you recognise her?' Jack asked his wife.

'Yes I know her face; I couldn't tell you her name.'

'Well she is going to be missed by someone and

soon,'
'I kicked her dog, God forgive me.'
'Why?'
'I didn't notice it coming in when I turned around Jasmine was petting it. It all happened so fast, I just panicked and lashed out. Then the woman came in I turned away so she couldn't see my face which was stupid really.'
'I didn't mean why you kicked the dog I meant why should God forgive you,' said Jack. 'In case you haven't noticed Candice we are officially evil. Get into the fucking house woman; we need to make a plan on what we are going to do next.'

8

It was easy for Anna to close her eyes and think herself into Jack's van. She was getting the hang of moving about in her spirit body. The first thing she did was to look at the clock as soon as Jack switched the engine on. It was 2.24 in the morning. The drive took forty-five minutes to get to a building site with the name Sutherland Construction on the gate, in a town called Pavesway. She had been in this town a lot as this was where her friend Karen Chalmers lived. Jack got out, keeping the engine running he ran over to gate and unlocked the padlock; he got back into the van and drove into the site. There were some houses nearly finished and some in the early stages of build. Jack drove until they came to one that looked like it was just getting started; he got the van reversed up as close as he could to the soon to be house. She hoped that maybe a security guard would turn up because she knew that he was just about to bury her body. He got out of the van and walked away. There was a couple of security lights dotted about, they did not illuminate the site by any stretch of the imagination, all they did was cast vague eerie shadows from the part built houses over the rough land. Anna felt despair and misery at the whole scene; she wanted to be elsewhere; however, here is where she thought she needed to be. She heard another engine start and peered into the near darkness to see Jack coming back in a small digger.

That's going to be a house. He's going to bury me under a house. Once he digs the hole and buries me it will not be noticed. He will make sure of that. They must be ready to pour the concrete foundations here any day that's why he chose this spot. How convenient for them.

The pipe work and the hardcore had been already put down for the house, also the hardcore for the garage two meters to the left of it. It was the garage space that Jack was interested in. That way there was no pipe work to disturb, the membrane and reinforcements would not be compromised if he stayed away from the edges. He drove the machine over to the garage space and started digging. He used the arm of the digger at full stretch to reach away from the side. The hardcore was only 100mm thick and was down 300mm from ground level waiting for the concrete to do down on Monday morning. It really didn't take him that long to get down to a decent depth for which to throw the body in and that is exactly what he did. He opened the back door to his van which was only ten feet away, dragged her body over to the hole and just threw her in as if she were a bag of rubbish. He went back to the van, grabbed the bag with the white suits and blood stained wipes and threw that in on top of her plastic wrapped body. Jack then jumped back into the digger then started filling in the grave. He discarded some of the dirt on the pile that was already sitting to the left of the soon to be garage. Once he had finished he drove the machine back to where he had got it and walked back to his van. He jumped in then turned the van round so that his headlights were shining on the hard core where he had just buried her and went to the back of the van again, he returned with a spade. He had to replace the hardcore on top of the grave. There was a pile of it sitting ten meters away to his right. It took him six journeys with his spade until he was satisfied that he had enough. He stood back looking at his handiwork. It looked a bit raised where the grave was.

'Fuck it,' he said to himself.

He levelled it out with his spade, scattering the hardcore around as best he could then started stomping all around the area. He was glad he had put his wellingtons on as it was raining and getting a little dirty underfoot. Anna laughed out loud at him when he slipped and fell all his length on the ground.

'Serves you right, you monster,' Anna said out loud to Jack, of course with no response.

Once he was satisfied the ground was flat and appeared to be undisturbed he returned to the van and spread a dust sheet on the driver's seat before he got in to save the seat from getting dirty from his clothes.

I'm not getting in that van with him again. I have a much better way of getting back anyway. I just hope this is not my final resting place. It's down to me to make sure they are caught and the Innocent is saved. The police finding my body would be a bonus, although maybe that's a long shot. Who knows what will happen, I never thought for a minute I would be in this situation, just goes to show, you never know what's in front of you.

She watched as Jack drove away. Then she closed her eyes.

9
Friday 15th November

Jack got back to his house at 6.45 am; he would have liked to have been back sooner. He spent more time that he wanted making sure that the ground was flat. The building site is opened up at eight by one of his trusted employees John Morrison. No one needed to go near the burial site today, the concrete foundations were going down on it on Monday morning and he would be there to oversee it himself. He just hoped that nothing would look out of place in the daylight. He took his mobile from his pocket and made a call.

'Hello John just to let you know I won't be in until about ten this morning been up all night with a dodgy stomach.'

'That's cool; I will keep the troops busy until you get here. Is there anything specific you want doing this morning?'

'No just carrying on with the roof on house number seven and eight. We will get the foundation to number nine done first thing on Monday.'

'No probs. I spoke to the decorators last night; they said they can start the site on Tuesday.'

'That's great John, thanks for doing that for me. I will see you soon. Bye.'

'Bye.'

Candice came into the kitchen where Jack stood all muddy and looking very tired.

'How did it go,' Candice asked her husband.

'How the fuck do you think it went?'

'I'm just asking, no need to snap my face off.'

Jack started to take his clothes off, shaking his head in disbelief at his wife. Once he had removed everything he had on apart from his boxers he strode out of the kitchen, along the hall and into the bathroom where he took an extended shower. When he returned Candice was filling the washing machine with his dirty clothes.

'I took your wellies out to the outside tap and washed them, they are sitting on the top step at the back door.'

'Oh thanks.' Jack said sarcastically to his wife.

'What's done is done Jack. If you didn't have a criminal record then we would have been able to adopt rather than go through all this.'

'It's not my fault, well maybe the adoption thing is, but we tried the IVF three times without success maybe we were just not meant to be parents.'

'Oh I know I was meant to be a mother, it is the only thing that is missing in my life. You think it is easy for me to see all the young mothers out there pushing prams up and down. Half of them don't even deserve to have kids and you know it.'

Jack didn't answer her. He knew some people didn't deserve to have children; there was nothing he could do about that. He went over, put the kettle on then started to make some toast.

'Let me make you a proper breakfast, how about some bacon and eggs?'

'Sure, I'm away to get dressed.'

He stayed in the bedroom until Candice gave him a shout that his breakfast was on the table.

'I'm going to take this out to our guest.' Candice said walking towards the back door with a plate covered with tin foil in her hand.

'Just make sure your careful this time, do everything right.'

'I think I have learned my lesson.'

Jack picked up his knife and fork and started eating his breakfast. Candice was back in five minutes.

'I just pray that nothing looks out of place where I buried that woman.'

'Everything will be fine Jack, you are worrying over nothing.'

'I don't want to start another argument. I just don't know how you can be so flippant over all this. At the end of the day the both of us could end up in prison, probably for the rest of our lives.'

'It won't come to that everything will work out darling, just you wait and see.'

'I wish I had your confidence, how is the girl this

morning?'

'She is obviously a little traumatised with everything that happened last night. Her eyes are all puffy and red because she has been crying, but she will be fine.'

'You really are just not getting it are you, you silly cow. There is no going to be fine for her. We will have to kill her once that baby is here. You know all this, we planned all this. Why oh why do you keep deluding yourself that there is going to be a good outcome to all this.'

'There will be, we will have our child.'

'I wish we had never started with this.' Jack said with worry in his voice.

'Well it's much too late to turn back now; we need to stick to the plan Jack.'

Their plan was to wait until January, by then the baby would not be far away from being born. Candice would move up to the house they have in the countryside ten miles away from Inverness. The house belonged to Jack's uncle; it was inherited by him when his uncle died as his uncle was a bit of a hermit and had no family of his own. Jack was surprised he got left the property; he really didn't know Uncle Fred all that well, he thought the house would be sold with the proceeds going to some cat charity; Fred liked his cats more than he liked people. They had been renting the house out, but gave their tenants six months notice as soon as they abducted Jasmine which would work out perfect for them. Jasmine's body would be buried in the large garden at their country place, how they were going to kill her was not something they had thought much of, but they knew the time would come.

Jack would stay behind; put the house and business on the market. He would dismantle the sound proofed shed and get everything in order at this end then he would go join Candice at the weekends, then permanently as soon as the business was sold. He was a seasoned builder, he was sure he would find a job with a construction company in Inverness. They would tell friends and family that they had at last been accepted for adoption, although Jack and Candice had tried and failed their friends and family didn't know that. They would live happily ever after with their new family.

They sat finishing their breakfast and drinking coffee in silence until it was time for them to go to work; Candice had a late start of half-past nine today as she had covered for a colleague last week.

'I'm sure if they had noticed any disruption at the site I would have had a call by now.' Jack said wearily.

'I told you everything will be fine,' his wife answered him. 'Just go and get the day over with.

You look so tired. It's just as well you finish early on a Friday.'

Jack got up without another word, kissed Candice good-bye, and left with Candice close behind him.

10

When Anna opened her eyes she was back with Jasmine. The young lady looked terrible and was no surprise after what she had gone through. She was huddled under the duvet sobbing furiously. Anna felt terrible for her. She could not begin to imagine how this girl was feeling.

I need to start thinking about what to do next. I need to go see how my family are. I need to try and contact someone, somehow. I hope and pray that I don't let that child down.

Anna sat at the bottom of the bed, in her way of thinking she was keeping Jasmine company even though Jasmine could not see or hear her. Anna looked at the place on the floor where her body had been. There was no trace that it had ever been there, all the blood was gone, but the sight of it was etched in her brain. Candice had done a fine job of cleaning up. Anna could not smell anything; she thought if she could she would smell all kinds of chemicals.

She had been sitting there for a while before the door opened, in walked Candice the monster with a plate with foil over it, bolting the door behind her.

'Good morning Jasmine,' she said to her prisoner.

'Is it?'

'Well here is your breakfast that should cheer you up.'

'Will it?'

Jasmine didn't like to upset her captors. She didn't like it when they sedated her, she thought it might be doing damage to her child, but she was in no mood for this evil woman this morning.

'I will leave it here on the floor then,' Candice said bending down placing it within Jasmine's reach. She stood for a couple of minutes just staring at Jasmine before she turned around abruptly and left locking the door behind her.

As soon as she had left Jasmine pulled up the sheet on the bed to reveal the thin mattress, she started picking at the top corner as if she was looking for something. Anna stood up and moved to the top of the bed, she was curious to see what she was up to. Jasmine found the small hole in the covering of the mattress that she was looking for and pulled out a small silver disk about three quarters of an inch in diameter. Anna moved closer still so she could get a good look at what it was. The girl was turning it over and over in her hand as if she was trying to polish it with her fingers, then she laid it flat on her palm and stared at it. That's when Anna leaned right in and saw it was Rex's tag from his collar, there was his name in the engraving. She knew on the other side would be her mobile number in smaller writing than Rex's name to fit it on the disk.

Oh my word I can't believe it. This girl must have been thinking quickly to snatch that from our dog. I knew it was loose, I'm glad I didn't fix it or maybe it would not have been so easy for Jasmine to get off the collar in the little time she must have spent with Rex.

'Look what I have baby,' Jasmine spoke in a shaky voice with a little touch of triumph as if she had gotten one over on the Sutherlands.
She rubbed her stomach and put her head back with a slight smile on her face.
'When we get out of here and I have got to believe that we will, I will tell the police about what happened to the lady, maybe this will be proof that she was in here with us. I hope that the dog is ok. I hope he made it back home and someone is taking good care of him. When you are old enough I will get you a dog, we can call it Rex.'
Anna listened to Jasmine talk to her baby, after everything this young woman had endured it sounded to Anna that she hadn't given up, that she still had hope for a future outside of this prison.

I need to go check on my family and Rex. I don't

think the evil pair will come back to her for a while. Maybe I should go into them first, listen to what they are saying, that is my priority after all.

Anna thought of them and using her usual magic was a second later standing in their kitchen. They were sitting at the dining table finishing off their breakfast. She wanted to shout at them. Tell them what she thought of them. She knew it would be a waste of time. She knew she had to put all her efforts into the job she came back to do. They weren't saying a word to each other. She sensed that maybe things were a little tense between them. The woman kept stealing a look at the man; he would not meet his eyes with hers. She stood there for about fifteen minutes with not a word said so she decided it was time to go elsewhere.

I can't try to contact anyone until tonight so I might as well go check on Tom. This is getting me nowhere.

It felt good to be standing in her own living room though the sight of her parents and husband squeezed her heart, it was as if a sumo wrestler had picked her up and gave her a bear hug, getting tighter and tighter.

I should never have come here. There is nothing I can do to ease their pain. They all look terrible; they must have been up all night. I can't bear to see them like this.

'I can't take this anymore I'm going to call the police station. We have been out looking all night with no joy, we have not heard a peep from the police,' her father said.
'I will do it George, about time we knew what they are doing about this,' Tom declared.

So they have called the police. I wonder where Rex is. I hope he is here, not out there wondering about hurt somewhere. My mum looks bad, I knew she would.

Anna went over and sat beside her mother just to be near her even though her mother did not know she was there.
Tom lifted his mobile; he dialled the number For Hallington Police Station.
'Yes hello, my name is Tom Ross, I'm calling about my wife,' before he could say anything further the man on the other side interrupted him.
'Oh Mr Ross this is Inspector Halliday, I am familiar with your case, my colleagues have filled me in. I take it your wife has not returned?'
'No she hasn't. I need to know what's going on, my father in-law and I have been going around the streets all night looking for Anna, there has been no sign and no one has contacted me.'
'I was hoping she would have turned up before

this. I was just going to give you a ring to fill you in,' Inspector Halliday said before continuing. 'We went around Hallington Park last night as did we go around the route which you and your wife walks your dog. We are going back to the park this morning, there is CCTV on the main gate on Main Street if she did happen to go in there last night then we will know one way or another. If we see her going in on the CCTV then we will search the park immediately. There isn't any other public CCTV on the route we think your wife took. We may get lucky if any of the private residences on the route have it. We called all the local hospitals; there was no one of your wife's description admitted. Sergeant Stephen Rooney will be in contact with you after we have been back to the park. In the meantime if you could make a list of Anna's close friends and family it would be appreciated. I know that you have already contacted a couple of them last night, the sergeant will probably want to speak to some of them himself.'

'Alright I will. Has this sergeant got my number?'

'Yes and your address.'

'Thank you I hope to hear from him real soon.'

'You will bye.'

'Bye.'

Tom hung up the phone and filled his in-laws in

on what was happening. Anna was there to hear it all as well.

'I wouldn't go into The Green at night,' Anna said out loud, her words falling on deaf ears.

'I will put the kettle on; maybe make us all a bit of toast. You and George can get started on that list for the police.'

'That sounds great Ruby,' George answered her thankfully.

Tom went into the drawer under the coffee table and took out an address book then lifted Anna's mobile from the top of it. He went to the sideboard, removed a notebook and pen from one of the drawers on it and handed the address book to George. Tom started going through her mobile.

'What friends should I include, just close friends?'

'I would say so Tom, I don't think they will want the number of every person she has on her phone.'

'That was a stupid question.'

George started looking through the address book, matching the address for the number that Tom was writing down.

'Do you think I should put something on Facebook? A lot of people do that when someone goes missing, I see them all the time,' Tom asked George as if looking for approval.

'Maybe, if you think it would help then anything is worth a try. Maybe we should run that by the police before you just go ahead and do it. They have procedures.'

'That makes sense.'

Anna sat taking in everything that was being said. She could hardly believe it was her they were talking about. She felt so bad for her family having to go through this; she knew that there was going to be worse coming for them.

What if they never find out what happened to me? What if my parents go to their graves still looking for me? How long will Tom look for me? I'm thinking all wrong here; I shouldn't be thinking like this, I should be trying to save the Innocent One. That is my mission. If they do find me then it would break all their hearts knowing I was murdered. I don't know what would be best for them, knowing or not knowing. I need to get back to Jasmine I will have plenty time to think a lot of things through while I'm there with her.

Ruby appeared back in the living room.

'Here's the coffee,' she said putting a small tray on the coffee table. 'The toast is just coming,' she left the living room and returned to the kitchen.

'She's not holding up too well is she?' Tom commented to George

'No she's not. She wants to call Clara; I don't want to worry her yet. Not until we definitely know that we have got something to worry about.'

'I really hope Anna turns up soon. I don't know what I would do without her.'

'I don't know what any of us would do if anything has happened to her son.'

Ruby came back with the toast. The three of them got stuck in putting a list together for the police.

11
Wednesday 7th August 2019

Jasmine had been a little worried about telling her parents she was pregnant. She was only eighteen and was meant to be starting college in two weeks time; she was going to do an accounting course, following in her mother's footsteps. She wasn't sure if that was going to be possible now that she had a baby on the way. The father of the child was Glen Norton; he too was eighteen, he was going to Edinburgh University the week after she was meant to start college. Jasmine was not sure she was going to tell him about the baby, their relationship was casual; she did not want to put pressure on him, although she knew he had a right to know. A long hard think about what to do for the best was in front of her.

It was half-past five, Jasmine was in the waiting room at the Brownhill Doctors' Surgery, waiting on her turn. The room was square with chairs along two walls and kiddies toys along the wall below the window. Next to the door was a television which was not on, All three walls were covered in posters about all kinds of illnesses, information on breast feeding, and mental illness to name a few. What was left to see of the walls was painted magnolia. She saw a notice for patients to switch off their mobiles so she did so.

Jasmine heard her name being called so stood and went in to see the doctor. She had already been here to have a pregnancy test; she reckoned she was two months gone. She hadn't had a scan yet that would tell her for sure, she was waiting on the appointment coming through, that might not be for another few weeks the doctor had told her. Jasmine was here today because she thought she had a urine infection, it was driving her up the pole.

Candice Sutherland had made the appointment for Jasmine Brown on Monday when she had called the surgery. Candice finishes at four every second day and would be sitting in her car waiting for Jasmine on her way home. This was the chance she was waiting for; Candice had access to the patient's records, she had been looking for a young pregnant woman for months to carry out her plan. The shed was all ready and waiting. She had told Jack about this girl on Monday night when he got home from work. Jack was a little dubious about it. She convinced him it was a chance she could not pass up.

Jasmine was right. A urine infection it was, the doctor gave her a prescription for a course of antibiotics, with it folded up and put in it her shoulder bag she left the surgery. If she hurried she could catch the chemist before it closed at six, it was only a five minute walk. She came out the surgery gates and turned right into Park Street, past the entrance to Canter Avenue then left into Upton Road, took another left into Pine Road, crossed the road and entered Smith's Chemist. Candice had passed her a couple of times on route, watching and waiting. She was a little nervous, but she had made up her mind that this was the one.

Jasmine came out of the chemist and crossed the road and turned right into Upton Road, crossed this road and waited at the bus stop. She was exhausted, all she wanted to do when she went in was go to bed, but the night was the night she was going to break the news of her pregnancy to her parents. She sat down on the wall in front of a modest little cottage and wondered how this was all going to pan out for her. She knew her parents would want to know who the father is. Then they would probably insist that she tell him right away. This would be the most sensible thing to do and was starting to think of how she was going to break the news to Glen. She knew he could only take the news two ways; he would either be happy or angry. He had no right to be angry she thought, it was him that had slipped the condom off that night during sex, although she wasn't sure this was the actual time she fell pregnant, it could have happened before then. Only the scan would be able to tell her. He apologised afterwards, looks like it was a bit too late for apologies. Jasmine was happy about the baby; the only thing she was thinking about was how other people around her were going to take it. There was no question in her mind from day one that she was going to keep it. She already loved this baby more than life itself. Taking a tissue from her bag, she dabbed at her weeping eyes unaware that she was being watched.

Candice saw the girl crying and took her chance there and then. She knew Jasmine would recognise her from her job as receptionist at the doctor's, if she couldn't trust her, then who could she trust? Candice pulled up in her White Ford Focus then put the window down.

'Can I give you lift Jasmine, you look a little upset dear?' Candice asked her as if butter wouldn't melt in her mouth.

Jasmine looked up with tears rolling down her face. She could hardly deny that she was upset though she wasn't sure that she wanted any company.

'I will be fine thanks,' she answered.

'Oh come on you can't sit at a bus stop crying, it's just not right. Come on I will take you home.'

Jasmine knew this woman; she had seen her nearly every time she had been at the doctor for years.

'Ok Mrs Sutherland if you're sure and I'm not putting you out.'

'Call me Candice please. Mrs Sutherland makes me feel so old,' she said to Jasmine with a big smile on her face, trying to put her at ease as Jasmine got in the car and put her seat belt on.

Candice pulled away from the bus stop slowly. 'Where do you live then, I can remember names, but I couldn't possibly remember every one's address as well,' she said with a little laugh trying to lighten Jasmine's mood.

Jasmine was grateful for the lift, although it would take a lot more than this to lift her spirits.

'Belford Avenue, if it's too far out your way you can drop me at the next bus stop.'

'Don't be silly dear I offered so I will take you.

Jasmine was still crying, she was trying her best to stop. It was useless she had opened the flood gates.

'Do you want to talk about it?' Candice asked her.

'I wouldn't know where to start.'

'A problem shared is a problem halved so they say. I don't know who they are, but people keep talking about them,' Candice said being her most charming.

This seemed to amuse Jasmine a bit; she gave a small smile through the tears.

'Tell you what, why don't we go to my place, have a cup of tea and if you want to talk about it you can. If you don't well that will be fine as well you can't go home in that state, you can just hang out for a while and compose yourself then I will take you home,' Candice said in her most caring voice.

'I would like that, if you're sure I'm not keeping you from anything.'

'Don't be silly Jasmine. You look as if you need some time to think about what is bothering you, I will listen if you decide you want to share it.'

'Thank you so much. You are so kind.'

'My husband won't be back until late tonight so we won't get disturbed dear.'

'I will call my parents when I get to your house then, tell them I'm at a friend's. It is a lie I know, but a small one.'

'That sounds good. At least you let them know where you are unlike a lot of the youngsters today. They must be so proud of you.'

'I don't think they would be if they knew.'

'Knew what, 'Candice asked, although she already knew what the girl was talking about.

'I need to tell someone so I will tell you; maybe you could give me some advice.'

'If I can, I will do my best. We are nearly at my house,' Candice said as she turned left off Bison Street into Main Street where her house sat.

Jasmine felt comfortable in Candice's company, thought that she could tell her anything. Candice had fooled this young woman and she was feeling pretty pleased with herself.

'Here we are,' Candice announced when she pulled into the driveway.

'You have a lovely house.'

'Thank you, it takes a bit of upkeep, the garden at the back is large, but I like to do bit in the garden.'

She drove the car right up to the front of the garage. Both women got out and headed around the back of the house to go in the back door.

The back garden was large, roughly about twenty metres square. Running along the side of the garage was a raised, brick flower bed with an assortment of different flowers. The lawn ran from the edge of the path along the back of the house right up until two metres from the back fence where it was met with an array of non flowering plants and shrubs, then over the back fence was Hallington Park. There were trees at the side of the garden opposite the garage, this side of the garden also bordered with Hallington Park. In the far corner stood a brick shed.

'Your garden sure is beautiful. Does your husband help you with it?

'Yes he does his share, which is less than my share,'

Candice said with a laugh.

Jasmine smiled as Candice opened the back door, the two women went inside.

'I will put the kettle on, I've got some pasta in a tomato sauce in the fridge would you like some?'

'I would love some if it's not too much trouble. I haven't eaten since breakfast,' Jasmine said.

'It's no trouble at all. You sit down, I will spoil you rotten.'

'Thank you again for all this.'

'You don't need to thank me dear. I'm sure you would do this for someone else if you needed to.'

'Yes, but I really do appreciate it.'

Candice was all a flutter inside. She was nervous and excited at the same time. She knew she had to act fast before Jasmine had a chance to call her parents. She took the tub of pasta out the fridge, put some into two bowls then put one of them in the microwave.

'I'm just going to the loo, would you mind taking this out when it's ready then put the other bowl in for two minutes?'

'Yes of course, it's the least I can do.'

'Be back in a sec.'

Candice left Jasmine in the kitchen and went straight to her bedroom. Jack's friend Adam, who gets called *get anything Adam* had purchased some Chloroform from the dark web for Jack, he did warn Jack that is was toxic and volatile, but Jack had never thought that it were ever going to get used. Just like the shed he had prepared, it was all to keep Candice happy, make her believe that this plan was a possibility. But Candice was going to use it and the shed. She went into the bottom drawer of the five drawer set and took out the bottle and a cloth she had put in there with it. She put the amount onto the cloth that Adam had suggested then held it behind her back, making sure it was kept well away from any of her own breathing apparatus. She then went into the toilet and flushed it to make it sound good then went back to the kitchen. Jasmine was standing in front of the microwave doing what was asked of her.

'Have you called your mum yet?

'No, I think I will do it just now.'

That's when Candice swooped. She took three long, fast strides towards Jasmine's back and pounced on her. Before she had a chance to react the cloth was covering her face. Candice had her other arm around her, holding her as tight as she could. Jasmine could not hold on to her consciousness, her legs folded beneath her then everything went black. Candice was pumping with adrenaline, this was actually happening. She took Jasmine's weight in her arms as much as she could and lowered her to the floor. She had to call Jack. He would probably be on his way back; she had lied to Jasmine about her husband being back late. She would need to call him. They would need to keep her unconscious until it was dark enough to take her to the waiting shed. Not that there was many neighbours to see, just the back of the four in a block council houses on the street to the right of them in Parkway Lane

'Jack I've only went and done it,' Candice proclaimed to her husband as soon as he answered his mobile.

'Done what?'

'I've got the girl I was telling you about.'

'You have got to be kidding me.'

Jack was dumbfounded. Never in a million years did he expect this plan to come to any fruition. He thought he was putting the pretence of it there for Candice, she kept on and on with her insane plan. He did not want this to happen; now it seems it was much to his disappointment.

'No she's lying on our kitchen floor,' she said with a sense of pride in her voice.

'I will be home in fifteen minutes.'

'See you then, love you, bye.'

Jack got home and saw the girl lying there on the floor.

'How long will she be out?' He asked his wife.

'I don't know. When she starts to come round I will give her another sniff of the chloroform.'

'This is unreal Candice.'

'I can't believe it myself. Our dream is coming true.'

'Well it's too late to turn back now I suppose.'

'You don't seem happy about his Jack.'

'It just seems a little drastic. I mean it was fine talking about it, it's all so very real now.'

'Well as you said yourself it's too late to turn back now.'

'As soon as it is dark enough we will put her in the shed. Just remember Candice this is serious so we will need to be very, very careful.'

'Don't worry everything will be hunky dory.'

'Where's her phone?'

'It's in her bag there on the table. It's switched off.'

'You didn't switch it off did you?'

'I know some things. I know when you switch a phone off it pings at the tower. It was already off or out of juice.'

'At least that's one thing less to worry about; I will dump it in the river at the edge of town when I'm going to work in the morning. You can burn the rest of her things and the bag itself in the log burner.'

They waited until half-past eleven that night before they carefully lifted the woman out to her new home. Jasmine had indeed started to come to a couple of times. Candice was ready for this with the chloroform. After they put her on the bed and shackled her wrist to the bed post they double checked that everything was secure and there was no possible way she could escape.

The first time Jasmine opened her eyes and found herself in the shed was the most depressing day of her life. She couldn't believe how cool Candice was that day when she had brought her food for the first time.
'Where am I?' Jasmine shouted at her.
'In the sound proof shed at the bottom of my lovely garden, so there is no point in screaming or shouting for help because there is no one to hear you my dear.'
'Why?'
'You have what I want.'
'What's that then?'
'I want your baby of course, what else have you got?'
'How do you know I'm pregnant?'
'I work at the doctors', sweetheart I know a lot of things.'
'Did you plan this?'
'Yes and keep your voice down or I will be forced to sedate you, not that anyone can hear you anyway, I will not have you speaking to me like that.'

'Oh yes I can, you are the one that is in the wrong here, you lured me here, you were being nice to me, I thought I could trust you, then you go and do this,' Jasmine said through gritted teeth.

Candice took the food with her, was back out the door and had it locked in a flash. Jasmine shouted when the door was open, it was not open long enough to do anything. In the days and weeks that followed she learned that the monsters were in control. She was sedated a couple of times for her outbursts and they kept food from her to punish her. She was furious, but she knew it would do her no good to show it.

12

Sergeant Stephen Rooney arrived at the Ross house at 10.10 am. The front door was opened by
Tom, he was immediately invited in. The sergeant was a slim, tall man standing at six foot three inches. He was forty-four years old; however, if you had to guess his age you would guess a little older. He had a full head of grey hair, cut short at the sides, with a little length on the top. His eyes were blue and small, framed with rectangular silver glasses which sat on a long thin nose.

George was at home feeding their cat Fluff and Ruby was up in the spare room having a lie down, who could blame her, she was exhausted as was Tom which showed on his appearance. He had a bit of stubble going on, dark circles under his eyes and his hair was in disarray.

'I'm Sergeant Stephen Rooney, I'm here to update you, I believe you have a list of people who I can contact who know Anna,' he said to Tom getting straight down to business.

Ruby walked into the living room and sat down next to Tom.

'Pleased to meet you. Tell me you have good news for us,' asked Tom.

'I'm afraid not. We have checked the CCTV at Hallington Park to no avail.'

'I knew that would be a waste of time as I told the officers early this morning she would not have gone in there at that time of night especially by herself.'

'Yes that may be, you have to understand Sir we had to check it to rule it out.'

'I suppose so', Tom answered with a sigh.

'There is CCTV in the shop on the corner on Westfield Street and Parsons Way, do you know it.'

'Yes that is Omar's shop, he's a good guy.'

'I'm heading there when I leave here to have a look. A Constable is going round the route your wife was most likely to take to see if we can spot any private residences with a camera and I would like to take Anna's mobile phone with me if that's ok with you.'

'Sure why not, it's not as if she is using it. I'm sorry I'm tired and worried, I'm being snappy. It's not your fault you are here to help.'

'That's quite alright Sir, we know that people can get frantic when they have a loved one missing. I have a few questions for you and Mrs Anderson.'

'Go ahead, please,' Ruby urged. 'And please, call me Ruby.'

The sergeant took a few seconds as if he was contemplating whether or not to ask his questions. He did not want them jumping to any conclusions, although he needed to ask.

'A girl by the name of Jasmine Brown went missing here in the town in August, I believe from the reports that you were one of the last people to see her Ruby.'

'Yes I work in Smith's Chemist; she came in not long before closing to fill a prescription that day. I served her; she was talking to Lorraine Jackson and her two children. She was trying to make the younger kid who was in a pram smile, Lorraine's older girl had a unicorn and she was talking to the little girl about it.' Ruby paused for a moment said. 'You think this is connected to Anna's disappearance don't you.'

'Anna has not been missing long enough to consider that she won't come home, it is a long shot to say they could be connected at this stage, we are just concerned that two young woman have gone missing in the space of just over three months from the same area. As I said I have read the reports and the statements that were made at the time. We will have to check if there was any connection between Jasmine and Anna, through work or on a social level. Tom you said Anna goes to the gym to do a spin class every week.'

'Yes she did I mean she does. Anna doesn't know that girl or she would have said something at the time when the girl went missing,' Tom answered adamantly.

'I hear your dog came home injured and is at the

vets.'

'Yes he did, the vet is doing an x-ray to check his ribs. I've to give them a call at eleven,' he paused to look at his watch. 10.20. 'I hope he is alright. Wish I knew what happened to him. My first thought was maybe he had been knocked down by a car, maybe the vet will be able to shine some more light on it when I call them.'

'Would you mind giving them a call just now? I would be interested to know if the vet thinks he may have been knocked down,' Sergeant Rooney asked.

'Yes of course I will. Be right back.'

Tom grabbed his phone from the coffee table and went into the kitchen.

'I'm glad I have you on your own Ruby. I have a sensitive question to ask.'

'Go right ahead.'

'Do you know of any infidelity by either your daughter or your son in-law?'

'I can vouch that my daughter has not strayed within the marriage, I don't know about him. She confided in me last night that she thought that Tom was having an affair. She hopes he's not because she really does love him. Did you know they are going to Lanzarote in a few weeks?'

'No I didn't.'

'Well she is hoping it is going to be a fresh start for them. Maybe getting away just the two of them will rekindle the romance.'

'Is there any evidence that he is having an affair?'

'Not that she told me of, I think it was more a feeling she has rather than anything else.'

Sergeant Rooney found this information interesting. He may have to look into the husband's activities he thought to himself. They sat in silence for a moment or two until Tom returned from the kitchen.

'Katie Irvine, the vet I saw last night stayed on this morning to do the x-ray herself, she went home at nine o'clock. I spoke to Michael who said that Rex has a couple of cracked ribs. It should heal on its own through time. They are giving me anti-inflammatory tablets for him and I can go pick him up anytime.'

'That's great,' Ruby said relieved.

'Did Michael say of any possible causes for his injuries?' Sergeant Rooney inquired.

'He said that we may never know what happened to him.'

'That's all for now, if you could get me her mobile and the friend's list please.'

'Yes, sure,' Tom said getting up to go into the kitchen to retrieve the phone from where it was charging on the worktop. He came back with the mobile, lifted the list from the table and handed both of them to the policeman.

'Thank you,' the officer said before standing up.

'As soon as I have anything I will call.'

Both Ruby and Tom thanked Rooney then walked him to the door.

George was coming in the gate with milk in one hand and bread in the other when they opened the door.

'You must be Sergeant Rooney,' George said.

'And you must be Anna's dad if I'm not mistaken. Your wife and son in-law will fill you in on what's happening Sir,' then over his shoulder he said, 'Try and get some rest, you all look like you could do with.'

'We will try. It won't be easy,' George answered for them all.

Ruby and Tom sat at the kitchen table as George made some coffee while they filled him in on what the police were doing.

'You didn't ask that policeman about putting it on Facebook,' Ruby commented to Tom.

'Shit I forgot, I will ask him when he phones me. I need to go pick Rex up.'

'Oh, have you called the vet?'

'Sorry George I meant to say. Yes the sergeant asked me to do it while he was here because he wanted to know the outcome. Rex has cracked ribs and will be on tablets for a week or so.'

'That's not so bad, did you phone your work this morning to tell them you were not going in.'

'Yes, I told my boss I was not well, not what

is actually going on. I will need to phone him back, tell him the truth; I don't want him to find out from another source. I should have just told him this morning, I'm not thinking straight.'

'None of us are dear,' Ruby commented.

They sat for a while until the coffee was gone. Tom left to get Rex. Once he was gone Ruby told her husband about what Rooney had asked her when Tom was in the kitchen phoning the vets.

'Did you tell him what she had told you?'

'Yes of course I saw no point in lying.'

'They will start to check him out now. They will start to think he has something to do with her going missing.'

'Don't be silly. Tom would never hurt her like that.'

'We know that, they don't. They will pick him apart.'

13

PC Nicole McMillan was meeting Sergeant Rooney at the Day-Today store to check the CCTV. The young woman was new to the force and was surprised when asked to do a solo task. The sergeant had asked her to go around the route they thought Anna had took and check if any of the houses had cameras up. There were three on the street names she had been given. There was one on Parson's Way, another on Bison Street and one on Westfield Street. No one was home at any of the addresses. There were three shops on Main Street, a hairdressers, a Chinese take away and a small grocery, two of the three had cameras on the inside, none had them on the outside.

'Hello Nicole, how did you get on?' Rooney inquired when they met outside the shop.

'Three houses, no one in, here are the addresses,' she said handing him a piece of paper.

'Probably at work, we will try them later. In the meantime we will go check the one in here,' he said starting towards the shop.

Nicole was medium build and height, with long, blonde hair, blue eyes with perfectly manicured eyebrows. She looked right at home in her uniform and she wore it with pride. Being in the police force was all she ever wanted to do. Everything she did was done with the utmost effort.

'Mr Mohammad?' Rooney asked the man behind the counter.

'Yes, if you would like to come through, I will show you the footage I was called about this morning. I believe you would like to see between nine and eleven last night,' Omar said as he came out from behind the counter, his son went in to cover the till for him.

'Has there been a bit of trouble?'

'Nothing to worry about at the moment Sir,' PC McMillan took the initiative.

They went into the back room; Rooney sat on the seat that was in front of the monitor then asked Omar, 'Could you leave us to have a look please.'

Omar agreed and left the room, they could tell he was not happy about it. He wanted to know what was going on. The room was cram packed with stock for the shop; the only floor space was what little there was around the cheap desk they were at.

'Right, time here on the screen is 8.58 pm. I will press fast forward and stop if we see any movement.'

'Ok, I've got my eyes peeled boss,' PC McMillan said from behind his left shoulder.

He stopped the tape at 9.03.

'The shop closes at nine, so that is the owner

going home.'

'Yes, there he goes.'

The next bit of activity was at 9.06, he took the tape off fast forward. They saw two girls of about thirteen walking by the shop coming from the Main Street direction; they crossed the street just outside the shop. The tape was put back on fast forward. Rooney stopped the tape another couple of times seeing youngsters probably going home. Then at 9.49 they spot Anna. They rewound the film around a minute before she appeared on the screen and watched her walk past the shop with her dog towards Main Street, although there was a chance she went down Morcombe Street before that. Nothing out of the ordinary they thought. They watched it three times before going back to the front shop and asking Omar if they can get a copy of it.

'Of course anything I can do to assist,' Omar said as he hurried into the back and came back a few minutes later with a memory stick for them.

'Thank you Sir,' Rooney said before they left the shop.

Outside the shop he said to his colleague. 'We will go back to the station I want to show this to Inspector Halliday before I call Mr Ross. We know now that she did indeed take the dog a walk, she could still have come to harm when she got back home. Between you and me, I have a couple of scenarios. First Anna confided in her mother that she thinks it might be possible that her husband could be having an affair, although she has no proof of it. If he confessed or if she found something then maybe there could have been a confrontation. Second the dog may have been knocked down, not my own theory, although a possibility. The vet can't be sure what happened to him, what if Anna was mowed down with her dog and the person who did panicked and took the woman with them. There have been no reports of her at the Hospitals.' He paused then went on. 'Just ignore me; we don't have anything to go on yet. I'm babbling here.'

'Yes Sir.' His colleague said trying to hide a smile.

14

How long have I been sleeping? It can't be that long surely, Ravi told me I would only need three hours. Tonight I'm going to start my quest to try to find someone with whom I can communicate. It won't be easy, the main problem I face is, who? I will start with my nearest and dearest I suppose that is if they are sleeping at all.

Anna had been sleeping on the floor of the shed right next to the shabby bed. She was not uncomfortable in the least, apart from the fact had she could not feel the physical things there was the usual inch she had between her and whatever she walking on or sitting on, like sleeping on air she thought. No one had come into the shed since Jasmine had got her breakfast. The poor girl was looking at Rex's name tag again. Maybe she had some sort of hope pinned on this, Anna didn't know, anything that could give this girl a shimmer of hope was worth holding on to considering her position.

Jasmine had finished the book the monsters had given her and was hoping she would get another, she had already read more than a dozen books since she had been in her prison, there was nothing else for her to do. To them she was just an incubator, not a human being. They fed her three times a day, changed her toilet bucket daily, she was given a basin of hot water and soap with fresh clothes a couple of times a week, Candice would unchain her for the length of time it took her to change the t-shirt, which wasn't long at all. Jasmine once tried to overpower her, she didn't have the strength. Candice told her if she tried it again she would kill her, so Jasmine didn't attempt it. The boredom was the worst thing to her, she had heard of people being held captive for years and wondered how on earth they could cope with it, she thought of her parents and Glen every day, thinking what they must be going through. Hoping that they don't think she ran away with not a thought for them. No, she thought they would not think her capable of intentionally giving them that kind of heartache. Jasmine often envisioned her captors making some kind of mistake then she is able to get her freedom, so far they were much too careful. They had too much at stake to make an error.

This is dire in here, yet there is nothing much I can do at the moment to achieve my goal. I'm only staying here trying to be a friend to this girl, but I'm an invisible friend. She has no clue anyone is trying to help her. If only she knew someone knows of her ordeal. Even if she learned about me, would it give her any comfort? Would she even believe it? I know I wouldn't.

Anna was jolted from the questions she was

asking herself by Jasmine, she was talking to the baby again.

'I totally think you are a girl. I'm going to call you something unusual. A name no one else has considered yet. I don't know what yet; however, I have plenty of time to work it out. I will let you know as soon as I do.'

I wonder how much more this girl can take, apart from being pregnant she physically looks alright, although it can't be good for her stuck in here with no fresh air and getting no exercise. It's her mental well being that I'm worried about; I sure hope she is strong enough to stand this until I can get around to helping her, who knows how long it will take me to find someone who can help. That's if I find anyone at all. I can't think like that I need to be more positive.

'If you are a girl then you will be a princess and if you are a boy you will be my little prince,' Jasmine was still talking away to her bump.

This is crazy. I can't stand listening to her planning for the future as if she is the one who is going to get to name that baby. The only one that can make that happen is me. I stand between her and the future she could have. I need to save them. I'm going to see the evil ones to see if I can find something out.

Anna stood before Candice. She was at work, answering the phone at the doctors' surgery as

if she didn't have care in the world. The clock on the wall read 11.43 am. Candice finished her call and started tapping away at her keyboard.
'I take it your going home for lunch,' her workmate Susan at the other desk in the reception asked.
'Yes, I made some homemade soup last night; I am looking forward to a nice big bowl.'
'Lucky you, I've got my usual boring sandwich with me.'

I bet Jasmine will be getting some of that soup for her lunch as well. I wonder what time this lunatic gets her lunch. I suppose I can wait. I have nothing else to do.

'Did I tell you we are trying to adopt.'
'No.' Susan answered Candice a little surprised.
'We tried IVF a few times without success; this is the last option for us. We have done all the paperwork and had the adoption people out to the house for a couple of visits. You know to make sure we are suitable.'
'Well I hope it all goes well for you both. If anyone deserves it you do. You two will be wonderful parents.'
'Ah thank you Susan that means a lot to me,' she said as the phone started ringing.

The lying rat, she is planting the seed. She has all this figured out. This deceitful, evil scumbag needs to get caught. Would her friends even believe how much of a bad apple she really is? I don't know any of them; she seems to have Susan fooled for starters.

Anna waited by her side until 12.30 lunch time, she then went to Jasmine. She waited with her until Candice appeared with the homemade soup.

The homemade soup is real I thought for a moment that maybe that was made up as well. I wouldn't believe a word that came out her lying mouth. She angers me so much. If I were alive my stomach would be churning about now.

'Here we go dear, some lovely soup for you.'
'Why can't you have a heart and let me go,' Jasmine pleaded with her.
'You know that is not going to happen dear.'
'Well stop calling me fucking dear; it gets right on my nerves.'
'A bit touchy today are we dear.'
Jasmine turned away from her. She really wanted to scream at her, she knew Candice would take the food away if she did. Candice left the soup and disappeared out the door with her well practiced procedure

Jack Sutherland was in the site office which was a portacabin when Anna turned up beside him.

The poor lamb looks exhausted as well he should after what he was doing half the night. I take it nothing at my burial site seems out of place to anyone.

'If I could I would spit in your face right now,' Anna said out loud, silent to everyone else.

'How's your stomach now?' John Morrison his second in command inquired.

'It's not too bad now; I might even try a bit of lunch soon.'

'Do you want to go home? I can take care of things here.'

'No, that won't be necessary. I'm sure I will survive the day out.'

'If you are sure you can manage. You need to phone the Council Offices to find out about the authorization for the street lights.'

'I know, they said on Tuesday that the specifications and drawings were nearly complete. I will do it after lunch.'

'You can't sell these houses until they are up,' John said stating the obvious to the seasoned builder.

'I *have* done this before John,' he responded sarcastically.

'I know I'm sorry. I'm sure you have everything in hand.'

'I have a company waiting for the go ahead, it has taken a little longer than normal, but I have been assured there will be no problem.'

'Ok, you are the boss.'

'How would you like to be the boss?'

'What do you mean?'

'I told you I inherited that house up by Inverness.'

'Yes.'

'Well we are moving there in a couple of months.'

'Wow I didn't see that coming, well done you. Are you asking me if I want to buy the business?'

'I was thinking of selling. Now I want to keep it, let someone run it for me, that someone being you if you agree to it. Of course there will be a pay rise. You would do all the day to day stuff; I could do the legal stuff like chasing up planning and authorization that kind of thing. I'm sure I can make an office in that big house in the country.'

'Yes I would love to,' John accepted happily, stood up, walked over to his boss and shook Jack's hand. 'Thank you I won't let you down.'

'You had better not,' Jack said jokingly.

'Are you selling your house here?'

'Yep, we have no plans to come back here so why keep it, it will free up a fair bit of money for the finer things in life,' he said laughing. 'I'm too tired tonight, but how about going to the pub tomorrow for a pint to seal the deal?'

'Sounds good to me,' John agreed.

Listen to him making his plans. Well not if I have anything to do with it. This makes my blood boil.

Jack made the decision to keep the business without consulting Candice. She would not be happy he thought. Nothing he does makes her happy. Maybe this baby will change her for the better.

15

Sergeant Stephen Rooney was asked inside the Ross home by Tom when he knocked on the front door at 1.10 pm on Friday afternoon.

'Mr and Mrs Anderson not with you?' he asked as he entered the living room.

'They went home, Ruby is done in. They are going to phone their eldest daughter Clara, let her know of the situation. Have you any news?'

'I checked the CCTV from the shop; Anna was spotted walking by with the dog towards the direction of Main Street at 9.49 last night. There are three houses in the area we have found to have security cameras. We will check these out tonight when people are more likely to be home. We checked earlier. They were probably at work. We will contact people from the list you gave us after she has been missing for twenty four hours. Don't want to alarm anyone unnecessarily.'

'Her business partner Sam knows she's missing and a couple of her close friends.'

'That's fine; I would expect you to have called a few people at least.'

'Should I put a post on social media? I see posts about missing people all the time.'

'Not yet, it is a bit too early for that. You may do it tomorrow if she's not back. We will do it on our page too. It may turn up something helpful.'

'Will I find out tonight if Anna is on these other cameras?'

'You will find out, maybe not tonight Sir,' the sergeant answered.

'Something has happened to her I know it.'

'You need to stay positive Mr Ross. She could walk back in that door with some weird story to tell,' the officer said light heartedly.

'I suppose you could be right.'

'Have you had any sleep?'

'No, I can't even think about that.'

'Well maybe you should, you are no good to anyone if you are dog tired.'

Rooney noticed Rex in his bed in the corner next to the sideboard.

'So this is Rex,' he said standing up then walking towards the dog.

He bent down and gave Rex a pat on the head.

'If only you could talk my friend, you would be able to solve a mystery for us. How is he doing?'

'He doesn't seem to want to move much, who can blame him.'

'I'm going back to the station. I will contact you if we uncover anything. In the meantime please try to get some rest.'

Tom walked the policeman out and then went up the stair. He was going to take the sergeant's advice and try to get some rest.

Inspector Alan Halliday and Sergeant Rooney

sat at a cluttered desk opposite each other in the incident room at Hallington Police Station. The room had seven other desks; three of which were occupied by other officers. The building had two storeys; the first floor had the public desk, the staff canteen, three interview rooms and a few cells. The offices were on the second floor. The Incident room had plenty natural light flooding in due to the large windows on two walls. The other walls were painted white, a long time ago by the look of them. Details of Anna Ross were on a whiteboard next to the two policemen.

'So what's the next step Alan?'

'I think we should search the park tomorrow, she may have been dragged in there through one of the side gates that have no CCTV on them at the top end of Parson's way. It's a long shot, although it's possible. After you told me what her mother told you about Anna's suspicions about her husband having an affair maybe we should get a search warrant for their house especially if we get a hit on the residential camera on Bison Street, she was nearly home by then.'

'I thought he was maybe to blame, the more I think about it the more I think that he didn't have time. He called the in-laws just after eleven. Anna would have got home at 10.25 give or take. Do you think that would be enough time to do the deed then get composed enough for the aftermath?'

'Yes I do Stephen. If he did do something to her he is certainly brazen enough having the police in his house. Let's wait until you and PC McMillan have checked those cameras tonight.'

'It all depends on what side of the street she walked down if we see her on it or not.'

'Yes that's true.'

'She could have been knocked down when her dog was hurt then taken away by the panicked driver,' Rooney suggested.

'Of course that's another possibility. We need to whittle down the scenarios. A search warrant and a search of the park will do this. We need to hope you get a result on the cameras tonight. Then we may be able to rule something out.'

'I can't rule out a connection to Jasmine Brown,' Stephen said.

'Quite right, it annoys me that we never got anywhere with that case, we may never know what happened to her. I mean a few people saw her at the doctors' and the chemist, then nothing, strange. I still pray that we get something on her. With the amount of time that has elapsed my hope is fading.'

The police got a warrant to see Jasmine's medical records a week after she hadn't been seen. That's when they found out about the baby, they couldn't share this information even with her parents, their hands were tied. This made them think that maybe she had run away. After there had been no sightings of the girl they were at a dead end.

'I hope they are not connected. We have found nothing on Jasmine, I'd like to think we won't let the trail go cold on Anna,' Stephen said wearily.

'We won't. No stone will be left unturned.'

Stephen smiled inside when the inspector said this. He was well known for his proverbs. His colleagues believed he knew every one of them; this earned him the nickname of The Proverb King.

16

Anna had been back with Jasmine for a while, but nothing was happening here, not that she expecting anything to transpire so quickly, she knew this would not be solved anytime soon.

I feel like I'm wasting precious time sitting here doing nothing. There's not much I can do until everyone is asleep. I might as well check on Tom, I will walk around; at least it will pass sometime.

She thought herself outside the shed. It was raining, although none of it seemed to be falling on her. When she reached the monsters gate she realised she was immune to the rain.

This make is waterproof. Result. I'm sure there is more to it than that. That's another question for Ravi when I eventually see him again.

She turned right outside the gate to the corner of Parkway way lane where Billy Barclay stays. She thought of him, then it struck her that he was the last person apart from her killer to see her alive.

I wonder if many people know I'm missing. I wonder if Billy knows.

Anna crossed the road where the entrance to Bison Street was not far away. She walked down this street, crossed the road at the end and entered Drayton Street. Across the road at the bottom of this street was her house. Both Tom and her cars were in the driveway. She thought herself into her living room where she was very pleased indeed to see Rex in his bed.

'Oh Rex you made it home. You're alive. I can't believe it. This is the best bit of news I have had since I died,' she laughed through her tears of joy.

Rex wagged his tail a little she was sure of it. She approached him slowly and bent down to him. She thought he was looking at her until she turned around to see Tom coming into the living room.

Rex must have heard him coming down the stair that's why he was wagging his tail. How stupid I am to think he knew I was here.

She moved out of the way as Tom came closer to their pet.

'How are you feeling now boy? Do you need a pee? Come on we will go out into the back garden.'

He took a few steps then turned around and patted his thigh to entice Rex to follow him.' Come on boy.'

With a touch of reluctance and a small grunt Rex got up slowly. Anyone could see he was in pain. He followed Tom into the kitchen then went out into the garden when Tom opened the back door.

He's limping. He got hurt; at least he is back here where he belongs. Tom looks terrible, no wonder, Mum and Dad must be at home, they must have called Clara by now, although knowing them they will be reluctant to worry her.

Tom stood in the same t-shirt and jogging bottoms he had on last night. His stubble was growing dark and his hair was a mess. He did manage to get a couple of hours sleep; he did not feel any better for it. He looked at his mobile, no missed calls, no texts, the time was 4.05 pm. It was still raining; the sky was starting to darken. He stood at the sink watching Rex in the garden.
'Anna where are you? Please come back to me.'
'I'm here Tom,' she said walking over to his side.
'I should have treated you better. I should have made more of an effort. I didn't know how lucky I was to have you,' Tom whispered, loud enough for Anna to hear him.
Rex came in the open back door, went straight for his food bowl then got tucked in.
'At least you still have your appetite,' Tom said to him.
Tom went into the living room and sat down; when Rex came through he lifted the dog up beside him.
'I'm going to spoil you boy.'

He took Rex's head in his hands and gave him a big kiss on the forehead. That's when Tom noticed his name tag was missing from his collar.
'Where's your tag?'
Tom looked around on the couch, found nothing.
'You stay here I will be back just now.'
Tom went into the kitchen to have a look then decided to check the garden. It was a touch on the dim side so returned to the house for a torch. The grass had not been cut for a while, but was not that long. He methodically went up and down the garden to no avail.
'I will check it again in the daylight,' he said to himself

He has noticed the disk is missing. I hope he doesn't spend too long looking for it, he won't find it.

Tom went back into the living room and went to sit beside Rex.
'When did you lose it? Was it when you got hurt?
'That's it Tom. You are getting warmer, although it's not anywhere you will find it,' Anna commented to her husband wishing he could hear her.
'I need to call Katie Irvine to see if she saw it on you. If she didn't this could be a clue.'
Tom picked up his mobile and called the vet. The woman who answered said her name was

Mary, she said that Katie would not be in until six for the nightshift which made sense to him. Tom left his name and asked Mary if she could get Katie to call him as soon as she came in. She agreed, they said their goodbyes then Tom hung up.
'That's another wait and see scenario. I'm going to walk around the route anyway. You can't come with me boy I think it might be too much for you.'
Tom went into the hall for a jacket then left by the back door. Anna went with him. He searched the pavement as he walked along for Rex's name tag; it was too dark by now to be able to spot something that small. He tried anyway. He got to the corner of Morcombe Street and stopped. Sergeant Rooney had confirmed that Anna had come this way. They didn't know for sure if she went along Morcombe Street or went on to Main Street they only saw her go by the shop on the CCTV. Knowing Anna Tom was sure she went the long way so headed on for Main Street still combing the pavement with his eyes in the gloom with Anna right beside him. The traffic was at its busiest at this time with people going home from work. The drizzly rain had stopped, but it was bitterly cold.
'You won't find me or the name tag honey,' Anna told her husband who of course was oblivious to the fact that she was even there.

Tom's mobile rang; he took it out his pocket. It was Ruby.

'Hello Ruby,' he said answering it.

'No news from anywhere then?'

'No nothing. I'm walking around the scheme again. I don't how significant it is, Rex has lost his name tag. I'm waiting for the vet to call me back. I need to know if he had it on when he was in there, he may have lost it when he was injured or whatever happened to him. I will tell the police when I speak to them which hopefully will be soon. They are checking out the houses with the security cameras at six so I hope the sergeant will call me after that to let me know the outcome,' Tom relayed this to Ruby all in the one breath.

'We will come over to your house in a bit. I have some homemade lasagne.'

'That sounds great. I should be home in twenty minutes or so see you soon, bye.'

'Bye son, see you soon.'

Tom put his phone back in his pocket; he was half-way along Main Street. He started thinking of all the bad things that could have happened to Anna. A mugging gone wrong, a rape, a murder, a rape and murder, some lunatic out of his face on drugs not knowing what he was doing or a hit and run.

'Stop thinking all this shit Tom, you don't know what happened,' he said to himself under his breath.

Yes think the worst Tom because the worst happened.

Tom reached his gate with no name tag found and more importantly no sign of Anna, it was a long shot, he knew that, still he had to try. Five minutes after he got in George and Ruby turned up, the latter with the lasagne in her hand.

'I will put this in the oven, be about forty minutes.'

'Thanks Ruby. Oh and Sergeant Rooney said I should get Anna on social media in the morning, said the police will probably do it too.'

'Why not now,' George demanded.

'The police are still hopeful that she will turn up. They probably need to wait twenty-four hours before taking it public, they have a point I suppose,' Tom answered.

'She has got a bit of explaining to do to her old dad when she does turn up,' George said trying to lighten the mood.

Tom's phone went again, this time it was Sam, Anna's business partner.

'Hello Sam.'

'I'm so sorry to bother you, I need to know if there is any word on Anna I'm worried, 'Sam said sounding a little flustered.

'Nothing yet I'm afraid, the police are checking out a few things tonight. I'm hoping to hear from them soon,' Tom explained.

'Promise me you will phone me or get Anna to phone me when she comes home. I know this may sound silly, I have called her phone a few times today.'

'The police have it Sam.'

'Well I feel even sillier now.'

'Don't Sam, it just proves how much you care for her and yes I promise I will phone you as soon as I have any news.'

'Thank you; hope to hear from you soon then.'

'You will bye.'

'Did you fill in Clara?' Tom asked his in-laws.

'Yes we did. She did not take it well as we imagined. She is coming to our house tomorrow night. Peter is home tomorrow afternoon. He will stay with Jamez and Clara will drive up here,' Ruby told him.

Clara's husband Peter Quinn often worked away from home, never for more than two nights at a time. He sells pharmaceuticals for a large company and made that one of the conditions before he took the job. Their daughter Jamez is four years old and the living image of her mother. They live in Newcastle; however, often come to visit and stay with Ruby and George.

'That's good, by then we can only hope that Anna will be home. Are you two going to stay here tonight?' You're more than welcome.'

'I am, George is going home for the cat tonight,'

Ruby answered.

Anna stood watching and listening to her husband. She didn't want to go back to that drab shed, although she knew she had to. So she took another look at her loved ones then closed her eyes.

Anna took up her usual position at the bottom of Jasmine's miserable bed. All she had to do now was wait until everyone was asleep then she could start her work.

Jasmine had no means in this little prison to determine the time. She just knew the time roughly by the meals she was given. Jasmine had some idea of the length of time she had spent in this hovel by the size of her bump and how much colder it seemed to be getting.

'Your granny and granddad don't know you exist yet. Well I don't think they will. I really don't know what has happened outside of this pathetic shed since we came in here,' Jasmine was talking to the baby again. 'If the police know by now then maybe they do too.'

This is breaking my heart. I wish I could talk to her, not that I think it would give her much comfort to know that a soul is trying to help her, or maybe it would. I think I will try Tom first tonight, then my parents, then Clara. After that I'm just stabbing in the dark really. I wish it was bed time so that I can get started.

'The witch will be in with dinner soon I think,' Jasmine said.

Witch is too good a word for her.

Anna went into the monsters' house to see if anyone was home. Jack was standing in the kitchen cooking dinner. The radio was on; he was humming away to how deep is your love by The Bee Gees as if kidnapping someone and keeping them hostage was an everyday occurrence. Anna went over to have a look at what Jasmine would be getting for dinner tonight. It was stovies; Anna never really cared for that dish when she was alive.

At least that girl is getting a wholesome meal tonight. I suppose if they give her something she doesn't like she needs to eat it anyway. She must feel like she wants to give up, but can't for the sake of her little one.

Jack didn't like to go to the shed much. It made him feel worse than he already did. He was trying to block the guilt out, it wasn't working, all he could think of was the girl they had in the shed. He knew Candice didn't care a jot for the girl; all she wanted was the baby. He loved Candice with all his heart or he thought he did. He couldn't believe how cold she had become, how void of feelings, no empathy, no compassion, just a single track mind to get what she wants. He knew he crossed the line by killing the woman that stumbled across their secret. Jack now wished he had said no to this crazy plan from the get go.

Anna went back to Jasmine. She had Rex's name tag out again staring at it as if it was magically going to transport her out of here. Anna took up her usual spot to wait for bedtime.

17

Sergeant Stephen Rooney and PC Nicole McMillan approached Tom's front door in the pouring rain. Before they could knock Tom opened the door.

'Please come in, I heard a car so looked out and saw it was you. I hope you have some good news for me.'

Once they were settled in the living room the sergeant gave them the news.

'I'm afraid we have no further information that shines any light on Anna's whereabouts. We know for sure now she went to Main Street. The residential camera in Parson's Way shows Anna walking past at 9.51 pm last night. We didn't really need to check the camera in Westfield Street as we saw her on the one in Parson's Way, we checked anyway they informed us they have not long moved in and have not had it connected yet.'

'You must be talking about Shannon and Ryan Cuthbertson,' Ruby said.

'Yes, I take you know them.'

'Shannon is the Trainee Pharmacist in Smith's Chemist where I work. She has been there for a couple of months now.'

'It's a small world after all. They seem to have their hands full with that little girl of theirs.'

'Her name is Harper and yes they certainly do.'

'Enough of the chit chat Ruby, I want to know about the other camera,' George interrupted
'Yes, let's talk about that,' Tom added.
'Sorry,' both Ruby and the sergeant apologised at the same time.
'The camera on Bison Street is very much in full working order; unfortunately it only covers one side of the street. If Anna had walked down the other side of the road there is no way it would pick her up. So as it stands we are assuming that she went along Main Street and came down Bison Street, although there is no way to be sure.'
'So we are no further forward then,' Tom said disappointed.
'We are drafting in all the officers we can get to do a search of Hallington Park tomorrow, if Anna is not back that is. We are closing it off to the public.'
'I told you she would never have gone in there at night.'
'Voluntarily perhaps, we have to consider that maybe she went under duress.'
Ruby gasped and put her hand to her mouth, then said, 'We don't want or need to think about that sort of thing, not yet anyway.'
'We need to cover all bases I'm afraid,' the sergeant told them giving a glance over at PC McMillan.
He was hoping for some help on this, PC

McMillan took the hint.

'Everything we do is to rule things out, especially if we don't have many leads on a case.'

'Someone must have seen her last night. Tom is going to put it on Facebook first thing in the morning hopefully someone will see it that has some sort of information,' George said.

'As will the police Mr Anderson. At least social media has some good uses,' PC McMillan added.

'I don't know if this has any significance, but Rex's name tag is missing from his collar. I called the vet, she wasn't there. When she called back she said it wasn't on him when he was at the surgery,' Tom said.

'Can the vet be sure?'

'Yes, she had to take the collar off for the x-ray.' The sergeant took out his note pad and said.' Describe it please.'

'It's a silver disk with Rex on one side and Anna's mobile number on the back.'

'As you said it might not be important, sometimes it's the smallest things that make the difference. When was the last time you noticed it being on his collar?'

'I can't say. It's just something that you always expect to be there. Wait, it was definitely there on Wednesday night, he was scratching himself and I remember Anna telling him to do it more quietly, it was jingling about when he was scratching. She was on the phone to her friend

Fiona.'

'See it is amazing what you can remember when you need to,' the policewoman stated.

'Well we will be going now. I hope you all get a better sleep tonight, you all look done in if you don't mind me saying,' Rooney said as he stood up to leave.

'I'm not sure we will,' said Ruby also standing to walk them to the door.

After the police had gone Tom and the Andersons sat in silence not knowing what else there was to say, all they could do now was to wait for Anna to show up.

18

When Jasmine's dinner was brought to her Anna was pleased to see that it was a generous portion, she was more pleased that it was accompanied by a chocolate bar.

At least they are taking care of her dietary needs, shame about the rest of her needs or rights as a human being. I wonder what time it is now. It is Friday night people tend to stay up later when the weekend comes round.

After a few hours sitting with Jasmine Anna popped home to see the time and to check up on her loved ones, Tom was sitting on the couch with Rex. The sight brought tears to her eyes, she could not bear to see the pain she was causing her family, even if it was unintentional.

Is he here all alone? Maybe Mum and Dad went home for a sleep; they must be exhausted with what they are going through. I will try the spare room you never know.

Anna went upstairs to the spare room where she found her mother asleep.
'Anna Anderson,' Anna said to her mother with no response.
'Anna Anderson,' she tried again and waited.
She stayed there for ten minutes saying her name over and over again, nothing happened.

Well that's one person that I can score off my list. Dad must be at home, I will try him next.

She went back downstairs to the living room to find Tom crying, cuddled up to his dog.
'I wish I could take this pain away from you,' Anna said to her husband. 'I wish I had gone the short way round on my walk and none of this would have happened.'

If I had went the short way round I wouldn't know about Jasmine. I wouldn't be helping her. One life for another I suppose. This was meant to be. It has got to mean something, a reason behind it. I still can't make total sense of it.

She went to the kitchen to check the time it was 9.32 pm.

Is that all the time it is. Mum is sleeping early, she must be knackered. No one is going to be sleeping yet, I might as well go back and see Jasmine not that it is going to help her, me sitting there doing nothing.

Anna went back to Jasmine. The young woman was fast asleep. There was a new book for her to read on the floor next to the bed. Anna missed whoever came in to deliver it. She sat on her usual spot at the bottom of the bed and let the tears come. She was unsure why she was crying; she had lots of reasons though right now she wasn't sure which one was upsetting her the most.

I need to stop this blubbering, it's not helping one little bit. I'm feeling sorry for myself I think. I shouldn't be, I've accepted what has happened. I need to pull myself together. Ravi was right about the boredom, I'm on my first night and I'm feeling it already.

'Anna Anderson,' she said out loud into the room.
Anna was startled and excited when Jasmine started to move in her sleep.

Oh my, is she hearing me? Can it be real?

Anna let Jasmine settle again and said her name again. This time Jasmine mumbled in her sleep. Anna was amazed by this. She never thought she would be able to communicate with someone so fast.

Maybe I'm getting excited for nothing here. Even if I can make her hear me how is it going to help her? Even if I can't help her I can give her hope at least.

Anna said her name again to be certain. Jasmine mumbled again.

I think she can hear me

Emotion crashed over Anna like a huge wave all at once. She was laughing and crying at the same time. It was a few moments before she could compose herself enough to talk to Jasmine.

'I don't know where to start Jasmine. I'm the woman you saw murdered right here in this shed. My name is Anna Ross, formerly Anna Anderson. I am here to try and help you and your baby. I don't know if I will succeed, but I will give it my all and more. I don't know how much if any of this you will be able to understand, it is the weirdest thing that I have ever had to do. What I'm trying to say is just hang in there; I know this must be extremely hard for you, keep the faith that you may get a happy ending.'

Anna sat on the bottom of the bed for another couple of hours waiting to go and try someone else who might be able to actually physically help her. The monotony was really starting to grate on her; she knew there was nothing she could do about that. She was here to do a job, and she was determined to get it done.

Anna popped home to check the time again. Tom was still up. He had his jacket; trainers and a hat on, the jacket and hat looked damp.

He must have been out looking for me. If only I could tell him that it's useless to go around the streets. There's nothing he can do really, he must feel terrible. If the shoe was on the other foot I don't know that I would be able to function at all.

Rex was on the couch next to Tom, so Anna sat down next to them. She felt as sad as she had ever done seeing him like this. She put her hand on Tom's and felt a similar, but not the exact same sensation as when she touched Jasmine. She pulled her hand back and just stared at her loved one. Once again Anna got emotional.

I feel like I've cried nonstop since I died. Hey! There's a line I never thought would ever be true. As much as I would love to spend more time here I need to move.

She went into the kitchen to check the time. It was 11.50 pm.
'It's late enough now, time to get started.'
Anna went straight to her Father's bedroom, he wasn't asleep. Anna had rarely seen her Father weeping, he was sitting up in bed crying with their cat Fluff lying beside him.
'Get some sleep Dad,' Anna said.

What a state he's in, it's all my doing, well not really my doing. No matter where the fault lies the point is he is devastated.

Anna didn't hang about she left to go to Clara. Clara was sleeping in her king size bed alone as Peter was away on business. The bedside table lamp was on so Anna could see how red and puffy her eyes were, her skin looked paler than normal against the freckles dotted around on her face. Her red hair was sprawled across the pillow like the tentacles of some alien creature. 'Anna Anderson,' Anna said over and over with a few minutes between each time, there was no sign of contact being made.

I don't know what I'm doing. Should I try my entire family first? I need to have patience I suppose. I knew this was not going to be easy when I took it on. It may just be impossible.

'Pull it together, you have only just started, it's going to be a long, lonely journey, you need to do this,' Anna stated to herself.
She was just about to go back to her dad to see if he was asleep yet when she noticed that she was standing in front of Clara's mirrored wardrobe and that she had no reflection.

What can I say; things keep getting stranger and stranger. Now that I think about it I'm not surprised I have no reflection, I am dead after all.

Anna went back to her father. At first she thought he was sleeping now because the light was out, she could still hear him sniffling in the dark room. She left and went back to Tom. He was in the exact same place as he was before.

Who do I try now? These three people could be anyone, anywhere.

Anna started to feel disheartened. She went outside and started to walk the route she had done the previous night. It wasn't raining now which of course made no difference to her. She stopped suddenly then went back to her gate.

I will need to do this house by house. I will start from my house and do a street at a time. I don't know how long this will take, I would say it doesn't matter, but it does, that baby is depending on me.

Anna went to the house to the right of hers and thought herself in the gate. She walked to the front door then thought herself through that. When she got inside she walked up the stairs to find the room doors closed so she thought herself on the other side of the first one. Anna stood in Malcolm Tate's room, the teenage son of her neighbours. She said her name over and over, there was no acknowledgement.

He might be too stoned to make any kind of response. I smell it when he is smoking weed out his bedroom window when his parents are out.

Anna went to the other bedroom. The small light on the wall at the side of Mrs Tate's side of the bed was on as she was reading. Her husband was asleep, she said her name a few times and again she had no contact. She went to the next house over the fence. She didn't know these people's names, all she knew was it was a young couple with twin girls, who kept themselves to themselves. The same happened, no acknowledgment, so she worked her way along the street, house after house with no luck. Some people were sleeping, some were still awake and one house was having a small party, it was always the same outcome. No contact.

What am I doing? Is this all I can do? I can't even write down the houses that I need to return to because some of the people are awake and I certainly can't remember them all. Am I to keep going around and around in circles? I only have two people left if I'm correct in thinking that Jasmine can hear me.

Anna did the rest of Browning Street and half way up Parson's Way. She then realised that people were starting to get up to start their weekend, so she returned to the shed with Jasmine. She lay down on the floor beside the bed and went to sleep disappointed.

19
Saturday 16th November

Tom had eventually gone to bed at 3.15 am. It was now 7.50 am and he was up and on Facebook putting on a post about Anna. Ruby was at the sink doing what dishes there was to be done. After she had finished she lifted her mug of coffee from the worktop beside her and went to sit next to her son in-law at the kitchen table.

'Let me see it then,' she said to Tom.

Tom turned around the laptop to show her, there was a picture of Anna that had been taken in Hallington Park in the summer. She had a flowery, red, cotton dress on, she had a good tan. Most of all she looked so happy. The tears came to Ruby's eyes before she could even start to read what he had written.

'That's a great photo Tom.'

'Yes it is. It's my favourite.'

Ruby read what Tom had written, she was so overcome she excused herself and went to the bathroom.

George let himself in the front door with his key and came straight into the kitchen.

'Have you had any news from the police yet?'

'No, I'm going to call them soon I think.'

'Where's Ruby.'

'Up in the bathroom, she got upset when she

seen this photo,' Tom told George as he turned the laptop around to let him see his post.

'It sure is a good photo of my little girl.'

'We can only hope that we get some sort of response from it, someone has got to know something.'

'Someone does know something that we can be sure of.'

Ruby returned dabbing her eyes with a tissue.

'I will go to the shop soon and pick something up for breakfast. In the meantime, do you two want some more coffee?'

'Yes, please,' Tom answered.

'Make mine tea please darling,' said George.

At 8.15 the door went. It was Sergeant Rooney with PC Nicole McMillan.

'Mr Ross with your permission we would like to search your house and car please,' Sergeant Rooney said when Tom answered the door.'

'Why, I have nothing to do with this, you lot really should be out doing your job by finding my wife.'

'Sir, this happens when people go missing under strange circumstances, we have a warrant just in case you refused.'

By this time Ruby and George were at the front door, along with three more officers and a forensic woman who had come out of their cars and made their way to the house.

'Of course you can do your search, he has

nothing to hide,' George announced protesting Tom's innocence.

'Yes, just do it,' Tom stated.

'We would also like you to come to the station for some questions if you don't mind,' Sergeant Rooney said in his most authoritative voice.

'Sure, let's go,' said Tom with a degree of resignation.

'Mr and Mrs Anderson here will take care of things this end for you I'm sure.'

'Of course we will,' Ruby spoke up.

'PC McMillan and I will accompany you. I will leave these other officers here to do the task in hand.'

Tom walked down the path and out the gate to the waiting car with the sergeant and PC close behind him.

'You have nothing to worry about Tom,' Ruby called after him.

'I know,' Tom answered.

Tom was led into interview room number two when he arrived at the station. He was expecting to see a two-way mirror and some recording equipment, there was none in here. The room was pretty much bare except for a rectangular table with four, red plastic chairs sitting at it, there were no windows and the walls were painted off white.

Sergeant Rooney and Inspector Halliday came into the room with a coffee for each of them.

'Please take a seat Tom. This is just an informal chat, no need to worry,' Inspector Halliday spoke first.

Alan Halliday was a big man in stature; he was six foot three and weighed two hundred and forty pounds. He had black hair with only a few specks of grey showing, light blue eyes and a pale complexion. He had a large nose and his mouth was so small underneath it looked like it didn't belong on his face. Inspector Halliday was fifty-two and looked every day of it.

'I have done nothing, but I fear if I had nothing to worry about I wouldn't be sitting here.'

'You know Tom, a lot of people have been hurt by someone they know, and you are here today to rule you out and nothing more. We have a tough job sometimes. Sometimes all we can do is start to eliminate people until we get some leads, we can't just wait for a vital piece of information to fall into our lap. We need to take action as soon as we can, it would be unfair to the victims to sit about and do nothing, you do understand don't you?' Rooney spoke this time.

'When you put it like that then of course, I suppose I would be complaining if you did nothing.'

Inspector Halliday slid Anna's phone across the table to Tom.

'We are finished with your wife's phone. We found nothing of any importance on there to help us. One thing I must ask you about and you can tell me it's none of my business if you like. In your texts to Anna you call her a *treek*, what exactly do you mean by this?'

'Oh it's silly really; it's a combination of trendy and geek. She can be a bit of a geek over a few things, but she's not a typical geek in the way she dresses and looks, not that geeks have a typical appearance, you know what I mean, so that's what I call her, affectionately of course.'

'Of course,' Inspector Halliday answered.

Tom was starting to relax a little. He took a sip of coffee. He put it back down on the table, it was clear he did not care much for the taste.

'Sorry about the coffee, I guess us lot are used to it by now,' said Rooney.

'It's ok; I've already had a couple this morning. I put a post about Anna on Facebook this morning; I hope it gets some response.'

'I hope it does, I must warn you that you may receive some false information, it's amazing what some people will say they have seen when they haven't,' Sergeant Rooney said.

'That's something I have thought of. I know I need to be realistic.'

They sat for a minute in silence. Rooney was trying to pick his moment.

'Tom I'm just going to come out and ask you. Are you having an affair?'

Tom sat and stared at him for too long, to the

policemen he was admitting his guilt.

'Tom, you are having an affair, aren't you?'

Tom looked down for a while then lifted his head to reveal tears in his eyes.

'I was, I put a stop to it a few weeks ago. I came to my senses when she asked me to leave Anna. That was just not going to happen.'

'The grass is never greener on the other side,' Halliday said sarcastically.

This latest proverb from the Proverb king didn't go unnoticed by Rooney, instead he chose to ignore it and carry on.

'If this other lady hadn't asked you to leave Anna would the affair still be going on?

'No, the guilt was eating away at me. I realised how stupid I was being, I could have wrecked everything between Anna and me. I love Anna and I'm glad I came to my senses.'

'Anna suspects you were having an affair,' Rooney said.

'Is that a question?'

'No, she suspected you.'

'How do you know?'

'Let's just say we have been busy finding out about Anna.'

'Tell me, who told you?'

'That doesn't matter now. All that matters is that we find her as quickly as possible.'

'I will make it up to her when we do.'

'Tom I must ask, do you think it's possible that

Anna could have harmed herself in any way?'
'No, she would never do anything like that.'
'Even if she thought you were playing away?'
'She didn't know for sure, because if she knew she would have confronted me.'
'Did you confess to her about the affair Tom?'
'No I told you, I ended it weeks ago, and as far as I was concerned Anna knew nothing.'
'Did she have any other problems that were worrying her?'
'Nothing, she seemed normal to me'
'Right then we will leave it there for now.'
'Are you still going to search the park?'
'As soon as we are done at your house, there will be a few other officers joining us from Goldfield Police Station in Edinburgh. We are going to close the park and have a good look around.'
'Can I go home?'
'Not yet Mr Ross, as soon as we are finished at your property you can go,' said Halliday who had left most of the talking to Rooney.
The police officers left Tom in the room and went upstairs to Rooney's desk.
'What do you think?' Stephen asked Alan.
'I don't think he has done anything to be honest. We will know for sure if the search at his house comes up empty, I will be surprised if they find anything to incriminate him. I think our best hope at the moment is the search at the park or if the Facebook post gets any hits.'

'Tom has put one on and so have we so if we get anything from it it's a bonus.' It won't take long to search his house it's not that big and the forensics have not much to check either. I'm hoping they will be done for half-past ten, and then we can get to the park.'

'I'm off for some breakfast, you coming?' Halliday asked Rooney.

'No, I've got a sandwich, I will eat it here while I go through what notes and information I have, see if I missed anything.'

'An army marches on its stomach,' Halliday said before getting up and leaving.

PC McMillan came over when she saw Halliday leaving. 'Anything I can do to help?'

'Sure, take a seat,' he responded as he passed over some paperwork to her. I'm just going over it as if it's the first time I have seen it. Four eyes are better than two.'

The two of them sat there going over and over everything they had, swapping pieces of paper so that both of them had checked it. They shared the sandwich the sergeant had brought in and some of the terrible station coffee. They found nothing. Sergeant Rooney's phone on his desk rang at 10.20; it was one of the officers at Tom's house to say the search was over and that they had found nothing of importance.

The sergeant and the PC went straight down to the interview room where they had left Tom, they told him the news then took him home much to his delight.

The sergeant instructed the officers at the house to take a break and be at Hallington Park at half-past eleven. Then he called Goldfield Station to tell them he was ready for the extra bodies he was getting from there to help search the park. By the time they got there it would be around half-past eleven, all the officers could be briefed all at once before going in. PC McMillan and Rooney went to the main gate to the park to wait for the others.

Tom went into the living room; Ruby went straight over to him and gave him a cuddle.

'It's my fault. I'm sorry.'

'What is your fault?'

'I told them what Anna told me on Thursday night, that she had suspicions that you are having an affair. I'm so sorry I shouldn't have said anything.'

'It's all right Ruby, sit down I have something to tell you.'

Both Ruby and George listened to Tom without saying a word as he told them about having a bit on the side. He told them that it was over and that he would never have left Anna for her, the look on their faces told him they were disappointed in him before they even responded.

'I knew it. Anna would not have said as much if

she had any doubt. How could you do that to her, she has done nothing but love you,' Ruby did not hold back.

It was George's turn. 'Why you dirty rat. When Anna comes home she will be coming back to stay with us.'

'That's her decision George. I will make it up to her. I love her so much. All I want is for her to walk in that door so that I can make amends. I know I have hurt her, I promise you both here and now I will never hurt her again.'

'We need to find her first, so why do we all concentrate on that for the moment then see what she wants when she gets back,' Ruby said stifling a sob.

'Ok, just know that I am so sorry.'

Ruby and George went home ten minutes later, telling Tom to call them if he got any news, they were angry with him and he knew it.

20

Anna woke up with Candice bringing in breakfast for Jasmine. She could not bear to look at her so closed her eyes and popped home to see her kitchen clock, her go to place to see what time it was. She was unprepared for what she saw. Her parents were in the kitchen sitting at the dining table; it was the police searching the place that got her panicking a little. The back door was lying open so she went outside to find a woman with a white suit on in Tom's car.

What the hell is going on here? Where is Tom?

She thought of Tom and closed her eyes then was right beside him in the interview room. He was alone. She stayed with him until the policeman and woman came to get him. She went back to the house to wait on him getting back there and that's when she heard all about his affair when he was telling her mum and dad. She knew it. Her gut instinct was right about him. She was boiling over with rage now she knew for sure.

I knew it. Now everyone knows it. How could I have been so stupid to stay with him and not say a word when I knew there was something amiss? I'm just a silly wife that dotes on her husband. I need to get out of here.

Within seconds she was back with Jasmine. She didn't know what time it was, that mission was wrecked by all the information she just had to digest. She had never felt such anger. She paced the small floor space that she had in the shed, mumbling to herself until something Jasmine said to her baby softened her mood.

'We have a Guardian Angel baby. I don't think I was dreaming. I'm sure she came to me last night to tell me she is going to help us, her name is Anna.'

Anna stopped mid-pace, a smile spreading widely across her face.

It worked. It really did work, I thought it did, but was not totally sure until now; this is the best thing to happened to me since I died.

At 11.30 am Sergeant Rooney was standing at the main gate to Hallington Park in the drizzly rain. It showed no sign of stopping by the look of the dark grey, overcast sky above them. There were fifteen other police officers in attendance both from Hallington Police Station and Goldfield in Edinburgh. They were there for one reason and one reason only, that was to search the park as thoroughly as possible for any sign of Anna Ross.

'You all know why we are here and we have a hard task in front of us especially in this shitty weather, but we need to give this our full attention. I know quite a few of you are here today on your day off doing overtime and would rather be someplace else. The sooner we get the job done the sooner you can all go home. That does not mean we can rush this in anyway. We will start in the left of the park as we go in this gate; we will be in a line six feet apart until we hit the far end then move on to the next strip on our way back until we are done. There are no bodies of water in here so that should make this search a little easier. You all have markers with you, if you see something then use them. Caroline Adam the Forensic Technician who helped us out earlier at the house will bag anything that is found. Just give her a yell if you use a marker. I know you have all probably done searches similar to this in the past, but we all need to know where we stand. Has anyone any questions before we begin?' Rooney's speech was said with total authority.

After receiving no questions he said, 'Good we start in five minutes.'

Rooney walked over to Caroline to say hello, it had been a while since he had seen her before this morning. She was a petite woman of thirty-six, long, dark hair which today was bundled up under the hood of her white forensics suit. She had large brown eyes, a small, perfect nose, full lips and tanned skin.

'Well hello, how are you doing? Never got much of a chance to talk earlier,' Rooney asked.

'You know me Stephen I never complain, I am going to moan a little about this blustery weather today though. I heard your divorce came through. I like Gail. We still keep in touch from time to time.'

'She said I was married to the job, you know how these things go. Have you bagged yourself a man yet?'

'As a matter of fact I have, we moved in together just last month.'

'Spill the details then.'

'His name is Peter Dunbar; he is thirty-eight, tall, dark and handsome, more importantly he has the best personality.'

'You have really landed on your feet then.'

'Sure have Stephen, just goes to show you are never too old to find love. You will again, I'm sure of it.'

'I hope you are right. Right I think we should get started in here then,' he turned and said to the gang, 'Showtime.'

They all went into the park, went to the far left and made a line.

'Go,' Rooney shouted so everyone could hear him.

The line moved slowly forward. All eyes downward trained on the ground, eager to find something, like a dog that can smell a treat. The same drizzly rain was still coming down on top of them. They all had the same standard police issue waterproofs on. In unison they edged their way methodically across the park. Time was against them as the nights were coming in fast; they had to go as quickly as possible without compromising the quality of the search. They plodded on despite the rain all determined to find something linked to Anna.

At four o'clock the search was called off, the light was just too dim to see properly anymore.

'Right, that's it for today, this will need to be completed in the morning,' Rooney announced to the group.

Caroline had been walking behind the group collecting the items that were discovered. Bagging and tagging them to take to the lab at Goldfield Police Station to have a look. If something could not be eliminated as being Anna's then they would be shown to her family to identify them.

Rooney waited for her back at her car.

'Anything interesting in any of the bags you have?'

'We have a grand total of ten items so far, a lipstick, a gold necklace, a pair of glasses, did she wear glasses?'

'No.'

'Well I guess we can rule that one out straight away. We also got a slipper, a glove, a set of keys,

a t-shirt, a throw away lighter and two earrings that are not a pair.'
'At least something was found, I'm still hoping she will still turn up fine and dandy, as the time goes on the chances are getting slimmer.'
'I suppose all we can do is hope for the best. I will take this stuff to Goldfield Station and log them, I want home early, going out for dinner tonight.'
'You will be here tomorrow won't you?'
'Wild horses and all that, see you tomorrow Stephen.'
'Yes will do, enjoy your meal.'
When Caroline had pulled away Rooney got on the phone to Inspector Halliday.
'We only got three quarters searched before it got dark enough not to be able to do a proper job. We will need to resume tomorrow.'
'You know the old saying Stephen, don't put off until tomorrow what you can do today. I suppose Mother Nature put that out of the question today. I will get on to the Chief then to see how many bodies we can get tomorrow, you know how he feels about overtime especially on a Sunday.'
'Sure just do what you can Alan, we can't let this one get cold like it did with Jasmine Brown.'
'I hear you. I feel the exact same way. I will call you as soon as I know.'
Rooney went to see Tom to let him know about

the search, there was no answer at the door. It had been a long day so he decided it was time to go home even though there was no one there to go home to.

Billy Barclay got home from work at 6.20 pm, his wife Kate was there waiting for him with Tom's Facebook post open on her tablet.
'You will never believe it Billy.'
'Believe what?'
'This,' she said putting the tablet in his lap as he sat down in his favourite armchair in their living room.'
Billy read and re-read the post, Kate was right he couldn't believe it.
'This can't be right I spoke to her on Thursday night.'
'It says there that was when she went missing; maybe you should contact the police.'
'I will go and speak to Tom first; I want to get all this straight from him.'
'Do you want to have your dinner first I was going to order take away?'
'No, I need to get round there; I couldn't eat just now even if I wanted to.'
'Well I'm coming with you.'
'Let's go then.'
They both went out to their old, faithful blue mini and drove around to Tom's house, even though it was only a short walk away.

Billy knocked on the door and waited, there was no answer so he knocked again a little louder. This time the door opened and Tom stood there with a bath robe on.

'Sorry Billy I was in the bath,' but before he could say another word Billy interrupted him.

'I saw Anna on Thursday night. I was talking to her.'

'Come in I need to know everything.'

Tom, Billy and Kate went into the living room.

'It's true what we saw on Facebook then?' Billy asked.

'I'm afraid so. Where and what time did you see her?'

'It was after 10 pm on Main Street.'

'Did she seem ok to you?'

'Yes we just spoke about the dogs and she mentioned you are going on holiday. She was walking in the direction of my house I was going the other way. I should have turned back, walked with her. I just didn't know. I so sorry Tom, what are the police doing?'

'They were searching the park today. They searched my house this morning. I haven't heard from them since then.'

'I think we should call them right now,' Kate said.'

'Yes of course, I will get my phone and Sergeant Rooney's number.'

Tom went to the kitchen and retrieved what

he needed, then came back through and made the call without saying another word to his visitors. It went to voicemail so Tom hung up and called again straight away, this time Rooney answered.

'It's Tom Ross here, I have someone here who was talking to Anna the back of ten on Thursday night.'

'That's great Tom. I will speak to this person first thing in the morning. I can have their details?'

'I will let you speak to him just now,' Tom said and handed the phone to Billy.

'Hello officer I was the one that saw and spoke to Anna the other night.'

'Give me your name and address and I will come and get a statement from you first thing tomorrow if that's ok.'

'That's fine I'm not working tomorrow, my name is William Barclay, everyone calls me Billy, my address is 3 Parkway Lane.'

'That's close to Halligton Park isn't it?'

'Yes Sir.'

'Can I come see you around eight in the morning?'

'Yes of course.'

'Great see you then, can you put Tom back on please.'

Billy passed the phone back to Tom.

'We never got the full park searched today, so

we will be back out there at nine tomorrow to get it finished.'
'Was anything found?'
'A few items were found. Once we search the rest we will see what if any of these items could be linked to Anna. If there is then we will ask you and her parents to identify them. I will call you tomorrow when the search is finished, bye for now.'
'Bye.'
Tom thanked Billy for coming to him. He saw them out then went back into the living room where Rex was in his dog bed.
'That's a more positive piece of news boy, the Facebook post paid off. Let us hope we get more.'
Tom called Anna's parents to fill them in on all that was happening. It was George who answered; he was a bit frosty towards him at first. He thawed out a little after he heard that someone had seen her. He told Tom they would come round in the morning with breakfast and Clara who would be there later and wanted to see him. They ended the call. Rex came slowly out of his bed, walked into the kitchen then to the back door. Tom followed him, opened the back door then went upstairs to put on some clothes. He had nowhere to go and nothing to do except go around the route they think Anna took again. This was going to be the third time

today; it made him feel like he was doing something, he got dressed for the weather this time, called Rex back into the house and left.

Anna had not left Jasmine's side since she found out about Tom's affair that morning. She had slept on and off all day. She kind of knew what time it was roughly, Jasmine's meal times were pretty consistent so far, which was a good thing in Anna's mind. Candice had just brought in her dinner, which was spaghetti tonight; the evil bitch had even brought yet another book and a packet of crisps, Jasmine had thanked the monster, although she showed no warmth towards her captor.

I will need to go see Tom at some point, not tonight. I will go and see my parents, I've got a feeling they will be at their own house tonight and if there are not then they are more forgiving than I am. I wonder if the police have got any further in trying to find me. They never got very far in finding Jasmine.

Anna sat on her spot at the bottom of the bed, watching Jasmine reading and munching on her crisps after she had finished her dinner in the dim light. It was just as well the shed was small; the light would not have lit a larger room quite as much as it did this one. Anna decided to go in and hear what Candice and Jack were saying; she wanted to be kept in the loop as much as possible.

They were sitting in their kitchen at the table with their dirty dinner plates in front of them in conversation about Jasmine and Anna.

'Did you hear what I just said?' Jack growled at Candice.

'I heard you. There is no need to panic. We can still do this.'

'What if the police come chapping our door asking to have a look around, what then? If we say no they will think we are hiding something and if we say yes and they want to know what is in the shed then we will really be screwed.'

'Look, there is no reason in the world why they would want to come here and start digging around.'

'You saw them today searching the park; we both know it is likely to do with the woman I murdered.'

'They must be looking for her of course, but they haven't found Jasmine yet have they?'

'We need to cut our losses on this one Candice, before we both end up in prison.'

'What is it you want to do, murder her and her child?'

'No I don't, it's the only way out of this I can see before we get caught red handed. I can't go back to prison and the plan was to kill her anyway, not that I want to, this has all been forced upon me.'

'We are sticking to our plan; we have come too far to get nothing out of it. I don't want to hear another word about it tonight.'

Candice got up and cleared the table then went into the living room. Jack followed her.

'I told you I'm going for a drink with John tonight?'

'Yes you did, what time are you going?'

'I said I would meet him about eight in the Dirty Dog.'

'Fine, I'm tired tonight so I won't wait up darling.'

'Suit yourself.'

They both sat in silence until Jack switched on the TV.

They can't kill her, Candice won't let him. I need all the time I can get to find someone who can help. The police searched the park for me. I wonder what they think has happened to me?

Anna went back to Jasmine to wait until it was time to go and do her job.

21
Sunday 17th November

Rooney made an early start; he wanted to get as much done as he could. He was going to his sister Vera's house at three o'clock; she was always nagging him to go, saying she hardly ever saw him anymore, which was true. He only ever saw his sister and brother at special occasions which was a shame as they were always a very close family when they were growing up. Vera's two teenage sons took up most of her time these days, his brother Stuart has a daughter who is married with three kids of her own so his grandchildren keep him pretty busy. Rooney wasn't blessed with children during his marriage. He wanted them, it just never happened. He thought he still had time to meet someone and maybe become a father.

Rooney knocked on the door at Three Parkway Lane; Billy Barclay opened the door to him, they did their introductions then Billy invited him in. Billy lived in an upper flat of a four in a block. It was a council house which Katie and Billy had purchased from the council twelve years ago, long before the council put a stop to people being allowed to buy their houses from them. The two men climbed the stair and walked along the hall to the living room where Kate sat reading Tom's Facebook post yet again.

She stood up when they entered and tried to make herself useful.

'Can I get you some coffee or tea perhaps officer?'

'Sure I would love some coffee please, thank you.'

While Kate busied herself in the kitchen, Rooney got down to business.

'Right, start from the beginning and tell me everything, don't leave out anything, some little detail could be important,' Rooney said opening his notepad.

Kate was back with a coffee each for the three of them; she put them on the coffee table then sat down next to Billy who was in the middle of telling the policeman his detailed account of his meeting with Anna on the night she disappeared.

After Billy had finished giving his statement he said, 'I Hope you find her and quick. I'm very fond of her you know.'

'We are doing all we can, we will be back in Hallington Park today to resume the search we started yesterday. Lack of daylight prevented us from doing it all. This information you have given us will help narrow a few things down hopefully.'

'Has this anything to do with the other missing girl from August, I know her mother Sheila,' Kate spoke with sympathy in her voice.

'At the moment we have no reason to believe that these two cases are related.'

'Sheila has not gone back to work yet, I don't know if she ever will.'

'I didn't know that. It's been a month since I spoke to her. I will pay her a visit, but I'm afraid I don't have any new information for her.'

'She's in all the time, hardly ever leaves the house. I think she is waiting for her daughter to walk back through the door and she wants to be there if she does, which is understandable,'

'I can understand that. If you remember anything else Billy no matter how irrelevant it may seem please get it touch,' Rooney said handing him a card with his details on.

'I think I have told you everything, but yes, if anything else comes to mind I will call you right away.'

Rooney left there and headed straight for the main gate to Hallington Park.

Rooney was there before anyone else arrived. Inspector Halliday had called him last night to let him know that there would be eight officers joining him in the second part of the search today, nine including Caroline Adam from forensics. He sat in his car contemplating all the details he could remember of the Jasmine Brown case. He felt guilty for not being in contact with her mother after what Kate Barclay had said to him. He decided he would go visit her today after the search. He believed he would have time before going to his sister's house, if not he would make the time.

The rest of the troops started turning up at 8.50 am; Rooney was outside his car waiting for them. He did a head count at nine, all present and correct.

'Right, most of you were here yesterday; however, I see a couple of different faces, so I will catch you up. We searched around three quarters of the park yesterday; we will do the rest hopefully in a few hours today, let you all get back to your station or your families for those of you doing overtime. Let's get this done.'

Taking the lead Rooney entered the park got everyone in their places then they started.

Anna went back to the shed around 7.30 am after a night of more disappointment. She lay down on the floor next to Jasmine's bed, sleep would not take her. Everything was going around and around in her head.

I wish I didn't find out about Tom having the affair. I wish I could find even one of the two people I have left to contact. I wish I had just let Rex out in the garden that night. All these wishes, what's the point, there is nothing anyone can do to turn back time. The funny thing is now all I have is time, although that baby doesn't. I wonder if it's a girl or a boy. I really want to know what The Realm is like; do your loved ones that have passed on already meet you there? Do they welcome you with open arms? Can you look down on your loved ones that are still down here on earth? Do you get to watch over them shaking your head when you know they have made a mistake? I think I need to hurry up and get the job done here then I will find all this out first hand and then I can stop wondering.

Sleep took her half an hour later.

The search went the same way as it had the day before, with military precision. There were three items found today, a purse with nothing in it, a red scarf and a half used bottle of sun screen which was prised from a tangle of long grass by Caroline after an officer gave a shout and put a marker down. It went the same way as the other items found on the search, put into plastic bags then tagged for further inspection. Once the search was complete the officers dispersed to their cars after being thanked for their time by the sergeant. Caroline was waiting for him at his car.

'Well that's another job well done Stephen.'

'Sure is, I'm glad that part is over and the woman was not found in there.'

'Do you think she is still alive?'

'I would like to think so. The more time marches on the more likely that she isn't, although it is still early days. Between me and you her husband admitted to us yesterday that he was having an affair, said he put an end to it a few weeks ago. I believe him when he says he finished it, the question is did Anna find out about it and go off somewhere to make him sweat for a few days.'

'Does she have other close family?'

'Yes, her parents live close by, she actually confided in her mother the night she disappeared that she thought Tom her husband had a bit on the side.'

'But she didn't know for sure?'

'I believe not, if she did just bugger off to get away from him, if I were her parents I wouldn't be too happy with her for putting them through all this worry. That's the only thing that makes me think she didn't go off voluntarily.'

'I see your point. Have you contacted her close friends or is that a stupid question.'

'Of course we have, we haven't contacted her business partner yet, I am going to do that in person tomorrow. How was dinner last night then?'

'Great thanks, no drinks though I knew I was out here again this morning.'

'What are your plans for today then?' Stephen inquired.

'I will take what we found back to the station

and get them logged then home to a hot bath and a bit of relaxation. What about you?'

'I'm going to my sister's. First though I need to go and see Jasmine Brown's parents Sheila and Phil.'

'That's the teenager that went missing a few of months ago.'

'Yes, when I was speaking to a witness this morning his wife started to tell me that Sheila is not doing so well. I have not been in contact with her for a while and I will tell you this for nothing it makes me feel as guilty as hell.'

'I don't envy you that one.'

'I can see it far enough. At the end of the day I need to do it for their sake to let them know we haven't forgotten about her. The truth is the trail went stone cold, it's as if she was plucked up off the planet.'

'You are not suggesting an alien abduction by any chance?' Caroline said with a little laugh trying to lighten his mood.

'Well if it was aliens which I don't believe for one minute that it was, at least she might be alive and well.'

'That's true pal, I'm off then enjoy your time at your sister's. I will call you tomorrow morning as soon as I have sorted out the items found.'

'Great I will wait for your call bye.'

Stephen watched her as she got into her car and drive off; he got into his and made his way to twenty-three Belford Avenue.

The Brown's house was a charming, picturesque semi detached old sand stone building with ivy covering half the frontage. Rooney sat in his car, he was dreading going in, he knew he needed to even if it is to ease his own guilt. He got out and walked up to the front door and knocked half hoping that no one was in. The door was answered by Phil Brown.

'Sergeant Rooney. Have you got news of Jasmine?' Phil inquired with a tinge of hope in his voice.

'Unfortunately Mr Brown I don't I have just popped round to see how you two are doing.'

'Oh I see, come in Sheila is in the living room, please go through.'

Rooney had been in this house a few times so knew his way to the living room.

'Hello Mrs Brown,' he said to Jasmine's mother when he walked into room.

Sheila Brown quickly got to her feet, 'Is it Jasmine? Have you found her?'

'No we haven't as I told your husband I have just called round to see how you are doing.'

'If I'm honest I'm not doing very well,' she said, her voice starting to quiver.

'I don't mean to upset you Mrs Brown.'

'I know you don't, I can't seem to help myself, Jasmine is our only child, it's as if half of me is missing without her. Is there no new news on Jasmine at all?'

'I'm afraid not Mrs Brown.'

'Please call us Sheila and Phil; I think you have known us long enough to be on first name terms. Would you like some tea sergeant?'

'Yes please Sheila.'

Sheila went into the kitchen to make the tea.

'She isn't coping great at all,' Phil informed Rooney.

'So I was hearing.'

'Who told you?'

'Kate Barclay I believe your wife knows her well.'

'Yes she does, known her for years.'

The two men sat in silence until Sheila returned. She sat a tray on the coffee table and told the two men to help themselves.

'I want to be the one to tell you that another woman has gone missing locally.'

'What, do you think this could in any way be linked to our girl?' Phil asked.

'At this stage we can't say one way or the other, but I didn't want you to hear it on the news or from someone else and start jumping to conclusions.'

'If it is related I assume you are doing all you can to find this woman while the trail is warm then it might lead to Jasmine being found.' Phil said.

'Let us not jump the gun, yes we are doing all we

can to find this woman, we still are looking for Jasmine as well. Just because we have not had any fresh evidence does not mean that we have given up on her.'

'I wasn't suggesting that you had sergeant, it's just so hard on us not knowing if Jasmine is alive or dead.'

'If we do get a sniff of any news then you will be the first to know.'

'Who is the woman that has gone missing?' Sheila asked

'I might as well tell you as you will find out soon enough, it is Anna Ross do you know her?'

'I don't think so.'

'Her mother Ruby Anderson works in the Smith's Chemist.'

'The poor woman, I know exactly what she is going through.'

The three of them sat drinking their tea, exchanging small talk for half an hour until Rooney left to go to his sister's.

Anna was in the shed most of the day. After her failings to make contact the previous night she was eager to get started again.

I could tear my own hair out with the boredom. Ravi was right and then some about that. I've got to keep positive though, I know it will happen, I just need to keep at it until it does.

Anna had a lot of strange thoughts going through her head all day. Too much time to think about what was important and what was not. She had thought if it was possible that aliens could exist, she dismissed this as a no. She wondered a lot about The Realm again, what it would be like when she eventually got there, this seemed to be on her mind too much of the time.

I think I will go see Tom and my parents before I go out on the job tonight, I need to get out of this shed, I feel so guilty leaving Jasmine here all alone in this depressing place. I need to see what time it is anyway so I will go visit Tom just now.

Anna thought of her kitchen and she was there. She heard voices coming from the living room so went straight through. Tom was sitting on the floor rubbing Rex's belly gently, her parents and Clara were on the couch.
'So did Billy talk to the police?' George asked Tom.
'Yes he came round this morning after Sergeant Rooney had gone to his house to take a statement.'
'That's great at least they can start to piece things together,' George said.
'Yes it's something, I'm hoping beyond all hope we get some more information from the Face-

book post. Listen since you are all here I just want to say how sorry I am about the fling. I love Anna with all my heart, it was a silly mistake that should never have happened,' Tom said sheepishly to Anna's family.

'We have told you Tom, all we care about now is getting Anna home, whatever she decides to do will be down to her,' Ruby said.

Rex struggled to get up and went into the kitchen.

'I will go let him out in the garden, poor soul,' Clara spoke for the first time since Anna arrived and it was great to hear her voice.

'Have you called Sam back yet? Ruby asked Tom.

'Yes I called today, with no news there was not much to say.'

Sam must be worried about the business, I know if the shoe was on the other foot I would be too. More importantly they know Billy was the last person to see me; he has spoken to them. It wasn't far from there that I came to my untimely death. I am going to go to Billy tonight I will try him first; I don't know why I hadn't thought of going there before this. In all likelihood it won't work, it is somewhere to start tonight.

Anna sat for a while listening to her loved ones talking about her for a while. All she wanted to do was hug them all and tell them she loved them, tell them what had happened, ask them to help Jasmine. If only it was that easy. She went into the kitchen to do a time check. It was 8.20 pm; she left her own house and went back to the hovel that housed Jasmine until it was time to go and try to make contact.

Anna left the shed and went back to her kitchen to check the time; it was 10.30 pm, late enough she thought to try people on a Sunday night. She went straight to Billy's house and stood outside first, the light in his living room window was still on. She thought of Billy, a second later she was standing in front of him. He was sitting watching TV with Kate; Buster was on the floor in front of the gas fire that was on at a low heat. The dog was lying on his back with all our paws pointing to the ceiling, he looked more than comfortable.

They are still up. I was hoping I could try him right away tonight, might have guessed things would not go my way, I can't wait on them going to bed. I could be out trying other people. I will come back later.

Anna left Billy's and started where she left off the night before. She found it tedious getting knock back after knock back from people she didn't even know. That's when she realised that she had not had the chance to try Tom or her father yet, she had not seen them sleeping since she found herself in her current situation which was a bit worrying for her. She immediately went to Tom first, she found him in bed and asleep at last. She couldn't stay mad at him and she didn't know why, but she had forgiven him, she still loved him more than anything. Rex was not on his usual spot at night on the bottom of the bed.

Poor Rex he must really be suffering if he is not able to make the stairs, I will go see him before I go.

'Anna Anderson,' she said out loud to the silent room.
No response from Tom.
'Anna Anderson,' she repeated.
Still there was no sign at all that Tom had heard her. She sat on the bed, well not entirely she was hovering her usual inch. She wished she could get into bed beside him and snuggle up to her husband; she wanted nothing more there and then. She said her name over and over again willing Tom to hear her, it didn't happen.

Oh Tom I miss you. I still love you and I always will. I wonder if he is going to work tomorrow. Now that's plain silly I know him, maybe not as much as I thought I did. I don't think he will be at work, I'm sure he would have spoken to his boss before this. See you soon sweetheart.

Anna went down to the living room to check

up on her dog He was lying in his bed all curled up fast asleep. She went for a time check, it was 11.35 pm.

I must have been sitting with Tom longer than I thought, that is the quickest the time has gone since I died. Time to go see Dad then, hopefully I will have a little more luck there.

Luck did not seem to be on Anna's side at all. Her Father was asleep, it was the same scenario she had with Tom, absolutely nothing.

That's another one scored off the list in my head.

Anna left her parents' house and made a beeline back to Billy's. This time the couple were in bed sleeping. The bathroom light had been left on and the room door was quarter way open so a soft light illuminated the room enough for Anna to be able to see better than she had been in many of the bedrooms she had visited over the last couple of nights.
She stood there staring at the couple for awhile wishing it was her and Tom lying there. Thinking how content the couple before her seemed. Buster was on the floor in his own bed, giving off a slight snore now and then.
'Anna Anderson.'
Billy grunted and turned around.
'Anna Anderson.'
Billy turned again.

'Anna Anderson,' Anna said again, hope and excitement rising in her voice.

Billy started moaning and getting restless. He was turning from one side to another then settled on his back. He was now mumbling something that Anna could not make out.

'Anna Anderson.'

Billy was kicking the covers off himself and Kate, still mumbling. To Anna it looked like he was having a bad dream.

'Anna Anderson,' Anna spoke again feeling bad, also full of anticipation.

Billy let out a shriek and sat bolt upright awake, waking up his wife with the commotion.

'What's going on Billy? Did you have a nightmare honey?'

'Yes I think so; I think I was dreaming about Anna.'

'What happened in your dream?'

'I don't know, I can't remember a thing about it, it's strange usually you recall something especially when you just wake up. I've not zilch.'

'Lie back down, go back to sleep.'

I think. No I know I have done it. I have contacted someone that can help. I couldn't be happier about that, although I feel bad for Billy. I should be ecstatic just now, full with joy that I can start to help that girl and baby, Billy is going to suffer through this I can see that now.

Anna left the Barclay house there and then; she decided Billy had had enough for the night. She knew she was going to put a lot of pressure on him. She also knew that Billy would help out anyone if he could. It was difficult for her to put someone through this; however, it had to be done. She would come back tomorrow night and torment him some more, she had plenty time to work out how she was going to go about it.

Anna went back to the shed to a sleeping Jasmine.

'I have enlisted someone else to help us; it might be a bit tricky. I will find a way.'

Anna was not expecting an answer, so was shocked when she got one.

'That's wonderful,' Jasmine said in her slumber.

Jasmine just answered me. How is that even possible? I suppose at this stage anything is possible. Or maybe she is dreaming of something else.

22
Monday 18th November

Rooney and PC McMillan entered Anna's shop at 9.10 am; it was next to the precinct in the Town Centre on Barnes Road. There was no one behind the small counter and there was not much to look at in the shop itself, there was a couple of mannequins dressed in clothes that looked unfinished, a female one in one corner and a male in another corner, most of the work they did was done in the back of the shop out of sight. The windows however, were decorated with the most fabulous curtains, brown and teal done with a thick blackout fabric. Sam does most of the curtain making and is extremely proud of them. The floor was tiled in yellow and brown with an old fashioned look to it, a look that was making a return to what was fashionable.

'Hello,' Rooney shouted through the half open door that was behind the counter.

'Just a moment,' a man's voice answered.

A few seconds later a tall man appeared from the back of the shop. He was in his late thirties with a thick head of brown hair, blue eyes, a small nose and mouth. He was wearing faded jeans and a sleeveless dye dipped t-shirt with every colour of green you could imagine on it. Glasses and a measuring tape hung in front of him tethered around his neck.

'I'm hoping to speak to Sam Thomas,' Rooney said.

'Well you are now,' answered Sam.

Rooney seemed a little taken aback.

'Oh sorry, please excuse my ignorance I was expecting Sam to be a woman for some reason.'

PC McMillan put her head down slightly and gave a little smile amused by the sergeant.

'Don't you worry about that; it's not the usual type of work for a man. However, I love it and I'm good at it.'

'I'm Sergeant Rooney; this is my colleague PC McMillan.'

'You are here about Anna; I'm beside myself with worry, I wasn't sure to open up this morning or not.'

'Is it fifty-fifty here with the business with you and Anna?'

'Yes, we have been here for nearly four years now, business is booming.'

'When was the last time you spoke to her?'

'It was when we were closing up the shop for the night on Thursday.'

'Did she seem ok to you?' Rooney continued with the questions while PC McMillan took some notes.

'Yes she seemed fine, nothing out of the ordinary.'

'Have you spoken to her husband?'

'Yes, he is devastated you know.'

'So Anna never mentioned anything to you that something might be bothering her?'

'No, nothing at all, I would like to think that if she had any problems she would talk to me. Wait a minute I'm not one for gossip, a few weeks ago she did say that her and Tom were drifting apart a little, I thought that had been sorted out because she never mentioned it again.'

'This is not a question I have asked her family. Do you know of any enemies that Anna may have?'

'None, Anna is a wonderful person, well liked and loved by all who knows her. Find her please.'

'We are doing our best Sir, if you think of anything that may help however, small please give me a call.' Rooney said handing Sam a card.

'Of course I will.'

They said their goodbyes before Rooney and the PC left the shop.

'You never said a word in there Nicole'

'You had it all in hand Sir; you asked everything that needed to be asked.'

'You need to start coming out of your shell a little more, when you are with me questioning someone don't be afraid to let yourself be heard.'

'Yes Sir, I will keep that in mind.'

The officers made for the Ross house when they left the shop, Nicole was driving. Rooney sat beside her deep in thought. When they arrived at the gate Rooney told Nicole why they were there and to do most of the talking. He told her he would jump in if he thought she needed any help. Tom answered the door with Rex at his feet.

'Good morning Mr Ross, may we come in?' asked Nicole taking the lead as she was told.

'Yes, please.'

The three of them went into the living room and sat down.

'The dog seems a bit better,' Rooney said.

'Yes he is, moving about a little more. Is there any news?' Tom asked impatiently.

The sergeant looked to the PC.

'We found a number of items in the park, so we would like a sample of Anna's DNA if that's possible Mr Ross.'

'I will get her toothbrush and hairbrush, will that be good enough?'

'Yes they should be quite adequate.'

'Tom left the room and was heard by the officers going up the stairs. He returned after a short moment with the before mentioned items. PC McMillan produced a small plastic bag from her pocket then held it open so that Tom could drop the items into it.

'There are a few items we found in the park

that we can rule out like a pair of glasses for instance, you might be asked to identify some of the others if need be, this hopefully will happen in the next day or so,' Rooney said to Tom before realising he was taking over.

'Someone sent me a photo of a woman they thought was Anna after seeing my post on Facebook, it wasn't her, it looked nothing at all like her.'

'It happens all the time Mr Ross,' PC McMillan said taking the lead back from Rooney.

'I know I was told about false information, I am still hoping for more. Have you been to see Sam Thomas yet?'

'Yes as a matter of fact we were there just before we came here; he had nothing to add to what we already know.'

'I was half thinking that maybe Anna had confided something in him that she didn't tell anyone else, they are close you see. The only reason I see that she is missing is that some evil fucker has done something to her,' Tom spat with anger.

'We don't know that for sure Mr Ross and I know you're angry, but that won't get us anywhere will it?' Rooney said this time.

'I know, I know, it's all so hard to deal with.'

'We will take our leave now, we will be in touch.'

The two police left and went out to the car.

'Sir I have a question, stop me if it sounds silly. We haven't checked out the woman Mr Ross was having the affair with, could this be a case of a woman scorned?'

Rooney sat in silence for a few minutes taking this in. He hadn't thought of this at all. Why hadn't he, it could be possible he supposed, unlikely he thought, but possible.

'You know Nicole that's a very good question, come on we are going back in.'

They got back out the car, back up the path to the front door and knocked. Tom answered nearly right away.

'I saw you getting back out your car, have you had some information?'

'No Sir, can we come back in, we need to ask you a few questions,' Rooney was taking control of this.

When they were all seated as they were before Rooney started.

'This may be a sensitive question for you. Does your mistress know your wife?'

'Yes she does. Why?'

'In what context does she know her?'

'She is one of the receptionists at the Leisure Centre, Anna goes there. They often chat so I've been told.'

'Who told you Anna or the other woman?'

'Both of them told me, that is one thing about women they talk to each other then about each

other. No offence,' Tom said gesturing to the PC.
'Why are you asking me about this?
'We are going to need this other woman's name please,' Rooney said sounding insistent.
'Why, you don't think she had anything to do with Anna going missing do you?'
'Don't you think it is possible?'
'No I don't, I think that is absolutely absurd.'
'I'm going to need the name.'
'It's Rebecca Blacklaw.'
'Do you have a home address for her?'
'56 Blane Road.'
'Is that here in Hallington?'
'Yes I know where it is,' PC McMillan answered before Tom had a chance.
'We will be contacting her Mr Ross. We would appreciate it if you didn't speak to her first.'
'I won't I haven't spoke to her since I broke it off, I really do think you are wasting your time there.'
'That maybe Sir, you understand we still need to check out every avenue.'
'Yes of course,' Tom said flatly realising that as much as he didn't want them to go near her they had to.
Rooney and the PC left for the second time that morning to return to their car.
'Well done Nicole that was good thinking. Now let's go see this Rebecca Blacklaw.'
'She might be at work.'

'We will try her at home first.'

They pulled up outside the address given to them by Tom for Rebecca Blacklaw. It was a semi detached, two-bedroom house. The garden was neat and small at the front, no flowers or plants just grass. There was a brown wooden fence around the perimeter of the garden. The path was made up of slabs; the front door looked as if it had been freshly painted brown, nearly, but not quite the same colour as the fence. They rang the door bell a few times before it was answered by a woman with short, blond, bobbed hair. Her makeup was immaculate and had stunning blue eyes; she was medium build and was about five-foot-five.

'Rebecca Blacklaw? the sergeant asked.

'Yes what can I do for you? It's not every day I have the police calling.'

'We would like to ask you a few questions about Mrs Anna Ross.'

'Why?'

'Can we come in?'

'I was just on my way out actually.'

'This won't take long, it's important.'

'Ok.'

She stood back holding the door open; once she closed it she pointed to a door motioning for her visitors to go through. They entered into a long room; it was a living room at the front with a dining area at the back. The living space was all cream coloured, the suite, the carpet, the curtains even the walls were cream. The cream theme continued into the dining area, the dining table in here was dark brown glass which contrasted with all the cream beautifully. The room was decorated with expensive looking ornaments dotted about in perfect placement.

'We know that you were, how should I put it, seeing Tom Ross,' Rooney started.

'Oh, if you know that then you will also know that he finished with me a few weeks ago.'

'Yes we are aware of that. How well do you know Mrs Ross?'

'I don't know her on a personal level; she comes into the Leisure Centre a couple of times a week, I sometimes chat to her now and then.'

'Did you chat to her before you started seeing her husband or did that come afterwards?'

'Before I met him, I think if I knew at first it was her husband then maybe I would have stopped it before it started, she is a lovely woman. I didn't know he was married at all for the first couple of weeks, then I noticed that when I was trying to make arrangements with him he would come out with all sorts of weird and wonderful excuses so I asked him straight out. He admitted it. I should have put a stop to it then, I was hooked.'

'How long did you see him for?' Rooney inquired taking his time to get round to the important questions.

'Five months give or take.'

'Anna Ross is missing.'

'Seriously, is she?'

'Yes since Thursday night, can I ask where you were on Thursday night?

'You can't think that I had anything to do with that do you?'

'We are covering all possibilities.'

'I was here; my new boyfriend who is not married might I add was here. He stayed over.'

'I am going to need his name and number.'

'Yes, fine.'

She walked out of the room and came back in with a piece of paper in her hand then gave it to Rooney.

'Here you go, Anna is a nice woman I really hope you find her soon,' Rebecca said sounding genuine.

'We are doing our best; we will go now, let you go to where ever it is you are going, we will see ourselves out.'

Back in the police car Rooney looked at the piece of paper. It had the information he had asked for.

'I don't think she had anything to do with it, we will check out her alibi anyway,' Rooney said solemnly to PC McMillan.

'I don't think she had anything to do with it either, at least it is something scored off the list. She wasn't long in finding a new guy that's for sure.'

'I was thinking that myself.'

'Maybe she was not that fond of Tom, if she was as hooked as she said she was she would not have entered into another relationship quite so soon, take it from me.'

'You have a point there.'

They headed back to the station. Rooney filled in Inspector Halliday on the morning's visitations as they sat in the canteen drinking coffee.

Anna had been in the shed for what seemed like days, she was getting cabin fever. She knew how difficult this challenge was going to be, but it was harder than she ever thought possible. She didn't know how this young woman beside her had the strength to keep going, the only reason that was apparent was the baby she was carrying. Anna was certain that if she was in the same position she would have quite literally went crazy before the same length of time Jasmine had been in her prison. Night time could not come quick enough for her; she was so impatient to get back to speak to Billy, it was all planned out in her head what she was going to say to him tonight. She felt so bad for Billy; he was going to suffer. She hated herself for having to be the one to do it. Jasmine picked Rex's tag out of its hiding place.

Oh there she goes again with that tag, I can't blame her really. It is all she has to a connection to the outside world in a way. I will speak to her tonight after I have been to see Billy of course. I might as well go see what time it is, maybe do a bit of visiting.

Anna went to check the time in her usual place. Tom and her parents were sitting at the table in her kitchen having dinner. It was 6.10 pm.
'How's Rex been?' George asked Tom.
'He is making a good recovery, actually thinking about taking him out for a very short walk tomorrow if he is willing that is.'
'Clara said sorry she couldn't stay for longer, Peter needs to go to work tomorrow so she had to get back for Jamez,' Ruby told Tom.
Anna went to find Rex to see how he was. She found him at the bottom of the stairs in front of the radiator all stretched out fast asleep. This put her mind at rest a little; he seemed as if he was getting back to normal. She went back to the kitchen then regretted it as soon as she heard what her loved ones were talking about.
'So the police asked you for your girlfriend's details?' it was George asking.
'Yes, they said they were going to speak to her, make sure she had nothing to do with Anna

going missing, a waste of time if you ask me, she couldn't possibly have anything to do with it.'
'You were a total ass to get involved with someone else in the first place,' George again.
'I know you have mentioned it a few times. Again I am so sorry for what I have done, if I had a time machine I would go back to change it all.'
'Now, now boys, play nice. We have been through all this, we all know it will not help anyone to drudge it all back up again, 'Ruby scorned.
'I know. The least he can do is to tell us who it is before we find out from someone else,' George said.

Yes tell him Tom, I want to know who it is as well. Or maybe I shouldn't know.

'We will find out Tom, the truth usually comes out in the end,' Ruby stated.
'It is Rebecca Blacklaw.'
'I don't know her, is she from Hallington?' Ruby asked.
'She stays here now, she is originally from Glasgow, she moved here after her divorce.'

I can't believe it; she spoke to me every time I saw her at the Leisure Centre. What a witch. I hope she feels as guilty as sin now.

'Well if she did have anything to do with it the police will soon find her out,' Ruby spat.

'I can honestly say I don't think for one moment that she did,' Tom retorted

Well he is right she didn't have nothing to do with it, but she has hurt me emotionally, acting all friendly towards me to my face, then having it away with my husband behind my back, not that Tom is totally blameless. I have heard enough for one night, I'm going to walk back to the shed the route I took on my last night alive.

Anna went to her gate. The rain was falling moderately; she started on the replica of her last journey. She got as far as the end of Browning Street and the corner of Ashton Drive and that's when she saw him. A man with a make on was standing on the opposite side of the road on Ashton Drive waving at her. He was a small dumpy man with greying hair. She was elated that someone could see her. She stood there smiling, not thinking about lifting her hand to wave back. He started crossing the road to her; still she just stood there smiling.
'Hello there,' the man said as he reached her. He looked as happy to see her as she was to see him.
'Hello,' Anna said hesitantly.
His make was darker than hers, although he was older; if Anna had to make a guess she would have said he was around fifty years old. She noticed that his face was scarred badly with what she presumed was acne.

'My name is Frank, Frank Wood.'

'Anna, Anna Ross,' she said with a smile.

'How long have you been down here?'

'Four days give or take, and you?'

'It seems like a lifetime. It has been four and a half months. Can I ask why you are here?'

Anna couldn't help herself; she had someone to talk to at last. She told Frank the full story; he listened to every word with fascination.

'Now that is a mission,' he said.

'What about your mission.'

'Are you sure you want to hear this, it's a long story, I can give you the short version.'

'Of course, I have time to kill as you can imagine.'

'In that house over there,' he gestured with his hand to a house at the edge of Ashton Drive. 'That's my biological mother's house. When she was eighteen she fell pregnant with twins, me and my brother Richard. She gave us up for adoption; I didn't know we were adopted until after I died. Our adoptive parents are dead; they died in a car crash a few years ago, a drunk driver in the other car. Richard still doesn't know he was adopted. My mission is to reunite my mother and brother. My guide in The Before told me that my mother's biggest regret is giving us up, she has not led a great life since then, she never fell in love again, she never got married. My guide Fenza told me that she is so sad, that the only thing that would give her a little happiness in her life before she dies would be to get my family reunited.'

'Did she not try to find the two of you?'

'No, and Fenza told me she will never try, she does not want to upset us in anyway even though it makes her so miserable. She has tried to take her own life a couple of times over the years. Fenza said if she really wanted to kill herself she would have succeeded.'

'What about your father?'

'He died before we were born, got into a fight, the other guy gave him a fatal blow. Fenza said that is the reason my mother gave us up, thought she couldn't cope with us without him. I have thought about it and I think it was the grief or losing him that made her give us away. What my mother doesn't know is that she has four grandchildren, I have one child and Richard has three. She also has two great grandchildren. If I can pull this off then she need never be lonely again.'

'Can you communicate with people?'

'What do you mean?'

'Well I can communicate with people in their subconscious, like when they are sleeping. I can only do it with three people, I have found two already.'

'Wow, I wish I was able to do that.'

'Have you tried?'

'No, I didn't know anything about it, Fenza told me I can move things, pick small things up, put them under my make where they can't be seen and move them to a different place.'

'Right well we have different powers then. It's so weird to be able to have a conversation with someone.'

'It sure is, hey maybe we could help each other out. I was told it was against the rules, that two shades will be added to my make if I help another soul, if I succeed then I get ten shades removed, I'm doing the maths, seems like a no brainer.'

'I was told the same; you do have a valid point though. I will need to think about it. Will I be able to find you here then?'

'Yes Anna I'm always here, please come back to see me soon.'

'I promise I will even if I decide not to help each other.'

Anna walked on with a spring in her step. She had a lot of pondering to do; she had plenty of time before she went to Billy tonight.

It was so good to speak to someone; I missed conversation more than I thought I did, I think we should help each other out, what is the worst that could happen. Yes we will get two shades added to our make; however, the quicker we get our tasks done the quicker we get back to The Before, the quicker we get to work on getting our makes clean, the quicker we can get into The Realm, that is the main objective here. I can't wait to see what it will be like. How do they fit everyone in? Will we be separate from animals? Will there be animals? Of course there will be animals there has got to be. The thing is I don't know, it's all in the unknown for me. I really hope it won't be long before I get to experience it all.

Anna had been back in the shed for a few hours; Billy was on her mind. She felt guilty for putting him through what she was going to have to do to him. She had no option unless she found her third person; she knew Billy and she knew he would do all in his power to help.

The plate from Jasmine's dinner was still sitting on the floor; she missed whichever monster had brought it in to her earlier. Jasmine was huddled under duvet eating a chocolate bar. Anna did not feel hungry, although she thought she would like to taste chocolate again, she loved hot tea and a bar of chocolate. She would let the chocolate melt slowly away to nothing a square at a time in her mouth. Jasmine had not long finished brushing her hair and tying it back again, it was greasy and dirty. Anna wondered if her hair had been washed since she had been put in here. Anna closed her eyes against the injustice of Jasmine and went home again.

Tom was on the couch with Rex, it seemed to be their thing now. Anna went to check the time, still too early, only 9.45 pm. She went back to the living room and sat there with Tom, he had the TV on, it didn't seem as if he was watching it, he was suffering.

'What to do Rex?' I think we will let you out then we will go to bed. I wish I knew where your mummy is.'

'I'm right here, sitting next to you, wanting to hold you, wanting to pet our dog.'

Tom didn't move to let Rex out; he sat there staring at the TV screen. He stayed there like that for nearly an hour before he moved. Anna sat there with them crying. Crying because of how lost her husband looked. Crying because she would never get the chance to kiss him again, crying for her parents who she knew were devastated.

Why does death need to be just as hard as life? What can I do to help my family?

Anna went to the clock it was 10.50 pm.

I will go to Billy's; I will just hang out there until he falls asleep if he isn't already.

When she reached Billy's, Kate was in bed. Billy was still up; sitting at the kitchen table with a beer in his hand, Buster was on the floor at his feet. Buster looked wet on his underneath.

Billy must be on his four days off, that's if he still works continental shifts. I wonder when he starts back, he must not be long back from a walk with Buster going by how wet he is. I hope he goes to bed soon, I want to get started. I'm being too impatient, I know it. I need to relax, let Billy get a little peace and quiet before I put the pressure on him.

Anna kept casting a glance at the clock displayed on the front of their cooker it seemed that the digital numbers were stuck; the time was going by so slow for her.

It would have been better if he was sitting watching a movie or something, the time would be going in a little quicker. There I go again with the moaning. Did I moan this much when I was alive? Is that what drove Tom into the arms of another woman? I need to leave and come back later this is doing my head in.

Anna went back to the shed, not that time went any faster there. She thought she would get a sleep then go back to Billy, by then he would surely be in bed. She lay down on her usual spot on the floor and tried to sleep, an hour later she was still awake. Ravi had told her that she would not need as much sleep, for her it was just a way of whiling away the time. Not tonight though, she had too much going around in her mind, she knew it would be a waste of time trying to nap.

I thought I had it worked out in my mind what I was going to say to Billy, it has disappeared, why can't I remember all the things that I wanted to say? Will he know that it's me trying to invade his sleep? Of course he won't what I am thinking, although Jasmine knows my name, she said it to her baby. Maybe if I annoy Billy long enough he will know that it's me.

Anna went to Billy; at last he was in bed asleep.

I wonder how many beers he has had; I hope it doesn't affect the quality of contact I can make.

'Anna Anderson.'
Right away Billy started to squirm in his slumber.
'Billy this is Anna Ross. I need you to help Jasmine Brown; she is being held against her will in a shed in the garden over the fence from your back garden. You probably know the people who are holding her.'
Billy changed his position.
'You need to keep an eye on that shed in your neighbours' garden; you need to help that girl. You are the only one who can help. Please Billy do all you can.'
Billy woke up; he got up then padded barefoot to the kitchen with Buster at his heels.

He poured himself a glass of water and looked out the window into the darkness. He turned around and leaned his lower back against the sink unit.
'I think I'm going crazy Buster. Maybe I should have stayed off the beers tonight.'
Buster just sat there looking at him.

He definitely hears me; however, I feel as if I'm not getting my message through clear enough. How long will I need to torment him before he gets the message? I feel like I'm haunting him. Is that what I'm doing?

Billy went back into the bedroom, again with Buster following him.
Anna stayed in the kitchen wondering what needed to be done.
'Ravi,' Anna said out loud.
She stood there waiting; she was going nowhere until her guide showed up, forty minutes later Ravi was before her.
'Yes Anna what can I do for you?'
'Hello Ravi, I'm glad to see you. How long will I need to annoy Billy? I feel so bad for getting him involved in all this.'
'I have been watching your progress Anna and I must say you have done remarkably well so far; however, these things take time. You will need to visit Billy as much as you can, do not feel bad Anna you are doing a good thing here. Billy will

feel great if he gets to save The Innocent, but you have not mentioned The Innocent to Billy yet, you have only mentioned Jasmine Brown.'

'Why can I communicate with Jasmine if it doesn't help me to save The Innocent?'

'It may not be helping in any way that you can see, but it is helping in some way. It is giving Jasmine more hope that you can know. It is helping her to endure what she is going through hence making her calmer then in turn keeping the baby calmer.'

'I see what you mean. I'm sorry to have bothered you, have you any more advice you can give me?'

'Sorry Anna I have told you all I can.'

'Do you think I should look for my third connection or work only with Billy on this?

'The decision is only yours to make Anna. I must go now; I have a few other souls to see. I hope to see you again soon.'

Ravi disappeared as quickly as he appeared. Anna went to see Billy; he was lying on his side turned away from Kate playing some game on his phone.

He can't sleep now.

Anna returned to the shed not too pleased with herself. She wanted things to move faster than what they were. She wanted to get to The Realm more than anything, the longer she was down here, the more the longing for The Realm became. She felt that once she done her best here she would be going home, home to The Realm. Of course she would have work to do in The Before; it would take her one step closer.

23
Tuesday 19th November

Rooney called Tom at 8.30 am and asked him to accompany him to Goldfield Police Station in Edinburgh to identify a couple of items found in the park. The sergeant picked Tom up at nine.
'The forensic lady that was at the park with us was busy yesterday afternoon. As a priority we had her do the park items as soon as possible, the last thing we need would be to let the trail go cold. Just so you know we are all over this.'
'I know you are doing your best, I am truly thankful, I wish I could do more to help. Anna's parents have got posters printed; we are going around the town to put them up when I get back.'
'That's a great idea, keep you busy.'
'I'm going back to work tomorrow; do you think it is too soon?'
'No I don't, there is nothing you can do sitting in the house.'
'Ruby and George said the exact same thing; you will call me right away if you hear anything though won't you?'
'Of course I will. When is Ruby going back to work?' Rooney asked remembering that Mrs Brown never went back to work after Jasmine went missing.
'I don't know, George told her to go back tomor-

row that he is here to hold the fort as he put it, she was having none of it.'
'She will go back in her own time I suppose.'

When they reached the station Rooney took Tom to see Caroline Adam.
'Good morning Caroline, how's tricks?'
'Great, how was it at your sister's on Sunday?' she asked.
'Fine, she always was a good cook. This is Mr Tom Ross; I don't believe you have met.'
'Just call me Caroline Mr Ross.'
'Well just you call me Tom in that case.'
The room was small, painted white with a small table and no chairs. On the table were two clear plastic bags one had a gold chain with a gold thistle on it. The other contained a set of keys, two Yale keys and a larger key.
'Ok, so you can pick these items up in the bags, I couldn't get conclusive DNA from these items, which might mean they have been out in the elements for some time, although they don't look rusty. We ruled out a couple of items, there are a few still to be tested, we wanted you in here as soon as possible to see if these look familiar.'
Tom picked up the necklace and turned it over in his hands a few times in the bag, he knew right away this was not Anna's. He didn't need to pick the keys up to know that they were not

Anna's; Anna had left her keys in the house.

'No, neither of them belongs to my wife.'

'Are you sure?' Caroline asked.

'Yes, I am totally sure, I don't know if it's a good thing or a bad thing.'

'What do you mean?' said Rooney.

'Well, I don't know anyone that has gone missing before. I don't know if I should be happy or sad that I don't recognise these items. I mean if I do see something that belongs to Anna in the items from the park that means more than likely that she was in there that night. I know she would not have gone in there at that time of night of her own accord, which makes me think the worst. Then if I don't verify anything then we are no further forward to finding her.'

'I see the point you are trying to make Tom, but you have got to stay positive.'

'That's easy to say, my wife has been missing since Thursday night with no indication of what happened,' Tom snapped

'I know it can't be easy for you, we are doing all we can.'

'I know I'm sorry I know it's no excuse for biting your head off. I'm just not sleeping great at all.'

'That can be expected. I will take you home now,' Rooney said.

Tom and Rooney sat in silence on the journey back to Browning Street.

'Ruby and George are here,' Tom said as they

pulled up to his gate and he saw George's car.

'That's right you said you are all going to put posters up.'

'Yes I want to make sure you can't walk down any street in this town without seeing Anna's face.'

'Well say hello to Mr and Mrs Anderson from me, and good luck it, will be a tiring day for you all.'

'It sure will, the sooner we get started and all that, bye for now.'

Tom got out the car feeling exhausted and shrunken, he checked the time on his phone it was 10.25 am. A long day stretched out before him and he hoped he had the energy to deal with it. Ruby and George were in the kitchen with the back door open for Rex.

'Do you want something to eat before we go out?' Ruby asked.'

'Coffee please,' Tom answered.

'Have you had something to eat this morning?' George inquired.

'No, I'm not hungry.'

'Put some toast on for him Ruby, he needs to eat,' George instructed.

'Where are the posters?' Tom asked.

'Out there in the car, we are meeting a few of our friends from the bowling club at the precinct at eleven; they are going to give us a hand. We have four cars including yours and six people including you, we will meet there and split up, what streets we don't get done today will get done tomorrow,' George said.

'Sounds good, how many posters did you get?'

'We got five hundred, lots of paste and brushes. Don't worry we have everything we could possibly need, wrap up well it is quite cold out.'

After being forced fed the toast and quickly drinking his coffee he called Rex in from the back garden then got ready to go.

'Right I will follow you and Ruby.'

I need to go see Frank today. We need to put our heads together, figure out how to help each other out. I think it's going to be harder to get through to Billy than I thought, I will keep at it. I will go tonight and every other night until it works.

Anna was bored out her skull; she had checked the time a little earlier, it was 11.30am, Tom wasn't in; however, she was happy to see Rex walking a lot better. She reckoned it was nearly time for Jasmine to get her lunch, so she waited until Candice brought it in. She didn't need to wait long.

'Hello dear,' Candice said to Jasmine as she entered the shed closing the door behind her.

'Hello,' the young prisoner answered.

'We have a cheese, onion and tomato sandwich for lunch today.'

'Oh great, any chance of a cup of tea with that

please, I haven't had a cup for a while?'

'You know I decide what you have, this not a hotel I'm running here, I have already got a bottle of water for you,' Candice said throwing the bottle on the bed next to her.

'It was just a thought; pregnant women get notions for certain foods you know.'

'I know that, do you think I am stupid.'

'No of course not, I'm sorry I won't ask for anything again.'

Candice put the sandwich on the floor next to the bed and left without another word.

I don't know how Jasmine stays so calm with her, I would be screaming at her. They really have ground her down in here; she only wanted a cup of tea, surely that is not too much to ask. There is not much I can do to get her tea, I can keep trying to help, time I went to see Frank I think.

Anna decided to walk round to fifty-eight Ashton drive where Frank's mother lives. She stood outside on the pavement staring in the window. It felt wrong for her to go inside without being invited in by Frank; she felt like she would be trespassing on another soul's territory, so she waited until Frank saw her then came out.

'You are a sight for sore eyes Anna.'

'I could say the same thing about you.'

It was true, Anna didn't realise it until she saw him, she truly was so happy to be in his company again, to be able to be heard, to be able to be seen, small luxuries that are taken for granted when you are alive.

'I think we should help each other Frank, we have nothing to lose.'

'Well I'm glad to hear it little lady.'

'The problem is I don't know how we can do it yet.'

'You can communicate can't you?'

'Yes, but it's not that easy, I will need to keep at Billy saying the same things over and over until it sinks in. I called my guide last night he told me I need to mention The Innocent to him, so that is what I will do.'

'How about my power, can you think how I can help myself with that, I will admit I wasn't the smartest man when I was alive. All I'm doing at the moment is going between my mum and Richard. I have practised with my power I know it works; the thing is I haven't figured out how to use it to my advantage yet.'

'Letters,' Anna said the idea popping into her head out of nowhere.

'What, what letters?'

'Posted letters, start moving their mail.'

'I'm not getting this.'

'Take Richard's post to your mum's house and take your mum's post to Richard's house.'

'How will that work.'

'I don't know that it will, it's the only thing I've got at the moment, what if Richard takes the mail back to your mum's, they could meet.'

'Yes, that could work; I will start in the morning, thanks Anna.'

'You have to remember it might take some time. You might need to keep doing this for a while for it to pay off.'

'I know Anna, I have nothing but time on my hands. I wish I could help you.'

'If I think of something I will let you know.'

'How would you like to come in and see my mother?'

'I would love that,' Anna said before they both disappeared into the house.

May Simpson was old for her age, her hair reached chin level and was pure silver grey, she wore glasses that had the thickest lenses that Anna had ever seen, her skin was creased with wrinkles, she had no teeth in which maybe put an extra ten years on her. The house itself was old fashioned and in desperate need of a coat of paint. The couch was a corded green fabric thing with two matching chairs, the carpet was also green, a bit thread bare and looked as if it hadn't seen a vacuum for a couple of weeks. The curtains were cream with a white net curtain underneath, the kind of window dressing that Anna always associated with old women. There was no coffee table, a dirty cup sat on the floor next to where May was sitting on one of the chairs.

'This is my mum,' Franked announced proudly.

'She has a very kind face,' Anna said not knowing what else to say.

'I know she looks old, I put it down to what she has been through.'

'Yes, that would have a bad effect on anyone.'

May stood up and went into the kitchen taking her dirty cup with her. She was well dressed which took Anna by surprise. May had on a black knee length skirt, black shoes and a white blouse; she had silver stud earrings in and a silver heart necklace.

'What do you do all day here with your mother?'

'Well she likes old movies, which I watch with her, she likes her magazines and crosswords. I lean over her shoulder and tell her the answers when I know them; she can't hear me of course.'

'Sounds as if you are not as bored out your head as I am then, maybe I should be doing more of that stuff, I feel bad when I leave Jasmine alone for too long by herself.'

'Can I come and see the girl?'

'Yes why not. I will warn you it is a miserable, depressing sight.'

'I can handle it I'm sure.'

'Ok we will walk around; I'm trying to pass the

time until I can visit Billy again tonight.'

They thought themselves outside the house then started walking.

'This is the route I took the night I was murdered,' Anna told Frank.

'It must stir up some bad memories for you then.'

'You know, it's not that bad at all, I think I have totally accepted what happened to me and I really am focused on helping The Innocent now.'

'You are a good person Anna you deserve to get to The Realm as soon as possible.'

Anna stopped walking; they were walking towards the bus shelter at the end of Morcombe Street not far from Omar's shop.

'Look,' she said gesturing towards the poster on the bus shelter. 'It's me.'

They both took the last couple of steps to reach it a little quicker.

'Someone is desperate to find you.'

'That will be Tom and my parents. I bet that's where Tom was when I popped in earlier, he wasn't there.'

It had all the details about when and where she was last seen along with a decent photo of her. The telephone number for the police was at the bottom.

'I wonder how many they have put up.'

'No amount is too many,' Frank said.

'Come on let's go.'

They continued on their walk until they reached the monsters' house. They saw three more posters of Anna on light posts on the way.

'It's around the back,' Anna told Frank.

'They walked around the back of the house, they both stopped outside the shed door.

'Are you sure you want to see this, it is my murder scene as well. It's all cleaned up now, but when I came back down I came down in this shed with my dead body lying there in front of me.'

'No way.'

'Way.'

They both thought themselves on the other side of the door and a second later they were in the middle of the pitiful scene. They had come at a bad time, Jasmine had her basin of water and was struggling to wash her intimate bits with her bump in the way; Frank took a very quick look around and left. Anna thought herself outside the shed where Frank was waiting on her.

'Well that was awkward,' said Frank.

'Yes, well maybe I should have gone ahead for a peek. I take it Candice is home a bit early from work today since she has been back in the shed.'

'That would have been a good idea. I never want to go back in there again Anna, it is very disturbing.'

'Indeed it is, I have no option, I wish there was more I could do for her.'

'You are doing all you can.'

'I know, it still feels like it is not enough. I'm going to visit the monsters that did this; do you want to see them?'

'Why not, nothing can be as bad as what I have just witnessed.'

Anna and Frank went into the kitchen of the Sutherlands. There was no one there so they went to the living room. Candice was there, Jack was nowhere to be seen.

'Jack must still be at work I take it.'

'She looks normal,' Frank declared.

'They are normal in every other sense. They both have jobs and live normal lives apart from their big, dark secret out in that shed. I wish they would talk; I want to know what they are up to. Maybe I should spend some more time with them.'

'I know I wouldn't want to be in their company.'

'I'm going to see Tom. We can walk again, it's on the way to your mother's house, let's get out of here.'

They said goodbye at Anna's gate. Frank disappeared from Anna's sight; he obliviously didn't want to walk the rest of the way. Anna went straight to the kitchen it was 4.10 pm.

Time has gone quicker today, probably because I

have had someone to talk to.

Anna could hear her loved one's voices coming from the living room so went to join them. They were talking about Anna, her mother was crying.

'Something bad has happened, I just know it, if she were in a huff about the affair which she has every right to be might I add then she would have been back before this. She would have let us know she was alright, we would have heard something,' Ruby said through the tears.

'The posters might do some good,' said George trying hard to keep her spirits up, he knew himself, he knew his daughter, something had happened.

'I will call Sergeant Rooney in the morning, find out what's happening,' Tom added.

'I thought you are going back to work tomorrow,' George asked.

'I am, although I'm sure I will be able to phone whoever I want to under the circumstances.'

'Of course you will, remember to phone us with the latest news.'

'That goes without saying George, as soon as I'm off the phone from the police you will hear your phone ringing, I promise you that.'

'We will do the rest of the posters in the morning, only one hundred left to put up, we made good progress today,' George said.

'I'm making pasta for a quick dinner tonight hope that's alright?' Ruby asked.
'That sounds great, you are a star. You still ok to take Rex home with you two tonight?'
'Yes, I bet he misses going to work with Anna.'
'I just can't leave him in all day by himself, when Anna didn't take him to work she always came home at lunch time to see him and let him out.'
'He has us to do that now, until he is back to his old self we will have him stay with us, Fluff will just have to like it or lump it,' George declared.
Anna was happy that her family were working things out between them; she left her comforting home for the depression of the shed.

Anna hung about in the shed just being with Jasmine for as long as she could stand it. She went back home and sat with Tom until he went to bed at 10.45 pm; there was no sign of Rex in the house then remembered her parents were taking him tonight. She went to their house to be sure, right enough there he was sleeping in his bed at the bottom of their bed on the floor. Fluff was on her parents' bed at her dad's side, that cat was a real daddy's girl. Seeing that Rex was ok she went straight to Billy's to see if he was sleeping yet and he was. Kate was in bed. She was reading a book by Dean Koontz by the light of a bedside lamp at her side of the bed.
'Anna Anderson.'

At once Billy started to move about in his sleep, once he had settled Anna tried again.

'Billy it is Anna, there is a girl being held captive over your back fence in your neighbours' garden. They are evil Billy, the girl is pregnant and that baby is an Innocent.'

Billy turned and started to mumble inaudibly.

'Billy, please find a way to help The Innocent you are the only hope that the girl and her baby have. Please do all in you power to bring the Sutherlands to justice. They need to be punished for what they are doing. I implore you to be very careful, the last thing I want is for you to be harmed in any way.'

'Anna,' Billy shouted a second before he woke with a start.

'Have you had another bad dream darling, you shouted Anna were you dreaming about Anna Ross,' Kate asked a little startled.

'I think I was. I don't really know, I can't remember exactly. It's strange it was a dream we both know that, it seemed like something else, I don't know what, just something different.'

I'm getting through to him, or at least I think I am. I must be doing something right, maybe Ravi was right all I needed to do was mention The Innocent, sure I have a ways to go. I'm on the right track I know it.

Billy got out of bed then walked out the bedroom door with Buster by his side as usual.

'Could you get me a drink of water please?' Kate asked.

'Sure honey, be back in a minute something I need to check.'

Billy went into the spare room, the one at the back of his house. It is spare now, but it still had a lot of his son Arran's things in it. Arran moved in with his girlfriend at the beginning of the year. They had only been going out for three months and Billy did not agree with his decision. He thought it was too soon, Arran was too young at the tender age of twenty, but Arran and his girlfriend Kirsty had proved him wrong, they were getting on brilliantly in their private let flat at the other end of Hallington. Billy had told them on more than one occasion that if they were serious about each other to get the money together for a deposit on a place of their own, no point in renting when you could be buying he would say. They listened to his advice and opened a joint account for that very purpose.

Billy went to the window, opened the blinds; he didn't put a light on in here, he had the light from the hall which he had put on when he came out of his bedroom. Billy peered out to his neighbours' garden; the only light out there was the lights coming from The Green which was not enough to illuminate their garden to be

able to see anything properly.
'I will take a look at that in the morning,' he mumbled to himself, just loud enough for Anna to hear him.

He really heard what I said. I can't believe it, I could save The Innocent or rather Billy could, I could get to The Realm pretty soon.

Billy left the room with Buster leaving Anna standing there alone in the dark, not that she minded one little bit, she was over the moon with her progress. She decided that plenty had been achieved tonight; she would leave Billy alone until tomorrow, that way she felt as if she wasn't putting too much pressure on him. She went back to the shed for a well deserved sleep.

24
Wednesday 20th November

Tom had only been at work for just over an hour when his mobile rang. He was up a ladder so came down to check who it was; it was Rooney so he called him back straight away.

'Hello Sergeant Rooney this is Tom Ross.'

'Hello there, I called to ask if you are available to come to the station. It seems that someone has seen one of your posters yesterday; they called us as soon as they saw it claiming that they saw Anna in the precinct on Monday afternoon, we have checked the CCTV and we have spotted someone that does look like her. We knew which cameras to check because the person who came forward was very precise about where in the precinct they spotted this woman. I don't want to get your hopes up Tom; it won't hurt for you to take a peek.'

'I will come straight away if that's ok with you.'

'Yes of course, ask for me at reception.'

Tom went straight to his boss Paul as soon as he hung up from Rooney.

'I need to go to the police station Paul, I have not to get my hopes up, but they have a sighting of someone that looks like Anna apparently.'

'Yes, go. Listen Tom, take the rest of the week off, you came back to work too soon. I will call you on Sunday, we will take it from there; let

me know how you get on today though.'
'Of course, phone you later.'

Tom turned up at Hallington Police Station forty minutes later. He had been working in Pavesway, unknown to him that Anna was buried in that very town.

Tom went in and asked for Rooney. He only waited for a few minutes before being taken into an interview room where Rooney and PC McMillan were waiting for him. The room was larger than the interview room he had been in previously, it had the same table and chairs, the same decor, the only difference was that a screen had been set up for him on a smaller table to one side of the room, the two chairs that sat in front of it were occupied by the two officers who stood up to greet him when he walked in.

'Thanks for coming so quickly Tom,' Rooney said.

'I wouldn't be anywhere else after your call.'

Tom went over and sat eagerly as the screen jumped into life prompted by PC McMillan. The picture was grainy, although Tom recognised it clearly as the precinct, the time on the screen read 12.04pm.

'Right, you need to watch here outside Semi-Chem at 12.07,' PC McMillan instructed.

Tom kept his eyes firmly on the spot where

he was told, just as the PC had said among the other shoppers a woman of Anna's description appeared from the shop. Tom shifted forward on his seat until he was sitting on the edge; once the woman vanished from the screen the young PC replayed the scene for him. It was played four times before Rooney spoke.

'What do you think?'

Tom's heart sank like the Titanic; although he had watched the film several times he so much wanted it to be Anna.

'It's not her, it does resemble her, but it's not her. She has on similar clothes, that woman on the screen has a little lighter hair than Anna that I can tell. That woman does not have Anna's walk. I can tell people a mile away from their walk, Anna says it's my gift apparently.'

'I'm sorry for getting you in here for nothing; you understand we had to rule this out.' Rooney told him.

'I understand I'm glad you did. It shows me how hard you are looking for her.'

'With that in mind, I would like you to go back to Goldfield Police Station with me tomorrow to have a look at a few more items found in the park.'

'Yes, what time?'

'Are you working tomorrow?'

'No, I'm off work for the rest of the week.'

'How about eleven o'clock then?'

'Eleven is good for me.'

'What are you doing this afternoon Tom?'

'I was going to help Ruby and George with the rest of the posters if they haven't finished; it has worked already even though it was a false alarm. Why?'

'We contacted the local news station about doing a piece tomorrow night. They would like to come to your house today for a small interview for it,' Rooney said enthusiastically.

'Really, I would be happy to if you think it will help in anyway.'

'It can't hurt put it like that, would three o'clock be good for you?'

'I will make it good.'

Tom left the police station feeling deflated that it was not Anna on the screen, but positive about the news story. It made him feel that everything that could be done was being done to find his wife. As soon as he got back to his car he called Anna's parents to tell them everything that had happened and was going to happen. They were as impressed with the police as Tom was. Tom went home to tidy up for the TV station coming. After he tidied up he called his parents to let them know what was happening, they seemed concerned, only not enough to come back to Hallington and support him. They had their own lives which were a world of away from Tom's own. He believed that there was nothing important enough to bring them back. Of course they loved Anna; however, Tom knew from childhood how selfish they could be. All he had were Anna's family. That would have to be enough for him.

At three o'clock Tom looked out his window when he heard a vehicle pulling up and right enough right on time it was the TV station. It was a white transit van with red lettering on the side. A young woman of about the same age as Anna came out the passenger door, a man of about forty came out the driver's door. He walked to the back of the van and came out with a decent video camera. By the time they reached Tom's front door he had it open ready to greet them.
'You must be Mr Tom Ross,' the woman said.
She was quite tall, around five-foot-ten, medium build with short brown hair. She was dressed smartly in black trousers and a white shirt with a black trench coat lying open.
'Yes,' Tom answered. 'Please come in.'
He held the door open for her and in turn the man coming in with the camera, who was as thin as a stick insect and very light on his feet, springing up the front door steps with the camera as if it weighed nothing at all. He had dirty, blonde hair and gold framed glasses. He was as pale as anyone Tom had ever seen, Tom

wondered if he went outside at all. They all gathered in the living room. The camera man dropped the camera then made off out to the van.

'William is just away to the van to get some lighting, he will get the equipment set up then we will be ready to go. My name is Jill by the way,' she said holding her hand out to be shaken.

Tom shook her hand and said, 'Pleased to meet you, I hope this will help find my wife.'

'I can't promise anything, it certainly won't hurt.'

William was back in a flash, had the equipment set up in no time. He didn't speak; he just got on with his job. With everything in place the interview could begin.

Tom sat on one side of the couch with Jill on the other out of screen shot. She asked him all the details of Anna's disappearance. Tom answered them all fully with nothing left out. Once they were finished William got to work taking all the equipment back to the van, which he did as fast as when he was bringing it in, still not saying a word.

'Check out the news at half-past six tomorrow night. You will be on it Mr Ross,' Jill said.

'Thank you so much for coming here and doing this, I hope it gets some response from the public.'

'We can only hope,' Jill said before saying her goodbyes and leaving.

Tom got straight on the phone to George and Ruby; he informed them on the interview and when it was going to be aired.

'Are you two coming over?' Tom asked after he had told them all the news.

'Yes we are bringing Rex back to see you, Ruby has made some homemade steak pie for dinner,' George said.

George had the phone on speaker, after Ruby had heard the news about Anna she went to get everything prepared to take to Tom's. George took the phone off speaker and said quietly so Ruby could not hear him. 'Ruby has had a bad day today; she could barely contain the tears when we were putting up the rest of the posters. I think it is starting to get real now. It has been nearly a week with no word from Anna,' George confided.

'I wish there was more I could do, there is nothing I can think of.'

'We are all doing what we can.'

'I can keep Rex here, I don't think I mentioned Paul gave me the rest of the week off, I have to phone him on Sunday, take it from there.'

'That's great son, see you soon.'

Tom was chuffed that George had called him son. It seemed to Tom that his in-laws were starting to forgive him.

The wretchedness of the shed was more than Anna could handle, although she was dead she still thought of herself to be the lucky one compared to Jasmine that is. Anna had now come to think of her afterlife as part of her life, she was looking forward to going into The Realm more than anything. She knew that helping The Innocent was the right thing to do, the fact that if she succeeded she would get to The Realm even quicker made her more determined to do it. Dinner time had brought Candice into the shed with sausage casserole for the prisoner. Jasmine cleared her plate then fell asleep right after. Anna decided she would go find Frank; she was in dire need of a conversation. She didn't know what Ravi would think of her spending time with another soul, she was going anyway. She thought of Frank's mum's house and was there.

'Frank,' Anna called into the window.

No one else could hear her; it occurred to her that she could make as much noise as she wanted.

'Frank,' she shouted again after a few moments. She was ready to shout again when she jumped a little with fright as she saw Frank appear at her side.

'Hi Frank you gave me a start there.'

'It is weird getting used to all this jumping about from place to place. I would never in a million years have guessed that I would be here after I died doing what I'm doing.'

'You and I both. How are you doing with the letter moving?'

'There was no mail for my mother today; Richard already had his letters when I got to his house. I will need to be quicker tomorrow; I will be on the street looking out for the postman, waiting for him to drop the post in their doors. I will be on it.'

'Sounds great, hope you get success from that soon.'

'How about you, how is your mission coming along?'

'I am making progress with Billy Barclay, did I tell you about him? Anyway he is hearing me, I am getting a reaction so I will just need to plod along with it in the hope that something big happens soon.'

'Have you thought of any way that maybe my power could help you?'

'Not yet, I keep racking my brain trying to think of how it could help, I'm stumped, I will keep thinking.'

'Well remember I'm here to help if you do come up with something.'

'I know Frank, I really do appreciate it. How's is your mum?'

'She's fine. I have found out quite a bit about her life from when her friends come round, as far as

I'm aware there is only two, well two that I have seen since I have been in her life.'

'Two friends, she really must be lonely.'

'Fenza never told me a great deal about her, although I have found out that she worked in a textile factory, sewing men's garments for most of her life, until she was made redundant ten years ago. Then she volunteered in a charity shop, she packed it in only two years ago, so she worked until she was sixty-seven. She goes to the bingo a couple of times a week, the sad thing is it sounds as if she has kept herself to herself apart from a couple of close friends most of her life.'

'I know that may sound sad to you; some people like a solitary life, some people have lots of friends, no true ones. Sounds like your mum has few friends, but they are real loyal friends,'

Anna said all this in the hope that it would make Frank feel better and it worked.

'You know Anna you are right. You have a very wise head on your shoulders.'

'Thank you, I don't think anyone else has ever said that to me before.'

'You're welcome; I am only saying it as I see it.'

'So what are you doing tonight Frank?'

'Mum has bingo tonight so I might tag along with her and her friends.'

'Why don't you come with me? See what I'm trying to do, maybe you could think of some-

thing you could do to help me.'
'Really, you would let me go along with you?'
'Of course that is why I'm asking, to be quite frank Frank, I could really do with the company,' Anna said and they both laughed.
'Ok then let's go.'
'We will walk, it will pass some time.'
'Fine by me, where are we going?'
'My house first, I want to check on Tom, we can see the time there as well.'
'Lead the way sweetheart.'
They walked back along Browning Street, when they reached Anna's house they went in. In the living room Tom, Ruby and George were talking about the TV Interview.
'Oh my word Anna, you are going to be on the news, it must be comforting that your family are pulling out all the stops to find you.'
'Yes it is, I'm afraid they will never find out what happened to me. I'm afraid that they will never get any kind of closure.'
'I'm sorry I wish there was something I could do to help.'
'Don't worry about it.'
'Watch this,' Frank said before walking over to Tom and waving his hands in front of his face. It still amazes me that no one can see or hear me.'
Anna laughed and said, 'I'm starting to realise you are just a big kid at heart Frank Wood.'
'I sure am. This is crazy that we can stand here

in front of them, have a full blown conversation and they have no clue.'

'It is very surreal.'

Anna noticed Rex in his bed at the side of the sideboard.

'There's my dog, he seems to picking up nicely from his injuries.'

Frank stepped closer to Rex and bent down, 'I want to pet him I love dogs.'

'Have you ever tried to touch your mum?'

'No, I didn't think it possible.'

'Ravi told me that I could walk through a wall, well I say walk he said I would need to drag myself through and it would take me a long time. He said it would drain the energy out of me practically, but I touched Jasmine's and Tom's hands. I got a strange sensation.'

'You actually touched them?'

'Well my hand went through theirs so no not really touch, you know what I mean. I meant to ask Ravi about it, I forgot. Hey try to touch me.'

'Why? What do you think will happen?'

'Let's find out.'

Frank and Anna both held out a hand and put them together, their hands just went straight each others. No sensation all at.

'Nothing, so you have been talking to your guide?' Frank asked moving on from the useless experiment

'Yes I called him; I needed to know if I was

doing something wrong, he told me I was making great progress.'

'Wow, you have done a lot more in the days that you have been here than the months that I have.'

'Try it Frank, call Fenza, ask if there is anything she can tell you that will help you, it's worth a try. Touch your mum, see if you get the same sensation as I got, you have nothing to lose at this late stage of the game.'

'I will, tomorrow, you have taught me a lot tonight Anna, we must hang out more often.'

'Anytime, if you need to go and call your guide or to try to touch your mum I will understand.'

'No I said I would come with you tonight and that's what I'm going to do, as I said I will do it all tomorrow, although I don't think I'm going to try and walk through any walls anytime soon.'

'I am. I want to experience it all. You should too.'

'Ok, I will make a deal with you we will both try when the other is present, a bit of support and encouragement.'

'It's a deal.'

'I'm going to do a time check, be back in a sec.'

The living room door was closed so Anna popped to the kitchen and was back in a flash.

'It's 8.35, maybe a bit too early for Billy to be in bed.'

'We could always go visit your murderer.'

'You know what Frank that is the best idea I have heard all day.'

They left Anna's house and walked round to the Sutherlands', went inside. Candice and Jack were sitting at the kitchen table with empty coffee mugs sitting in front of them.

'I told you the police would not come snooping around,' Candice said.

'I think it is a little too early to think we are out of the woods just yet,' Jack replied.

'Oh you always worry when there is nothing to get your knickers in a twist for.'

Jack didn't find this amusing at all, Anna could tell by the look on his face.

'Candice, I have murdered for you, I am keeping an innocent, helpless, pregnant girl in a shed for you the least you can do is show me an ounce of respect.'

'Just for me, you will be a big part of this baby's life as well Jack, you will be a father.'

'I'm quite happy without kids, so yes this is really all for you,' Jack said getting irritated.

Candice stood up, pushed away her chair, stormed out of the kitchen.

'Fucking stupid woman,' Jack mumbled when she was out of earshot.

'All is not rosy in this household,' Frank commented.

'I'm hoping Jack flips his lid with her, I haven't

spent as much time with them as maybe I should be, I think the guilt is getting to him,' Anna replied.

'I will keep my fingers crossed for that. He is evil, there is no way a normal Supreme fearing person would do what he did.'

'Anyway, Billy lives over the fence in the next street, it's time we paid him a visit.'

Billy was in Arran's old room when Anna and Frank caught up with him. He was looking out the window into the darkness of Sutherlands' back garden.

'Look Frank he is checking it out, I must really be starting to get through to him,' Anna said with a touch of excitement in her voice.

'Well done, it certainly seems so.'

What are you doing in here Billy? You have been in and out of here all night.' Kate came into the room pulling his attention away from the window.

'I don't know. I'm being silly I think.'

'I wish you would talk to me, tell me what is going on.'

'I don't know myself, it's just a feeling I have today. It's weird. I'm going for a shower then going to bed.'

'I will make you a nice cup of hot chocolate darling; do you want to drink it in bed?'

'Yes that sounds great, shame I am back to work tomorrow when you have the day off.'

'Que Sera Sera.'

When Billy got out the shower he went into his bedroom to find his hot drink waiting for him on his bedside table. He got into bed, lifted the book he was half way through, got comfortable and shut the rest of the world out.

Kate was in the living room about to watch a movie so Frank and Anna settled down with her to watch it, they both agreed they deserved a little treat and concurred that by the time they watched it Billy would be asleep ready for Anna to resume her work.

Ten minutes into the film Anna said, 'I feel guilty, Jasmine is in that horrible shed and here I am watching a movie.'

'What could you possibly do to help her at this moment? I will tell you, absolutely nothing, so switch your mind off for a while, and watch the movie.'

'I will try.'

When the movie finished Anna went straight to Billy to see if he was still awake, much to Anna's delight he wasn't.

'Anna Anderson,' she said.

Billy started to squirm about immediately.

'It's Anna Billy, listen I know you have to go to work tomorrow so I will not keep you long tonight. Keep looking into your neighbours' garden; you will see what you are supposed to soon enough. I am asking a lot; please you need to save The Innocent Billy. Keep an eye on that shed, keep an eye on those people who live in that house, just do what you can. See you tomorrow night.'

Anna went back to the living room where Frank was watching the TV alone.

'Where is Kate?' Anna asked.

'She is down the stair letting the dog out in the garden. She must be getting ready to go to bed as well.'

'At least she has the sense not to take the dog for a walk at night by herself like I did.'

'Anna stop it, none of this is your fault. Are you done here?

'For tonight anyway yes.'

'Well I'm going to my mother's I will see you tomorrow I hope.'

'Of course you will.'

'You don't need to stand outside shouting next time, just come in.'

'I will.'

With that they both disappeared to different places.

25
Thursday 21st November

It has been a week since I was murdered. It's been a long week. Maybe I should be more like Frank, he entertains himself well, I think he just wants to be around his mother; maybe he is not as keen as me to get into The Realm. Of course he has never known his real mother; it must be difficult knowing that one day he will have to leave her behind, at least he knows that they will meet again in a much better place. It must still be early, no breakfast has been brought in yet and Jasmine is still sleeping, although I couldn't blame her. Her slumber was restless, moving about and moaning most of the night, that bed must be doing nothing for her back, not to mention the lack of exercise. Soon to be mothers are meant to keep themselves healthy and fit, what chance has Jasmine got of doing that.

Anna was plucked from her thoughts by someone entering the shed. It was Jack, much to Anna's surprise. He lifted the bucket being used as Jasmine's toilet, replaced it with an empty one and left again without Jasmine waking up. Twenty minutes later he was back with a plastic carrier bag. Jasmine woke this time and looked as taken aback as much as Anna was to see Jack. Jack took as little to do with the girl as possible; Jasmine knew there must be a reason why Candice the witch was not here.

'Candice is ill, so you won't see her today,' Jack announced.

'Nothing too serious I hope,' Jasmine answered him sarcastically.

'Whatever it is I'm sure it will soon pass.'

'There was I hoping it was something more serious,' Jasmine retorted.

'You watch your mouth.'

Jack put the carrier bag onto the bed beside his prisoner then left the shed with haste. Jasmine emptied the bag as soon as he had left. Inside much to her delight she found a flask of tea, two chocolate biscuits, two bottles of water, a sandwich and a sausage roll.

'This must be to do me until dinner time,' Jasmine said to no one.

So Candice is ill, that is a shame, not. It must still be early; Jack will be going to work so he has brought Jasmine that bag of goodies to keep her going. At least there is tea for her; it will put a heat in her.

Anna lay down and went to sleep knowing no one would come in here until dinner time. She had not slept all night; she had every kind of thought going around in her head.

Tom sat at the kitchen table with his laptop open in front of him. He was on Facebook looking at a post that Missing People had put on about Anna; Sergeant Rooney must have contacted them. It seemed to Tom that Rooney was doing all he could possibly do to help in the search for his wife and he was grateful. He went to his own post, reading all the comments that people had written. Most of them were wishing him luck to find her. A few were sharing their own experiences with him; all he was looking for was comments that had any information on Anna's whereabouts. He went through them all, there was nothing he felt useful, so he closed the laptop, and looked under the table where Rex was lying.

'Are you going for a small walk today?'

Rex wagged his tail then came out from under the table. Tom went into the hall, came back with his jacket and a beanie hat, after he put them on he went to reach for Rex's lead. He was puzzled at first as to why the lead was not over the back of the chair, he had not needed it when Rex was under the weather, and that's when he remembered Anna was the last one with the lead.

'I can't believe it, why did I think the lead would be there? I wasn't looking for it for the past week because I didn't need it. I never even gave it a second thought; I suppose I have had other things on my mind,' Tom was talking to Rex who by this time was waiting patiently at the back door ready to go.

'I will need to go buy you a new lead first boy.'

Tom opened the back door; let Rex out into the garden.

'This will have to do for now boy.'

Tom took a few poo bags from one of the drawers, he had not cleaned the garden of dog dirt for a few days; it was starting to look like they had a pack of dogs staying there. Tom stepped outside, the rain felt cold on his face as it immediately showered him, coming down sideways with the wind behind it. He turned his face away and hunched his shoulders before turning and heading straight back into the house. He watched Rex in the garden, the rain didn't bother him. He went about his usual sniffing routine as if it were summer. When Rex had finished and was back in the house Tom took a towel from the airing cupboard in the hall and dried him off.

'Right, I'm going out to get you a new lead, I promise I will take you a walk and clean the garden when the rain eases up a bit.'

Tom lifted his car keys, wallet and phone then left the house.

Anna woke to find Jasmine talking to the baby again; she had the name tag out and was holding it by the edge up in front of her face between her thumb and index finger rolling it back and forth.

'See baby, this is what a detective would call a

clue. If someone has noticed it is missing then they might be searching for it. Oh I know they won't find it here, if they find me they will find this as well, it is evidence that the lady was here.'

'I'm still here Jasmine; I'm with you every step of the way from now on kid,' Anna said.

If only I could have a conversation with her as I can with Frank. I think I'm bored; I'd hate to think how bored and lonely this young lady is. I can't bear to see her in these conditions, I hope I get to see her out of here and living the life she should be living, free, clean and healthy with a baby to look after. I wish I could have fallen pregnant, it was all Tom and I wanted a while back, the notion seemed to have left him, now I know the reason why. If we did have a child and this still happened to me I wonder if Tom could manage on his own? He wouldn't have to; my parents would help him of course. Why am I thinking all this, it didn't happen and never will now? I'm letting my mind wander; I need to think of things that are going to help me help The Innocent.

Anna left the shed, walked round to see Frank; the driving rain again had no effect on her. She stood outside his temporary residence and gave him a shout. Frank had told her just to go in; she didn't want to impose; however, after no response from Frank she went in. His mother was still in bed, awake, sitting up in reading a magazine with a cup of hot tea steaming next to her on a bedside table.

She has the right idea on a morning like his. Where is Frank though? He can't be far away I suppose.

Anna left the house and went walking around the streets in the hope of bumping into her new friend. She was desperate for a conversation, since she met Frank it had gave her a new lease of life, or death as it was. She walked for about an hour before she spotted him. He was on the trail of the postwoman.
'Frank,' she called across the road, he was in Walker Terrace just off Drayton Street.
'Can't talk, need to keep up with the postie. Don't want to miss her posting a letter at my brother's or my mum's.'
'Well I will leave you to it then, I will catch up with you later at your mum's.'
'Yeah sure thing, this woman has a van around the corner; I think I should maybe sit in the van until she gets near their streets. Why didn't I have that idea earlier?'
'Well you have it now. Good luck.'
Anna went home; the time on the kitchen clock was 10.25 am. She could hear Tom in the living room talking so she went to see who it was. It was just Tom and Rex in here. Tom was taking something out of a plastic bag, it was a dog lead.

A new dog lead, I never even gave that a second thought, Tom must not have either until Rex was ready to go for a walk which must be today.

'Right boy, I will take you for that walk now, don't worry we won't go far on your first day.' Tom said to Rex.

I will go with them, like the good old days when I was alive.

Tom and Rex went out the back door the traditional way, Anna waited until they were outside and used her unconventional method. When they got outside the gate Tom crossed the road into Drayton Street, the postwoman's van was parked halfway along the street, Anna waved to Frank when she walked by, he was sitting in the front seat carrying out his own idea. Tom turned right into Westfield Street, he only walked about a third of the way along before turning back.

'That's enough for your first walk; we will do the same tonight,' Tom spoke to Rex.

The rain had eased a lot, it was only spitting now, but it was really cold. Tom walked with his shoulders tensed and hunched. The sky was dark grey with the threat of another downpour looming.

He should have warmer clothes on, yes he has a hat

on, but he really needs to put on a warmer jacket, he has a few to choose from. I suppose it's not something that is at the fore front of his mind at the moment.

'I'm so sorry to hear about Anna Tom,' it was Arlene Ferguson the postwoman who was speaking to him.
'I was in a world of my own there. Thank you it is a very difficult time for us.'
'I bet it is, I saw your post on Facebook and I couldn't believe it. Anna is a lovely person, when I take letters into the shop if I'm on that route I always stay in there too long blethering.'
'The police have been great; they are doing all they can, please share my post.'
'I already have Tom; I will do it again and again if I need to.'
Frank came out of the van, he was getting impatient.
'This will take all day if she keeps talking to people all the time, every time she see's someone she knows, there she goes again,' Frank said to Anna doing the talking sign with his hand.
Anna was laughing so hard at him she could not answer. She just stood shaking her head before getting herself together enough to say 'You know something Frank you are hilarious even when you are not trying. You have time on your hands, chill out.'

Frank started laughing now, it started Anna off again. It was only when she heard Tom's next words that it got her attention.

'I will be on the news tonight at half-past six, doing an appeal to help find Anna,' Tom told Arlene.

'Well I will tune in and tell everyone I know to do the same, the more people that see it the better. Hope it brings good news, see you later.'

'That will be a lot of people judging by the amount of people she has spoken to today,' Frank said.

Anna never heard him; she heard yesterday that an appeal was to be on TV, she didn't think that much about it until now, she was concocting ideas of how she was going to watch it, she knew Tom would be watching, and her parents, there was no way she was going to miss it.

'Are you ignoring me,' Frank said sounding annoyed.

'I'm sorry, what are you saying?'

'Oh it doesn't matter.'

'Do you want to come and watch it with me?'

'Of course I will, what time is it on.'

'Half-six, meet me outside my house at six o'clock.'

Tom had walked away and Anna hurried to get by his side again. Frank went back into the van to wait on Arlene. Once Anna had walked Tom and Rex back to her their gate she went back to the shed.

Jasmine was sleeping, so Anna spoke to her.
'I'm going to be on the news tonight. The police and my family are pulling out all the stops to find me. I am doing all I can to help you Jasmine, it may take some time, so I need you to hang on in there.'
Jasmine did not stir when Anna spoke to her.
'That's weird, she is not responding to me.'
Anna moved closer to her and watched her chest to make sure it was rising and falling, it was.
'Why are you not showing any sign that you can hear me?'
Anna sat on the bed waiting for Jasmine to wake up, after what Anna thought was an hour or so she went to her kitchen, it was 2.20 pm. She went back to Jasmine and waited on the bed for another while until Jasmine woke.

Thank goodness she is awake; I was starting to think there was something wrong with her.

It didn't take long for Anna to notice that there *was* something wrong with her. Jasmine was moaning and groaning, Anna could tell by the look on her face that she was ill. Jasmine started heaving over the edge of the bed vomiting into her toilet bucket.
'Oh my word, are you all right?'

Of course she is not alright, she can't hear me anyway. No wonder she is ill, she is sleeping right next to her toilet, no one should need to do that especially when pregnant. They two evil scum of the earth people need to pay for this. Wait a minute Candice is ill as well maybe this is some sort of bug that is going around, I take it Jasmine caught it from the witch.

Anna went into the Sutherlands' house to find Candice in bed out for the count.
'Anna Anderson,' There was no response.
'Anna Anderson,' still nothing.
Anna went back to Jasmine; there was nothing she could do to help the girl. Jasmine settled back down and fell asleep again.

Maybe that's the best thing she could do. I hope when the monster comes back in here later he will do something to help her. I bet Candice has all the medicine and stuff she needs to keep her comfortable. Lying in there in a nice, big comfy bed without a care in the world, while Jasmine is out here in a prison unable to help herself or ask for help. It's a disgrace.

Anna thought of Billy and was there beside him. She turned up on the bus that Billy was driving. The bus was quiet with only a handful of passengers, most of them pensioners, mostly women. Billy seemed deadly serious; she had never seen him at work before, she never took the bus anywhere. She sat down on one of the front seats and stared out of the window trying to work out her location. They passed by the building site where her body was buried and Anna recognised it immediately.

'Arrrgghhh,' Anna hurled a scream out into the near empty bus.

She stood up, started pacing up and down the aisle, rage bubbling up inside her; she was clenching and unclenching her fists, with the presence of sheer anger on her face.

'Why, why did I need to come here at this precise time and see that place? I'm dead, things could not get any worse or so I thought. Is The Supreme punishing me?'

Anna was quick to sit back down when the bell for the bus to stop went off; the last thing she wanted was for someone to walk through her. She didn't know exactly what would happen, she was taking no chances. She was super annoyed so she went to see Frank. She stood outside the house where his mother lived and shouted, still not wanting to take it upon herself to enter the house, she didn't wait long until Frank appeared. She told Frank what had happened, standing there with her arms and hands making all kinds of gestures, she was agitated and harassed.

'You need to calm down Anna.'

'I know, but I can't, I'm totally fuming.'

'I can see that. You are not helping anyone being in such a state. The best thing you can do is concentrate on the job at hand.'

'I'm sorry; I came here shouting the odds about what has happened to me. How did you get on today?'

'Great actually, I took a letter from Mum's and put it at my brother's house.'

'Good, you will need to do it every day until we can think of something else that might help.'

'I know it won't be easy, but I will do it.'

'About your power, can you pick up anything?'

'No just things that don't weigh a lot, I tried a cup, my hand went straight through.'

'What about doors can you open them?'

'No tried it, same result, hand goes right through. It seems it's only small or light objects I can move. It's strange I must have this power for a reason, if not for moving the letters then something else that I have no clue about yet.'

'We will work it out, you still coming to my house to watch the interview?'

'Yes, wouldn't miss it for the world.'

Frank vamoosed from her side, but was back in a few seconds.

'It is 5.15 pm, you want to walk round just now and wait. I like your house.'

'I need to check on Jasmine before I go, she was sick today, Candice is ill as well. It was Jack,

who brought in her breakfast this morning, when I went to Candice she was in bed sleeping.'
'You go and check on her and I will meet you at your house then, don't think I want to go back to that shed, it's so depressing.'
'Welcome to my world Frank.'
Anna went to the shed, Jasmine was in a terrible state, she had used a lot of her toilet roll blowing her nose, there was a pile on the floor and her nose was bright red. She was coughing and holding her throat as if it was sore, her eyes were red and watering. It didn't seem as if any of the monsters had been back into the shed to see her.

Frank said it was 5.15, it shouldn't be long before someone comes in here, I think Jasmine needs a doctor, I know that is not going to happen.

Anna went into the Sutherlands' house, Jack was in the kitchen. He was heating up ready meals in the microwave. When the first one was ready he put the second one in. He lifted a carrier bag and the first ready meal then headed out the back door. Anna was back in the shed waiting when he arrived. He opened the door and slipped in as fast as they always do, but was taken aback when he saw the state of his captive.
'What the fuck is wrong with you?'
'I'm ill are you blind,' Jasmine spat.

'No, I don't know what to do,' Jack said with panic in his voice.

'I need a doctor, I'm pregnant or have you forgotten.'

'No I haven't forgotten. There is no way in hell are you getting a doctor. I will go get you some cough medicine and paracetamol, and anything else I can lay my hands on.'

'Will you empty that bin, I have been sick, it stinks.'

'One thing at a time, here there is your dinner and some water and crisps in the bag, I will be back shortly.'

Jack left the shed flustered; he went straight in to Candice.

'Jasmine is sick. She says she needs a doctor.'

'Of course she will say that, she will have the same as me, it's a bug and a cold rolled into one by the feel of it.'

'I'm going out to get her something; your dinner will be ready. Can you take it out the microwave?'

'I don't feel like eating, but yes I will get it.'

'Great I'm off.'

Jack left the house and went to Smith's Chemist before it closed at six. He got a cough bottle, cold and flu tablets and some sore throat lozenges, he would also give Jasmine some of the paracetamol that Candice has. When he got back to the house he grabbed an empty bucket

and the paracetamol then went straight out to the shed. He was worried about the girl; he was feeling guiltier about her than he was letting on to Candice. He knew he couldn't let her go, that didn't stop him from wanting to. Candice started all this and he was drawn in, in too deep to reverse it all now, if he could change it he would. Jasmine was glad to see him when he went in.
'I can't eat the dinner, I can't stomach it. What did you get me?'
He passed the bag to her and she opened it immediately, she took out the cough bottle taking a swig right away.
'Go easy with that, the last thing you want to do is take too much.'
'What do you care?'
'I'm just saying you don't want to harm the baby.'
'You two are the ones that are harming me and my baby, keeping me in here chained up, seeing no daylight, the only way I roughly know what time it is, is when I get my meals. I get no exercise and I'm eating my meals right next to where I go to the toilet. It's not healthy.'
Jack didn't say another word, the guilt was eating in at him; he went out of the shed and back to the house.

The pressure is getting to him. Maybe he will crack,

one can only hope. I want to get to my house, but I don't want to leave this poor girl all alone.

Anna went to Frank who was standing at her gate waiting.
'I need to go back to the shed and watch over the girl, she is not looking good. Will you go watch the interview and tell me all about it?'
'Of course I will, I don't fancy being in your shoes right now.'
'Thanks Frank, I owe you one.'
Anna was back in the shed within seconds. She knew there was nothing she could do to ease any of Jasmine's suffering from her illness; she just couldn't let her suffer alone.

I will need to pile the pressure on Billy tonight, I know he is working and I feel terrible for doing this to him, but Jasmine and this baby come first to me. I need to up my game.

Anna waited in the shed with Jasmine for what seemed like hours. She went home to her kitchen; it was 9.25 pm. She left there, went to give Frank a shout. Frank was at her side in no time.
'Well what was the interview like?'
'I watched it; I'm starting to wish I didn't. I can't get the sight of your mother out of my mind. She was in a terrible state; it might be just as well you didn't go watch it for yourself.'
Anna closed her eyes and pinched the top of her

nose between her forefinger and thumb. There was too much problems coming from all roads today.

'I can't handle this, don't tell me anymore about it, I'm sorry I wasted your time getting you to watch it, I can't take any more today Frank.'

'What can I do to help?'

'I wish I knew.'

'What are your plans now?'

'I'm going to Billy; I need to go all out from now on.'

'Will I see you tomorrow?'

'Yes of course, I will find you.'

'Not too early, I have a postwoman to chase.'

'Ok. Bye.'

Anna went to Billy's, he was in bed with the light out, he wasn't asleep yet. Kate was in the living room watching Anna's favourite show, so Anna decided to give herself a bit of down time and watch it with her. After the show ended Kate got the dog lead which Buster must have heard because he came out of the bedroom and padded into the living room where Kate was putting on her Jacket.

'We are not going far Buster,' Kate said to her dog.

Kate and Buster went out for a walk, so Anna went to Billy, he had fell into a slumber.

'Anna Anderson.'

Billy turned over and moaned.

'Billy, there is an Innocent in the shed in your neighbours' garden over the back from you. Their names are Candice and Jack Sutherland. There is a young woman who is pregnant with an Innocent being held captive there and they need your help urgently. You need to help them Billy, you need to find a way. At the moment you are their only hope, I'm sorry for having to put this on you, you are the only person who can hear me that can do anything, please help.'

Billy woke up slowly, not with a start, just as if he was waking up naturally. He pulled the covers off him and went into the spare room at the back of his house; he went to the window peering out into the darkness. After a few minutes he walked away from the window shaking his head.

'I'm going insane.'

Billy went back to bed, he could not sleep. He picked up his book and started to read, that was no good. He got back up and went back to the spare room window.

'Someone is trying to tell me something.'

He heard Kate and Buster coming back in from their walk; Buster's cold nose was against his hand a moment later.

'There you are, my shadow,' Billy said to his dog.

Kate came into the room. 'What the hell are you doing in here again? You should be in bed, remember you are up at five.'
'I know I'm just going.'
Billy went back to bed; it took him a long time to fall over.

26
Friday 22nd November

Jack came into the shed with Jasmine's breakfast and lunch; he left then came back five minutes later with a basin of hot water, a towel and clean underwear. He never said a word to Jasmine, Jasmine never said a word to him. He left as quickly as he came.

Well that was awkward; I take it Candice is still in bed ill. I think I will go in to have a listen to what they are saying.

Anna went into their bedroom where Jack was sitting at the bottom of the bed; Candice was in bed looking like death itself.
'We need to change the sheets on her bed and her clothes, I never noticed until this morning, it really is starting to stink in there' Jack told Candice.
'We will change the bed sheets and give the place a right good clean tomorrow; hopefully I will be feeling a bit better by then.'
'I can't wait until this whole thing is over.'
'I know me neither; we will have our child and be miles away from here. How is the girl today?'
'She looks like you, ill. I never spoke to her, she never spoke to me. Can't blame her after everything we have done to her, she must totally hate us. I know if the shoe were on the other foot I

would be full to the brim with anger.'

'What's done is done Jack; we still have the worst part to come. We will get through it. We have to.'

'Don't remind me, I'm scared of what's to come. I don't know if I could kill her when the time comes.'

'Don't start with that carry on Jack, it needs to be done we both know it.'

'I think you should do it, I killed that woman in the heat of the moment, don't get me wrong it had to been done, she saw too much of our crime, I don't want to do it again.'

'Don't be such a pussy, if it comes to it and you haven't got the stomach then I suppose I will have to do it. You are the so called man you should be doing it.'

'So called man, what the hell do you mean by that?'

'Nothing, I'm sorry I should never have said that.'

Jack got off the bed and went out of the room, lifted his van keys and left for work in a mood.

Seems to me that all in not rosy in the Sutherland household. I'm still hoping that Jack will crack. Maybe I should try to make contact with him; I don't think I have tried him yet. I can't remember. I will try tonight anyway, maybe if I could haunt him enough he will turn himself in.

Tom was on the phone to his boss Paul when Anna arrived home at 9 am. Anna heard Tom recite everything that happened in the search for her, all the things she knew and a couple of things she had missed. She walked towards Rex who was in his bed by the sideboard.

'Rex, you seem much better now baby,' Anna said to him bending down to get her face closer to his. All she wanted to do was snuggle up with him, it seemed to Anna that it was a life time ago that she last did it. Tom came off the phone, dialled another number.

'Hello, this is Sergeant Rooney'

'Hello this is Tom Ross, I was wondering if you could fill me in on what's happening.'

'To be honest Mr Ross we have no new leads, which is why we are going to try a door to door, try to see if we could maybe jog someone's memory of that night. Some people are not on Facebook or listen to the news; there could be someone out there with information and don't know it.'

'When is this going to happen?'

'Today Sir, we are going to concentrate on the streets your wife took on the night she disappeared.'

'Will you call me if you get anything?'

'You will be the first to hear. Speak soon, bye.'

Tom was just about to dial another number

when his phone rang, it was Sam.

'Tom could you possibly spare a few minutes to come and see me please, it's about the business.'

'Can't you handle it, I don't have any knowledge of your or Anna's job, I mean I know what you do, but I couldn't do it'

'Tom I can't do all this work on my own, I can't replace Anna I know that. I want to keep this business going for when she gets back so I will need to get someone in to help me. I just wanted to run it by you first.'

'Sam, you do whatever you need to do, I have total faith in whatever decision you make.'

'That means a lot to me. I won't let you or Anna down; phone me if you get any news.'

'I will do, bye for now.'

'Bye.'

Tom phoned George to tell him what the police were doing next, there was no answer. Both Ruby and George walked in the front door seconds later.

'Didn't answer the phone because we were here,' George told Tom.

'Yes I can see that now.'

Tom informed them of what the police were doing next over breakfast and coffee, not that there was much to tell them.

Sergeant Rooney was at his desk, PC Nicole McMillan and PC Graham McCartney from

Goldfield Police Station were with him.

'Thanks for coming out here Graham, I appreciate it,' Rooney said.

'Just following orders Sir, I believe Inspector Halliday requested me because I know the family a little.'

'Well we three are going door to door today; we will do a street at a time on the route Anna took the night she disappeared, I have a photo here for each of us. If anyone can give us any information we will count that as a bonus. It was late and dark, the weather was miserable so many folk would have stayed indoors. She must be somewhere, someone knows something. She didn't vanish into thin air.'

'What's the next step if we come up empty today?' PC McMillan asked.

'I don't know yet, we will need to take this one step at a time for now. Right let's go.'

It was four o'clock in the afternoon before Anna left the shed to find Frank. She found him where he always was.

'How did you get on this morning?' she asked.

'Richard's wife Eloise gave the letter I brought from my mum's back to the post woman today, so when she put it back in Mum's I took it back to my brother's. Richard got more mail; Eloise got it put straight in her hand so I never had a chance there. How is Jasmine?'

'She is much the same today as she was yesterday; although she has not been sick today, which to me looks like a good sign.'
'I hope she feels better soon.'
'Yes me too, it's bad enough seeing her chained up in that prison, to be ill on top of it is too much to bear.'
'I take it you are going to see Billy tonight then?'
'I sure am, tonight and every other night, I need to get tougher with him, I do feel bad, but I need to put Billy's welfare out of my mind and just think about how it will all help The Innocent.'
'Do you want to come in and watch some TV?'
'I shouldn't really.'
'Oh come on Anna there is nothing you can do until tonight.'
After a bit of coaxing from Frank Anna gave in and took a much needed break from the drudgery of the shed. She stayed there for a couple of hours before the guilt took over again and she returned to Jasmine's side.
Jasmine's toilet bucket was changed, the sheets hadn't. The remnants of her dinner lay on a plate on the floor at the side of the bed. Jasmine had the name tag out, moving it around in her hand every way possible for a while then put it back in its hiding place.
'Need to keep that safe baby,' Jasmine said.

I will speak to her later when she can maybe hear

me, I think she needs to hear that I am still here and fighting her corner, it's all I can do to give her some hope.

Anna waited by the girl's side for some time before going to see Billy. It was only 9.20 pm when she got there, Billy was already snoring away.

'Anna Anderson.'

Billy moaned and groaned in his sleep.

'Good, you can hear me. I need you to save The Innocent Billy; I need you to keep watch on the garden out your back. Jasmine Brown is in that shed and she is pregnant with an Innocent. You need to save them; you need to do all in your power. You need to uncover what your neighbours are doing in that shed. They are evil people I bet you know them, you probably speak to them. It's the Sutherlands Billy.'

Billy writhed about for a moment then settled back down.

'DO YOU HEAR ME BILLY,' Anna shouted in frustration.

Billy shot up into a sitting position with a shriek.

'See you tomorrow Billy.'

27
Saturday 23rd November

The ground was white with frost; the first flickers of snow were starting to fall. The last week or so had been milder and wet, although the wind still felt bitter, winter was definitely on its way. There had been a few frosty mornings at the beginning of the month, a couple last month and even one or two at the end of September. Now the change was noticeable. The snow would come and go now until February or March. Rooney hated the winter, the cold, dark mornings didn't agree with him at all. He sat in the kitchen of his modest one bedroom flat sipping hot coffee and eating toast. The house he shared with his wife was now occupied by her and her new boyfriend; she bought him out of his share. He didn't want the house; he wanted a fresh, new start after the divorce. Somewhere that didn't remind him of his wife, he soon came to realise that memories follow you anywhere you are or go.

His kitchen was not a bad size and was bright and cheery, with red and yellow walls. All the appliances were white, as was the floor. He kept it clean and tidy as he did with the rest of the flat. Here is where he spent most of his weekend mornings when he wasn't needed at work. He would sit at the white table with the morning paper and not move until he had read it from front to back and completed the crossword. He shoved the paper away and lifted the phone from the table he had a call to make.

'Hello Mr Ross.'

'Hello sergeant, any news?'

'The door to door threw no further light on the situation I'm afraid. An old lady said she thought she saw Anna walking by her house on the night in question however, she can't be sure, says her eyesight is not that great.'

'So where do we go from here? What's the next step?

'We will be discussing this case at our meeting on Monday to see if there are any other avenues we can try. In the meantime we can only hope that some of the media coverage turns up something.'

'Thank you sergeant I know you are doing all you can. Call me if you hear anything at all.'

'I will. Bye'

As soon as the call ended Tom told his in-laws the latest. They had been there since 8 am, it was now 9.30. Ruby had insisted that she come over and do some housework for Tom, she wanted to keep busy and George had something he wanted to say.

'Are you going back to work on Monday Tom?'

'I have to phone Paul tomorrow, but yes I was thinking about going back.'

'That's what I thought. We will take Rex on Sunday and keep him with us until Friday, he still needs looked after.'

'I don't want to lose him, you have a point. I get him for the weekend though right.'

'Yes of course.'

'How will Fluff deal with him being there so much, will that be a problem?'

'We know there is no love lost there, she will need to get used to it.'

'Thank you George, I'm glad someone is thinking about things like this, I feel as if I can't get my mind around anything at the moment.'

Ruby had been in the kitchen and now rolled into the living room with the vacuum.

'Right you two go into the kitchen for a while let me see to this place.'

The two men did what they were told and went into the kitchen with Rex at their heels.

Anna knew that Candice was feeling better because she was in the shed with Jasmine's breakfast. It was full English with toast on the side and a flask of tea.

Maybe she has a conscious after all. That's more like it, a decent hot breakfast. It's the least she could do.

'Got a big day today Jasmine, we are going to give your little palace a good clean.'

'Little palace are you having a laugh?'

No there is no conscious there, I was wrong.

'Now now, watch your tone young lady, you know we can do this the easy way or the hard way,' Candice warned her.

Jasmine said nothing; she started on her breakfast instead.

'I take it you are feeling better today as well?' Candice asked and again Jasmine said nothing.

'I will be back in half an hour, give you time to get that breakfast down you,' Candice said and left.

True to her word Candice was back in half an hour with Jack in tow. Jack had a basin of hot water; Candice had clean clothes, shampoo, conditioner and a couple of towels.

'That hair is getting a treat today, I will help you wash it first, and then you will get more water to clean your body.'

'Why wash my hair now?' Jasmine asked.

'It stinks in here, we will be cleaning everything.'

Jack left and came back with more hot water; he left again and came back with clean bed covers and an extra fleece blanket. After her hair had been washed it was a bit of a chore to brush it, it was knotted and tangled, with a lot of effort Jasmine got it feeling good again. They left her to clean her body in private, but they had to be there when they unchained her to change her clothes. Jack turned his back and stood by the door as Candice unchained her and helped her to change then chained her back up by the wrist. There was no point in Jasmine trying to struggle, there was nowhere for her to go with Jack on guard. Once that chore was finished Jack left and came back with a hair dryer. He unplugged the halogen heater and used a small extension cable for the hair dryer to reach Jasmine. Both of them stood waiting in the shed until Jasmine had finished drying her hair then told her to stand as near to the top of the bed as possible. They changed the bed covers swiftly and efficiently. Jack lifted her toilet bucket and left, Candice gathered all the dirty laundry and gave them to Jack when he came back with a brush and dustpan. Jack left again while Candice swept up, after she had finished she left with the brush and dustpan then came back with a mop five minutes later. No bucket of water just a wet mop, Jasmine could smell the disinfectant from it as soon as Candice brought it in. Candice went from side to side along the small floor, finishing at the door and left. Jack came back ten minutes later with an empty toilet bucket.

'There. Nice and clean, you must feel better now you have had a good clean.'

'Sure, a good clean, the only thing I ever

wanted,' Jasmine said sarcastically.

Jack never said another word; he could not chastise her for being cheeky after everything they had done to her. It would be too cheeky of him.

Anna had been the shed the whole time the cleaning was going on, dodging them when they were doing their chores. She did not know if it smelled cleaner, both the shed and Jasmine herself looked a lot better. Jasmine settled down under the duvet and her new fleece blanket then went to sleep.

That big breakfast and feeling clean must be a change for her. The poor soul is worn out.

Anna went home to see how her loved ones were doing. Tom and her parents were in the living room, Ruby was on the phone to Clara, filling her in on the latest news. Tom and George were listening to Ruby's conversation, butting in when they thought Ruby was missing something out. Anna noticed that the house work had been done and knew that her mother was responsible for it. After looking for Rex she found him in the back garden, sniffing about. The back door was closed, probably done so on its own accord with a little help from the wind. They usually always kept the back door open when Rex was out, they had heard about many peoples' dogs being stolen from their gardens and they didn't want to take the risk with Rex. Not that he was a pedigree or worth the money that some dogs are worth, it's just because they loved him and couldn't bear if some nasty person took him. It wasn't long before Tom came into the kitchen, opened the door and shouted him in.

'It's cold out there today boy, you can't be out there too long, you are still recovering. I will take you a walk later.'

Once Anna was satisfied all was in order in her house she went to Billy. He was on a break, sitting in his bus eating a sandwich and drinking coffee from a thermos. He looked tired, that was of no surprise to Anna. She knew that she was the reason that he was tired however, she couldn't let up on talking to him at night, the sooner he found out what exactly was happening the sooner The Innocent would be saved and the sooner Anna could go to The Realm. It was on her mind a lot, getting into The Realm, being at peace with nothing to worry about. She wondered a lot of what the place will be like; she had so many questions unanswered in her head on the topic. She knew it was a waiting game until all the mysteries of it would be solved. She left Billy and went seeking Frank, she could not find him.

He must be out chasing that postwoman, I will

catch up with him later.

Anna went back to be with Jasmine, she was still sleeping so Anna lay down and went for a nap herself. She was woken up by Jack bringing in Jasmine's lunch; Anna left her to it and went home. It was 1.45 pm when she checked the time. No one was at her house, even Rex was not there, so she went to find Frank again. He was standing outside his mother's house when she walked around.

'Hello there,' Anna greeted him.

'Hello there yourself Anna, how are things with you today?'

'The shed was given a clean, fresh bed covers and an extra fleece blanket, clean clothes for Jasmine, they even washed her hair.'

'Wow it's a good day for her then.'

'It's never a good day for her in her position.'

'I'm sorry I didn't mean it like that, I just mean it's a better day for her today than yesterday.'

'It's ok Frank I know what you mean. How did you get on this morning then?'

'Great, two letters moved from Richard's to my mum's and one from my mum's to Richards.'

'That was quite productive.'

'I need one of them to go to the other's door. I know that it might take a while, it will happen sooner or later.'

'Yes it will, no one said any of this was going to

be easy.'

'Want to come in, see what my mum is watching, kill some time.'

'I was told to acknowledge other souls; we are spending a lot of time together. Do you think we will get in trouble for it when we eventually reach The Before?'

'Maybe, they already told us the consequences for it, I think it is worth it.'

'Ok, let's go see what is on the TV today.'

May Simpson was watching a DVD, an old movie called Seven Brides for Seven Brothers. Anna and Frank had missed the start, but got the gist of what was going on fast enough. Anna loved the movie and when it finished she was hoping that May would put on another, she didn't. She put the DVD back in its case, made a cup of tea and settled down with a Sudoku book.

'Has she got more movies like that?' Anna asked Frank.

'Yes she has loads, all musicals.'

'Well the next time she plays one come find me.'

'I will, I promise.'

Anna went back to the makeshift prison. She wished she could spend all her time with Frank doing fun things. She knew by doing that she was drifting away from her mission and that just could not happen.

What do I say to Billy tonight? Do I keep repeating myself? Maybe I will shout at him again tonight that seemed to do the trick last night. It's still early, what am I to do now? I know what I am doing is important, it is so tedious. Frank seems to be enjoying this more than me, although he's not the one who has to watch Jasmine in her misery. He gets to spend time with his biological mother, find out all about her and her life, not that she has had a great life. I suppose that is why Frank is here, to try and improve it. I wish I could think of something I could do to help him, maybe I could plant the seed with Billy. No I don't think I can. Ravi told me to mention the Innocent to get Billy to take heed, I don't think it would work to mention Frank's mother, in fact I'm sure of it and I don't think Ravi would be too chuffed with me if I tried. I Know Ravi is watching, he said as much when I spoke with him, he knew the progress I had made, he knows everything. I hope that he is not disappointed in me for spending time with Frank.

Jasmine took Rex's name tag out and was playing about with it in her hands as many different ways she could think of. Rolling it between her fingers, tossing it from one hand to the other, then trying to keep it balanced on its edge on the palm of her hand.

She is more bored than me; at least I can leave this

pit whenever I want. She is literally stuck here day in, day out with only her unborn baby for company. Life sucks for her.

Anna watched her play with the disc, Jasmine started to flip it.
'Telephone number for heads and Rex for tails, eh baby,' Jasmine said to her bump with the nasal sound of the cold in her voice.
She flipped the disc, 'Heads,' again 'Heads,' again, 'Tails.'
She done this for about ten flips not doing it very high, then she started to get cocky and started to do it higher and higher.
'Heads, tails, tails, heads.'
Anna watched with anxiety as she flipped the coin.
'Stop it, what if you don't catch it, stop it, you are going to drop it' Anna said to her unheard.
No sooner than Anna had said the words, the disc came down Jasmine fumbled to catch it, it hit off the metal frame on the top of the bed then hit the floor and rolled over and stopped when it hit the halogen heater.
Jasmine was frantic, she stood up and stretched as far as her chain would allow her, it was no good and she knew it. She had tried to reach Anna when she lay dead on the floor, it hadn't worked then, it wasn't going to work now.
'Stupid, stupid, stupid,' Jasmine said over and

over hitting the palm off her hand against her forehead. 'How could I be so stupid?'

Anna went over to the disc and bent down. 'I told you, not that you could hear me, but I told you,' Anna said.

Jasmine was crying loudly as if she had just heard some devastating news.

I knew it meant a lot to her, I just didn't know how much. The problem is what if one of the monsters find it? Will they think it has been there on the floor since the night they killed me? I don't think so they cleaned up pretty well then and then they cleaned today. If they think Jasmine has had it then will they punish her? What to do.

Jasmine was sobbing uncontrollably.

'Please stop, we will fix this I don't know how yet, let me think,' Anna pleaded.

Anna sat on the end of the bed with her head in her hands trying hard to figure out what to do, Jasmine's crying was making it so much of a chore. Anna thought herself outside the shed to get a bit of quiet to think. She stood there in the gloom of the monsters' back garden, pacing up and down on the grass, well just above the grass. It wasn't raining tonight; she knew it was cold even though she could not feel it. She paced there for while before it came to her, and wondered why it didn't come to her straight away.

Frank. Frank could lift the disc. I need to get him right away.

Anna thought herself straight into May's house and found Frank there sitting on the couch. May was on one of the chairs; both of them were watching TV.

'Anna what's up?' Frank asked when he saw her.

'You need to come with me right away.'

'Where are we going?'

'The shed.'

'Why, I hate that place.'

'Jasmine has dropped Rex's name tag, trying to be smart playing heads or tails, anyway that doesn't matter I need you to pick it up, it is out of her reach.'

'Ok let's go.'

They were in the shed in seconds, Anna showed Frank where the name tag was.

'Where am I putting it?' Frank asked.

'I don't know I hadn't thought of that.'

'What will Jasmine do when she notices it's missing?'

'Again, I don't know?'

Jasmine was staring at the disc; the crying had subsided a little.

'We can't move it with her watching it that was one of the things Fenza told me. It would appear to someone that something has just disappeared in front of their eyes so my power will not work if that is the case,' Frank told Anna.

'That makes sense. We will need to wait until she is sleeping and do it then.'

'Again, where am I going to put it? Are we going to give her it back?'

'I don't know I will need to ponder that one. In the meantime pray that one of the monsters don't find it when they come in. That's the last thing I need or should I say what Jasmine needs.'

'What a conundrum we have here,' Frank commented.

'Do you think we should give her it back?' Anna asked.

'I don't know, what else can we do with it?'

'It is evidence in a way, it being here proves to me anyway that Rex was here. I don't know if the police would share my opinion.'

'What if we give her it back, she would not know how it got back to her and she knows that the people who snatched her would not give it to her.'

'Maybe she will think it was me, it might give her more hope. I know if she got it back then she won't be flipping it in the air again,' Anna said.

'Anna what if we gave it to Billy?'

'That is a great idea or is it? If he found it would he take it to the police? Would they then suspect him?'

'What if I sat it on his bedside table?'

'Then he will think he is going out of his mind

and he certainly wouldn't take it to the police in that case.' Anna said frustrated.

Anna and Frank stood there in silence, both of them trying to think it through.

'What if we got it to the police ourselves, it has Jasmine's finger prints on it,' Frank suggested.

'Well that would prove a connection between Jasmine and me maybe, but they still would not be able to find out what happened to either one of us from that. Oh Frank I don't know what to do. Why don't we move it to a safe place until we decide what to do for the best?'

'Ok, we will take it to my mum's.'

'Lift it as soon as Jasmine takes her eyes of it,' Anna said.

Jasmine was still looking at it ten minutes later; Frank was starting to lose patience.

'Why won't she stop staring at it?'

'Frank it is all she had as a link to a world outside away from this hell hole.'

'I know, I'm sorry, poor girl.'

Jasmine screamed in frustration then pulled the duvet over her head. Before Anna knew what was going on Frank had scooped the name tag under his make and vanished. Anna went straight after him to his mother's house.

'That was fast, I didn't even know what had gone on until you were gone,' Anna said a little amazed at his quick thinking.

'Where shall we put it then?' Frank asked, he

was more just thinking out loud.

'You know May better than me.'

Frank sat the name tag on the carpet just at the side of the couch.

'It will be fine there for a while my mum only vacuums once a week on a Wednesday,' Frank informed Anna.

'I will need to think about what to do for the best. Will you move it for me later when I have given this some more thought?'

'Of course Anna anytime, you know where to find me.'

'Thank you for everything; I will be back as soon as I know what to do with it.'

After a long time of considering what to do and visualizing every outcome of where to put the name tag Anna decided she would get Frank to drop it in Billy's jacket pocket. She had a plan. She would tell Billy it is there or try anyway. She thought maybe if he saw it then it would trigger something in him to realise that she needed help, that an Innocent needed help. Ravi told her she was making great progress; she wanted this done and fast. She wanted to go home to The Realm more than anything now; she wanted well away from the trials and tribulations of being on Earth. The pressure of helping The Innocent was getting to her; the decision she just had to make was tough for her. She thought that she was doing the right thing; she hoped she was doing the right thing.

Anna had been sitting on the bed in her spare room for how long she did not know. She needed to get away from everything and everyone to find the resolution of where to put the name tag without any outside influence. If she had went to the shed then maybe she would have given the name tag back to Jasmine because Jasmine would still be upset about losing it in the first place.

Anna went to the kitchen it was 8.10 pm. Tom was in the living room with Rex. Rex was up on the couch lying on his back next to Tom who was rubbing his belly absentmindedly while watching TV.

All is well here; my two boys seem contented sitting there. I will go see my parents then I will get Frank.

Anna went to her parents' house; it was a twenty minute walk or a five minute drive from her house. A three bedroom semi-detached in a street where nothing ever happened, this is where she grew up and was very happy here. Her parents were sitting at the dining table in kitchen; Ruby had a glass of wine in front of her barely touched, the rest of the bottle sat next to the glass. George was drinking beer out of a pint glass with his name on it; Anna had bought the glass for him a few years back. The kitchen was barely large enough for the table, Ruby had insisted on it when they first moved into the house, the table they sat at just now was only a couple of years old, a square pine table with four faux leather, brown chairs. The kitchen itself was dated; the cupboard doors were also pine and had been there since Anna could remember. The walls had been painted a few times over the years. The tiles around the top of the worktops had been changed less frequent, and both tiles and paint were a dark yellow at the moment.

'Are you not drinking that wine Ruby?' George asked.

'I thought I wanted it or needed it, turns out I'm not in the mood.'

'You know she will turn up one way or another, sooner or later.'

'I know, it is the not knowing that is killing me. It makes me appreciate Clara more now. I wish she lived closer to us. I am going to suggest that she move back to Hallington or somewhere close, see what she says. I miss Anna so much; from going to seeing her every couple of days to not seeing her at all is too hard.'

'I feel the exact same way honey.'

'What can we do now to find her George?'

'We will need to wait to see what comes out of this meeting with the police that Tom told us about.'

'I suppose. I'm going around to see if any of the posters need replaced, the weather had been wet some of them will be ruined.'

'We will do it together.'

Anna wanted to pull out a chair, sit down beside them and insist that she share her mother's wine. That was not to be so she left them and went to get Frank and the name tag.

Frank was sitting on the couch in his mother's living room. Anna had stopped standing outside shouting on Frank, she felt more comfortable just going in now that she had done it a couple of times.

'I knew I would find you here,' Anna said.

'Where else would I be? Have you made a decision about the name tag then?'

'Yes, I am or should I say you are going to put it in Billy's Jacket pocket, it's the best way I can think of to help The Innocent. If we gave it back to Jasmine then that wouldn't help, maybe if Billy finds it, it might help him to realise that something weird is going on.'

Frank went over and picked up the name tag from where they had left it earlier. 'Ok let's go do this.'

They both left there and appeared in Billy's living room at the same time. Kate was sitting playing some game on her tablet; Billy was nowhere to be seen.

'Where is his jacket?' Frank queried.

'I don't know. We will have to find it, if it's anything like my house all the jackets will all be hanging up together somewhere.'

It didn't take long for them to find them; there was a coat stand at the top of the stair.

'I can't see the jacket he was wearing the night I was killed.'

'Does it need to be that one?'

'Well at least I know he wears that one.'

'By the way where is Billy?'

'He must be out with Buster, either that he is in bed, it seems a little early for that.'

Within seconds of her uttering the words they heard the door open. They looked down the stairs to see Buster first then Billy come in and close the door. He was wearing the jacket that Anna was looking for.

'That's the jacket.'

They stood aside until Billy had climbed the stairs and took off the jacket and hung it up. Frank then dropped the name tag into the pocket.

'No turning back now,' Frank said.

Thank you, what would I do without you?'

'How long do you think it will take him to find it?'

'He loves that dog. He is out in all weather walking him so hopefully not long at all.'

'I never had a dog, but I can see the appeal. Richard is allergic so we never got one when I was a child, although we did have a few goldfish from time to time.'

'Yes, you told me you loved dogs when I introduced you to Rex. Tell me about your family Frank. How did you die? I can't believe I have never asked you?'

'Heart Attack Anna, the worst thing was I was at work when it happened.'

'Where did you work?'

'I was a fork truck driver in a warehouse over in Greenside Industrial Estate at the other end of town.'

'Were you scared?'

'Yes I was. I never got a chance to say goodbye to my wife Gina or my daughter Sarah.'

'Do you go and see them?'

'Yes every day.'

'Why did you not mention it to me?'

'You have enough on your plate, anyway my wife and I were split up, there was not much love left in the marriage. Sarah is fifteen now, not a kid anymore, they are doing just fine without me.'

'I am sure they miss you Frank.'

'I think my wife was seeing someone else before I died.'

'I am sorry you died so young, you are here with me and for that I am grateful.'

'You died younger than me, a lot younger.'

'Yes, but I was murdered, took before my time.'

'Did you want kids Anna?'

'Yes, we were trying, it wasn't to be.'

'What are your plans for the rest of the evening?'

'I need to stay here until Billy goes to sleep. See if I can get through to him, that's all I will be doing every night for the foreseeable future.'

'There is no post tomorrow, so if you would like to hang out that would be great. I could show you my daughter and maybe watch a movie with my mum if she puts one on.'

'That sounds good Frank, I will come look for you.'

'See you then,' Frank said before vanishing.

Billy went into the living room, said hello to Kate then went to the spare room. He did not know why, he just went there and went straight to the window. He did not switch any light on as he wanted to see into the garden at the back of his. The light was not great. The only illumination was coming from the lights on the edge of the green. He could make out the layout of the garden in the gloom, he could see where the buildings were, where the grass and bushes were.

'What is over there? Why do I need to know? I'm going off my head, I must be.' 'The last of my days on at work tomorrow so maybe I can get a better nosey about in the daylight on Monday, that's the problem with starting work when it's dark and finishing when it's dark, no daylight hours at home.'

Billy did not realise he was talking to himself until Kate asked him.

'Are you talking to yourself? It can't be Buster he is in the kitchen getting a drink.'

'Yes I suppose I was. Hey do you know where the binoculars are? The ones Aaron used to use?'

'Why, what do you want them for? And why are you looking out that window again? Is there something going on that I need to know about?'

'No, yes, no I mean I don't know. I think I am going off my head. I don't know why I want to look out there, I feel drawn to it. Don't ask me why, I don't know, just humour me, where are the binoculars?'

'Ok they are in the loft. You are acting strange, but yes I will humour you, if you find something out there let me know.'

Billy went into the hall and used the pole to pull down the ladders to get into the loft. The loft had laminate flooring down and a light fitted. It was used for storage and was handy as there was not much cupboard space in their flat. He found what he was looking for after a ten minute search. He came back down, replaced the ladder and the pole then returned to the spare room where he proceeded to take the binoculars out of their case. He fixed the focus on them then took a peek at the garden in question. He still had the same view just a little closer so he went into the kitchen stepped over Buster and took a look out of that window. He could only see the back door of the house over the garage roof.

'It needs to be the spare room window Buster,' He said to his dog. 'Not much of a view of that garden in here.'

Anna had witnessed all that Billy had said and done since Frank went to his mother's and she loved it. She finally knew that Billy was starting to listen to her, that he was finally taking some action to help. Feeling happy Anna went back to the shed to check up on Jasmine. The joy she felt moments before drained out of her as she witnessed the misery Jasmine was in. Jasmine was sobbing her heart out. Anna guessed it was because she had lost the name tag, although her whole current situation was enough to make even the hardest hearted person cry. Anna sat with Jasmine until she fell asleep.

'Anna Anderson,' Anna got nothing.

'Anna Anderson,' Jasmine started moaning and weeping in her sleep.

'I'm still here. Don't worry about losing the name tag too much, I have it. Well I don't have it now. I will try to get it back to you once it has served its purpose. I took it to try to help you and your baby out of this terrible dilemma you are in. Please be aware that you are not on your own, I am here,' Anna told the distraught girl.

I hope that gives her some comfort. It's all I can say to her just now. I know it hurt her to lose the disc, if it moves Billy into action the way I think it will then it will be worth it even though Jasmine might not feel that way, time to go see Billy again.

When Anna turned up at Billy's bedside after sitting with Jasmine for a while both Kate and him were in bed and out for the count.
'Anna Anderson,' Anna said, it stirred Billy immediately.
'I know that you can hear me Billy, The Innocent is waiting for you to help. You now know there is something going on in that garden I saw you with the binoculars, I saw you at the back window, you need to keep at it Billy, you need to be alert and observant, most of all please be careful. These people are dangerous, you may speak to them I don't know, believe me they are capable of anything. The last thing I want is for them to hurt you. They are evil monsters Billy. Please take care.'
Billy was moving about so much it woke Kate then she woke Billy.
'What the hell is going on Billy, were you having another bad dream?' Kate asked when she shook him awake.
'No I don't think so, I can't remember.'

'Well you have been sleeping mighty restless of late, I'm a bit worried. Maybe you should get an appointment on with the doctor, get checked over.'

'I'm fine; I would still be sleeping if it wasn't for you waking me.'

'Well sorry for being worried. Next time I will go sleep in the spare room,' Kate said angrily.

'No I'm sorry, I'm just a bit cranky, go back to sleep honey.'

They both turned to face away from each other and went back to sleep.

Going back to the shed was the last thing Anna wanted to do so she went for a walk, a very long walk, she walked all night and only went back to the shed when the day was starting to break.

28
Sunday 24th November

The weather was pretty miserable; there was no frost or rain this morning. A thick fog hung over the town like a cloaked evil ready to pounce with an unexpected doom. Frank walked through it. He thought if anyone could see him he would look like a very shady character indeed what with his make and all. Frank was on his way to see Anna; he wanted to walk, to get his idea straight in his head before he shared it with his spirit buddy. If his plan succeeded then he would be back in The Before in no time. He reached the shed, he didn't want to go in, knew Anna could not hear him from within what with the sound proofing so he had no choice. He went in and told Anna he would meet her outside.

'Hey how are you doing,' Anna said to him a few seconds later.

'I have been out walking all night staging an idea in my head; I need to run it by you. I think this is what will blow my mission wide open.'

'I have been out walking all night also running things through my head; the main reason behind it was I didn't want to come back here. Here I am rattling on when you have got a breakthrough, I'm sorry what is it?' Anna said when she knew Frank was getting annoyed.

'Don't be sorry, I'm just impatient because I need to share this. My mum has a silver heart shaped locket that has a baby picture of my twin and me in it, it's not on a chain, she keeps it in the top drawer of a chest she has in her bedroom. She took it out last night, left it open on the bed while she went to the toilet and that's when I saw it.'

'Is this the first you have seen it?'

'Yes.'

'What is your idea with it?'

'I could take it to Richard.'

'I don't think that is a great idea Frank.'

'What makes you think that?'

'She will be gutted once she spots that she has lost it.'

'Oh I never thought of that, you are right, you have just seen how upset Jasmine was after losing the name tag.'

'The outcome might be worth it though. Will Richard know that it is the two of you?'

'That's the only problem I could foresee. If he doesn't notice that it is us then I would be upsetting Mum for nothing. Maybe that was not the best idea I could have come up with.'

'Well if you decide to do it I support you,' Anna told him.

'Are we still going to hang out today? Is there anything in particular you would like to do?'

'There is nothing I can do until tonight, so why

don't we try walking through a wall today?'

'I know I said I would; now I'm not so sure. We got warned it would drain us.'

'I will do it, you can watch and then if you want to try then I will watch you.'

'Ok Anna, where do you want to do it?'

'Anywhere, how about your mum's house, if that's ok with you?'

'Sure, I will race you,' Frank said before disappearing.

Anna was seconds behind him; they were in May's living room.

'Pick a wall.'

'Right, what is behind this wall,' Anna said pointing to a free piece of wall space.

'That's her bedroom.'

'Yes, but is there any furniture at the other end, don't want to make it too difficult for myself.'

Frank walked into the bedroom and came back.

'Nothing that side, you have a metre free that side.'

'Do you think I should go at it with speed or put a hand through and go slow?'

'Go slow Anna, better than rushing in.'

Anna stepped up to the wall feeling nervous and a little daring. She put her right hand fingers to the wall; they started to melt into it and then stopped. She pushed her hand in further with some force; very slowly the wall took her hand then started on her wrist. She could feel no sensation of touching anything; it was as if there was nothing there, the wall seemed to hold her. She pushed harder; the wall took her wrist then started on her forearm.

'Go into the other room and see if you can see my hand at the other side,' Anna asked Frank.

He went and came back, 'I can see the tips of your fingers and they look like they are part of the wall, like a statue or something. They look like plaster.'

Anna shoved harder, it didn't seem like she was moving through the wall any further. After ten minutes of trying she was up to the elbow in wall.

'Do you want to stop?' Frank asked. 'How do you feel?'

'I'm not stopping, I feel ok.'

She put her right foot to the wall and put pressure on it leaning into the wall, driving herself through. Frank was standing there mesmerized; he could not believe the sight in front of him.

'I am going to have to try that. What are you going to do when it comes to putting your head through? Are you going to keep your eyes open?'

'I don't know yet, I will be doing it soon, I will need to make up my mind shortly.'

Another fifteen minutes had past. Anna had her arm all the way through up to her neck and her leg up to her thigh.

'I'm going to close my eyes and maybe open them halfway.'

'Anna, be careful please.'

'I will, what's the worst that can happen; we weren't warned not to do it, just that it would take a while and drain us.'

'Do you feel drained?'

'Tired, not drained, not yet anyway.'

She closed her eyes and started to force her head through. Frank's eyes grew wide as her face melted into the wall, he went into the bedroom for a peek then he came back through and watched as Anna's full face was eaten up by the wall. She opened her eyes when she knew they would be in the wall, she saw nothing but darkness so she closed them again. Another fifteen minutes elapsed before Anna opened her eyes and her head was on the other side of the wall. She glanced down to see half her body in the bedroom and could hardly believe the spectacle before her. Frank was back in the bedroom waiting for her to finish her challenge.

'Frank what the...this is the most bazaar thing I have ever seen.'

'Yes I know it's strange, you need to start pulling now.'

'Well I hope it is easier than pushing, I'm feeling very tired now Frank, it's as if the wall is sucking all the energy out of me.'

'Well you can't stop now.'

She strained to yank and tug herself through the rest of the wall. Her left hand and left foot were the only body parts left to come out. She gave it all the energy she had left for one final heave and came out of the wall with that much momentum she went right through Frank who was standing at her side then fell on the floor exhausted.

'You went right through me then, I didn't feel a thing.'

'Sorry, I felt nothing either,' Anna said sleepily. 'I need to rest.'

Anna shuffled herself over to the bottom of the bed out of the way in case May came through and fell asleep.

'Anna, Anna,' Anna could faintly hear Frank's voice as if it were echoing around in a small tunnel.

'Anna, Anna,' She could hear his voice getting clearer and louder.

'Anna, wake up,' Frank was saying with concern. That's when Anna finally fully awoke and realised that Frank was worried.

'What's wrong?'

'I thought I was never going to wake you. You have been sleeping for eleven hours nearly.'

'What, that can't be Ravi told me I would need three hours.'

'We were also told that dragging ourselves through a wall would exhaust us, exhaust you it did. I was starting to panic.'

'I'm not doing that again that's for sure, I advise you don't try it.'

'Not a chance after that.'

'What time is it?'

'10.15 pm.'

'The best of it is, I still feel tired. I need to go check on Jasmine then go visit Billy.'

'Well after you do that, get some more sleep, I will see you tomorrow.'

'Ok Dad, 'Anna said with a laugh and vanished.

Jasmine was awake when Anna got back to the shed. Anna could hardly believe what she was seeing. Jasmine was sitting against the wall with the duvet pulled up doing a word search.

The monsters have given her a pencil; I can hardly take it in. Why wait all this time to give her a pencil and a word search book. Maybe she had one before I got here for all I know. I'm glad she has something to keep her mind active; it can only be good for her, poor girl.

Once she was satisfied that Jasmine was as ok as she could be under the circumstances Anna went to Billy. Both Billy and Katie were in their living room. Buster was in the hall all sprawled out across the floor. Anna settled on a chair in the living room with Billy and Kate; she was planning on staying here until they retired for the night. There was no TV on; they were sitting talking about Billy's work.

'So were you out doing the Sunday Service run or were you on maintenance today?' Kate asked Billy.

'I was on maintenance. I would much rather be out doing the driving, but I have to take my turn I suppose, it is only once a month. It used to be worse when we had to manually check the tyre pressure, now with the power of technology that is a thing of the past. We have sensors now that alert us to any inconsistencies.'

'Too much information darling, I'm interested in your work, just not that interested.'

'Ok I will shut up.'

'I see you have moved one of the dining chairs to the window in the spare room.'

Billy had been waiting for Kate to mention this to him and was all ready for it with an answer that he thought might pacify her.

'I am taking up bird watching. Harry at work is getting me into it, he is in a club, he gave me a book with the different kinds in and I've got a notebook to write down all the ones I see.'

'Is it not better in the summer or spring for that sort of thing?'

'Yes, by the time spring comes around I will be off the starters block.'

'You are turning into an old man,' Kate informed him.

Billy has this all planned out. He is taking me seriously. I don't think I will annoy him tonight; I will see him tomorrow, he wouldn't be up this late if he had work in the morning. Maybe he will spot something in the daylight.

29
Monday 25th November

The meeting was held at Goldfield Police Station in Edinburgh at 9.30 am. In attendance were Sergeant Rooney, PC McMillan who Rooney insisted be there, Sergeant Jackson Gardiner, Chief Inspector Laura Aird and Detective Inspector Norman Mathieson. They were in a small conference room on the first floor. It was a comfortable room with a large table with black faux leather chairs, tea and coffee supplies were on the table along with mugs and an assortment of biscuits. The walls were painted light grey and dark grey. Grey, hard wearing carpet covered the floor. Files sat in front of each of them with all the details they needed for their meeting. They were at the meeting for several reasons, one being the disappearance of two young women, Jasmine Brown and Anna Ross. They got all the rest of their business out the way then started to discuss the two vanished women.

'Right, I have read everything up to date on these two cases; I must say I was expecting more progress. Why have the two of them not been seen?' Chief Inspector Aird asked the room.

Chief Inspector Aird was a no nonsense kind of woman. She always got straight to the point and expected others to do the same with her. At fifty-two she had not lost her looks or her figure, she was five-foot-six with dark brown hair with warm caramel highlights. Her eyes were large and brown; she had a beauty spot just above her top lip and her makeup always looked as if a professional had applied it each morning.

'Well the easy answer is I don't know. We have done all we can with social media, the husband of Anna Ross did a TV interview which was aired on the local news. Her family have also put posters up all around the town and as I believe they are continuing to do so. We have done a door to door with a photo of her. We searched the home she shares with her husband and the park that she frequents with her dog,' Rooney replied.

'Can we rule out the husband for sure?' Aird asked.

'Yes.'

'Jasmine Brown has been missing for a while now with no trail left behind her. Could there be a connection?' Aird continued with her questions for Rooney.

'There was no connection that we could find.'

'Does anyone else have any ideas on where to go next with this?'

The room was quiet for a few minutes before Detective Inspector Mathieson spoke. 'I have read the notes for the cases. On the one hand you could think they are connected if there is some lunatic out there hurting young women and if that is the case then I don't think he will stop at two. On the other hand Anna Ross could have been hit by a car and been killed. The killer could have took her body with him or her, I read here that her dog was injured, but made it back home, if say for instance that Anna was attacked, the dog could have been trying to protect her and been injured by the attacker. Jasmine Brown is a total mystery if these two cases are not connected. I think the best way forward from here is to go back to the door to door with photos of both women. Post on social media again, keep it at the fore front of the public's minds; we don't even know for sure that a crime has been committed.'

Mathieson was an exceptional officer with a string of arrests under his belt. Although he was fifty-four his age had never slowed him down. He was at the gym three times a week to keep in shape; he had a full head of black hair with only slight signs of greying. His face was handsome with dark brown eyes housed by attractive brown framed glasses and dark skin. One could be mistaken in thinking he was ten years younger than he was. He was tall at six-foot-three and had a lean muscular body.

'It's true that we don't know if a crime has

been committed, both women have reasons for wanting to leave, as we know, but the general population don't know Jasmine is pregnant, maybe she was too scared to tell her parents or doesn't want anything to do with the father of the child. Anna's husband was having an affair, she suspected it, perhaps she wants to make him sweat,' Sergeant Gardiner commented.

Rooney listened to what they had to say before he spoke. 'I believe that yes, Jasmine has a reason for getting out of dodge, but I don't think for one moment that Anna would put her parents through this heartache unnecessarily. They are a close family, she even confided in her mother about her suspicions with the affair.'

'If I may,' PC McMillan spoke for the first time in the meeting.

'Go ahead, by all means,' Aird told her.

'The last time we did the door to door a lot of the doors we chapped the residents were out, if we do it again we should take note of the no answers and go back until we speak to everyone. It may be talking to one person, the right person that could open this case up.'

'Widen the area by few streets; you think you know the exact route Anna took. We don't know exactly what happened to the dog, she may have had to go after it if it got away,' Norman Mathieson added.

'That's a lot of hours of manpower. Nicole I

want you and PC Graham McCartney solely doing that, you know the case and PC McCartney knows the family a little. Make your lists, go to every door and find the right person. Stephen, I will speak to PC McCartney and tell him to report to you at Hallington tomorrow morning for the foreseeable future. Nicole, be sure Sergeant Rooney is notified right away with any information you find out no matter how small. We can't let this slip, we have two families in turmoil over this,' Aird commanded.

'Are we to widen the area for door to door then as the Detective suggested?' PC McMillan asked.

'Yes, go an extra three streets each way, see where that takes us.'

The meeting was over at 10.40 am.

When Anna awoke she felt refreshed and hoped that yesterday's antics would not have any more effect on her. She went home to check the time, it was 11.10 am, Tom was not there, neither was Rex.

Rex was at her parents' house until Friday night and Tom was back at work after agreeing with his boss Paul that he would go back, take it one day at time.

Frank was on her mind so Anna went to May's to find him. She was starting to sense a theme today as neither May nor Frank was there either.

What is it with everyone today, no one is around. Frank must be out chasing the postwoman again. I can't blame him after all he is on a mission. I will wait here, he will be back soon.

She waited and waited and eventually when the clock on May's mantelpiece read 1.30 pm she thought of Frank and was there in front of him. He was in a hospital standing next to a bed that May occupied. There were three other beds in the room with elderly ladies in them.

'What happened,' Anna asked Frank.

'Last night we were sitting going through some old photos, well she was I was lurking over her shoulder. She got up to go out of the room and fell onto the floor, couldn't get back up. Luckily her mobile was within her reach, well not quite she had to do a bit of crawling, sort of like a out of shape Army Cadet would do under rope net ting in the mud, it was a horrible sight, I was so worried. I heard her telling the paramedic when the ambulance turned up that she was feeling dizzy and sick. Apparently she has low blood pressure, they are keeping her in here until it goes up a bit.'

'Has she had this before? That's a stupid question, how would you know.'

'I do know. I have been listening to every word that has been said about her and to her since she got here. She has had low blood pressure on and off for the last five years.'

'Well you are quite the detective. I take it you never got any mail swapped over this morning?'

'No, but I have something better.'

'What?'

'When we were checking out the photos, Mum held up a picture with Richard and me as babies and Mum in it. It seems like it was taken in the hospital a day or two after we were born. When she had finished looking at that one she turned it over onto the pile that she had looked at and that's when I saw the writing.'

'What writing? I'm in suspense here.'

'Well on the back it says, May and her twin boys Richard and Frank. It isn't my mum's writing. I know her writing now and it is a colour photo which I believe were fewer than black and white in those days.'

'So you are thinking of taking that to Richard? Is it the same photo of the one in the locket?

'No, so I'm starting to think that Mum didn't give us up straight away, I will need to ask Fenza about that.'

'Well you two still have your birth names; maybe if you were given away straight away your new parents would have changed your names.'

'That's what I was thinking, I need to plant more of Mum's mail at Richard's house first, let the name May Simpson sink in then hit him with the photo.'

'Where is the photo?'

'After Mum got settled in here at the hospital I went back and took it. I hope you don't mind I put in your house.'

'My mum has been doing housework for Tom, where did you put it?'

'Under the bed in the spare room, I reached under about six inches and laid it there, there is no valance sheet on the bed, it was easy for me, I don't think it will be found unless someone looks under the bed.'

'That's good; there is nothing under the bed for anyone to go searching for so it should be safe.'

'Anyway, how are you feeling after your escapades yesterday with the wall?' Frank asked.

'Well I slept all night, I feel back to normal, if you call this normal. Who is the woman visiting your mum?'

'That's her friend Judy, Mum called her this morning, she came straight here.'

'It's good that she has someone to rely on. It will be even better when she gets reunited with her family.'

'It will change her life so much for the better, you have no idea.'

'I will catch up with you later Frank, I'm off to see Billy.'

'Sure thing, I will see you later.'

Billy was at the spare bedroom window when Anna caught up with him. He was sitting there with his binoculars, a note book and pen and the bird watching book his workmate given him. He was not interested in bird watching and didn't know a starling from a chaffinch, but wrote in the notebook anyway about seeing a pigeon and a seagull; he had been there since Kate left for work at 8.30 am. He was writing things about birds in the front of the notebook for the benefit of Kate, he was saving the back for comings and goings in the back garden of his neighbours. There was already one entry in the back of the notebook, that was Candice going to the shed at 12.55 pm with a carrier bag and a bucket then coming back out with the carrier bag and a bucket. Billy thought that she had put something in the bucket in the shed because it seemed to him that the bucket was empty on the way in and it seemed not to be on the way out, it was the way she carried it that gave the game away. He wrote all this down in as much detail as he could even the part about the neighbour unlocking and locking the shed. This didn't seem that strange to him as everyone locks their shed, he didn't write down when Candice left in her car. He was only concentrating on things that involved the shed.

Now that's what I'm talking about, he is getting in-

volved with this now. I hope he finds Rex's name tag soon .That should give him an extra push. It's a pity it gets dark early and I know he will be trying to hide this from Kate, who wouldn't try to hide it she would think he was going off his head.

Billy sighed and looked at his watch, it was 3.10 pm. He had eaten a sandwich and had a coffee at the window at about twelve o'clock. Buster was walked at 7.30 that morning and had been out in the garden twice since then. Billy craved a bit of chocolate so left his post and went to the kitchen; he made a cup of tea and took a chocolate biscuit out of the tub in the cupboard, Buster was sitting in front of him wagging his tail, he went into a different tub in the same cupboard and gave him a few treats.
'Give me time to eat and drink this then I will take you out,' Billy said to his pet.
Buster seemed pacified by that and went into spare room in front of Billy, jumped up on the bed and lay down.
'You are a good boy,' Billy said as he took up his sentry at the window.

If he is going out with Buster then I am going with him, if he finds that name tag I want to be there to see his reaction.

Half an hour later Billy got ready to go out. It was dry, but cold; he put on a hat, scarf, gloves and the very jacket that Frank had put the disc in. He waited until he got to the gate to put the lead on Buster; he went out the gate and turned left then left again onto Main Street. He stopped, pretending to tie his lace outside his neighbours' house, he wanted a nosey about the back garden, but was too anxious in case one of the people who lived there came home and caught him. How would he explain it? He stood back up and carried on along Main Street.

'You want to go into the park Buster?' he asked the dog.

'Ok, we will,' he answered for Buster.

At the gate of the park he put his hand in the same pocket as the name tag and pulled out a couple of poo bags for the dog. The disc fell on to the pavement, he heard it and peered down to see what it was, he tried to lift it with his gloves on, couldn't get any leverage on the edge. He took off his right glove and picked it up. Billy turned it over and over in his hand with a puzzled expression on his face.

'Did that just fall out of my pocket? Surely not, but I heard it fall. I am starting to go mad. This is Rex's, how could it possibly get in my pocket?' He said to Buster, who was waiting impatiently to get into the park.

Billy put the disc in the front pocket of his jeans, put his glove back on and continued into the park with his dog. He didn't stay long in the park; he wanted to get home to inspect the name tag more closely.

'Come on Buster time to go home.'

'Billy walked briskly back home, once inside and settled back at the window he took the name tag from his pocket and laid it flat on the palm of his hand.

'That say's Rex.'

He turned the disc over to see the number.

'Should I ring it, is it Anna's number or Tom's? If I take it to the police would I become a suspect in Anna's disappearance? I can't take the chance, but I have nothing to hide. Should I take it to Tom? What will I say when he asks me where I found it?' He was talking to himself; Buster came into the room assuming he was talking to him.

He sat the name tag on the window sill and leaned over with his elbows on his knees and his hands on his forehead.

'What to do, I have done nothing to Anna. I like Anna. How the fuck did this get in my pocket? I met Anna that night did I do something to her? Did I black out and do something? This is torture. What can I do? I think I am going crazy.'

Oh no. What did I do? I didn't think this through properly. I didn't think for a minute what effect this would have on Billy. I can't undo this, I will talk to him tonight, get through to him that it is me who is talking to him, that might be a long shot, although I will try.

'Maybe it is time I told Kate everything that is going on with me. She will tell me to go to the doctor that's for sure. What if I tell her about the name tag? She might think that I have done something to Anna. Did I do any harm to Anna? Did I hurt Rex?' Billy continued talking to himself.

What have I done? This is too much for him; he was going to check out that shed without me putting that disc in his pocket. This may send him over the edge.

Billy sat there in the same position until he heard Kate come in from work at 5.20 pm; he stood up and met her in the hall on her way in.
'There is something I need to tell you, come in and sit down,' Billy said.
'What is it? What's wrong?'
'Just sit down woman,' he said as he led the way to the couch.
Once they were both seated with Anna standing at the door Billy started.
'I found this today,' he said handing her the name tag.
'This is Rex's, where did you find it exactly?'
'Well that's the strange thing it fell out my jacket pocket.'

'How the hell did it get in there?'

'I don't know Kate, I wish I did. I have been driving myself crazy wondering where it came from. I am starting to think that maybe I blacked out that night Anna disappeared, maybe I hurt Rex and did something to Anna.'

'Don't be silly; you are not capable of such an action, I think I have known you long enough to know what kind of a person you are. Anyway you would have been acting strange when you came back that night, you weren't. In fact you were not away any longer with Buster than you would be any other night, I refuse to believe that you had anything to do with it. You should put that notion right out of your head.'

'There's more.'

'Tell me everything.'

'Well you know that I said that I have taken up bird watching?'

'Yes.'

'I haven't, I can't explain this very well. You know that I have had what you might call bad dreams of late.'

'Yes.'

'How can I put this? When I'm dreaming something or someone is telling me to watch my neighbours' garden that someone needs to be saved.'

'The Sutherlands' garden you mean? Now this is starting to sound a little far out there. So that is what you are doing in the spare room?'

'Yes, but after finding that name tag I don't know what to think, should I tell Tom?'

'No, tell no one, I don't know what to think or what to do at the moment; we will figure this out together. What is in your dreams, what do you see?'

'That's the thing I don't see anything that I can remember afterwards, I just believe that someone is talking to me.'

Kate believes in all that spooky stuff like tarot cards and spirits, she used to go to the spiritualist church in Pavesway every week, but hadn't been in a while. She was wide open to the idea that someone was trying to tell him something, get him to spy on their neighbours for some greater good.

'I am going to help you with this Billy; we will get to the bottom of it in no time. You are off work until Friday so you can keep watch until then, I will take over on Saturday. I know none of us will see what is happening on Friday, both of us will be at work; we will put all we have into this. If there is something to find we will do it together.'

'You would do all that for me? It is not easy I have been at that window nearly all day, I have a sore arse already, thank you darling,' Billy said getting a little emotional.

'I would do anything for you especially if it

means you keep your sanity. I'm going to start dinner you go and keep watch; you will not see much I expect because it is dark. We won't get anywhere if we don't put the work in. I will give you a shout when your dinner is ready.'

It was a cold, clear night and Billy could see a few twinkles of frost starting already on the grass and path of the Sutherland property as the outside light at the back door of their house was on. It reminded him of tiny shards of glass on the road catching the sun as he drove. He wished it was summer now; it would make it easier to do his spying work if the light nights were here. He stood up and peered down to the driveway of his people of interest, he had to press his face to the glass and look down at an angle to get a view. Jack's van was in the drive; Billy could see the nose of the bonnet of it from his position. Kate arrived beside him with a second dining chair.

'We will eat our dinner here on our laps, it will not be very comfortable, but we will be able to keep an eye out.'

'His van is there and the light at the back door is on,' Billy told her before she vanished back into the kitchen to finish dinner.

Ten minutes later Kate was back with a plate in each hand and two forks in her right hand stuck under the plate.

'Be back in a sec, going to get the juice.'

She was gone and back in no time. 'What else did I miss?' She asked as she sat down; put the two glasses on the window sill and took one of the plates from Billy that she had given him a short minute before.

'You have missed hee-haw, all is quiet.'

Billy put his plate of chicken carbonara pasta on the floor, got a pillow off the spare bed and put it on the chair before he sat down, picked up his plate and went about eating his dinner.

'Been stretching my back all day trying not to miss anything, this should do the trick. I forgot to mention the woman over there went out to that shed today; she had a carrier bag and a bucket, she came back out with a carrier bag and a bucket, it seemed that she had put something in the bucket when she was in there, she seemed to be carrying it in a different way. It's all in the back of the notebook,' Billy said motioning to the notebook on the floor.

'What time was that?'

'It was 12.55 pm.'

They finished their pasta; Kate took the dishes through to the kitchen then started rinsing them to put them in the dishwasher.

'Kate hurry up, put that light out on your way in here, we can't let them spot us spying on them.'

She hit the light switch on the way into the room. There was some light coming in from the hall, enough for her to make her way to the window. Billy handed her the binoculars that he lifted when he saw the back door open.

'The shed over there in the far corner, take a look.'

Kate caught Candice and Jack disappearing into the shed and closing the door behind her.

'Did she have anything with her?' Billy asked.

'It was the two of them. He was carrying a basin of what I presume to be water or a liquid of some sort, he was holding it precariously as if something might spill out. She had something in her hand and something under her arm. I don't know what it was. She opened the door he went in, she followed him,' Kate said.

'We need to write it down with the time.'

'Yes, I will as soon as we see them coming back out.'

They didn't need to wait long before the monsters left the shed and went back into the house empty handed after locking up the shed.

'What do you think?' Billy asked.

'I don't know what to think, not yet anyway. It is all a bit weird.'

'I know, but I also know that something bad is happening and we are going to get to the bottom of it, all we need is proof.'

'Well that is not going to happen overnight I'm afraid, we will have to observe them until we are sure of what is going down.'

'I'm glad you are cool with all this Kate, I was

worried sick wondering what you were going to say when I told you.'

'I love you, you have done nothing wrong, just remember that.'

Billy left Kate on sentry duty at 8.45 pm when Buster made it quite clear that it was time for his walk. When Billy came back twenty-five minutes later Kate reported that nothing else had happened. Kate went to bed at 10.30 pm leaving Billy at the window until 11.20 pm when he was sure nothing else was going to take place.

Anna had been with Kate and Billy in their home the full night; she knew what page they were on. It was the same one as her.

Billy will be ok now. He has Kate supporting him. I can't believe he told her everything, he did and I couldn't be happier. They must have an amazing relationship, Kate trusts Billy one hundred percent that is clear. I will give him a full night's sleep tonight with no interruptions from me. I was going to reassure him about the name tag. That can wait.

30
Tuesday 26th November

Anna spent the night in the shed with Jasmine, she was awake for half of it; she spoke to her in a reassuring voice anytime Jasmine fell asleep. There were a few groans, nothing to suggest that Jasmine was taking in anything that Anna was saying. Anna waited until Jasmine had got her breakfast and a fresh bucket before she went to catch up with Frank. There was no sign at May's house and no sign of May either. She went to the hospital, yes May was still there. Frank was nowhere to be seen.

He must be following the postwoman. I will come back here after lunchtime; he will surely be here by then.

She went back to Jasmine to kill a couple of hours.

Tom's phone rang; he answered it immediately in the hope that it was news about his wife. He was in the work's van having breakfast, his boss Paul was in the driver's seat beside him.
'Hello,' he said
'Oh hello Mr Ross, it's Katie Irvine calling from The Village Vets. I was just wondering how Rex is doing?' she asked.
'Hi Katie, Rex is doing well. He is staying with my in-laws during the week and coming home

to me at the weekend. I take it you heard about my wife?'

'No what about her?'

'That night, the night I brought Rex in, she has been missing since then, when she took Rex out a walk.'

'Jesus wept. I had not heard. I work a lot of night shifts. I am so sorry to hear that.'

'Thank you. Would you like me to bring Rex back in for a check-up?'

'No, if you think he is doing ok then we will leave it at that, if you have any concerns about him please give me a call.'

'I will bye for now.'

'That was the vet,' Tom told Paul.

'I know I heard every word, I am sitting right next to you, I just hope I don't get a private call because you will hear it all,' Paul said with a smile on his face.

'I was hoping that was going to be the police, they were discussing Anna's case in a meeting yesterday. They haven't called Anna's parents or me yet to let us know the outcome.'

'They will Tom as soon as they have something to say.

Paul had barely got the words out when Tom's phone rang again. This time it was Rooney. The sergeant told Tom everything that was said about Anna in the meeting, told him what was going to happen next. Tom thanked him and hung up.

'See I told you so,' Paul said then added. 'And yes I heard every word.

'I wish they could get a solid lead. I'm in turmoil thinking about what could have transpired the night she vanished.'

'Did you swallow a dictionary the morning,' Paul said with a grin.

Tom just smiled, amused by the comment, on the inside his mood was melancholy, he thought that he would never be happy again. He called George to let him know what the police were doing next.

Anna waited in the misery of the shed until Candice supplied Jasmine with lunch. She thought herself outside the shed and looked up at Billy's back bedroom window, she could barely see him, but he was there, hopefully writing the sighting of Candice in his notebook. She was happy that he was not that visible from where she was it meant that the monsters would not see him spying on them.

She left there and went to the hospital to find Frank and find Frank she did, hovering on the bottom of his mother's hospital bed.

'Frank, how are you doing? Have you been out with your postwoman this morning?'

'Yes and there are two police going door to door with pictures of you and Jasmine. I caught a glimpse of the photo of you when they were walking by me, so I went to the next door with them to see what they had to say.'

'What were they saying?'

'They showed the photos of you and Jasmine to the occupants and asked if they had seen either you or her, then they said that if they did see or hear anything to give the police a call.'

'At least they are doing something; my family will be delighted about that. Did you manage to put any of your mum's mail at Richard's?'

'Yes two letters, did I tell you I can only move one item at a time? Anyway for some reason my power only works with a single item. How are you getting on?'

Anna had a lot to tell him about Billy and the fact that Kate knows what is going on with him. She told Frank about how bad she felt when Billy thought he was going crazy when he found the name tag, she told him about the notebook and the sightings Billy had written in it. She was so thrilled that she had someone to share all this with, that she had found a real friend in Frank.

'What is your next step?' Frank asked Anna.

'I just need to do what I have been doing. I can't think of any more steps. I will speak to Billy tonight even if it just to make sure that he doesn't lose any momentum. What are you doing next?'

'My answer is the same as yours, do what I am doing until I feel the time is right to place the photo at Richard's house. We seem to be making progress doing the same thing over and over; if it's not broke don't fix it.'

'That's so true. Hey when is your mum getting out?'

'Going with what I heard it will be later today, her blood pressure is back to within a healthy range and that lady you saw yesterday visiting her is coming to pick her up, Mum is going to stay with her for a couple of days.'

'That's good news, you will be under no pressure to get to her post before she does for the next couple of mornings at least,' Anna said.

'Yes, and I hope she has a lot of post, I want this done as soon as possible, I am getting fed up with it all now, I just want to be at peace knowing that she has family around her. I have over stayed my welcome here.'

'I don't want you to go before I go, I know that I sound selfish, I don't want to be here on my own.'

'Anna you will be fine on your own. Who's to say that you won't go before me? You seem to be smashing your mission. I nearly forgot to tell you I saw another soul.'

'Where?'

'Right here in the hospital this morning. A man of about sixty-five, he was tall and going bald, his make was a lot darker than mine.'

'Did you speak to him?'

'I tried; he just looked right through me as if I wasn't there.'

'How many do you think are down here?' Anna asked Frank.

'Loads, well including us there are three in this hospital that we know of, so yes loads.'

'Life is not as strange as death. I still have trouble believing that all this is real. I sometimes think that I am dreaming.'

'Not just you, I do too. What you up to the rest of the day?'

'I will go between Billy and the shed, maybe pay the monsters a visit tonight. I hope they do a bit of talking I want to find out what their plans are. I'm off will catch you later.'

'I don't know where this friend of my mum's lives. I will see her settled there then I will find you.'

'Ok, Anna said before she took flight for the shed.

Anna stayed in the shed only long enough to check that Jasmine was going ok. She wanted to be everywhere at once. First she went to Billy who was sitting steadfast at the window watching his neighbours' garden.

Now that's what I call dedication, if only everyone could be like him, he is definitely one of the good guys.

She left there and went to see what Candice was up to, there was nothing much to see, the witch was hard at it working away at a computer screen. When Anna caught up with Jack in his office he was sitting staring into space, he seemed to have the world on his shoulders and he did. It was clear to Anna that he had more of a conscious than his wife.

I think I will try to connect with him; he looks like he is on the edge, maybe a gently push is what he needs.

Ruby was on the phone to someone when Anna reached her parents' house. Anna stood at the side of her mother listening to what she was saying and she realised quickly enough that her mother was talking to Clara. They were talking about Anna, saying things that already had been said, they had nothing else to say, they were still in a state of disbelief over what was happening. She went to the living room where her father was sitting on the couch with Rex by his side, Fluff the cat was on one of the two arm chairs curled up in a ball.

All is fine here. Fluff doesn't seem to be put out too much with Rex being here, which is good as I think he will be here most of the time now by the looks of it. I will go see Tom now, and then I can go back to the shed and relax until it is time to do some work tonight.

Tom had the first of the plaster on a wall in a room where Paul and he were working together. Anna didn't know which town or village she was in, she had thought of Tom and here she was. She could be anywhere. Tom's phone rang, he answered it right away.
'Hello.'
'Hello Tom it is Sam. I'm calling to let you know that I have someone starting in the shop tomorrow. I know she won't replace Anna, I wanted to give you the heads up first.'
'Sam I told you it was fine, with Anna not being there you are solely in charge.'
'I know what you said Tom, that doesn't make it any easier for me, half of this business is still Anna's.'
'I wish she were here to run it with you, but I know it is in the safest hands possible.'
'Thank you. Remember if you have any news about Anna let me know.'
'I will, hope to speak to you soon, bye.
Tom told Paul what the call was about with Anna listening to every word.

Poor Sam, I have not given him a second thought since all this happened. I will check on him tomorrow and get a nosey at the new recruit while I'm there.

Anna left there and went back to the shed; she had a nap and waited there with Jasmine until Candice turned up with her dinner. Dinner came in a plastic bag containing a plastic food bowl with Spaghetti Bolognese, a chocolate bar and a flask of tea.

'I will bring in your basin of water after you eat dinner, 'Candice told Jasmine then left taking Jasmine's makeshift toilet with her.

After Jasmine's little illness they seem to want to keep this shithole a bit cleaner. That's good for Jasmine, what's good for her is good for the baby.

Anna thought herself outside the shed to have a look up at Billy's window; she could see no one there. She went into Billy's house to find him asleep on the couch, Kate was nowhere to seen. Buster was lying on the floor outside the living room door, sparked out.

Oh no, I thought he was behind this, I thought he wouldn't stop until he had resolved it all. So he missed one sighting, I can't be too hard on him. I can't let things slide either. I need to wake him.

'Anna Anderson,' Anna shouted as loud as she could, Billy jumped three inches off the couch.
'What the hell,' Billy yelled.
He sat up and rubbed his eyes then peeked at his watch.

'Buster why did you let me sleep so long,' Billy said before getting up and heading straight to the window in the spare room.

Anna heard the front door open; Kate was in the room beside Billy in minutes.

'Where were you,' Billy asked Kate.

'I told you I would be later tonight, went down the precinct to get a few Christmas things. I left them in the car. What have you saw today?'

'The woman at lunchtime, I fell asleep so that is all the activity I have seen. I am starting to think that they are feeding something in there, maybe some kind of pet.'

'So are you trying to tell me that you are losing all that sleep and are doing all that worrying over some sort of pet that our neighbours have?'

'I don't know Kate, my head is wasted the now. What if it is a pet and we are wasting all this time sitting here marking down in a notebook every time they are feeding it. It makes me feel like an idiot.'

'You were so sure that something unjust is happening over there. I will go put the dinner on, go take Buster a walk and we will discuss this further when you get back.'

Billy left and took the dog a walk. When he got back in his dinner was ready for him at the dining table in the kitchen.

'Are we not eating this in the spare room,' Billy

asked Kate.

'What's the point if you are starting to think that there is nothing much going on over there? You were in such a state over this, now it seems as if you have changed your mind.'

'I don't know how I feel. I am so confused.'

'We will leave the neighbours in peace tonight; we will see how you feel about it in the morning. Deal?'

'Deal,' Billy said.

What is that it? I will need to step up the pressure on him tonight. By the time I am finished with him there won't be a single doubt in his mind.

Anna turned round to see Frank standing in the hall; she told him what she had just heard between the couple and told him of her plans for that night.

'What are you doing until then?' Frank asked.

'I want to visit the Sutherlands to hear if they are saying anything about Jasmine, then I will hang out in the shed until it is time to go torture Billy. How is your mum by the way?'

'She is good, nearly back to normal I would say. I have been to her house, moved a letter to Richard's, it was just junk mail, but it had her name and address on so it counts. Anyway Mum and her friend are going to watch a movie. You up for going to watch it, take your mind off things for a couple of hours?'

'Not tonight, I need to concentrate on my mission, I feel as if I have been slacking.'
'Ok Anna, if there is anything you need come for me, see you tomorrow,' Frank said then was gone.

Anna went straight to the monsters' house and found them both in the kitchen, Jack was sitting at the table, Candice was standing at the sink filling a bucket of hot water which Anna presumed was for Jasmine to get washed with and she was right.
'Lift that towel and come out to the shed with me,' Candice said to her husband.
'I don't want to go out there.'
'Tough, I need a hand. I will go back out later to retrieve this by myself; I want to fill a hot water bottle for her tonight anyway, it's meant to be a cold one.'
'Ok then.'
Jack lifted the towel and led the way out to the shed. Anna thought herself in the back garden and stood there watching them go into the shed then come back out minutes later. She glanced up at Billy's spare bedroom window, she saw nothing.

I knew he wouldn't be there. Billy is missing all this, I will remedy that tonight. I thought I was being hard on him; I have not been hard enough.

Jack and Candice settled themselves in the living room watching TV. Anna poised herself on one of the armchairs and sat patiently for any of the two of them to start talking about Jasmine. She waited and waited. They said nothing about their prisoner until Candice announced she was going to fetch the towel and bucket and give Jasmine her hot water bottle. The time was 8.45 pm on the clock on their fireplace wall. Anna had been there for some time and was not hopeful that this evil pair was going to say anything of interest so she left there and went to Billy's side. She was sure when she thought of Billy she would be standing in his house, she was wrong she was standing half-way down Main Street; Billy was lifting the mess Buster had left on the pavement. She walked beside Billy on the rest of his walk with Buster; it was a long walk tonight All the way down Main Street, down Parson's Way and Along Browning Street going past Anna's house, right along to Walker Terrace then back on to Main Street. He did the longest circuit he could do within the scheme. Once settled back in the house all Anna had to do was hang around until Billy went to sleep. It eventually happened at 12.30 am.

Right now is the time to get some serious work done here.

There was little light in the room; she could vaguely make out what was where. Buster she knew was lying on the bottom of the bed as she could hear him grunting and snorting gently in his slumber.

'Anna Anderson,' Anna said loudly into the room.

Billy started squirming.

'Anna Anderson,' she said even louder the second time.

'Billy I know that you have made a start to help The Innocent, you are starting to waiver. I know you found Rex's name tag; you need not tell anyone about it, I gave it to you to make you understand that you have to help that child. You have to keep tabs on your neighbours. They are evil; they are holding someone prisoner in that shed. The Innocent is in there and you have to save The Innocent Billy, there is no one else that I can turn to yet, you are in my opinion the best choice for the job. If I didn't think you could handle it then I would not be so persistent. Save The Innocent Billy. Be a hero.'

Anna had made her speech for the night.

'Billy, Billy,' she shouted at the top of her voice getting the desired effect.

Billy practically jumped out of bed, sending Buster on the floor in a hurry through fright and waking Kate up in the process.

'What is it,' Kate asked.
'I need to help. There is certainly something going on in that shed Kate, first thing tomorrow we are back on the case.'
'Ok darling, I am with you on it.'
'Thank you, I know I was changing my mind. I am positive now, someone needs saving.

My work here is done, even if it is just for one night.

31
Wednesday 27th November

The frost lay thick over every surface; it looked like the whole town had been generously dusted in icing sugar overnight. After Candice had been in to give Jasmine her breakfast and change her toilet Anna went outside. She checked out Billy's window only to see no one there. She went into Billy's house; he was there in the kitchen sorting Buster's meat into his bowl.

'Right there you go, I will take you a walk in a while,' Billy said to his pet as he laid the dish on the plastic mat on the floor.

He had taken Buster out to the garden when he got up half an hour before and lingered out there with one eye on the shed waiting for any activity, he had seen none. He had just missed Candice's morning breakfast visit. He made himself some tea and toast and headed to the back bedroom window where he held his position for fifty minutes before he took Buster for a walk. Anna went with him. When he got back he took up his watch at the window with a fresh cup of tea perched on the windowsill.

I wonder what Billy would be doing if he wasn't doing this task? It is taking up all of his spare time, but it is important. I am sure Billy will crack this.

Anna went to find Frank; she had nothing else to do all day. She tried May's house, no luck there. She thought of May and was there in front of her and her friend Judy, sitting at a dining table in what she presumed was Judy's house. The impression Anna got was that Judy was older than May even though she looked younger, May had not had an easy life and it showed. Judy on the other hand seemed to have had a better, easier life. Judy was tall and thin, her hair was straight, short and grey, well maintained. Her eyes were light blue and she was made up with a little make up. She was wearing navy trousers and a white cashmere jumper with sheepskin slippers on her feet. Anna looked around the house inside and out. The house was a detached sand stone, four bedroomed building which was kitted out with expensive furniture and fittings. It was the kind of house that neighbours would be envious of, the kind of house that any average person would hope to own. When she returned to where May and Judy were sitting at the dining table in the extremely large kitchen they had been joined by a man who Anna thought must be Judy's husband. He was not as tall as his wife and not as thin either. His brown eyes were framed by expensive silver framed glasses, he had on all shades of brown, his shirt was brown checked, the v-neck jumper on top of it was brown, his corduroy trousers were brown and he was even wearing brown leather loafers which looked old and comfortable.

'I'm going to the garden centre with Robert; he wants to look at wheelbarrows,' the man said.

'Ok, May and myself are going to the hairdressers then for lunch so won't be back before two,' Judy answered him.

'Well have a good time,' he said before turning and leaving the room.

'Gordon,' Judy shouted after him.

'Yes,' he said appearing back in the kitchen.

'Pick up some bird feed for the feeders please.'

'Oh yes, I knew there was something we needed.' Gordon said before leaving the room for a second time.

'You are so lucky,' May said to her friend.

'I know. I think you should stay here until after Christmas and New Year May. It would be great to have you.'

'I don't know. What about your girls and their families aren't they coming to stay?'

'They are coming for Christmas Day, they are not staying. I know Christmas is a month away, but we have lots of space here and I will feel a whole lot better if you are here with us while you recover.'

'Judy I have already recovered, it was only a bit of low blood pressure. I am over it now.'

'Oh please just say you will stay,' Judy pleaded.

'Ok. However, we will need to go to my place today to get some things for that long a stay.'
'No problem, we will go after lunch. So it's settled then, I am so happy I will have someone to have a sherry or two with on New Year's Eve, as you know Gordon doesn't drink.'

I don't know how this is going to affect Frank's plans; I will need to tell him when I see him. It is good for May to be here rather than in that house of hers all alone over the festive period. I wonder what Christmas will be like for my family? Will they even celebrate it with me missing in action?

Anna checked the time on the cooker in Judy's kitchen it was 10.10 am.

Frank will be out with the postwoman chasing down more mail to move. I will wait here, he will turn up eventually.

Anna was curious to find out how these two women had met so she stood next to them until they left for the hairdressers. 10.45, she had found out nothing, not that she was expecting to in such a short space of time. She sat at the dining table contemplating what was going to happen with her mission until Frank appeared at 12.40.
'Well hello there.'
'Oh hello, what are you doing here?'
'Looking for you, I have news for you.'

'Where is Mum?'

'She is away to the hairdressers, then lunch with Judy, after that they are going to your mum's to pick up some things because she is staying here until after New Year.'

'You are kidding me. What if Richard happens to go to her house with a letter and she is not there?'

'That's what I was thinking. What can you do? You will just have to hold on to that photo for a bit longer than you had hoped. Did you move any mail this morning?'

'Yes, Mum's voting card and a letter from her energy company, what's the point if she is not there?'

'There is every point. Richard will probably give them back to the postie or put them back in the post box for a while before he resorts to going to her door in person. Even if he does and she is not home you can still move the letters back again and again until she is back there, then you can move the photo and everything will work out,' Anna told him.

'That is going to take weeks, I want to get back up there as soon as possible, I am getting fed up with all this now, I want to go home,' Frank said referring to The Realm.

'You will soon enough, as soon as you do what you are meant to do, the same as me.'

'I'm sorry, how are you getting on?'

Anna filled Frank in on the set back with Billy and how she had rectified it with her visit to him last night.

'You think he will keep at it now?'

'I will keep at him until he solves this or goes crazy whichever comes first.'

'You want to go walking around the town with me; I have nothing else to do?'

'Yes I will, it seems like I have nothing else to do either, we might as well do nothing together.'

They left the house and walked in the direction of the Precinct, which was a ten minute walk away from Judy's. The shops were quiet, a little early yet for most of the Christmas shoppers.

'My shop is round the corner, I want to check out the new person Sam has working there,' Anna said.

'Who is Sam?' Frank asked.

'My business partner, did I not mention this?'

'If you did I can't recall. Has she hired someone?'

'He has hired someone.'

'Sorry I just thought it would be a female.'

'Everyone thinks that don't worry.

When they reached the shop they thought themselves on the other side of the door. There was an elderly lady who appeared to be in her eighties and a young woman of around twenty waiting at the counter, ready to be served. Sam entered the shop front with a clear bag with what looked like a coat inside and handed it to the young woman. Anna's heart skipped a beat when she laid eyes on Sam, she missed him so much and only realised now just how much.

'Here it is all spic and span,' Sam said to the young woman.

The young woman thanked him and exited the shop.

'How may I help you?' Sam asked the elderly lady.

She put a carrier bag on the counter and said, 'I need these trousers taken up an inch please, I would do it myself, but my fingers don't work half as well as they used to.'

'Let us see,' Sam said taking the trousers from the bag.

'He checked them out then said, 'It will be four pounds and can be ready Monday.'

'That's great,' the old woman said fishing her purse out of a black leather handbag she had looped over her arm.

She paid the money, thanked Sam then left the shop.

'So where is the new recruit?' Frank asked Anna.

'She must be through the back.'

'What are we waiting for? Let's go see.'

They both went at the same time; the new woman was busy at a sewing machine making what looked like to Anna as duvet cover.

'Do you know her? Frank asked.

'No I don't, she seems to know what she is

doing. Sam has made a good choice, maybe he knows her.'

'Well your shop is in good hands, let's go.'

Anna took a moment to look at Sam again before they left the shop. They continued on their walk, they didn't say where they wanted to go they automatically headed for the scheme where everything was happening for them. They were walking past the opening for Bison Street on Main Street when Frank spotted a police car sitting outside the Sutherlands' house.

'Look, I don't believe it.' Frank said pointing to the monsters' house.

Anna felt excitement rise within her when she saw it, they hurried along the road and came to a stop by the police car. They saw no police.

'Do you think they are in there? Do you think justice is about to be done? Be back in a sec.'

Anna thought herself inside the shed only to find nothing had changed. Jasmine was still there on that shabby bed. She was sleeping, a feeling of guilt washed over her.

I have been neglecting her. I have not spent as much time here with her as I should have, I have been out with Frank walking through walls and watching movies. I need to get my priorities sorted out. I have been doing what I can with my mission though. I will need to connect with her, try to reassure her, not right now I need to know what is happening with the police car.

She visited the Sutherlands' house then went back to where Frank was standing by the police car.

'You see anything?'

'No nothing I went into the monsters' house; there is no one in there.'

A few seconds later they saw two police come out of a gate a few houses along on the other side of the road.

'That was the same two I saw with the pictures of Jasmine and you. They must be doing to doors and asking if anyone has seen either of you. Come let's follow them.'

'Wait, I know this copper. I used to date him way back.'

'Well maybe because he knows you he will put in extra effort to get you found.'

'I hope so. You know I have never given his guy a thought for a long time, he looks good'

By the time Anna and Frank had caught up they had entered another gate and knocked another door. Frank and Anna stood and listened when the door was answered by an elderly gentleman.

'Excuse me Sir we don't want to bother or alarm you, we have a couple of photos here we would like you to take a peek at,' PC Graham McCartney said handing the man two pictures.

'Have you seen any of the two women in the past couple of months or so? These two women are missing, we urgently want to find them,' PC McMillan said this time.

The old man shouted behind him into the house, 'Betty, come here a minute.'

An old woman came to the door, saw the police and immediately asked, 'What's happened?'

'Nothing for you to worry about,' PC McCartney said, then asked her the same question that he had asked her husband showing her the photos. The elderly couple both stared at the photos together for a few moments before shaking their heads and saying that they were sorry, they had not seen either of the women. The two officers thanked them for their time and moved on to the next door with Frank and Anna following. The two police were shadowed by Frank and Anna until they returned to their car, where the two souls took up position on the back seat to hear what was being said.

PC McMillan had a notebook; Anna saw by lurking over her shoulder that it was a list of addresses.

'Fourteen addresses in Main Street that we need to come back to tonight, it's going to be a late one Graham.'

'Well we started at eleven so basically we are working backshift. We will go back to the station for lunch then tackle Parkway Lane,'

PC McCartney said starting up the engine and slowly pulling way.

'That's Billy's street right over there,' Anna said to Frank and pointed in the direction of Billy's house.

'Yes I know I have been there remember. Do you want to stick with this pair all day?'

'I think I will. I want to know if they are going back to the Sutherlands tonight and if they do I want to be there to hear what is said at that door.'

'I will stay with you; there is nothing for me to do anyway. Did you see their address in that notebook?'

'To me it was just a list, I don't even know their house number, the two of them work so I'm hoping the police get an answer tonight, that's if they haven't already. Candice goes home at lunchtime so maybe they got a response then.'

After lunch the two officers parked across the road from Billy's house and went to every door on the opposite side from his. When they had done that side, writing down the house numbers with no answer they crossed the road and made their way back up the street towards their car and Billy's house. They had no luck at all with anyone saying they had seen either woman. They must have been aware of the part Billy had played in the investigation because they didn't knock on his door.

'That's another street done and we are no further forward,' PC McMillan said to her colleague.

'What street do we have next?'

'Bison Street.'

'Right we will do that, break for dinner then we can backtrack on the houses that we got no answer at today. Does that sound like a plan?'

'It sure does.'

The rain started to come down, slowly at first, then with more clout, until it was pelting down sideways in sheets. The two officers returned to their car and put on their waterproofs.

'I hate the rain, although I hope this means that the temperature will rise a bit, it has been freezing all day,' PC McMillan said.

'I will agree with you there. I haven't been able to feel my feet for the last half hour.'

There were sixteen addresses in Bison Street and out of the thirteen that answered the door they got two people who recognised the photo of Anna. The first of the two was Mrs Shannon Cuthbertson, she told the officers that she was aware of Anna's case because she worked with her mother and that she had saw either Anna or her husband walk their dog by the house quite often. The other was an elderly woman who sat perched at her front window most of the day saw Anna the Sunday before she vanished walking past. Although theses were more positive results, they were not going to help the case in any way that the officers could see.

'What are the chances that we are going to uncover information that is going to be helpful in finding these women?' PC McMillan asked her workmate.

'I would say slim, but this is the job we have been given to do, it may not get us anywhere fast, there is a chance that we strike it lucky.'

'I suppose you are right, no I know you are right, someone knows something.'

'That's the spirit. Right back to the station for dinner then out to do the re-runs from today.'

Anna and Frank didn't go to the station with them; instead they spent an hour in the shed with Jasmine, much to Frank's protest. Anna popped into the Sutherlands' to check the time and see what was happening with Jasmine's dinner as she thought it must be about that time, she was right, Candice had just finished covering the dinner plate with tin foil and had a flask of tea ready in a bag to lift on her way out. It was 6.40 pm.

Anna followed her out and was happy to see that Billy was spying from the window. She got Frank and they headed out front just in time for the police car pulling up ten metres along the street, much to Anna's delight they got out and walked back to where Frank and herself was standing, they entered the Sutherlands' gate and knocked on the door. Anna and Frank were right at their side. There was no answer at the door. PC McMillan walked to the side of the house saw that there was a car and a van in the drive, reported this back to PC McCartney then he knocked on the door again, then again louder each time until the hall light came on and the door opened.

'Evening Sir. Don't mean to bother you. We are doing a door to door in the area to see if anyone has any information on two missing women from around here,' PC McCartney said holding out the two photos for the man to take and look at.

Jack took the photos and quickly glanced at them briefly before shaking his head and handing them back, 'I'm sorry I can't help I have not seen anything. The women don't even look familiar.'

'Are you sure Sir,' PC McMillan said taking the photos from her colleague and trying to hand them to the man.

'I'm sure,' said Jack refusing to accept the photos. 'If I see anything I will let you know,' he said closing the door.

PC McMillan put a card through the door and the two officers walked out the gate.

'Either he is extremely rude, has something to do that can't wait so he is in a hurry or he has something to hide,' PC McMillan said to her partner.

'You took the words right out of my mouth, I think this is one to mention to Sergeant Rooney,' he answered.

'Yes, indeed.'

'They suspect him of something,' Anna said to Frank with a tinge of excitement in her voice.

'They sure do, maybe we should go in there and see how Jack is reacting.'

Both of them went at the same time. It was a no brainer.

Inside the Sutherlands' house all was not well. Candice was sitting at the dining table in the kitchen, with her dinner sat out in front of her. There was a plate at the table for Jack, but he was not sitting down, he was pacing up and down troubled and aggravated by the police visit.

'We need to get rid of her and that shed right away, we have no time to waste,' Jack angrily said to his wife.

'I would see the point if the police were only at our door, but they are going to everyone's door Jack, it's their job. They don't suspect us of anything; they have no leads on either of the two women.'

'How do you know all this?'

'Mr and Mrs Fowler along the street told me when they were in the surgery this afternoon.

They told me the police were at their door with photos not long before they came for Mr Fowler's appointment. They were at their daughter's door as well with the same photos. They have nothing to go on, that's why they are going door to door.'

'It's only a matter of time before they have something.'

'What could they possibly find out? No one knows anything apart from me and you; we can't give up now when we are so close.'

'You want that baby, I get it, at what cost? It is all or nothing with you; I have been to prison, believe me it's not a great place to be.'

'Stop worrying. We will worry when we have something to worry about. Come on, sit down and eat your dinner, then we can deal with Jasmine's toilet, the water for her to get a wash and a change of clothes.'

Jack sat down, he was not hungry. He picked at the food and pushed it around his plate. He was worried, Anna could see that.

'Do you think he will crack?' Anna asked Frank.

'Maybe, I hope so; he certainly has problems with this. Come on let's get out of here. They are going out to the shed soon, we will go see if Billy is there to see them.'

Billy was not at the window, he was in the living room with his wife having another discussion about the name tag and the Sutherlands.

'What good am I doing with the watching? What can I say to the police? My neighbours are going to their shed a few times a day. I don't even know for sure what is going on. Do they have Anna in that shed? Is that why she can't be found? Have they someone else in that shed? That name tag is bothering me, I could have sworn it fell out my pocket, but how the hell did it get there? What if it didn't fall from my pocket? What if I imagined that and it was there on the ground before I got there, shouldn't I go to the police with it. It could be a vital part in the hunt for Anna. I don't know how, it could be.'

'Do what you are doing Billy, I have a feeling that if our neighbours are up to something, which I am sure they are, they will slip up and make a mistake sooner or later. As for the name tag, forget that it is there. Whether it was in your pocket or not, it will look suspicious to the police if you take it in now. The last person to see a woman who has vanished finds the name tag from her dog's collar, it is too coincidental. They will only suspect you, you have done nothing wrong and I know that for a fact. We will continue to do what we have been doing and see where it takes us.'

'Ok Kate, you are usually right. How long do we do this?' Billy asked.

'For as long as it takes to either find out what is going on. One way or another we need to see this through.'

Anna disappeared for a second and appeared again.

'Frank that name tag is on the windowsill in the spare room. It is time we took it out of the equation. Maybe it was a bad idea from the start putting it in Billy's pocket; I'm messing with his head a little too much.'

Frank and Anna both went into the spare room at the same time. Frank lifted the name tag and asked 'Where will we take it?'

'Under the bed in my spare room along with your photo, keep all our stuff in the one place.'

'As good a place as any I suppose.'

What are your plans for the rest of the night?'

I am going to see all my family and try to think of a way to get Mum to go back home, or my plan will be on hold for over a month.'

'I am going to spend some time in the shed with Jasmine then I am going to reassure Billy tonight that he is on the right track.'

'Ok I will drop this into your house, I will see you tomorrow. Bye.'

Anna went to the shed, where she sat at the bottom of the shabby bed watching Jasmine cry.

32
Thursday 28th November

Anna spent most of the night watching Jasmine sleeping and crying. The situation was taking its toll on the young woman, Anna could see just how much. Anna took some time out from Jasmine during the night to visit Billy. She spoke to him for twenty minutes going over what she had already told him and reassuring him that he was following the right path. She knew he could hear her, how much was getting through to him was out of her control. All she could do was plug away at him night after night like a great tormentor.

Tom was up early as he wanted to put a fresh appeal on Facebook for Anna. It had been a fortnight since her disappearance; he wanted to feel as if he was doing something, anything that could help find her. He sat on the couch in the living room with tears dripping from the end of his nose onto the keys of the open laptop sitting on his knee. He looked around while wiping his face on his arm as he did so. He was alone, no Anna, no Rex. He missed them both. At least he will have Rex at the weekend to keep him from going insane with the loneliness he thought. He posted a heartfelt article then went to get ready for his working day. He had not been to the shop for food, he was living on takeaways this week and he decided that would change tonight as he was planning on going to the supermarket then making a homemade meal for himself. Ruby had been brilliant with him, bringing dinner over and having it there with him a few times. He knew he had to start standing on his own two feet and look after himself a little better than he was doing. He left for work feeling depressed, but hopeful that the day would be the day that Sergeant Rooney would call him with some news; Tom decided if he had not had a call for twelve o'clock then he would phone him.

PC McMillan and PC McCartney clocked on at eleven, instead of going straight out door to door they came to the agreed decision to check out the owner or owners of fifty-two Main Street. They had taken down the registration numbers of both vehicles at the address; they were going to do a little snooping with the help of a couple of colleagues. Once they had what information they could gather they went to see Sergeant Rooney. He was on the phone and held up a finger as if to say wait a minute. He finished the call then turned to the two PCs.
'What's up? He asked them.
'We had a strange one last night at one of the doors we went to.' PC McCartney answered.
'Strange how?'
'Well the man briefly glanced at the photos be-

fore saying he hadn't seen them, he was eager to get the door closed to be rid of us.' PC McCartney said.

'Maybe he was busy, had something on the cooker, babysitting, missing some of his favourite TV shows. People are strange, that doesn't mean they are up to something untoward. Did you check him out?'

'Yes, the Transit van that was parked in the drive is registered to Mr Jack Sutherland; the Ford Focus that was there is registered to his wife Candice. He has his own company Sutherland Construction; she works at Brownhill Doctor's Surgery.'

'Hold up. She works at Brownhill Surgery?'

'Yes is that important?' PC McMillan asked.

'I don't know. That was the second last place Jasmine Brown was seen. Is there anything else about them that I should know about?' the sergeant pressed.

'The man, Jack he has a prison record, got six years done three and a half for GBH,' PC McCartney informed him handing him the information on paper.

'This still does not prove that he has done anything to any of these two women. Leave it with me, in the meantime I want you to go into Brownhill Surgery, preferably at a time that is most likely that no one will be away on lunch and show the receptionists the photos. Be sure to mark any response that comes from Mrs Sutherland. I know there is no proof of wrong doing here and you are following your gut, there is nothing wrong with that, many a case has been solved by gut instinct, its gut instinct with a little digging that sometimes leads to evidence.'

'Yes Sir,' both PCs said at the same time and left the sergeant with the paperwork and his thoughts.

Tom called Rooney ten minutes later to find out if there was any progress, much to Tom's disappointment the sergeant had nothing to report. He gave Tom an update on what they were doing; from Tom's point of view apart from the door to doors nothing else was being done.

Anna stayed with Jasmine until after Candice had served her lunch before she went to find Frank. She did not need to look far; he was at his mother's side once again.

'Hello Frank,' Anna greeted her friend.

'Hi, what you been up to?'

'Not much really, I have been with Jasmine all morning. If I am being honest I don't think she is doing so well, when she isn't sleeping she is crying, it breaks my heart.'

'Is there anything I can do?'

'I don't think so. I am doing all in my power to get that young lady her freedom; it is out of my hands. I'm relying on Billy to get this solved. How are you doing? Did you move any mail this morning?'

'There is no point, there was nothing at Mum's this morning to move anyway. I need Mum to go home, by the look of it I think she is settled here for now.'

'It seems an awful long time for her friend to ask her to stay, have you found out yet how they know each other?'

'No not yet. I'm hoping the more time I spend here the more I will find out. Let's face it she will be here another five weeks, which is a long time for me doing nothing. I need to find a way to get Mum to go home, I just can't think of anything.'

'Keep moving the post back and forth; your mum will be going back to her house to check on it surely, even if it is once a week, she will need to get her mail you would think. If there is a pile of post there for Richard every time she goes then it may encourage her to go to his house.'

'I suppose I need to keep at it; there is nothing else I can do. I did have one idea.'

'What's that?'

'Move the photo of Mum, my brother and me to Richard's and then move it wherever he goes. Do you think that would play games with his mind?'

'Yes, it's a great idea, he will get the hint eventually, I hope.'

'Oh you have a cruel side Anna. I will move it tonight.'

'If it's any consolation I don't think for a moment that your mum will stay here all that time, she seems too independent for that.'

'Well I hope you are right, it would make this a whole lot easier for me if she was at home. What are you up to today?'

'I am going to visit my family and then spend the rest of the time with Jasmine. I will go annoy Billy again tonight; I don't want to, I have no option. I might also go see the monsters.'

'Well good luck Anna I will find you tomorrow, maybe we could hang out.'

'Yes I think that is a good idea, see you then.'

PC McMillan and PC McCartney entered Brownhill Doctors' Surgery at 2.30 pm. There were two women in the reception area and four patients waiting in the waiting room. The officers introduced themselves to the receptionists, told them why they were there and showed them the photos. The name tags on each of the receptionists told the PCs which one was Candice and the other was called Susan.

Candice looked at the photo of Jasmine while Susan had her eyes on the one of Anna.

'This young lady has been missing for a while. I

remember it well; I left work early that day. She had an appointment here after I left. The police came by then, there was nothing anyone here could tell them to help find her,' Candice said a cool as ice.

Susan spoke with sadness in her voice. 'This woman has not been missing long, I saw a post on Facebook about her, in fact I saw a new one on it this morning,' she traded pictures with Candice.

'I was on the reception with Mary Bryce when she was in for her appointment the day this one went missing,' Susan said with the photo of Jasmine in her hand. 'I remember it like it was yesterday. Mary does three to six every day which means Candice and I can go home at four every other day because we both start at eight.

'What's this woman's name?' Candice asked casually holding the photo of Anna.

'Her name is Anna Ross,' PC McMillan answered focusing on Candice's face; there was not a twitch of anything worth noting.

'Her mother works in Smith's Chemist, half of the prescriptions issued at this surgery go through there, but I don't know this young lady, I mean I may have been working when she has been in, not for a long time. Sorry we can't be of any help.'

PC McMillan looked at her watch, 'We will come back in a while to see Mary Bryce.'

When the two officers got back in their car PC McCartney called Sergeant Rooney and put him on speaker.

'Hello Sir.' PC McCartney said.

'What have you got?'

'Candice Sutherland was cool, showed no sign that she was involved in anything, she may be a good actress, I doubt she could be that good.'

'What did you think of her Nicole?'

'Much the same as Graham Sir, if she is involved then she did not show it whatsoever.'

'I have a job for you, where are you now?' the sergeant queried.

'We are outside the doctors' surgery waiting for the third receptionist to show up so we can show her photos.' PC McCartney answered.

'Yes, stay there and do that make it look good to Mrs Sutherland. After that come back here, I have taken an idea from Anna's parents, I have printed out some posters of the two women on it. I want you two to put them up around that house on Main Street, if Mr Sutherland has done something that he shouldn't have then I want him to sweat, I'm following your gut instinct. I have all the materials you need.'

'No problem Sir should be back there soon, PC McMillan responded.

They sat in the car until a woman they suspected was Mary Bryce walked into the surgery, waited a couple of minutes then followed her in. They were correct it was her; she had nothing to offer on the information front of any of the women much as they expected. They left the surgery and followed their instructions. They went back to the station and collected the posters from the sergeant and put them up around a quarter mile radius around the house on Main Street, all twenty-five of them. After this they went for dinner then resumed the door to door.

It was Jack that delivered Jasmine's dinner. It was a roast beef microwave dinner, a can of coke and a chocolate bar. Anna was not in the lightest of moods having watched the amount of crying that Jasmine had been doing the night before and today. As soon as he came in she started pacing around in what little space there was to do it.

'Just let her go free you evil, rotten to the core, poor excuse for a man, Can't you see the damage you are doing, sure you want a baby, but why go to this extreme to get one. You murdered me and you are putting this poor girl through hell, let's face it the outcome for Jasmine is not going to be good in anyone's book,' Anna ranted.

'Please Mr, let me go,' Jasmine spoke softly to her abductor.

Jack paused for a moment to look at her with

her pale skin and red rimmed eyes. Jasmine thought she could see some compassion and sympathy in his eyes, so she continued.

'I won't tell anyone I promise. I will tell everyone that I ran away because I was too scared to tell them about my pregnancy, that I have been living on the streets. I can't cope with how cold it is and with the pregnancy it is too much for me now. Please I have it all worked out what I will say.'

Jack shook his head slightly and left without a backwards glance.

'He has far too much to lose now Jasmine. Although if any of the two of them were going to let you go I suspect it would be him,' Anna said to the unhearing ears of Jasmine.

I never did go back and try to connect with him. That is a job for tonight. I will think hard on how to help Frank as well tonight. His mission is practically on hold as far as I can see until his mother returns home. I will get a good talk with him tomorrow; maybe if we put our heads together we could come up with something.

Anna sat with the prisoner until she thought it was late enough for Billy to be asleep which would not be late tonight as he had to be up for work in the morning. When she thought herself in his house she checked the time, it was 12.30 am. Billy was still awake. Both Kate and Billy

were in the spare room, not peering out the window, they were searching for something; they had the room nearly turned upside down.
'This is no good Kate; we have been in here for two hours. We are not going to find it.'

What on earth are they searching for that is so important at this time of night when he should be in bed for work tomorrow? Oh no I know, it's the name tag. I need to think things through more.

'Keep looking Billy it has got to be here. Only the two of us live here.'
Billy stopped abruptly, 'Do you think it is possible that Buster has swallowed it?'
'I never thought of that. It's a possibility yes. Do you think he will pass it or will we need to take him to the vet?'
'I don't know, but tomorrow when we take him out just let him out in the garden just in case.'
'Good idea, he doesn't get a walk until night time when we are both working anyway,' Kate reminded him'
'You will be home at lunchtime though.'
'Yes I always do when you are working.'
'Well he won't be getting a walk at all tomorrow if we can't find that name tag before then. I was worried about that disc. Now I'm worried about that disc and Buster.'

I need to fix this.

Anna went to Frank, who was of course with his mother; he was lying on the bottom of her bed like Anna does on Jasmine's and explained what was happening.

'You go back to Billy's, I will go get that disc and be there in a second.'

Frank was at Billy's as quick as he said he would be.

'What will I do with it?'

'Put it on the bed.'

Billy and Kate were still searching, at that minute both were on their hands and knees over by the window. Frank put it on the bed then Anna and Frank waited for it to be discovered.

'We need to stop Billy, it's just not here,' Kate said as she stood up and sat on the bed.

'I know, it's no good trying it doesn't want to be found.'

'It went the way it came; shrouded with mystery, best case scenario Buster has eaten it,' Kate said with defeat in her voice.

Billy got off the floor and sat beside her on the bed; he put his hand behind him and was just about to lay down when he felt it. He spun around to see it lying there.

'I don't believe it,' He said with glee in his voice, handing it to Kate.

'What are the chances? We have looked everywhere including on this bed a dozen times. I'm telling you something weird is going on. You need to get to bed. The mystery is solved,' Kate said.

Kate and Billy both went straight to bed. Anna decided she would leave Billy in peace tonight as it seemed he would not get as much sleep as he needed as it was.

'Thank you Frank, I need to start to think things through properly before carrying them out. You go back to your mother I will see you tomorrow.'

'Bye Anna,' he said and was gone.

Anna went to the shed and lay down on the bottom of the bed like she knew Frank would be doing again with his mother.

33
Friday 29th Novemver

Anna slept when Jasmine had slept throughout the night. Which wasn't very much as every time Jasmine woke she was crying which in turn woke Anna. Candice and Jack both came to the shed with her breakfast and a change of bucket for her toilet. Jasmine said nothing to them and them to her, strangers existing with each other with an outcome that would not end well for Jasmine and she knew it. Hope had deserted her and Anna could see that.

What else can I do? What avenue can I do down that I haven't already explored? I forgot to try to connect with Jack; I will need to remember to do that tonight. My memory seems to have left, it seems like I have brain fog. I made a decision to take the name tag away from Billy and look how that turned out, not well for him. I need to clear my head, get a firm plan in place then stick to it, but I'm restricted in what I can do. I know I have connected well with Billy, although what I say is not exactly what he hears, I know that much. He knows something is happening. He does not know the entirety of it. I need to walk and think.

Anna left the shed and started to walk the route to her house, not only was her own mission on her mind, but also Frank's. Despite the fact that she was deep in thought it was not long before she noticed a poster of herself and Jasmine, two photos side by side asking anyone with any information on either to call the police. Anna was happy that the investigation was still going strong. However, she had little confidence that the police would receive any information which would help solve the case. She stood and stared at it for a while before continuing her walk, she turned into her street and noticed Tom's car was there, her own was not.

He must have taken my car to work today, it does no good for a car to sit and do nothing. It just rots away at least that's what Tom always says. I don't even care about my car; the only thing I care about is getting that girl to safety, at the moment it seems impossible. I know there is no one at Billy's window as both Kate and Billy are at work today, it is only meal times that they are likely to see them going about their evil deeds anyway. I want to get to The Before and leave this world behind me more than ever. I wish it would be easy for me to call on Ravi and cancel this whole mission. I couldn't do that, not now that I am so involved, that would be taking the easy way out and I know there is no way I can give up now. I'm in this to the end one way or another.

The postwoman was on the opposite side of the street. Anna saw her van a few gates up so went to see if Frank was in it, he was. He came and stood beside Anna on the pavement.

'Have you moved the photo of your mother with you two as babies yet?' Anna asked.

'Not yet, I think I might hold off on that for a while, what I need is for my mum to go home.'

'Not long before the postwoman gets to your mum's house. What are you doing after that today?'

'There is nothing else for me to do.'

'Why don't we go to my house then and see if we can put our heads together, maybe come up with something.'

'Sounds a good a plan as any. We could walk together to my mum's just now; the postwoman will catch up to us. I don't need to follow her or even be at Mum's when she gets there, Mum is not at home anyway, I was just doing it for something to do. I hate talking to people and not getting an answer it can be so frustrating.'

'Tell me about it.'

'Arlene Ferguson, That's the postwoman's name, and let me tell you that woman can blether, she knows everyone and everyone knows her.'

'I spoke to her when she came into the shop with mail, although I didn't know her well.'

'I didn't know her, I know her now.'

They walked until they got to the gate of May Simpson and waited for what seemed like an eternity on Arlene. When Arlene reached the house she had post for May. Frank and Anna went inside to wait on it being put through the door, before it was they could hear voices outside so went back out to find Arlene talking with May's next door neighbour.

'May is not in; I'm keeping an eye on her house while she is at her friends staying. She was in hospital for a couple of days, her friend Judy insisted that she go there and stay until after Christmas and New Year. She will be back to collect her mail from time to time she told me,' the neighbour informed Arlene.

'She has good friends then. How is your grandson doing after breaking his arm?' Arlene asked.'

'Good, he gets the cast off next week, I have told him time and time again to be careful on that bike, but will he listen.'

'Typical youngster,' Arlene answered as she popped what mail she had for May through her letterbox. 'See you later Annie,' she said walking out the gate.

'Let's see what she got,' Frank said to Anna.

They both thought themselves through the door and saw that there were two letters sitting on the carpet on top of each other. The one on top was from the hospital by the look of it; Frank carefully got a grip of the corner and lifted it up. The one on the bottom was addressed to The Occupier and gave no clue as to where it came from.

'Is there any point in taking this to Richard?' Frank asked still gripping the letter from the hospital. 'It might be something important that she needs to see.'

'Take it to her. Maybe if you take all her mail to Judy's house she might see that as a sign and come home.'

'I doubt it, but I will take this one to her, be right back.'

Frank disappeared and reappeared after a moment.

'I left it on her bed.'

'Ok, come on we will walk back around to my house the long way, the police have put up a new poster with mine and Jasmine's picture on it I want to show you.'

They left May's house and started on their walk, they walked slowly with plenty of time to kill. They didn't see the point in rushing. Sometimes when you are with someone and nothing is being said the silence can feel awkward, not with these two, they were at ease with each other and felt comfortable saying what was on their mind or staying quiet. They said nothing the entire way up Parson's Way and onto Main Street until Frank saw something a little disturbing to him.

'Hey check that out,' Frank said startled.

Anna looked to where Frank was pointing

across the road and had to do a double take to make sure she was seeing what was there. It was another soul, their make was black. Anna felt uneasy immediately. The black make soul was facing the other way; it was standing at the entrance to The Green looking in.

'They haven't seen us, maybe we should think ourselves to my house,' Anna said a little too late as Frank shouted to the soul.

'Hello there.'

The soul turned around slowly to reveal it was a man, of what age Anna could not determine from across the road. The man waved and started to cross over to them.

'What are you doing? Do you not see the colour of his make, he is bad news I can sense it,' Anna said.

'Let's just listen to what he has to say. We have the time.'

As the man moved closer Anna could see that he was around forty years old. He had dark eyes and hair, his skin was as paler than the driven snow and contrasted a little too much with his other features.

'Hi there,' he said as he reached them.

'Hi, I'm Frank, this is Anna.'

'My name is Gavin Peterson. I was killed ten months ago and came back down here around about the same time. I will tell you just now there is no way I can help either of you. My guide told me the rules and if I help anyone that means that I will have two shades added to my make, the problem is if I even get one more added then that's it I won't be allowed to make amends in The Before. I don't know what happens to souls that have darker makes than mine and I don't want to know, all I know is I have a lot to make up for and I truly want to do it wholeheartedly. My mission is not easy, I have ten years to complete it,' he said holding nothing back.

'Ten years, that's a long time. What is your mission? Frank asked.

'Well I not proud of this now, I was part of group, or if you would rather, a gang of sorts from Edinburgh. One of the gang members I was with, murdered a young man and he is buried right here in this park. Don't worry he was definitely not buried alive so you don't have to worry about that if you were told the same rules as me. My mission is to make sure the body is found.'

'How long has he been in there? Frank continued with his questioning.

'Nine years give or take. I don't know how to get him found. I think I have been given an impossible task, don't get me wrong I am not asking for your help, I can't. This is something I have to work out, though it's not easy. My guide told me I have a power that will help me; the thing is he would not tell me what it is. He said this is the price I pay for being so nasty in life. Can I ask you one question?'

'Sure,' Frank said.

'What is your power?'

'Mine is I can lift light or small objects, hide it under my make and move them to a different location and Anna's is she can connect with people when they are asleep through their subconscious.'

'I don't believe that counts as getting help so thank you for the information,' Gavin said as he walked away and crossed the road then disappeared into The Green.

'He is evil, it is plain to see. You should not have told him anything,' Anna said.

'That maybe so Anna, but if he is trying to be forgiven for all his deeds, maybe he needs all the help he can get. I'm not saying we will see him in The Realm anytime soon, if he can pull this off then he might just get there eventually.'

Anna pointed out the new poster of Jasmine and herself; they saw another two of them on the way to her house. When they arrived they settled in the spare room ready for a brainstorm to crack open both of their missions. They sat there in silence, just thinking of what they could do, nothing came to them.

'Tell me about your brother,' Anna said

'What do you want to know?'

'Everything.'

'Well he will be fifty-one next April same as me, we don't look alike, he is taller and slimmer. Our facial features are quite similar. To see us together you would not know that we were twins, brothers maybe. His wife is called Eloise who he met at school, childhood sweethearts. Their eldest is Sasha; she has a three year old boy called Liam with her partner Mark. Next is Alex and with his partner Simone share a two year old girl called Vicky. John is the youngest at eighteen who still lives with Richard and Eloise.'

'What do Richard and Eloise do for a living?'

'Richard is an electrician, Eloise is an accountant.'

'Do you know what your father's name was?'

'Yes, it was Frank Ritchie.'

'Oh my, that is where your mother got your names from.'

'Weird huh, Fenza told me he is buried in a graveyard in Pavesway, that's where his family come from. I want to find the grave; I know the consequences so I won't. The thing is I don't think his family ever met my mum, if they knew then surely they would have supported her. Her parents obviously didn't or she would have kept us.'

'You are in the dark about all of what went on Frank, I am sure all will be revealed to you one day.'

'I could ask Fenza, though I have a feeling her time is precious, so I won't bother her, as you say one day I will know it all.'

They sat there for the longest time saying nothing, deep in thought. They were only brought out of their thoughts by the back door being opened; it was Tom home from work. The room was dark, but a little light came in when Tom put the stair light on. Anna always liked the dark, when she was trying to sleep even the smallest amount of light would drive her insane, hence the blackout blinds and the curtains that she made herself. It was only now that she realised that she wanted light, dark was too depressing, she was used to sleeping in the shed with the light on now. Was it because she was dead? She did not know.

'Tom must have been working late tonight; he is usually home early on a Friday.'

'What are you up to tonight?'

'I'm going to the monsters to see if I can connect with Jack I have been meaning to do it and never got around to it, if I can then maybe I can guilt him into turning himself in.'

'It's a long shot, is it not?'

'Yes, what have I got to lose?'

'Point taken. I'm off to see Mum, will see you soon and remember keep that thinking cap on.'

Anna went down to see Tom before leaving to

wait out her time in the shed. He was sitting on the couch staring into space; he had no expression on his face it was as if he was empty of all emotion.

'You need to snap out of this. I am dead, you are not, you have a life to live,' Anna spoke to her husband as if he could hear her.

He needs closure. They need to find my body, only then will Tom and my family be able to move on. That is something else I will need to try to remedy before I go home to The Realm.

Anna spent time with Jasmine before she went to Billy. She said the same things she had already said to him time and time again. There was not much more she could do, she only hoped that it would eventually lead to the outcome she wanted. She had no luck with Jack and Candice; she said her name over and over to no avail, she didn't expect anything, it would have been something more to work on.

34
Monday 2nd December

PC McMillan and PC McCartney stood before Sergeant Rooney at his request.

'Good work from both of you; you are doing a great job. I know that there is nothing to go on, but keep at it. It is not the most glamorous side to police work, although it needs doing.'

'We know Sir; patience is the name of the game in some cases. Have you anything more on Mr Sutherland?' PC McMillan asked.

'No more than we already know, I don't have grounds to have him watched, or his house searched, although we will pay him another visit in a few days, let the posters sink in.'

Jasmine had Anna for company for most of the day even if she didn't know it. The young lady was starting to look huge; sure she wasn't getting any exercise which certainly would not be good for her, not just for putting on extra weight. Her muscles were not being used the way they were supposed to be. She didn't have much leeway in moving about; she could stand up and take one or two steps in each direction before the chain on her wrist stopped her which was no space at all. The skin on the wrist that was chained was bruised, dark brown bruises that looked like they had always been there, much the same as the dark circles she had under her eyes. She was too young to have such signs of age on her face; she had been through more heartache over the last few months than some go through in their whole life.

Anna went to Billy's; Kate had been good over the weekend, staying at the post at the spare bedroom window while Billy was at work. They were sitting in the living room; Anna checked the clock on the wall above where Kate sat it was 7.40 pm. She knew she would be far too early to come and disrupt Billy's sleep; she just wanted to find out how they were doing.

'What are we going to do with the information Billy? If we go to the police just now we will be laughed out the place. We have no evidence that any crime has been committed,' Kate said.

'I have an idea, before I tell you I don't want you to freak out.'

'What is it?'

'I'm going over there tomorrow night to have a look around. There is enough light coming from The Green to at least see where I am going, I want a closer look at that shed. What type of lock and what that door is made out of, I will take a small torch.'

'What if you get caught? We don't know what these people are capable of.'

'I won't get caught; anyway you will be at the window watching me to sound the alarm if anything happens.'

'I don't like it Billy, but I think it is the right thing to do, how else are we going to move forward with this if we just keep staring out that window?'

'Good it's settled then, bring on tomorrow night.'

I will be here tomorrow night for sure; I will be with Billy every step of the way. I agree with Kate they need to move forward, it is dangerous for Billy I know how terrible these people are.

35
Tuesday 3rd December

Anna was excited and scared that Billy was going to the Sutherlands' garden tonight.

What if he did get caught? Kate would be there right at the window keeping watch, sure she would call the police if anything happens, that could be too late for Billy. It didn't take long for them to murder me.

She hadn't seen Frank for a couple of days so she waited until early afternoon to go and see him.
'Hi Frank, long time no see' she said to him as he stood behind the chair that his mother was sitting in.
'Hello Anna, I was just coming to see you. I have good news. Mum is going home. She told Judy only five minutes ago that she was missing her own space, but would come back here for Christmas dinner and after much persuasion agreed to stay on Christmas night.'
'That's great news your mission can come off hold.'
'Wouldn't it be great if I reached The Before for Christmas? I'm not even sure if Christmas is celebrated up there.'
'That would be great,' Anna said with some sadness in her voice which Frank detected.
'You will get there too soon enough, maybe even before I do.'

'I don't want to be down here on my own Frank. If you are not here I will fail, I just know it.'

'You don't give yourself enough credit. If it wasn't for you my mission would be nonexistent. It was your idea to move the letters; I had been here for months and not thought of it. Look how far you have got and you have only been down here for what, a few weeks. Come on Anna you will ace this with or without me.'

'Billy is going over to the Sutherlands' garden to check out the shed,' Anna told him.

'I take it you will be there and of course I will be there too, I know I won't be able to do anything, I will be there anyway. Hey maybe if I try hard enough I could kind of haunt them if they come out,' Frank said with a laugh which in turn made Anna giggle.

'Thank you I would love for you to be there.'

'I will meet you at Billy's at say 10 o'clock tonight, can't see him going before then.'

'See you then.'

Anne went to visit her parents; she was impatient for night to come, so she decided she would go around her family to fill the time. George and Ruby were in the kitchen at the dining table sorting through a fresh batch of posters with Anna's picture on them.

They will never give up; I need to get them closure. They can't spend the rest of their lives like this, searching for me.

'How many people do we have to help us with this tomorrow,' Ruby asked George.

'Five including us, Helen, Robert and Will, Helen is bringing her car so we can split up and get them up in no time.'

'Where is she George?'

'I wish I knew. All I know is that we will never give up until we find her. I'm going to take Rex for a walk, you want to come?'

'Yes darling I will.'

Mum is still not back at work. This is all my fault, I should have let Rex out in the back garden that night, I have been through this in my head many times, if I did that then there would be no one to help Jasmine. Talk about a no win, no win situation.

Anna closed her eyes and thought of her sister. Clara was standing at the blackboard in front of a classroom full of children, Anna was glad to see it. Being a teacher was what Clara had always wanted to do; she had the brains to do it.

I am glad she is getting on with life, although I know I will be on her mind, she has Jamez to think about, she needs to keep things normal for her. Maybe she will move closer to Mum and Dad now that I am not there, the only reason she moved away in the first place is because she knew they had me close by.

Tom was next on the list for Anna to visit; he was busy plastering a wall with the radio on in the background. Paul was with him in the room.

'You had any word from the police?' Paul asked.

'They are doing what they can, I suppose just not enough to throw up any leads yet.'

'What about your holiday to Lanzarote? It's on Saturday Tom, you haven't mentioned it. Are you still going?'

'Of course not, I tried to talk George and Ruby into going, they are having none of it, and I don't blame them.'

'Put it on Facebook. You might get a buyer for it.'

'A bit late for that don't you think.'

'Not at all, there is always someone looking for a bargain, just don't ask too much because if someone wants it, it will cost them to change the names. Are you coming in to work next week or are you still taking it off?'

'Do you need me in?'

'Always need an extra pair of hands; you know that, if you'd rather take the time, I'm not going to stop you.'

'I will come in, no point sitting around for the week, moping and giving myself too much time to think of all the bad things that could have happened to Anna.'

'I don't envy you. I don't know what would be running through my head if it was me, I can't even begin to imagine what you are going through.'

'It's a nightmare that I can't wake up from; I should have treated her better. It should have been me that took Rex for his walk that night.'

'Stop blaming yourself, what happened has happened, there is nothing you can do to change it.'

'That's the problem Paul, I don't know what happened.'

It's the not knowing what happened that is eating my family up. If they knew then they could grieve and maybe put all this behind them. I don't think they will be the same. They could learn to live with it if the ones responsible get what is coming to them.

Jasmine was crying again when Anna returned to the young woman's prison.

Crying again. I wonder what is going through her mind. I wonder if she knows that they will dispose of her when the baby is born. She must suspect it; maybe that's why she is crying more and more frequent, she knows that her time is running out.

Anna stayed with Jasmine until long after she was given her dinner and her toilet was changed. A new book was also delivered to her, Jasmine seemed grateful for it; she needed something to take her mind off the situation she found herself in. Anna knew this would be short lived as nothing was going to make Jasmine forget about her circumstances. Sure she could lose herself in the story for a while, as soon as she looked away from the pages the sad reminder of how her life was being wasted was all around her.

Billy and Kate were in the spare room when Anna arrived at 9.10 pm.
'I wish we could see into the shed, even with these binoculars the door is just at the wrong angle,' Kate moaned.
'If we could see into the shed the game would be up, we would know everything that we needed to know, nothing is ever easy,' Billy said.
'Are you sure you want to do this tonight?'
'Yes, I am going to take Buster a walk at eleven, walk past their house and make sure that all the lights are out, come back here drop the dog in and go straight over the fence there,' he said pointing out in the near dark at the building that was the Sutherlands' garage. 'That space at the back of the garage is perfect for not being seen, there are bushes all along their back fence that shares the border with The Green, if anyone comes out then I think I can get in between a couple of the bushes and hide. If that fails then

I will jump the fence over into The Green and make a run for it, no one is none the wiser.'
'You make it sound easy, but be careful and don't take any chances.'
'I won't, you will be watching anyway to make sure.'
'You bet I will and take what you get when you get back if you try anything stupid.'
Anna loved the relationship they had; they put her in mind of her parents the way they spoke to each other. Kate and Billy supported each other fully and you only had to see them together to see how smitten they are with each other.
'What if the lights are still on when you take the dog a walk?'
'Then I will wait until they are off, no matter how long it takes. I will take Buster out every hour if I need to, I must get a peek in that garden and a nosey at that shed tonight Kate.'
'Ok, I hear you.'
They sat there in silence straining their eyes out into their neighbours' garden, waiting and hoping for something different to happen, for something to take place that would tell them that there was something criminal going on over there.
'Hello Anna,' it was Frank showing up just like he said he would. 'It's ten o'clock on the dot, how long have they been sitting here?'

'I don't know. They were here before I showed up.'

'What time is he going over?'

Anna filled him in on the plan that Billy had told Kate.

'Well we can only hope that he sees something useful,' Frank said.

'I think maybe I should spend more of my time with the Sutherlands, I couldn't even tell you where they keep the key for the shed, I should know where it is and what kind of lock is on the shed door, but I don't know. I have neglected to find all these things out; these are things that I could have passed on to Billy, or tried to at least.'

'Make a point of it then, spend as much time as you can with them, just don't let their evilness have any effect on you.'

'I don't think that is possible. When is your mum coming home?'

'She's home already, so mission move all the mail I can move continues tomorrow with vigour.'

'When are you moving the photo then? Have you given it much thought?'

'Yes it's all I have been thinking about, I don't know, when the time feels right, whenever that may be.'

'The Sutherlands need to be caught for Jasmine and for the sake of my family they need to be caught for me too, so when the time is right you will need to give Jasmine that name tag back, it's the only proof that I was in that shed.'

'If Jasmine, sorry when Jasmine is rescued then she will be a witness not just that you were there, but to the murder and what about Billy? You know how much he searched for it the last time we took it.'

'I know. I will need to try and tell him when he is asleep, nearer the time of course that it is going to disappear again. I know Jasmine witnessed it all, I worry about what the police might think of her state of mind, if she has that name tag then they will need to believe her.'

'You have a point I suppose.'

Frank and Anna joined in on Kate and Billy's silence. Time seemed to have come to a halt. Anna paced up and down which she was doing a lot of lately.

'Right that's 10.55 I'm off out with Buster,' Billy announced to the delight of Anna.

Billy was away twenty minutes before he came back in the door.

'Right Kate, it's now or never. The lights in the house are out, if anything happens to me call the police, do not under any circumstances come over there. Do you hear me?' Billy commanded.

'I hear you darling, be safe.'

Billy kissed his wife, picked up a small torch

that was lying on the spare bed and left the house. He was all in black including hat and gloves. It was cold and wet so he had it in his mind that he was going to do this as quickly as possible. He went to the back corner of this garden and jumped over the fence into the garden of his neighbour to the left of him. He went to the fence where at the other side would be at the back of the Sutherlands' garage and climbed over. The grass was sodden underfoot, but he had suitable footwear on for the occasion. He landed awkwardly and went over on his left ankle; he shrugged it off and continued. Billy was not tall, kept low anyway, staying close to the bushes along the back fence. Kate was glued to his every move, what she could see of him, she could barely make him out shuffling along the garden, she could see enough to know where he was. Frank was with Billy, Anna stood at the shed door waiting for Billy to get there. When Billy reached the shed he pulled out the small torch from his pocket, had a glance around at the house, saw nothing so switched on the torch holding it as close to the lock on the door as possible. It was a wooden door on the brick shed; the door was newer than the shed. The lock was a typical one, or it was to Billy, he was no expert. There was also a padlock three inches below. He moved to the left hand side of the shed and started doing a tour of the circumference. The ground underfoot was uneven; this side of the shed had trees along the fence. Even though the leaves had already left the trees the branches were right against this side of the shed, forcing Billy to push his way through until he got to the back of the shed where he had a little more room. More bushes here, not as rough as the side, he came right down the other side and back to the door, took one more look at the door then made his way home the same way he had come.

'The shed is brick all the way around it with no windows at all. The door is wooden with a normal key lock and a padlock a few inches below it,' Billy told an eager Kate.

'How is this going to help us?'

'It doesn't, I want to break in then we will get to the bottom of this,'

'Are you crazy? You have never broken into anything in your life.'

'I know, I was thinking, maybe Jamie could give me some pointers.'

'Jamie McLaughlin?'

'Yes.'

'What has he ever broken into Billy? He is hardly skilled at breaking and entering.'

'What are you forgetting about Jamie?' Billy asked and stared at her waiting for the penny to drop.

Kate was frowning, the lines on her forehead

deepened by the process, looking at Billy as if to find the answer on his face. Then it clicked.

'He's a locksmith, I forgot,' Kate said with no jubilation in her voice that she had got it. 'You are not breaking in there, that's an end to it.'

'It won't hurt to talk to Jamie anyway, would it?'

'No, but let me make myself clear, you are not breaking in. Now come on it's time for bed.'

Kate left the room, Billy followed.

'See I should know where the keys are, I should know more about that shed than I do,' Anna said to Frank, who was staring out the window into the suspect garden.

'And what good would it do for you to know where the keys are?'

'You could move a key.'

'The Sutherlands won't let that key out of their sight, they will have it on them, there is too much at stake for them to be flippant about where they put it.'

'There I go again not thinking things through I'm sorry Frank, maybe I am depending on your power too much.'

'It's there for your use anytime. We just need to make sure what we do is for the best.'

'You got it; I'm going for a sleep. See you tomorrow?'

'Try and stop me.'

36
Friday 6th December

Sergeant Rooney sat at his desk deep in thought. The posters that he had asked the two PC's to put up had been up for days now, he presumed that Mr Sutherland would have seen then so he decided it was time to pay Mr Sutherland a visit, that would need to wait until later when he was sure the man would be in. Inspector Halliday popped his head in the door and motioned for Rooney to go for a coffee, the sergeant looked at the clock on his desk and thought now would be a good time for breakfast. Once the two policemen were seated in the canteen, the sergeant with cornflakes and coffee and the inspector with biscuits and coffee they discussed the case.

'Where are we on Anna Ross Stephen? Aird is coming in on Monday, thought I would give you a heads up.'

'I have no leads; the two PC's are still doing their door to doors. They have got nowhere as yet,'

Rooney said missing out the suspicions about Jack Sutherland. He knew they had nothing concrete on him; it would be foolish to mention it.

'They are still doing that?'

'Well they are nearly finished, they had a lot of doors to knock. It is just the two of them.'

'That's true. Many hands make light work. We just didn't have the resources to put more on it. There are other cases to deal with.'

'Oh I know; however, the two PC's are doing a thorough job, I trust they will not miss a trick,' Rooney assured the inspector.

'If a job is worth doing it's worth doing right,' Halliday said without even realising he had dropped another proverb.

'The mystery will be solved sooner or later; two women from one town, the truth will come out.'

'Well let's hope it is sooner,' Halliday said standing up with half his coffee intact. 'I will take this to my desk, forgot I have a call to make.'

Rooney sat there for a while even after he had finished his breakfast. He had the feeling that the only reason Halliday invited him for coffee was to mention that Aird was coming and to warn him he better have something for her. Halliday had not said it directly, although that is what he meant.

Jamie McLaughlin had agreed to come see his friend Billy before his wife Kate got home from work. Billy was back at work tomorrow; he wanted to find out if Jamie could help him have a peek in that shed without breaking in. Jamie showed up at 2.05 pm.

'Thanks for coming, I have an odd request that I don't want to explain, I know it is a lot to ask without even telling you why, I need to get a look in one of my neighbours' shed.'

Billy took Jamie into the spare room and pointed out the shed.

'You are not telling me why?'

'I can't in fear of sounding crazy, believe me I have good reason, at least in my head it is a good reason.'

'Are the people in just now?'

'No, but it is daylight. You aren't thinking of just walking over there right now are you?'

'I need a good look so yes I am. I will walk in the front gate as is if I am supposed to be there, I will have my tools with me, it will seem to anyone that sees me that I am there to do a job. Be back in five.'

Billy watched as Jamie brazenly went to the shed door with his bag to have a look. As promised he was back soon.

'The padlock is not a problem; the other lock is what we call a Mortice Sashlock. I can't do that one without maybe a little damage which means the owner knowing.'

'It was worth a shot, do you want a coffee for your trouble?'

'Sure, and a biscuit if there is one going, need to keep the strength up. I don't know why you need to get into that shed, I'm not going to pressure you into telling me, you obviously don't want me to know, just don't do anything stupid.'

'I won't, not yet anyway.'

The two old friends spent the next hour catching up before Jamie got a call and had to go.

Moving any mail that his mother got to his brother's house was easy for Frank. The problem was that the letters were few. He had moved the same letter twice in the last few days, Richard must have put it back into the post box after he had received it, Frank was ready to take it back to him fifty times if it meant getting this mission finished and getting to The Before. The days were getting longer, the boredom was hitting a peak, sure he had Anna, but she had her own things to deal with. She was spending most of her days at Billy's or with Jasmine. When the Sutherlands were at home at night she was spending her time with them. He could hardly blame her; she was more determined to get to The Before than he was.

The sergeant did not tell anyone that he was going to pay Mr Sutherland a visit, he would tell the two PCs of the outcome one way or another. Rooney waited until 7.30 pm before he knocked on the door on Main Street to be sure he was going to get an answer and indeed he did, he had the photos of the two women at the ready. The door was opened by Jack, Anna was right there beside him, but of course no one knew that. Over the last few days she had learned quite a lot about the Sutherlands, spending time with them had paid off in wisdom.

'Good evening Sir, I am following up on a door to door inquiry that is taking place in the area,' Rooney said politely handing over the photos.

'Ah the missing women, I told the other police that were here that I couldn't help.'

'So they have been here?'

'Yes, I was a little distracted when they were here, must have thought I was extremely rude and uninterested. My wife was out and I had something in the oven and I was waiting on an important phone call, you could say I was doing a fair bit of juggling,' Jack lied with a charm rarely seen from him.

'I'm here knocking on a few doors just to make sure that this area has been screened properly by the two PCs, we tend to check up on the people who are doing the checking,' Rooney lied this time.

'Nothing wrong with being thorough I suppose. My wife is in tonight, she has already seen the photos at the doctors' surgery where she works. The two young police were there last week.'

Candice came to the door; she had been listening to every word that had been said and decided that a little theatrics wouldn't go amiss. 'Jack why didn't you give me a shout, I thought it was the milkman collecting his money. Are you here about those poor women?' she asked Rooney.

'Yes, as I told your husband I'm just here checking on the checkers.'

'I have seen all the posters in the area, it makes you wonder where the both of them could possibly be, there were two young officers in my place of work just last week showing the photos to us. I know that Jasmine had been at an appointment at the surgery the day she went missing. I wasn't there at the time; it was my day to finish early. I'm sorry here I am talking away good style, would you like to come in?'

'No that won't be necessary Mrs...'

'Sutherland Candice Sutherland and this is Jack my other half.'

'Well it was good to meet you. If you do see or hear anything then please give us a call,' Rooney said.

'Of course we will,' Jack answered for them both.

The Sutherlands went into the kitchen where Candice poured out some fresh coffee, and sat at the table.

'Do you still think they know something?' Candice asked Jack.

'I don't think so; he declined your invitation to

come in. If he suspected us of anything I don't think he would have passed up that opportunity. It was a smart move to invite him in, I didn't think so at the time, now I do.'

'Sometimes you need to trust me; a little charm goes a long way.'

'I don't feel great about all this it is no secret, but now we have settled on a concrete plan I am feeling a little better, especially the part that you are going to do the bad deed with Jasmine and not me. That was the worst part that had been playing on my mind, I know I killed that other women, I never want to go down that road again.'

'I told you, you don't need to, I will do whatever it takes.'

Anna knew that Jasmine was going to be killed unless she and Billy could stop them. The Sutherlands had discussed the whole plan the night before, it seemed they had thought of everything or at least Candice had. Anna knew everything. She was right there when it was all being discussed. The country house they were moving to that belonged to Jack's Uncle Fred was being vacated on the twentieth of January by the tenant. Candice was going to hand her notice in at the Surgery over the next week as she wanted to give them time to find someone else; she would be finishing up work on the seventeenth of January. Jack had already told John

Morrison of his plans; he was ready to step into Jack's shoes whenever he was needed. All going well they would move Jasmine to the new house on January twenty-fourth where Candice would take care of her alone until Jack would come after he disposed of all the incriminating evidence in that shed and the shed itself. They wanted to leave no trace of Jasmine anywhere. They wouldn't need a shed where they were going; the closest neighbour was half a mile away, so Jasmine would not be heard even from inside the house even if she screamed her head off. Candice reckoned the baby would be due in February or early March at the latest and would get everything she needed when they moved. They seemed to have everything under control. Jack would drive the van with Jasmine in the back, Candice would follow in her car, she needed to make sure she could get out to the shops and not depend on having things delivered. The last thing she needed was people coming to the house before the baby was born. Once the baby was born they would tell what family and friends they have that they adopted. Up until then they would put off any friends or family that wanted to visit by saying that they were going on holiday or doing work in the house.

Not everything will go as they planned, for one

hopefully Billy will see the van being loaded up with Jasmine, that is if he hasn't solved all this by then, or if I can keep him interested, although I have a feeling he is totally invested in this now.

Rooney sat in his car for a few minutes before pulling away, he hoped that there would be something to chase here, the invitation into the home made up his mind about that, if they had something to hide then he would not have been asked in. Didn't mean the man wasn't up to something without her knowledge though; he thought it unlikely by the fact that he explained his actions the evening the two PCs were at his door. Mr Sutherland for the time being was in the clear, although he would not be completely forgotten by the sergeant; he can't just ignore the gut instinct of an officer after all.

Although Billy was up for work in the morning Anna still paid him a visit. Over the past few nights she had been trying to get the message through to him that the name tag would go missing again and that he was not to worry about it. That it would help and was for the best. She went over all the stuff she had done previously, it was a routine she had to keep up. After the first night she had told him about the name tag she was there with him the next day when he checked the window sill in the spare room, it was there, he just shrugged, so Anna presumed this meant that he had got the message, yet she could not be sure, time would tell.

37
Monday 9th December

Sergeant Stephen Rooney watched the rain pelting down outside the big widow from his desk. He knew the chief inspector had been in the building since 8.30 am, it was now 9.35, he knew it was only a matter of time until he was summoned to the conference room. He did not have to wait long, a few moments later the phone on his desk rang.

'Stephen, how are you this miserable morning?' Chief Inspector Laura Aird asked as Rooney entered the room.

'Not too bad Ma'am,' Rooney answered and sat down next to Inspector Halliday.

It was just the three of them in the room and Rooney was glad, he didn't need more of an audience when he told the chief that he had no leads in the missing women cases.

'So how are things?' Aird asked Rooney.

'Well we are on the brink of solving a spate of burglaries, hoping to make an arrest before the week is out. There is fair bit of vandalism going on, we have had numerous reports. It seems to be school kids by the sound of it. We will be sending a couple of PCs around the local schools to see what we can find out. I know the case you want to know about is the missing women, the truth of the matter is I don't have anything to go on,' Rooney said with a heavy heart.

'Is the door to doors not bringing anything in?'

'Not so far. Two separate, fresh appeals were put on social media this morning.'

'I want you to go through both cases from scratch, Detective Inspector Norman Mathieson will help you out, don't get me wrong you are still lead on the case, Norman will not be on this with you full time, but he can help. Talk to everyone that you did before and anyone that you think you should. Now, I know we got a warrant to see Jasmine's medical records because we know she was at the doctors' the day she vanished, we are not at liberty to reveal she is pregnant, but I think it maybe be time to tell her parents. What do you think?'

'They are in a bad place especially Mrs Brown, I think this may send her over the edge, the contents of her medical records is off limits, it's the rules.'

'Oh I think the way things stand, with it being, how many months since she was last seen, that we should perhaps bend these rules, ignore procedure and let her parents know. I know it won't be easy for them to hear, I think they have a right to know.'

'The truth hurts,' Inspector Halliday piped up for the first time since Rooney entered the room.

'That it does, I will tell them myself, and tell

them to keep the information under wraps,' Rooney said.

'That would be wise. You have my full support.'

Rooney took that as a sign the meeting was over and left the room to get reacquainted with all the details they had on the two cases. Rooney had sat at his desk the whole day apart from a break for a late lunch, making a list of people that he had to revisit. At the end of his shift, he changed out of his uniform and went to see Jasmine's parents. He thought that the news he was about to break needed a more personal touch.

'Oh sergeant I hardly recognised you without your uniform. Have you news of Jasmine? Phil Brown asked when he answered the door.

'Not on her whereabouts as yet. Can I come in?'

'Yes, sorry, of course,' Phil said holding the door open for him.

They went into the living room where Sheila was sitting watching TV.

'Who was it?' she asked turning to see Rooney.

'Sergeant it's you. Have you news on Jasmine?'

'We still don't know where she is. There is something that we would like to tell you about her condition when she vanished.'

'What is it? Tell us,' Sheila said impatiently.'

'She is pregnant or at least we know she was at the time of her disappearance,' Rooney revealed unwillingly.

'Pregnant, how far along is she? Why weren't we told at the time?' Sheila exploded with a string of questions.

'We don't know how far along she is, so we don't know if the baby has been born. We got a warrant to get access to her medical records because we knew Jasmine was at the doctors' the day she went missing. She had not been for a scan yet. You did not mention to us that you knew about the pregnancy and we were not at liberty to divulge that information.'

'So why are you telling us now?' Phil said.

'I am going to be honest with you, we are getting nowhere. I am starting from the beginning again with both Jasmine and with the other woman that is missing from this area. Do you think Jasmine ran away because she was pregnant, maybe scared to tell you?'

'No, no way. She would never have done that. Yes I admit she may have been a little apprehensive to tell us, after all she was young and just about to start college. Run away, out of the question,' Sheila stated.

Sheila got up from where she was sitting and left the room.

'That was maybe something you should have kept from us. This will set her back. She will worry even more now if that is possible,' Phil said.

'It was not my decision; my superiors thought

that maybe it could shine a light on why she disappeared. We need to explore all the reasons and facts.'

'Well it gives us something to think about. Is Glen the father? That was a stupid question, how is anyone meant to know that, he doesn't know. If she had told him surely he would have said something about it.'

'I will speak to him and everyone else again. In the meantime you cannot share this information with him or anyone else; it is for your ears only.

'Understood sergeant, now if you will excuse me I will need to go and try to comfort my wife.'

Rooney left them feeling disappointed. He knew they were not going to be happy about it, he wished that maybe it would ignite some idea as to where their daughter may have went, a revelation perhaps. Far too much to ask in a case like this, when they had a chance to digest the news if they had any ideas they would contact him.

Frank was with the postwoman all morning waiting for any mail that he could shift. He managed to get one from his mum's to Richard's and vice versa. His patience was wearing thin going through the same routine every day. The sooner he got this done the sooner he could move on. He found Anna in the shed just where he expected.

'Hello there,' Frank said to his soul mate.

'Hey there,' she responded sullenly.'

'What's up?'

'Check out Jasmine, she has been sitting there staring into space for hours, no crying, she hasn't touched her lunch or even drank her tea, and she loves tea. I think she is finally broken,' Anna stated pointing to the sandwich and flask on the floor by the bed.

'Poor girl, no wonder she is like that, all this is taking its toll on her. Did she eat her breakfast?'

'Yes, since then she has been like this, she needs to eat, it is not good for the baby to stop eating.'

'Anna it is one meal, I don't think it will have much effect skipping one lunch.'

'So far it is one meal; I just hope it doesn't last. I don't know, I think she looks angry today as if she has taken all she can take and is ready to explode; she has a strange demeanour about her. I should know I have spent a lot of time with her.'

'I would have exploded long ago being cooped up in this hell hole. Come on let's go for a walk, you need some time out of here.'

'Sure, why not.'

They walked the same route they usually took, down by Anna's along to May's and back up on to Main Street. They never spoke of their missions for a change, instead opted to talk about

The Before and The Realm. They both had ideas of what these two wonderful places were going to be like. They shared their views and hopes, taking it in turn to share their aspirations of what lay ahead. When they reached the Sutherlands' gate they stood for a while still deep in conversation, until Jack showed up in his van.

'He is home early; I wonder what time it is? I'm going in, are you coming?'

'Of course I am.'

It was 3.10 pm on the clock in the kitchen. Jack answered Anna's question of what he was doing home so early without saying a word. As soon as he entered the house he ran straight for the toilet and by the sounds that the two friends heard Jack had an upset stomach.

'This might sound silly, it sounds as if it is going to stink in there,' Frank said straight faced.

Anna roared with laughter, Frank joined in; they giggled and sniggered every time they heard another noise from the toilet. This went on for a while before Jack retreated from the bathroom pale and sweating.

'Deserves everything he gets,' Anna declared.

'You got that right. I'm off back to Mum's if you need me you know where to find me.'

Anna stayed where she was in the Sutherlands. Jack went to bed, he was up every half hour running to the toilet.

I hope it was not something that he ate in the house that is causing him this trouble. Jasmine eats the same as them almost, the last thing that girl needs is a bout of whatever it is that he has.

The idea to look for the keys to that damn shed had vacated her until now. There was a set of key hooks on the wall near the back door with three different sets on it, none of which looked as if they would fit the bill. One set had two Yale keys, another had three Yale keys and the third was a spare key for a car.

I don't even know what good it does for me to know where the keys are, it's not as if I could use them. Even If I managed to tell Billy where they are that means Billy would need to break in here before he could gain access to the shed, getting him into even more trouble. No it wouldn't, if he got into that little prison he would call the cops right away, get Jasmine and the Innocent rescued. He would be a hero. No the monsters use them three or four times a day, they must keep them close. Maybe they even have a set each, which would make sense, if they lose a set then the other would still have theirs. They must keep those keys on them. I know if I was evil enough to do what they have done then I would be keeping the keys on me, safeguarding them at all times.

Jack shouted on Candice as soon as he heard the door being open and closed. She went into the bedroom to find Jack pale, weak and in total misery.

'What is wrong with you?' she asked.

'Food poisoning I think. Had the runs since lunchtime, barely managed to make it home earlier. I had a burger yesterday as did John from a van near the site; he is the same as me.'

'I will get you some water just now; we might need to phone NHS 24 to get you an antibiotic, I take it you don't want dinner tonight?'

'Oh definitely not, that's the last thing on my mind.'

'I handed in my notice today. The plan is well and truly in motion. Right I will get the dinner on and then see to Jasmine.'

Anna shadowed Candice in the kitchen. Candice made an easy dinner, roast beef ready meals. Anna followed Candice to the shed and stayed there while Jasmine ate her dinner; she discarded the chocolate bar, but drank some of the tea from the flask that Candice had provided. Anna was glad that Jasmine had eaten her dinner, although she could see that her mood had not lifted. An hour later Candice was back with a fresh toilet.

'I will be back soon with wash stuff for you, wanted to give you a change of clothes, Jack is ill so it will have to wait, sorry,'

Jasmine didn't answer her; she just glared at her until she left.

I think more anger is building up inside this girl. As if she could get anymore irate. At least she has stopped crying, come to think of it I don't know if that is a good thing or a bad thing. Her hormones must be raging; it must be bedlam inside her head. What would be going through my head if I were her? She must know that they are going to have to get rid of her after the baby is born, she would be naive to think otherwise. Giving birth should be a joyous occasion for any mother, not for Jasmine it is a death warrant. I know I was murdered and this girl will be too, I didn't know in advance, she does. She is most definitely stressed beyond belief.

Candice came back with her water, soap and a towel. She laid them down in easy reach for Jasmine then left her alone once more. Anna went over to Billy's, Billy was not in. Kate was on duty at the window. She had the notebook in her hand, Anna peeked over her shoulder to see what she had written, the only light was coming from the hall, they leave the bedroom door open a little to give them some light in the room, not too much that someone would see them looking out. It wasn't enough to quite make out what was written. She saw that there was a small torch sitting on the floor at Kate's feet.

They must use that when they have something to

report in their book. Well Candice has been out at that prison a couple of times tonight already I hope they have noted all that. It can't be easy for Billy and Kate spending all this time doing this. They don't know what all this is about; I admire the both of them for what they have given to this.

At 10 pm Anna came back to Billy after spending a little time with Jasmine and visiting the monsters. Jack was in bed, so there was no conversation to listen in to in there. Kate and Billy were seated in the living room taking a well deserved break from their post at the window. Anna felt bad when she heard what they were saying.

'The holiday will just need to wait Billy.'

'I know, but we always go in January. I know that what we are doing might be important, or at least we are hoping it is. It's just that it would be good to get away.

'We will get a holiday as soon as we figure this out, whether it turns out to be of importance or not we will see this thing through to the end. Can you honestly tell me that you would be able to go on holiday and be able to relax, without giving a hoot about that shed?'

'You are right I wouldn't, you know me so well. I feel we have this huge responsibility and we don't know what it is or how to deal with it properly, it's like a burden, like a weight around my neck. There is something to discover over there of that I am sure. I only wish I knew precisely what it is and what to do about it because I can't wait to find out and get this whole episode behind me.'

'Billy, that was deep, I feel the same way. We will put this behind us, until then we will do what we need to.'

Anna hung about listening to them until they retired for the night. Billy fell asleep; she spoke the words she had said to him many times now about The Innocent and the recent addition of the name tag. She went back to Jasmine who was sleeping, so she spoke to her as well, trying to reassure her that all that could be done was being done and hoped that it was getting through to her.

38
Friday 13th December

Rooney stepped out of the house to a strong, bitterly cold wind gusting in his face, locked the door behind him and went to his car parked at the kerb, climbed inside and starting it up. The old, blue Ford Mondeo that he bought brand new way back in 2006 coughed and sputtered to life. It was time for an upgrade, he knew it. The engine warning light had been on for a few weeks now and was going to a local garage that his friend owns in the morning. The MOT was due at the end of April, he was planning on keeping it until then, but that depended on what his friend had to say about its condition. The problem was that he had a certain amount of sentiment for the car; it reminded him of his wife as he purchased it not long before they had got together, he had memories of them together in it.

He arrived at the station at 7.30 am, went in, changed and was at his desk for eight o'clock to collect the list of people that he needed to speak to in connection with the Anna Ross case. PC McMillan was to accompany him today, he was happy about that. He liked her, thought she had a great future ahead of her in the police force. They had already tackled the Jasmine Brown case this week, they had spoke to the people in the doctor's and the chemist, the last two places she was seen, they never learned any more than they already knew. Jasmine's parents were revisited; Sheila was not up to talking to the sergeant again. Phil informed him without too many words that they did not want to be bothered again until they had any solid information on the whereabouts of their daughter, Rooney could not blame them. They had put all their trust in the police finding their child and after all these months they were still in the dark. The door to doors on the cases had resulted in a big waste of time. Detective Inspector Mathieson as promised had a look at the details on the two cases; there was not a thing he could see that had not been seen already. PC McMillan approached Rooney's desk.

'You ready to get this done Sir?'

'Yes, there are not that many people to see to be honest, don't even know if anyone will be in, but yes I am ready. Before we start with the talking let's do some walking. I want to go the route that Anna was presumed to have gone that night. See if there is something that could have been overlooked.'

'You are the boss, boss.'

They went straight to Anna's house, got out the car and started on the route, walking slowly, taking in everything. Daylight was still not fully here; it wasn't dark by any means, at this time of the year it always seemed as if light was never fully engaged. They walked the route until they came to the Sutherlands' house, they paused outside.

'We were sure that man was hiding something,' PC McMillan said.

'I know. I've told you I went back and the two of them couldn't be any more open with me, it's good to follow your gut though Nicole, it will help in future cases believe me.'

'Are we going to see Billy Barclay first Sir?'

'Might as well since we are here.'

They knocked on the door at Parkway Lane. Billy answered the door right away. He had his jacket on and a dog lead in his hand, Buster was at his heels.

'What can I do for you?' Billy asked.

'We are doing a follow up on the missing woman Anna Ross,' Rooney told him.

'Come in please, the dog walking will just have to wait a while.'

Billy held the door open for them and let Buster out into the garden.

'That will just have to do him for the time being,' he said as he climbed the stairs behind the two police taking his jacket back off.

They settled in the living room, the two officers glad to be out of the cold for a spell.

'I told you all I know about that night,' Billy started the conversation.

'We are just double checking everything, so far we nothing to go on; until we get some sort of lead on the case it is at a standstill,' Rooney said.

Billy was tempted to mention the shed, but feared he might sound loopy, if the Sutherlands did have some sort of pet in there, like a snake. What would be their crime going out there a few times a day? They could not be done for looking after a pet so well. No he would keep his mouth shut until he had something solid to go on. If only the shed was at a different angle, when the Sutherlands opened the door then maybe they could get a better view in there with the binoculars, as it was they could not see inside to confirm that anything wrong was going on.

'Could you go over your story with us please?' PC McMillan asked.

Billy recounted every detail he could remember about that night, wishing with every word that he had walked Anna home. It did him no good to think like that, to wish that he had done something different. He was not psychic, there was no way he could have predicted what was going to happen. He still felt guilty that he was the last person to see her. After Billy had refreshed his statement the police walked back to their car outside Anna's house then went to see her parents. There was no point on knocking on Tom's door they knew he would be at work.

Ruby seemed pleased to see them when she answered the door, Rex was with her. He was wagging his tail looking for affection.
'Please come in. I will put the kettle, it's a miserable day I'm sure you could do with a cuppa.'
'That would be great Mrs Anderson,' Rooney said.
'Call me Ruby, please.'
Ruby led them into the living room then shouted up the stair for George to come down.
'Have you any news?' Ruby asked while waiting on her husband.
'Sorry, we are here to go through the case again,' Rooney explained.
George came into the living room, asked the same question that Ruby had and got the same answer. Ruby went into the kitchen to make the coffee leaving George to entertain their guests until she got back. Once everyone was seated and everyone had some coffee Rooney started on the subject of their daughter.
'So Anna was here the night she went missing?'
'That's right. She told me in confidence that she thought Tom was having an affair, which we have found out since then he was,' Ruby said.
'I know we have been through all this, I am going to ask again. 'Is it possible that Anna

could have gone away on her accord to get away from Tom or maybe to punish him, let him sweat a bit,' Rooney asked.

'The answer is the same as the last time, no she would never do that to us, to Tom perhaps, if she was sure that he was having an affair, at that time it was just a suspicion, she didn't know what we know now. If she had gone to punish him then she would have contacted us to let us know she was alright, tell us what was going on,' George answered.

'When were Tom and Anna meant to go on holiday?'

'Oh that has past, Tom cancelled it just days before they were due to go, he hoped that she would come back and they would be able to go, in reality he kind of knew that it wasn't to be. Even if she did turn up we would have told her about the affair, she would not have gone with him in that case. I'm not saying that she would not have tried to work things out with him, she loves him dearly. I just don't think she would have gone that holiday. He even asked us to go, it was out of the question,' Ruby said.

'We were hoping to get a lead from somewhere to point us in the right direction; the posters and social media have come to nothing so far. Until there is any new information I'm afraid we are at a crossroads so to speak,' PC McMillan said, much to the relief of Rooney.

'We understand. Is there nothing at all more you can do?' Ruby pleaded.

'I am going to see if we can get it back on the news for a fresh appeal, both Anna and the other woman that is missing from the area,' Rooney said.

'She must be somewhere. Someone knows something,' George stated.

'Yes indeed, we just need to find out whom, be assured we will not stop until we find her.' Rooney said.

There was not much more to be said so the sergeant and the PC left the house, returned to their car.

'People go missing all the time. Some are found safe and sound, some are found dead and some are never found at all. It's a crazy world we live in; I hope for their sake that we find Anna safe and sound, as the time goes on it is getting less and less likely. If only I was psychic,' Rooney said to the PC.

'If only, that would be helpful, it would also put most of us out of a job.'

They returned to the station where Rooney went to Inspector Halliday to get a fresh appeal on the news arranged.

When Frank reached his mother's house while following Arlene the postwoman, he found Anna waiting for him. Arlene posted the one letter for May; Frank picked it up straight away, put it under his make before May walked out into the hall to collect her post. She saw no letters on her carpet and with a confused look went back into the kitchen.

'She must have heard the letterbox go,' Frank said then had a quick glance at the letter. 'It's the same one that I moved two days ago; Richard is putting them back in the post box.'

'They will come here sometime to see the owner I'm sure, maybe it's time to move the photo,' Anna suggested.

'Not yet, Eloise thinks something strange is happening, it is, although I want her to be more curious. I want her to be a little spooked about the amount of letters they are getting for May Simpson.'

'You are wicked Frank Wood,' Anna said with a smile which in turn made Frank smile.

'You bet I am. How are things with Jasmine?'

'She is still the same; she needs a pick me up. That's where you come in. Think it is time you gave her back the name tag if you don't mind.'

'What about Billy won't he search for it again?'

'I have been connecting with him a lot about that, telling him that it will go missing again and not to look for it, that it will be where it is supposed to be. I hope I have done enough to convince him.'

'If you are sure we are doing the right thing this

time then I will do what you ask. I will take this to Richard, then get the name tag and meet you in the shed.'

'Sounds like a plan.'

Anna was only in the shed for two minutes when Frank appeared.

'Before I do this are you sure?'

'Yes, I think it will be good for her, maybe re-ignite a little hope.'

Jasmine was sitting under the duvet with her back to the wall at the top of the bed with her full attention on the book in her hand. Frank quickly got the disk out and tossed it on the middle of the bed. Jasmine felt it land because she immediately looked at it. Her eyes widened as she stared in disbelief at what she was seeing. She swiftly snatched it up and started crying. She held it up to her mouth and kissed it as if it was the most treasured procession she had ever had.

'How can this be? This cannot be happening,' Jasmine said through tears of joy.

She held it flat in the palm of her hand and checked the name on it was the same, then turned it over to check the other side.

'It is, it is the same one, but the bed was changed and it has been so long, how could it just turn up like this? Baby I have it back, we have our disc back, we have our proof that the lady was here,' Jasmine said rubbing her ever increasing bump.

'She is ecstatic. That was a good move for her anyway,' Frank said.

'This is the happiest I have seen her and if it gives her hope then yes, this was a great move. I will speak to Billy about it tonight again.'

Frank and Anna sat with Jasmine for the rest of the day, watching her put it in the slit in the mattress and bringing it out time after time. It was in her hand when Candice came in with her dinner, but it was not a problem, Candice had no interest in the young woman, she put her dinner on the bed then left without saying a word.

'Right time for me to go in and hear what the Sutherlands are saying,' Anna told Frank.

'Ok, I will see you soon, I suppose I will be watching soaps on TV tonight with Mum, I'm getting quite used to them now, maybe if I'm lucky she will watch a movie later.'

'Enjoy.'

The Sutherlands were sitting at the kitchen table eating their dinner, saying nothing. Anna went for a stroll around their house, thinking herself through doors when she needed to. Their decor was neutral in every room, plain and tasteful furnishings, the odd piece that looked out of place, an average house in an average street with a dark secret. She heard voices so returned to the kitchen.

'John wants us to join him and his wife at his

house tomorrow night for dinner,' Jack said.
'I don't like Fiona, but I will go, just make sure that we are not there all night.'
'Do you want to drive?'
'No you can drive or we can get a taxi, if I am spending time with Fiona then I am going to need a drink to get through it.'
'We will get a taxi then; I fancy a drink or two.'
'Is John ready to take over when you leave?' Candice asked.
'More than ready, he knows what he is doing.'
'Good.'
After dinner Candice returned to the shed with a clean bucket and to collect the dinner plate, then after loading the dishwasher joined Jack in the living room where they watched TV. They did not say much, just normal chit chat between a normal married couple. Anna remained there waiting to digest any piece of information they would give her, there was none, so when they retired for the night she went to Billy. She was fed up saying the same thing over and over again, although she knew it was the best way of getting through to him, so she mentioned the Innocent, the shed, his neighbours and of course the name tag, then went back to the shed to get some sleep of her own.

39
Wednesday 18th December

The fresh appeal for both women on the news had generated a couple of calls from the public; none of them came to be of any use. A man had reported seeing Jasmine in Edinburgh the previous month, when Rooney went to speak to him it came to light that the man was in his eighties and had very poor eyesight, he had apparently seen her passing by his house from his window, when questioned he confessed that the woman could have been anyone for all he knew. Another call was another sighting of Jasmine going into a shop in Hallington. When her photo was shown to the shop owner and their employees none of them could identify her. The CCTV for the shop had been recorded over, so it could not be checked. Rooney sat at his desk staring at the statement of a victim whose house had been recently broke into, but his mind was on the two missing women. He could not move on. He was stuck, not knowing what to do next.

'Someone knows something, that's what Mr Anderson said,' Rooney spoke to himself under his breath.

He hated being stumped on a case. Two cases really bugged him. The name tag was annoying him. If he could find that which he knew was virtually impossible then he would maybe have a starting point, but that would be like looking for bottle top in a scrap yard. Another thing that he would like to know that was irritating him was if the two cases were connected. Maybe if he could find some sort of link then he would have something to go on, there was nothing that he had detected.

'How do you fancy a trip out?' he asked PC McMillan who was two desks down.

'Sure. Where are we going?'

'The vets, something I need to check up on.'

PC McMillan drove to the Village Vet. Rooney told her on the way it was about the name tag that was on Rex's collar. The vets was busy. There were three dogs and two cats waiting to be seen, Rooney bent down to pet a black and white collie on the way to the reception desk.

'Hello, I'm wondering if you can help me out. A dog came in here on fourteenth of November late at night I was wondering if I could speak to the vet that took care of him. His name is Rex and the surname for that is Ross.

'Hold on, let me check,' the receptionist with Mary on a name tag on the front of her top tapped on the keyboard a few times and waited for a screen to load.

'It was Katie Irvine that seen him, there are five vets here, they all take a turn for the nightshift, Katie seems to do more than her fair share if I'm honest, think she likes the quiet. You are in luck she is on days this week. She is in with a pooch at the moment, if you would like to wait then I can catch her for you before she sees her next patient.'

'Yes, that would be great, in the meantime can I ask you if you have seen either of these woman,' Rooney asked showing her the poster with both women on it.

Mary stared at the women's faces with deep concentration, thinking hard, creasing her forehead.

'I'm sorry I have never seen this one,' she said pointing to the face of Jasmine Brown. 'I do know Mrs Ross; she has been in here with her dog, just not recently.'

'It was worth a shot,' Rooney said with a smile.

The two officers sat for ten minutes before a man with his rather large Alsatian came out of one of the consultation rooms. Rooney saw Mary lifting the phone, a moment later she waved for them to go into the room the dog and its owner had just vacated. When they entered the room Rooney's eyes widened, he was taken aback a little upon seeing Katie, he found her attractive. Both Katie and PC McMillan noticed and gave each other a subtle smile. Katie cleared her throat.

'How can I help you today?'

'Mr Ross brought his pet dog Rex in here on the

fourteenth of November late at night. He noticed the name tag from his collar was missing, and I know he has called to ask if it was on when Rex came in. I believe you didn't see it on him. Can you tell me if it has been found in here since then,' Rooney asked.

'No I'm sorry it hasn't. I would have called Mr Ross if it was found. Is Mrs Ross still missing?'

'Yes do you know her?'

'No I don't. They do bring their dog here, but has always been seen by another vet until that night Mr Ross brought him in. I have seen a photo of her on Facebook.'

'What about this woman?' Rooney said showing her the poster of both women, pointing to the photo of Jasmine.

Katie looked at the photo for a long moment then said. 'Yes I know her; it has been a couple of years since she has been in here with her dad and her cat. The cat had to get put to sleep. It was old. I believe they had the cat since before the girl was born by the way her father was talking. Poor girl broke her heart that day.'

'You must have a good memory for faces,' PC McMillan said.

'I do, an even better memory for the animals.'

'Well I think we have taken up enough of your time, we will go and let you get back to your patients,' Rooney said with a smile.

Back in the car PC McMillan fastened her seat

belt with a wide grin on her face saying nothing.

'What is up with you?' Rooney asked well aware why she was smiling.

'Nothing wrong with me Boss.'

'Out with it.'

'You fancy the vet and don't deny it. Your eyes near popped out your head.'

'Yes, I found her attractive; you would need to be blind not to see it.'

'Did you go there just to see her?'

'No, that is the first time I have laid eyes on her, it was a pleasant surprise. I am beating myself up about Rex's name tag, if it came off at the same time he was injured then it may be important, there is no chance of finding it. I think I am clutching at straws now.'

'We will get it solved Sir. It is only a matter of time.'

'That's the trouble, the longer they are missing well you know how it goes. Something else I want to know, are they connected.'

'If they were then we would have found out how by now.'

'Is there something we are not seeing though?'

'Sir, we are doing all we can do, stop beating yourself up.'

'There is one more stop I want to make?'

'Where are we going?'

'To see Anna's business partner Sam, I want to

show him the photo of Jasmine to see if she was a customer in there.'

PC McMillan drove to the shop on Barnes Road, parked the car and was ready to get out.

'You do all the talking in here Nicole.'

'If that's what you want Sir.'

Rooney handed her the poster, they got out and entered the shop. Sam was at the counter giving a garment back to a customer. He looked up and saw the sergeant.

'I will be with you in a sec sergeant.'

Rooney nodded. The customer left satisfied with the transaction.

'What can I do for you?'

'We would like you to take a peek at a photo if you don't mind; we would like to know if this woman was a customer here.' PC McMillan said as she handed over the poster with both missing women on it. Sam was overcome with emotion when he saw the poster; his eyes were drawn to Anna's face on it. He dug a tissue from the front pocket of his jeans and dabbed at his leaking eyes.

'I'm sorry, you must think I am a right drama queen, it's just that I miss her so much. If I knew where she was and that she was alright and could speak to her anytime I wanted then I wouldn't be in this state. It's the not knowing where or how she is that bothers me. How is the investigation going?' Sam asked.

'We are doing all we can, we will find her. The other woman there on the poster Jasmine Brown, is she a customer in here?' PC McMillan asked.

'I have seen her on Facebook alongside Anna, no I have never seen her in person.'

'How is business?'

'I had to take on an employee because there is too much work for one. I felt bad having to speak to Tom about it with all that he is going through, I did not want to do it without his permission.'

'I understand Mr Thompson that it must be hard to keep the place going on your own.'

'It is. Please call me Sam, everyone else does.'

'Will do, we won't keep you any longer. If you can think of anything that might be relevant please get in touch,' said PC McMillan.

'Yes anything at all,' Rooney repeated for good measure.'

They said goodbye and went to the car.

'Do you think Sam is keeping something from us?' PC McMillan asked.

'Why do you ask?'

'The way you reinforced that he should call us with anything.'

'I don't know, as I said earlier I am clutching at straws and I'm not fussy, any straw will do,' Rooney said with a chuckle.

PC McMillan smiled and shook her head,

started the car and headed back to the station.

Frank was moving the same letters over and over from May's to Richard's and vice versa. He had become quite fond of Arlene Ferguson the postwoman, she knows many people and speaks to most of them when she is out doing her job. He had spent a fair bit of time in her company. Even though they cannot converse Frank found himself looking forward to being in her presence, Frank found her humour and intelligence endearing. He had never followed Arlene home, he thought that was maybe a step too far, even a little creepy, he was curious to know who was in her life, the ring on her finger told him that she was married; he wanted to know what he was like to deserve such a woman. All the talking she had done in his company, she had rarely mentioned anything about herself, she was always asking after other people or their kids or grandkids. Maybe one night before he had completed his mission he thought he might go and find out who Arlene really is. He was sitting in her van thinking about it and watching her delivering mail to the houses in Morcombe Street through the windscreen.

'Boo,' Anna shouted at the window of the van giving Frank a fright.

'You so and so,' Frank said pointing a finger at

her then came out of the van to stand beside her.

'If I were not dead with a heart attack already then I would have been now.'

'I'm sorry I just couldn't resist it.'

'How is Jasmine?'

'She is the same as when you asked yesterday buddy, depressed.'

'Did you find out anything at the Sutherlands last night?'

'Nothing new, they are very quiet on the subject of Jasmine just now, if I didn't know any better I would say they knew I was in their house listening to them.'

'Don't be silly. I am the only one that needs to put up with you, don't get me wrong I do it gladly.'

'Thank you, I think.'

'What are you up to this afternoon?'

'Nothing, that's the trouble being dead, no work to go to, no housework to do, no people you can socialise with.'

'So I'm nobody,' Frank said with a smirk.'

'You know what I mean.'

'Do you fancy a walk around town after I have moved the letters, if I get any?'

'Why not, come to the shed for me when you are finished with the mail.'

'Ok see you then.'

Frank moved one letter from Richard's to May's

house, not much; but something he thought. He went for Anna, they walked to the precinct. It was far too busy with bodies. It was too much like hard work trying to dodge the herd of Christmas shoppers, so decided they would head for the quieter streets.

'Can't say I miss all the hustle and bustle of doing Christmas shopping,' Anna said.

'What do you miss apart from your family?'

'I never feel hungry, but when Jasmine is given a chocolate bar and I am there when she is eating it I yearn for the taste, normal food not so much. What about you?'

'I miss being able to do simple things, like opening a door, reading a paper without having to peer over someone's shoulder, having to read it at their pace. Most of all I miss my two favourite hobbies, doing jigsaws and playing golf.'

'I wouldn't take you for a golf player, it just goes to show how much I don't know about you still.'

'What do else do you want to know?'

'Everything I suppose, you are the best friend I have ever had.'

'Come on Anna don't get mushy with me,' Frank said with a mischievous smile.'

'Stop teasing me. Seriously though, it's funny how we go through life picking and choosing our friends when a stranger you pass in the street and never make their acquaintance could be an excellent friend, you could have more in common with that stranger than your friends or spouse even.'

'I think I know what you mean, let's face it if we were both still alive then we would never have been friends. We would probably never have met.'

'Exactly what I mean and it is sad.'

'It sure is.'

'When are you moving the photo? I think you should do it soon.'

'I was thinking about Boxing Day, get Christmas out the way.'

'That sounds good to me. By New Year your mission could be over successfully. I need Billy to know that the monsters are moving Jasmine on the twenty-fourth of January. I think it will be hard to get that piece of specific and important information through to him, it is imperative that I do because if he misses that date then all of his hard work will have been for nothing. He needs to see them take her from that shed; he will need to be rooted at that window. I don't know how he is going to out the Sutherlands that night, but he will need to, they can't be allowed to move Jasmine. The thing is I know if they take that van around to the shed and put Jasmine in it, she won't be seen from his window, the van will be in the way. I can give Billy all the information I can; it will be down to him in the end to get the job done.'

'I have seen that view of the shed from that window, you are right the view of the comings and goings will be blocked by the van. Maybe they will carry her or let her walk to the van.'

'I don't know how they will do it, Billy needs to be ready for whatever they do Frank; I don't want my mission to fail.'

'It won't. I know it.'

The sky above them was starting to darken when they reached the Sutherlands' gate. The rain was falling, the wind was getting a little gusty, not that it made one bit of difference to them, although they could still tell a miserable night ahead when they saw one.

'Good luck with Billy tonight Anna, I will catch up with you tomorrow. I'm going to Richard's tonight to spend some time there, I have not spent enough time with him since this all came about. I wasn't what you would call close to him when I was alive; I need to get to grips with his and Eloise's habits and routine so I know the best place to put the photo.'

'You have your work cut out for you there then.'

'I sure do, see you tomorrow.'

Anna went to the shed door and thought herself through it, when she got in there the place was in darkness, Anna didn't know what was happening so she thought herself outside then inside again.

It's the bulb in the lamp, it has given in. Thought I was going a crazy then.

When Candice came to the shed with Jasmine's dinner she opened the door, noticed the light was off then closed the door again immediately. She came back with a torch and a new bulb five minutes later to change it. She went back to the house and reappeared minutes later with Jasmine's dinner which was pasta. In a plastic bag there was a flask of tea, a bottle of water and a packet of crisps. Jasmine hoovered up her dinner with the plastic knife and fork which pleased Anna, the thought of the young lady not eating was bothering her. She knew that Jasmine needed to keep her strength up, not just for her, for the baby as well.

That poor girl is getting so big now; I wish I knew when the baby is due, not that it will make any difference babies can come early. I don't think I will bother going to the Sutherlands tonight, they are giving me nothing new. I know their plans could change so I will go back to them tomorrow night, I just feel as if I need a night off from Jack and Candice, they anger and annoy me. I will go to Billy; it is always nice to see him and Kate.

Billy was sitting at the table in his kitchen with Kate; the remnants of their dinner were on the plates in front of them.

'You take the first shift at the window, while I tidy up in here and take Buster a walk,' Kate said.

'No problem darling, at least I have not got work tomorrow so I can see what if anything has changed over there in the past few days in the daylight.'

'I know we are not doing this for nothing. I can feel it. If someone is in that shed we will be the first to know and the first to call the police.'

'I know you are right Kate, it's just the not knowing that is gnawing away at me. If someone is in that shed and I have a terrible feeling that it is Anna Ross then we have been watching that shed doing nothing for weeks now, when she is in there going through hell.'

'Wait a minute, we don't know for sure that anyone is in that shed, yes we have suspicions, that is not enough to go the police. We need evidence and to get that we need to watch, so come on get through there, I will relieve you when I'm done.'

Billy went to the window, it was 7.30 pm. He noted a bucket being taken to the shed at 8.15 and a few minutes later a bucket and something in a carrier bag was being taken to the house by the woman. Kate took over from Billy at 8.25; she noted a basin being taken to the shed. Well she thought it was a basin, they had seen it before and came to that conclusion. Twenty minutes later both the man and the woman went to the shed. The woman had another bag, what was in it was a mystery, they came back out and into the house ten minutes later with the bag in tow. Kate noted it all down.

'If only you could hear me, then I could tell you that they have just given her a clean toilet, a basin to get washed and as the both of them went out that must have been fresh clothes,' Anna said to Kate.

Billy relieved Kate at ten to let her go to bed for work. It was easier for them to take it in turns.

'Nothing else will happen tonight Billy, take it from me,' Anna said unheard.

Billy sat there at the window until 1.50 am, his eyes were clocking. He let Buster out in the garden and went to bed knackered. It didn't take long for him to drift off; Anna was right there ready to get her message across.

'Anna Anderson,' she said once and she knew she had Billy's attention.

'The night of the twenty-fourth of January will be a big night; there will be no sleep for you. All that you have been seeking to know will be revealed that night. That is the night you will save the Innocent. That will be the night that your neighbours will be caught out and you will be the one to do it.'

Billy woke up and checked the time. He sat on the edge of the bed for a while then lay down and went back to sleep.

I think I got through a little, I know I will need to go over what I have told him every night until that date just to make sure he gets the message. As soon as he knows for sure that something is happening on that date he will mention it to Kate, hopefully I will be here to hear it and confirm with myself that he knows what is happening.

40
Tuesday Christmas Eve

It was well into the afternoon or what she thought was the afternoon when Anna left the shed. She went to May's to find Frank, he wasn't there, neither was May. Anna checked the time it was 1.40 pm. May's white Christmas tree was sitting in the corner; it was beautifully decorated in red tinsel and baubles. She had seen the Christmas trees pop up in the windows over the last week or so making her feel as if she was missing out. There was no tree up in her house this year, her mother had no Christmas tree up either, she kind of knew that Tom and her parents would not bother this year, she could understand why. If it was one of them missing then she also would not be celebrating. She thought of May and was beside her in no time at her friend Judy's house.

That's right May is spending Christmas here. Frank must be at Richard's finding out all he can.

Anna thought of Frank, he was in Richard's house. Richard was not in. Eloise was there in the living room surrounded by Christmas wrapping paper and presents making her way through them one by one wrapping and sipping a Bailey's Irish Cream as she went.

'She has a lot do to there,' Anna said to her

friend.

'She looks as if she is enjoying it though,' Frank replied.

Their tree was twice the size as the tree in May's. It was a real tree kitted out with white and gold decorations. It was beautiful.

'Their tree is lovely.'

'Yes I agree. I have been to see Gina and Sarah today, well I saw Sarah, Gina was not home, I take it she is out last minute shopping. Sarah looked happy; one of her friends is round. They were playing music in her room. I wonder if she misses me at all.'

'Of course she misses you, how can you think any different.'

'This time of the year always made me feel melancholy. I just think it is a lonely time of year even if you are not lonely any other time. Ignore me I'm just being silly.'

'I went to see your mum at Judy's.'

'Is she there already, as soon as I found out that Arlene had no letters for Richard or Mum I came straight here, two days until I plant that photo and I still don't know where to put it? I have an idea that I will be letting Eloise find it, she seems more susceptible to the weird stuff.'

'Weird stuff? You have a way with words Frank.'

'What are you doing tomorrow?'

'I will visit all my family, but for the most of it I will be in that prison with Jasmine. I don't want her in there on her own; I don't even know if she knows it is Christmas tomorrow.'

'I supposed one day will be melding into the next for her, poor girl. I will be seeing my family as well. I will pop into the shed for a while to see you and Jasmine.'

'I will be happy to see you. Right I'm off for a long walk before my usual nightly routine.'

'Don't tell me you are spending the evening with the Sutherlands then you are going to see Billy.'

'You got it, can't keep up with this social life,' she said with a chuckle. 'Catch you tomorrow.'

Anna walked around the town for hours whiling away the time looking at all the Christmas lights. If she were alive she would be at home wrapping presents and having a glass of wine while she did so. Tom would be watching TV with a beer in his hand, he would ask her if she needed a hand, she would always say no. She would disappear upstairs to wrap everything she had bought him as a surprise, then bring them down and sit them under the tree. Tom would then question her about what they were, she never told. They usually went shopping together a few weeks before Christmas and would buy each other gifts when they were both there to choose them. Tom had learned that lesson early on in the relationship that Anna had a taste of her own and was best to let her pick what she wanted herself. He would buy her surprises as well, often her favourite perfume, her favourite chocolates and the things he knew for sure that she liked; he couldn't go wrong that way.

She thought of Tom and was there in front of him. He was at her parents' house; they were eating dinner at the kitchen table, fish and chips out of the chip shop. She wished she could smell the aroma of the food. She always found that smell so delicious.

'It will be a hard day tomorrow Tom, at least you will be here with us. We could not bear to think of you in that house all by yourself,' Ruby said between mouthfuls.

He is staying here tonight, that's good. My parents seem to have forgiven him for what he did and so have I mostly. I know my dad he does not forgive so easily, he is putting on a front for Mum's sake, he will not forget what Tom did. I am glad he is not on his own though.

The Sutherlands were sitting watching TV, both of them had a drink in their hands; they both seemed in good cheer. Anna sat on the opposite end of the couch from where Candice was sitting and watched the TV with them, waiting for them to say something about Jasmine, they didn't. The only thing they spoke about was the TV and Christmas presents, pretty boring stuff as far as Anna was concerned. When they switched the TV off for the night, Anna went to Billy's where the mood was sombre, she soon found out why.

'We have Aaron and Kirsty over all day tomorrow, how are we meant to keep an eye on that shed?' Billy asked Kate.

'We don't, tomorrow is Christmas day. We take a day off. If something is going to happen then it won't happen tomorrow. Trust me you deserve a day off.'

'I know you are right, I just feel so bad about it. If there is someone in that shed it means that they are spending Christmas Day in there when we are over here enjoying it.'

'You need to relax Billy, it is just one day.'

I am taking it he has not mentioned the twenty-fourth of January to Kate yet. I need to keep mentioning that.

Anna spent twenty minutes connecting with Billy after he had gone to sleep. She went over and over that date in January ten times before she was sure that was enough for the night.

41
Christmas Day 2019

Candice came to the shed with scrambled eggs and toast for Jasmine's breakfast along with a flask of tea. She also brought her a Christmas present. Jasmine looked surprised.

'A light breakfast this morning dear, need to leave plenty room for your Christmas dinner, Candice said.

'It's Christmas?'

'It sure is. I am preparing an excellent dinner for you.'

'That means I have been in here for four and a half months.'

'Never mind that open your present.'

Jasmine looked at the present that Candice had put on the bed beside her; she made no move to open it. The fact that she had been in there for so long stunned her, yes she knew she had been in here for a long time, she knew with the size of her bump that it had been months, to find out exactly how long and on Christmas Day knocked her for six.

'No lunch today, we are having a three course meal, it will start about two.'

'Oh, I am so grateful,' Jasmine replied sarcastically.

'Anymore of that and you have no dinner,' Candice retorted before leaving.'

Four and a half months of this. How is this girl still sane? Candice brought a Christmas gift. She should have acted normal as if it was just another day then Jasmine would not have known it is Christmas. It must be torture for her, she will be thinking of her family now more than ever. I wonder what the gift is; I hope it is not something that will bring Jasmine's mood down, although after finding out what day it is she will probably be on a downer anyway.

There were a few presents passed out at the Anderson's house, none of them seemed to hold anyone's attention. The atmosphere in their house was as depressing as the weather outside, cold and wet. They were up early and had breakfast with Rex getting more than his fair share from their plates. Tom decided to take Rex a walk, George insisted on going with them.
'I don't hate you Tom, but know this; I can't forget what you did to my daughter. She shows you nothing but love, for Ruby's sake you are welcome in our home anytime. When we get our girl back you will bend over backwards to make it up to her. Do I make myself clear?' George said calmly.
'I understand George I have been a bastard to her. I know she loves me. I don't deserve her.'
'I know you don't, when she turns up you have a lot of grovelling and crawling to do.'

'I will, I promise.'
They walked the rest of the way not saying a word. Tom knew where he stood; it was not where he wanted to be. That was where he put himself with his behaviour. When Anna went to see them George and Tom had just come in from their walk. Ruby was in the kitchen preparing what she needed for dinner. She was chopping vegetables and kept having to stop to sob into a tissue. Tom and George sat in the living room; the TV was on, although neither of them were watching it. The both of them seemed to be deep in thought. Rex lay on the floor between them after being rejected for a pet by the two of them.

Why did I come here? It is nearly as miserable as that shed, being here won't help them. It only makes me feel bad for them. I need something a little more cheery I think it is time to see my niece.

Clara and Peter were picking up the used wrapping paper from the floor in their living room. Jamez was sitting in the middle of it with toys and other gifts all around her.
'Are you looking forward to seeing your parents on Friday,' Peter asked Clara.
'In a way yes and in a way no, I am worried sick about Anna you know that and I hate being so far away from Mum and Dad when I know they are beside themselves fretting about my sister.

Jamez doesn't know what is going on and I want it to stay that way for now. I just hope that she doesn't sense or overhear anything about Anna that could upset her,' Clara said in a hushed voice so that Jamez could not hear her.

'We will need to tell her sometime.'

'She is too young to understand Peter.'

'That maybe, but we cannot protect her from this forever. She is going to ask where her Auntie Anna is when we go up there.'

'You are right we will talk to her tomorrow.'

'It's for the best Clara; best things are out in the open.'

Anna did not hear a word they were saying. She was too interested in watching her niece play with her new toys. She was going to miss her growing up, the thought tugged at her heart strings. She was sitting on the floor next to Jamez watching her face light up when she discovered something new in the jewellery kit she was playing with. Anna knew that Jamez would be moving onto the next toy soon and she couldn't wait to see her face light up all over again.

Frank stayed with his mother for a while on Christmas morning; she seemed as if she was having a good time with her friends so he chose to go and see Richard. Richard's youngest John was there along with his eldest Sasha with her husband Mark and their son Liam. The house was a mess with wrapping paper and gifts lying around, all Frank could see here was love. Eloise was doing her best tidying up, but was constantly being distracted with the festivities. Although he never saw his brother on a daily basis they always made a point of seeing each other at Christmas and on their birthday which of course they shared. They were different in so many ways, the same in others, they were told by their adoptive parents that Frank was born first and that was the cause of many a fight when they were younger when Frank used his piece of information to annoy his brother. However, what they did not know was they had been given false information; Richard was the oldest by seven whole minutes. Something caught his eye on the tree, it was his name, he was sure, and as he drew closer to the item he could see that indeed he did see his name on a shiny white bauble. Above it and to the right was another with Mum on it and even further up to the left was one for Dad. Tears trickled out the corner of his eyes as he tried to fight the emotion that was taking him by surprise; he couldn't so he just let it out.

He left there reluctantly to see Gina and Sarah and regretted it immediately. Gina was in the kitchen, heating up a pot of homemade soup with the help of her boyfriend Kevin, who it turns out is the complete opposite of Frank. Sarah was in her room applying make-up which Frank presumed she got for Christmas; new clothes were lying on the bed, beside her within easy reach on her dressing table sat a new phone. He went back down the stair and went to their tree, there was no such bauble for him on this tree. Frank stayed through the soup and main course, there was no mention of his name, which left him feeling lonely and unloved so he went back to Richards where he knew he was in their thoughts.

Anna pulled herself away from her niece after a four-hour visit feeling guilty that she left Jasmine alone for so long on her own on Christmas day, the depression of the shed had abandoned her for a while, it was back within seconds of being back in the shed. She brightened up when her best friend showed up.

'Frank, it is so good to see you.'

'You too sweet cheeks, how has your day been so far?'

'Good and bad, it was great seeing my niece; in fact that is where I have spent most of my time. Tom, Mum and Dad are really down as you would expect so I didn't hang about there, how is your day so far?'

'Well I have a bauble on Richard's tree which brought a tear to my eye; I am all but forgotten with Gina and Sarah. The boyfriend was there, I have no bauble there and my name was not mentioned once.'

'Just because they did not mention you when you were there doesn't mean that you have not been missed. They may not mention you. I bet they are thinking of you.'

'We will never know. Is that a Christmas present for Jasmine from the evil pair?' he said gesturing towards the gift which was now on the floor still unopened next to her plate which still had quite a bit of food on it.'

'It sure is.'

'Is she not eating again? That plate still looks kind of full.'

'We don't know how much was on the plate when it was brought in, you know what people are like on Christmas Day; they go all out and overdo everything especially the food.'

'That's so true. What are you up to tonight?' Frank asked.

'I am giving Billy the night off from my haunting, think I will spend some time here then go into the Sutherlands, see if I can claw a bit of new information from them.'

'Why don't you take the night off as well? It's not like you don't deserve it and I overheard Mum with her friend this morning, they are watching Calamity Jane and On Moonlight Bay with a bottle of sherry, a Doris Day spectacular, you up for it?'

'I really shouldn't, I should be trying to help her,' Anna said nodding to Jasmine.

'I understand, but all work and no play makes Anna a dull friend, come on it's one night and it's Christmas.'

Anna gave in and agreed to watch the movies; they both stayed with Jasmine long enough for Jack to bring in her dessert, take away her dirty plate and change her toilet. The gift from the monsters still lay unopened. Jack did not say a word about it or anything else. Frank and Anna arrived at Judy's at 7.45 pm, a little late for the start of Calamity Jane; they had seen it before anyway. Anna was more relaxed than she had been in a long time and she had Frank to thank for persuading her to come.

42
Thursday 26th December

Frank went to the shed to fetch Anna early; he had a photo to plant. He wanted to talk it through with his friend to come up with the best possible place to put it before he put the next part of his plan in action. He had no post to worry about today again, for that he was thankful. Anna was sleeping; he waited about with Jasmine until she woke up.

'Hi frank, I've not been sleeping long, have I?'

'I don't know I have been here for about twenty minutes at a guess; I left Judy's at seven, need to think about where to put that photo. Are you still up for helping me out?'

'I told you I will. I take it Jasmine has not had breakfast yet?'

'No evidence of it as far as I can see. What I can see is that she has not opened that present.' Frank said gesturing towards the present on the floor.

'Can't blame her, I would want nothing from that evil couple either.'

Jasmine was sitting with back against the wall under the duvet. She had the duvet flattened down on her big bump; she was rubbing it with both hands mumbling away, words that were inaudible to Anna and Frank.

'Does she do that often? It's a bit creepy,' Frank

asked.

'Now and then yes, and I agree it is creepy; however, this whole thing is creepy. Right let's go to Richard's house.'

'We should walk, it is still early, give us a chance to talk about it and give Richard and Eloise time to get up.'

'No probs.'

They both thought themselves outside the shed and started on their walk. Richard lived a half an hour away on foot, giving them time to discuss their missions.

'This is it,' Frank said stopping outside a semi-detached, white rough casted, up and downstairs house at twenty-four Bridge Road.

'Nice house. The blinds are still closed doesn't look like they are up yet,' Anna said.

'Well it is the holidays; we will go in and wait. You can get a good look around, find the perfect place to put the photo and when they get up you can gauge whether Eloise is as open to the weird and wonderful as I think she is.'

'What exactly do you mean by that?'

'It's just that some people believe in things more than others. Like some people would think things are a coincidence and some others think there is more to it, I think she is the one that will put this together. Richard is more how you do you put it, sceptical.'

'I see, you think she is far out there.'

'Hahaha, maybe a little, but she is very intelligent and alert. You will see her soon enough.'

They went inside, Frank showed Anna the Christmas bauble on the tree that he was so proud of. Anna started looking around. It was not long before she could hear someone moving around upstairs. Five minutes later Eloise came into the kitchen where Anna was. Eloise was a beautiful woman; sure she was fifty-three and had a few wrinkles just like anyone else. She had beauty that no amount of time would diminish. She had dark hair with highlights, large blue eyes and porcelain white skin. She was an average height and build and at the moment she had on a blue fleece housecoat with matching slippers. Anna watched her as she put on the kettle and took two cups from the cupboard then rinsed out the teapot that sat on the stove. She followed her into the living room where she opened the blinds then into the hall where she switched the thermostat for the heating up. Frank was right about her Anna sensed it right away; Eloise certainly had a special kind of presence about her.

'What do you think about my sister in-law,' Frank asked Anna as he followed her and Eloise back to the kitchen.

'I see what you mean; she is a very special woman.'

'Have you any ideas where we should put the

photo yet?'

'Why not right there on that kitchen table,' Anna said.

Before another word could be said Frank disappeared and was back in a minute. He waited for Eloise to turn her back and put the photo on the table.

'That was quick,' Anna said.

'No point in waiting when you know your next move.'

'It was my first suggestion; I never got time to think of anything better.'

'It's as good a place as any.'

Richard walked into the kitchen, went up behind Eloise, put his arms around her and kissed her on the neck; she turned around into his loving embrace. They kissed. Richard moved the two cups onto the table and got the milk from the fridge, a sugar bowl was already on the table; he retrieved two teaspoons from the drawer and sat down waiting for Eloise to pour. Richard was also in a housecoat and slippers, his were dark brown.

'The photo is right there in front of him. He can't see it,' Frank said.

'Give him time to notice it; don't forget he is just up.'

Eloise brought the teapot to the table and started to pour; she stopped and put the teapot down.

'What's the photo?' she said picking it up and taking a closer look. 'Where did this come from?'

Richard looked up from sorting the cups with sugar, took the photo that Eloise was holding out for him.

'Is that you and Frank with your mum?'

Richard looked at it with a puzzled expression.

'That is not Mum, so it can't be Frank and me. Where did it come from?'

'It was there on the table.'

She took it back and peeked at the back.

'What is the name on the letters that we keep getting in the door that are not for us?' Eloise asked. 'I can't remember, May something or another.'

'It's May Simpson.'

'Yes that's it.'

'Why?'

She handed the photo back to Richard and told him to read the back. She did not wait for a response, she went upstairs. Frank followed her; she went into the cupboard in their bedroom and lifted out a box, took the lid off and started looking through the photos that were inside. She found what she was looking for and went back to the kitchen with Frank behind her.

'Look,' she said taking the photo from Richard and putting the one she brought down from upstairs side by side on the table.

'That is you and Frank,' she said pointing to the photo from upstairs. 'And that is you and Frank,' she said pointing to the photo she found on the table.

'This can't be Frank and me, it says on the back May Simpson and her twins.'

'Take a good look, I am telling you that is you and Frank in both of the pictures.'

'It can't be,' he said gazing fixedly at them.

'Is there any chance you were adopted?'

'Don't be silly, I think I would have known before this if I were.'

'Not necessarily, would someone in your family know.'

'What family, my dad was an only child and my mum's only sister Grace has dementia and doesn't even know who I am when I visit. There is no one else.'

'What about Grace's children, your cousins Mathew and Hilary. They are a bit older than you.'

'I will see if I can get a hold of them on the phone later. How can you tell that that is Frank and me anyway, the one you found is in colour and the one I had is in black and white.'

'I can tell, I am positive.'

Richard stared at the photos, blinking deliberately and rubbing his eyes as if that was going to make him see better.

'You know I think you might be right,' Richard

finally concurred with his wife who was standing beside him impatiently waiting for him to see the obvious.

'We need to go see this May Simpson woman and find out what the hell is going on. Forget getting a hold of your cousins. We will get it straight from the horse's mouth if it is true. We still have a letter belonging to her so the address is not a problem.'

'We can't just knock on her door and produce these,' Richard responded nodding at the photos.

'If it is the same May Simpson then she will know about the photo with her name on it, she was there when it was taken. If it is a different May Simpson then what do you have to lose by asking. I believe there is something in this.'

'Ok, ok we will go this afternoon once Sasha, Mark and Liam go home.'

Eloise sat down at the table and put her hand on his and gave it a squeeze. They sat in silence and drank their tea.

'Wow, that was easy,' Frank said to Anna who was standing there agape at what had just happened.

'I don't believe it was that simple. You were right about Eloise, she is there and a little bit more.'

'What if Mum is not home when they go to her door?'

'Then they will go back, with something this big they will need to see it through.'

'You are right; it doesn't sound like Eloise will let it lie until it is resolved. Let's go to Mum's and see if she is home yet.'

May's house was empty, although it was still early. Anna saw that it was only ten to 8.50 am, so suggested they go walking to pass the time. They returned to May's at 12.15 pm, it was still too early to expect anything to happen yet. Richard said they would go in the afternoon, so they sat on the couch to wait either for May or Richard whoever came first.

'Go see your mum, see if she looks as if she is ready to leave,' Anna said.

Frank went and came back ten minutes later.

'You took your time,' Anna said.

'She is getting ready to go out alright, not here. Mum and Judy are going for lunch to some woman's house called Bianca.'

'What do you want to do?'

'I will wait here for Richard to show. I suppose I just want to make sure that he does.'

'I don't think he has a choice, Eloise will drag him if need be. I am off to be with Jasmine, come see me as soon as something happens please.'

'Of course I will. See you soon.'

Jasmine had the name tag out on the palm of her

hand when Anna arrived in the shed; she was also crying again. It was a sight that Anna had gotten used to.

Poor young woman missed Christmas with her loved ones, who like mine will be going out of their minds with worry. She has been missing for a lot longer than me. I wonder if they have given up any hope of ever seeing her again. I wonder if there is any way I could find her parents.

Anna closed her eyes and thought of Jasmine's room, nothing happened, she stayed where she was. She thought of Jasmine's parents, again nothing happened.

Is it because I don't know what Jasmine's room or parents look like. There must be a way to get there, to check up on them, I don't even know their first names. That's something I will need to think about long and hard. Frank is making good progress, in fact it is excellent. I am so happy for him, although I will be down here all alone when his mission is complete. How will I cope without him? I will just need to I suppose.

The door to the shed opened; both Jack and Candice came in with a basin of water, a towel and fresh clothes.
'Right Jasmine time for a wash and a change of clothes,' Candice announced. 'The usual drill, don't do anything silly, not that you could in

your condition and with the two of us to contend with.'

Jack turned his back while Jasmine got a wash down then the shackle was removed for her to change her T-shirt, the handcuff was put back on before she changed the clothes on the bottom half of her body.

'Open your gift, there is a book in there, lunch in half an hour,' Jack said before lifting her toilet bucket and they both left.

Jasmine opened the gift to find a pair of slippers and as promised a new book, which she started immediately. Jack came back to the shed with a clean bucket which held Jasmine's lunch an egg mayo sandwich, a flask of tea and a banana.

Jasmine had been doing the toilet in that bucket, I know they have washed it, but to bring her lunch in it is bang out of order, dirty pig.

Jasmine didn't seem to care that much. She opened the tin foil which housed the sandwich and took a bite barely taking her eyes from the page in the book she was reading. Anna sat with her for a couple of hours until her curiosity got the better of her; she went to May's to see what was happening. Frank wasn't there so she closed her eyes and thought of Eloise and was there in an instant. Richard and Eloise's daughter and her family were saying goodbye in the hall. There was quite a few bags for them to take, filled with gifts that they had received the day before. Mark made a few journeys to their car. After one last hug from their grandson Liam, Richard and Eloise stood at the door and waved as their car pulled away from the gate. Frank was there, Anna stood back to let him enjoy what little time he had left with his family, he would be going back to The Before soon if his plan worked out. Frank saw Anna and went to her.

'How stupid was I, sitting there in Mum's on my own. It dawned on me I wouldn't miss anything if I was right here with them,' Frank said.

'I never even thought of that. They must be going over to May's soon now that the family have left, the bad news is I was just there, she is not home yet.'

'As you said they will just go back. They will not give up until they get her in and speak to her. The worms will come spilling out of the can sooner or later.'

Anna laughed at his choice of words and shook her head.

'What?

'You are so funny sometimes and you don't even mean to be.'

Richard and Eloise came out of the living room and took jackets from the coat stand in the hall. Eloise grabbed the car keys along with the letter they had for May Simpson from the small table in the hall, they went out the door.

'Let's go to Mum's,' Frank quickly voiced a suggestion; he was gone just as quickly, before Anna could respond.

Anna went to May's where Frank was in the living room.

'Sorry Anna I'm just nervous I guess.'

'She is not here so you will need to save that nervousness until they actually get a chance to meet.'

'I know, you are right, but I want it to happen. I want Mum to have a family around her.'

'And she will have, if it is not today then it will be tomorrow.'

What if she wants nothing to do with them?'

'With what Fenza told you, she will welcome them with open arms.'

They waited until they heard a knock on the door, both Frank and Anna went outside. Eloise and Richard stood there on the path waiting for an answer, when no one came to the door they knocked again.

'No one is home, that is typical,' Richard said with impatience in his voice.

'Then we will come back later, if there is still no one home then we will come back tomorrow then every other day until we get all this cleared up,' Eloise answered in a calming voice.

They went back to the car, got in and drove home.

'I wonder what time Mum will be home,' said Frank.

'It doesn't matter Frank because Richard and Eloise will not give up.'

'Look.'

Anna turned around to see what Frank was getting at, there was May getting out of Judy's car, Judy's husband Gordon was out of the car and getting a few bags out of the boot. May walked up the path and unlocked the door and held it open for Gordon to take her bags in. He came back out and got back in the car. May stood at the door waving until they had driven out of sight.

'Would you believe it?' Frank asked.

'Well at least we know that when Richard comes back later May will be in. Just think you could be out of here by tonight.'

'As much as I will miss you Anna, I will be glad to get this all over with.'

'I know, I can't blame you, you have been here for months; however, I don't want to be here without you my friend.'

'You will be fine. Hopefully we will meet again up there someday.'

'I will look forward to it.'

'I'm going to wait right here until they come back.'

'I will wait with you.'

'What about your mission Anna?'

'I will visit Billy later; I gave him the night off last night so I am going all out with him tonight. I was going to spend some time with the monsters, they can wait until tomorrow and Jasmine isn't going anywhere is she? If all goes to plan this could be the last time I see you.'

'You will see me up there I am sure.'

'We can't be sure of anything now Frank. It is all in the unknown. Not everyone that dies is given the burden and opportunity to come back down here, in a way we are experiencing all that death has to offer.'

'I never thought of it like that before.'

At 7.30 pm there was a knock on the door. Frank and Anna glanced at each other; both of them went outside, it was Eloise and Richard with the photos and letter in his hand.

'Hello, can I help you?' May enquired when she opened the door.

'Em, er, I hope so,' Richard said.

May looked into Richard's eyes, she knew who he was. A surge of fear and excitement drenched her, she held onto the door frame to stop her from falling to the floor.

'Are you all right?' Eloise asked as she stepped forward to help May.

Yes,' May answered straightening up trying to compose herself.

'I keep getting mail for you,' Richard said holding out the letter. 'And I was wondering if you

could take a peek at these photos for me please.'
She took the photos and at once recognized herself. 'You better come in.'

Once they were all seated in her humble living room May started her story.

'His name was Frank Ritchie; he was eighteen years old when I met him. We both lived in Pavesway. We didn't know each other growing up, we went to different schools. We ran in different social circles until one night here in Hallington we met and fell in love. We met in Hallington Park. He was with a group of friends as was I, we started talking and realised that we were made for each other. I never had much of an interest in boys before then mainly due to my strict parents, so we started seeing each other in secret. April tenth 1968 that was the day we met and by the end of August I was sure I was pregnant, Frank was delighted, he asked me to marry him, I said yes. The only thing was we were scared to tell our parents, we knew we had to at some point. The weeks rolled by and I was getting bigger, but I was managing to hide it. The night before we decided to tell both our parents October twenty first, Frank went out for a night in Edinburgh with the lads as he put it and I never saw him again. Our friends knew we were in love, well the close ones anyway and it was one of his friends that came and told me the day after it happened that he was dead. He had gotten in a stupid fight, the other guy threw an unlucky punch and Frank was taken to hospital, he died later that night. I went to the funeral of course. I didn't make myself known to his family, I just couldn't do that to them when they were so full of grief. I went home and told my parents everything; they were great, said they would support me in any way they could. I was the youngest of five children, although I was the only one left staying at home, so there was plenty of room. I was eighteen; there was rather a big age gap between me and the next youngest sibling Margaret who was twenty-nine. My father always joked that I was the biggest surprise he had ever got. Anyway, Margaret is the only living sibling I have left; she hasn't spoken to me since the day I gave my babies away. I was preparing for one baby, back in those days you had to wait until the baby was born to know the sex, nothing like all the fancy scans you have nowadays. When two babies appeared it overwhelmed me, two boys. I named them both after their father, Frank and Richard, this photo was took when I was still in hospital, my friend Judy took it, I didn't know her then, she was a young nurse working on the maternity ward I was on. She was keen on photography and had a fancy colour camera; well it was fancy back then. We got on really well, always seemed to have something to talk about so we stayed in touch; in fact that was who I stayed with last night for Christmas. I am getting off course, where was I? Yes, I took the twins home and was alright for a few weeks, then reality hit, I was missing Frank terribly and was bitter that he would not see his children, I got depression and decided that I would give my babies up for adoption to a couple who would love them and give them a more stable home in which they would have a mother and father. Do I regret it? Yes I do, more than anything. I never met anyone else. For me there was only ever one man and that was Frank Ritchie.'

Richard, Eloise, Frank and Anna listened intently to what she had to say. There was silence for a few minutes, until Richard plucked up the courage to ask the question that was burning in his throat.

'Do you think I am one of your twins?'

'I know you are. You have your father's eyes, I saw him in you as soon as I opened the door. What is your name?'

'Richard Wood.'

'So they didn't change your name, that's good. I take it they didn't change Frank's name either then?'

'No, he was Frank.'

'What do you mean was?'

'I'm sorry to tell you this, Frank died earlier this year, heart attack.'

May was devastated, she began sobbing. Eloise went to her, kneeled in front of her and took her hands.

'On the plus side you have four grandchildren and two great grandchildren to meet,' Eloise told her.

May looked at Richard with tear stained eyes, he nodded in confirmation.

'I am not saying that you are not my mother, deep down I believe you are, I am going to have it confirmed, I'm sorry, it's just that I need to know for sure. I checked today, we could have the results of a DNA test back in a couple of weeks, if not sooner,' Richard said solemnly.

'Of course, anything,' May agreed. 'One question, how did you get this photo?'

'It was on my kitchen table this morning, just sitting there, no idea where it came from? Eloise answered.

'What about my letter? May asked.

'We have had a few letters for you, some we put back the post box, some we gave back to the postwoman,' Richard said.

'I have had a few letters for you too. I did the same,' said May.

'It's all a bit weird, I think there have been higher powers at work here to make all this happen,' Eloise commented.

'Frank, you did it, you completed your mission,' Anna said and turned to look at her friend.

Frank was overcome with emotion; the tears were flowing freely from his eyes.

'We did it Anna; I could not have done it on my own.'

'Frank, it's time to go,' another voice from behind them said.

They turned round to see another soul, one with a bright white make; she was stunning, jet black hair and light green eyes, pale skin and a wonderful smile.

'Fenza it's you, can I have a few minutes to say my goodbyes?' Frank asked.

'Yes.'

Frank said goodbye to his family even though they could not hear him then turned to Anna.

'I don't know what to say to you, you are my best friend, I will miss you so much. Thank you from the bottom of my heart. I hope I will see you again, if death is fairer than life then I will.'

'This is not the last time I will see you I know it, I love you Frank Wood, I am sure I will be up there soon.'

'I hope so Anna. By the way I love you too, bye.'

'Bye.'

There was no embrace, just words, that was more than enough. He was gone, just vanished as if he was going into the next room.

43
Friday 27th December

Anna woke up in the shed with Jasmine talking to her baby. She had tormented Billy for a full hour last night, she was feeling terrible about it, but good at the same time as she thought she had made progress and she knew Billy was not working today which eased her conscious further. Frank being gone was upsetting her more than she thought it would, although she knew this time would come; she knew she would have to see the rest of her mission out on her own. Today was a new day; she was more determined than ever to save the Innocent. She saw firsthand that a mission could be completed successfully, Frank done it and she would too.

Candice came into the shed with an empty bucket and a bag full of food.

'I have visitors coming today so I won't be able to come out until tonight when they are gone. Everything you need is in this bag,' Candice said bluntly.

Once Candice was gone with Jasmine's makeshift toilet, Jasmine emptied the bag on the bed. It contained a roll on sausage which she ate right away, a flask of tea, two bottles of water, four sandwiches, two chocolate bars and a packet of crisps.

A right old picnic she has there, no substitute for a

decent meal, at least she is getting fed. I need to go and see what visitors the monsters have today. It may not help me; I will try anything for a scrap of information.

Anna went into the Sutherlands' kitchen; Candice and Jack were at the table drinking coffee.
'How is the girl?' Jack asked Candice.
'The usual, she's not half getting big.'
'Did you give her plenty food to do her all day?'
'Yes, of course I did Jack, how stupid do you think I am?'
Jack ignored the question and asked one of his own instead, 'Is your gran coming with your mum and dad?
'Yes, do you think they would leave her in the house on her own? She is eighty-nine.'
'Well they do leave her in the house on her own.'
'Not for long and they will be here all day, they need to bring her.'
'Good I like your gran, she is straight to the point and never minces her words, and sure she is not as sharp as she used to be, her hearing is going, but she always has an interesting story to tell. Why are you always on the defensive? I ask you a question and you bite my nose off.'
'I thought you were going to moan about Gran coming as well as my parents.'
'Why do you always think the worst of me? I

have never given any indication that I don't like your family. You do it all the time, it is getting worse the older you get. You need to believe that people have got good intensions.'

'I don't want to argue with you.'

'Well you started it.'

'Well, I'm sorry, let's just enjoy the day.'

Jack left the kitchen, went into the living room and switched on the TV. Candice stayed in the kitchen until the door was knocked at 10.30 am. It was the visitors that were expected, Michael and Mary Davidson, Candice's parents and her gran, Mary's mother Beth Stewart. Hugs and kisses were exchanged on the doorstep then the visitors were shown into the living room where Jack got up and also welcomed their guests. Michael was in his early seventies. He had dark thinning hair with not as much grey as you would expect from someone his age, he wall tall and thin and had sharp features the same as his daughter. He wore dark brown framed glasses with grey eyes behind them. Mary was a total contrast to her daughter; she was short and dumpy and had hair so grey it was almost white. Her eyes were small and brown; she used to wear glasses, she had recently opted for contacts. Once seated and coffee and tea were served Christmas gifts were exchanged. It was a tradition for Candice's parents to visit her couple of days after Christmas;

Candice booked the day off work. Her parents always went to see Candice's sister on Christmas day because that's where the grandchildren were. Although Candice always wanted children she never resented her sister at all. She was the one person that Candice loved unconditionally. There was only a year between them in age; they were very close growing up. They had similar looks; their personalities though were chalk and cheese. Candice and Gillian were mistaken for each other often; it was always Candice that got into trouble for something or another.

'So when are you moving?' Mary asked her daughter.

'The end of January all going well, I have given a month's notice at work, Jack is keeping the business, he will work from home sorting out the legal stuff for his sites. John Morrison will be running things on a day to day basis; he has been with Jack for a good few years now, he has it all in hand.'

'When are you getting to adopt your child?' Mary questioned.

'I told you on the phone, the adoption agency has already said we are suitable, all they need to do is check out our new home. Then we wait,' Candice answered.

'We will visit at the beginning of February then. You said there is plenty of room so we could stay for few days; check the place out for ourselves.'

'You can't it will be too soon, there is a good bit of work to do before we can have people staying, I will let you know as soon as we have everything in order,' Candice said trying not to sound too off putting.

'Ok, it was only a suggestion.'

'You will get a good few bob for this place Jack,' Michael said.

'Should do; give us some money for bringing up the baby when we get one.'

'You may not be offered a baby,' Mary said.

'We said we would wait longer for a baby,' Candice answered.

'That may take a while you know,' Mary again.

'We know that Mum, we have waited this long, so we will wait for as long as it takes.'

'Did your criminal record not bother the adoption agency then?' Michael spoke to Jack.

'I was honest to them about it; they said it was a long time ago and that I have never stepped out of line since then, so they are more than happy to give me the benefit of the doubt. They said the checks they do are thorough and if they were not sure then they would have refused us,' Jack lied through his teeth.

'Have you seen your sister recently?' Mary asked.

'Yes, we dropped presents off for the kids last

Sunday; we stayed long enough for a coffee and a chat.'

Candice's mum sure likes to ask the questions. I wish she would ask her what she has in her shed. I think maybe that would be too much to ask.

'Is it too early for a Bailey's?' Beth asked out of the blue.
'No Gran, if that's what you want, that is what you will have,' Candice said, got up and went to the kitchen.

I don't think hanging around here is going to benefit my mission. They will never say anything out of place in front of her parents. The last thing I want to watch is an old lady getting drunk.

Billy was on sentry at the window; Kate was in the living room doing a little housework. Anna needed to know if Billy understood her new message that something was going to happen on the twenty-fourth of January. She needed to spend more time here to find out, even if he had the message already she would still deliver it to him every night until her mission either failed or succeeded.
She stayed with Kate and Billy for the rest of the day and into the evening. There was no mention of Billy being in the know about the date she had tried to put in his mind. They had taken turns at the window, although Anna knew they

would not see anything as the monsters had visitors and had sorted out Jasmine with food this morning.

Anna went back to the shed to check up on Jasmine, she was sleeping so Anna did the same. She was missing Frank terribly and the boredom she felt in her first few days back down here on earth with no one to talk to revisited her with earnest.

When Anna woke Jasmine was reading her book, she was in the middle of it by the looks of it. Anna wondered how Jasmine could see properly as the light in the shed was far from bright, she supposed Jasmine had younger eyes. Anna left and went into the Sutherlands' house again. She checked the time in the kitchen it was 7.40 pm.

I slept for longer than I thought, never mind it passed some time.

The house was empty, she went outside and noticed Candice's car was gone so she went to Billy; he was in the living room with a man Anna didn't know, they were having a beer. Kate was at the window. It seemed strange that she was here instead of in the living room when she had a guest. Anna was just glad that she was here keeping watch, not that anything was going to happen as the Sutherlands were out, she was glad that Kate and Billy were not giving up on this. She went back into the living room when she overheard the topic of conversation.

'So, the locks on that shed could easily be broke to get in,' Billy was saying.

'I'm a locksmith Billy, I can get into anything,' Jamie answered.

'I'm not talking about you, I am talking about me.'

'Tell me what is going on.'

'I don't know for sure that anything is going on, but I have reason to suspect it.'

'Billy, please tell me what is happening. I have known you for years. I know when something is bothering you?'

'Kate,' Billy shouted through to the room.

'What is it?' Kate said popping her head around the living room door.

'We need to tell him.'

'Tell him what?'

'About the shed and the twenty-fourth of January, he can help us with the locks.'

Anna was elated that the date in January had sunk into Billy, she had not been there to hear Billy mention it to his wife before, he had and it was the best she could hope for, she would still talk to him every night until that day came, she was taking no chances.

Kate nodded her agreement, grabbed a beer from the fridge and joined her husband and his friend. Billy told Jamie about the comings and goings from the shed and that he suspected something was going to happen on the twenty-fourth of January.

'What makes you think that something will happen on that specific date?' Jamie asked.

'I don't know how I know, I just know. You can't tell a soul about this Jamie, I'm serious. This has to be kept under wraps, as I said I don't know anything for sure.'

'Why don't we break into it tonight?'

'If we do that and they are not up to anything then we will get in trouble.'

'Ok, I will not say a word to anyone; for one thing if I did they would probably think I had finally lost it and you as well. I will be here on the twenty-fourth though, what better person to have on hand than a locksmith when you need to get into something.'

'Well if you want to be here you can. However, if something does occur it could be any time that day, morning or night,' Kate said.

'I will clear it with the wife and with work, is that a Friday?' Jamie asked.

'Yes I will need to get that day and the next day off, just in case,' Billy answered.

When telling Jamie about the shed they missed out a few details that would be considered very embarrassing if all this turned out to be one big misunderstanding. The name tag and the notebook that contained the details of the activity from the shed were not mentioned, or the fact that Billy thought that Anna Ross maybe in that shed.

I can't believe they have told someone. I hope this guy can keep his mouth shut. If he tells anyone and the Sutherlands get wind of it then this whole thing will be over. They will get away with it and if he breaks in and the Sutherlands catch him there is nothing to stop them from killing him too.

Anna spent the rest of the night at Billy's, waited until he was in bed sleeping then went over the same details with him again.

44
Monday 30th December

PC McMillan sat at her desk, with no other case to work on at the moment she was going through the details of the two missing women at the request of Rooney who had to go take a witness statement about a domestic abuse case. She had seen these files many times now, still nothing of any significance stuck out to her. The lack of any new leads was making it impossible to progress, but she was as determined as Rooney was to find these women. The gut instinct that she and PC McCartney had felt about Jack Sutherland had faded, it had not dissipated completely. She listened to what Rooney had to say about him the night he met him, she had a niggling feeling about him that would not entirely leave her. She had noticed that Mr Ross had put a fresh appeal on Facebook that morning. Different pictures of Anna with their dog and a sad insight into the way he was feeling not knowing what happened to her. She sat there until lunchtime going over and over the same things with optimism that something would jump out at her, nothing did.

Rooney was back and on the phone at his desk when she came back from lunch, she returned to the files and started studying them again.

'Nicole, we have someone downstairs who believe they saw Anna Ross the night she disappeared, you want to come with?' Rooney asked as he was passing her desk.

'Sure,' she said getting up from her seat and falling in step behind him.

A young man with blue jeans, a grey hooded top, a blue baseball cap and white trainers was pacing up and down interview room one when Rooney and Nicole went in. His brown hair stuck out from the sides of the cap, his eyes were brown and his skin was tanned. He was of slim build and average height.

'Please take a seat,' Rooney invited.

The young man sat down and the two officers took up the seats across the table from him.

'Can I have your name? Rooney asked.

'Ryan Doran.'

'How old are you? Rooney was doing the talking while Nicole was taking notes.

'Twenty-two, my address is three Topple Way Hallington.'

'Excellent that was my next question. Now I believe you saw Anna Ross on the night she disappeared.'

'I did, I was driving along Main Street. She was walking her dog.'

'Where exactly was she on the street?'

'I would say that she was about halfway along on the opposite side of the Green, near the hairdressers. The dog was off the lead. I was on the same side as The Green going the opposite way from Mrs Ross.'

'The Green? By that you mean Hallington Park?' Rooney continued with the questions trying to be as thorough as possible.

'Yes.'

'What time was it roughly?'

'Maybe about 10.15 give or take.'

'How sure are you that it was her?'

'I'm positive it was her, I mean I don't know personally, I worked with her husband Tom for a while. I am a plasterer.'

'Why has it taken you so long to come forward? This has been all over Facebook and has even been on the news.'

'I'm not on Facebook and I just got back from Gran Canaria yesterday. I have been there for six weeks doing a job for a couple my parents know. They bought a holiday home there, it needed a bit of work so my mate and I went there to do the work and get a holiday at the same time.'

'That's why you have the tan then?'

'Yes, it was hard work. We did get plenty time in the sun though.'

'Nice work if you can get it. So how did you find out about Mrs Ross when you got back yesterday?'

'My mum and dad told me about it, they are shocked because they said that was two women missing from here in so many months, that's when I knew I had to come in and tell you about it.'

'Did you notice anything odd about her or anything on Main Street that night?

'Nothing that sticks out in my mind, wait there was a man walking a dog as well, I passed him not long after I passed Mrs Ross; he was on the same side of the street as her going the opposite direction.'

'Is there anything else at all you can remember?'

Ryan sat for a few minutes in thought, 'No, sorry.'

'Ok Ryan, you can go, if you think of anything else please contact us.'

'I will.'

'One more thing before you go. Can I have your phone number and car registration please, make and model as well?' Rooney asked as he slid a pen and piece of paper across the table.'

Ryan left the two officers in the room after he wrote down the details he was asked for.

'What do you think?' PC McMillan asked.

'It doesn't give us any new information apart from the fact that he was the last person to see her alive and not William Barclay. The man with the dog he said he saw was William Barclay, we already knew about him talking to Anna the night she went missing. If she was hit by a car I doubt it was his. No one comes forward if they have something to hide, well almost no one. That will be your next job. Call round the garages; see if they have had anything in with the same registration over the last six weeks. We will go to his house later and have a look at the car anyway. We will say we have another question for him when we turn up unannounced at his door, talk to the parents if we can to check his working holiday story.'

'Right boss, I'm on it,' PC McMillan said as she got up and left the room.

At 2 pm Rooney went to PC McMillan's desk.
'How are you doing with the garages? He asked.
'No joy as yet boss, been through most of them within a ten mile radius.'
'Ok, let's leave that for now, we will go see him, hopefully he will be home. We can get a peek at his car while the daylight is still here.'
Rooney did the driving this time and was pleased to see Ryan's car in the drive when they pulled up at the address he had given. They got out and took a good look around the car before they knocked on the door.
'Hello, how can I help you?' A man in his early forties asked when he opened the door.
'Yes, I was hoping to speak with Ryan, I have a follow up question to ask him,' Rooney said.
'Please come in,' the man said and stepped aside.

'You must be Mr Doran, Ryan's dad,' Rooney said.

'Yes, it was me that told him he should go to the police this morning; he was away for six weeks. I presume he told you.'

'Yes he did, said he was working on a house.'

'Our friends have bought a house in Gran Canaria, hoping we get to spend some time there, I will just go get him,' Mr Doran said after he showed them into the living room.

They heard him going up the stairs then his footsteps on the way down.

'He will be down in a minute, he was sleeping, must be all that hard work catching up on him. I know he is young, but he is a great worker you know. I'm sorry, I need to ask. 'Do you know what happened to the two women?'

This was a question that Rooney hated being asked because he never had a decent answer.

'Our inquiries are ongoing.'

'That's all you hear about nowadays, people going missing, what is the world coming to?'

Ryan came into the living room rubbing his eyes and pulling on a Glasgow Rangers football top; he sat down next to his father.

'How can I help?' he asked Rooney directly.

'Sorry to get you up. I was wondering if you saw any other cars on the evening you saw Anna Ross.'

'Not on Main Street, it was quiet.'

'Did you notice any cars maybe parked with someone sitting in them.'

'I never saw any; I was not looking for that.'

'Well I will let you get back to bed, remember if you think of anything else give us a call.'

'Of course I will.'

'We will see ourselves out,' Rooney said as he got up and led the way to the front door.

'Well his story seems to ring true,' PC McMillan said on their way to the car.

'Yes, it certainly does, I just hope he comes up with something else that is potentially useful to us.'

They went back to the station. Rooney was feeling low.

The boredom was eating away at Anna, at least when Frank was here she had someone to talk to. Since he went she had not went to watch TV or a movie with anyone, most of her time was spent in the prison with Jasmine. The rest was spent between Billy and the Sutherlands. She went on walks around the route she took on her last night alive; she popped in and out to see Tom and her family, but did not spend any length of time with them. She wanted them to be alright, which they weren't; this would make her teary so she would throw herself straight back into her mission. She waited until after Jasmine had received her dinner and Candice had come back with water, a flask of tea and a hot water bottle and took the dirty plate away then Anna went with her back into the house. She had seen empty boxes appearing in their house over the last few days, now they were packing them. The Christmas tree had been taken down on Saturday and been put in a box, the rest of their stuff was following suit. Jack was packing breakables away with newspaper and bubble wrap and Candice joined him in the living room once she had filled the dishwasher.

'I hired a removal van for the eighteenth and nineteenth, that's the Saturday and Sunday before you go up. Paul is giving me hand; we will do a run each day of that weekend. We will just need to sleep in the spare bedroom that week and make do with the bare essentials,' Jack announced.

'No problem for me, I thought you let out Fred's house as furnished.'

'It is partially furnished; a lot of the stuff was old. I kept what I could.'

'We will have it the way we want it in no time.'

'You mean the way you want it,' he said with a smile.

'That's what I meant,' Candice said through a laugh.

They are in a good mood tonight by the sound of it;

they are usually taking a swipe at each other. Maybe this is how they normally are with each other; the stress of all their crimes maybe put them at each other's throats.

She stayed with them until they went to bed then went over the fence to Billy's. Billy was already in bed and sleeping. She said her usual speech to him then went back to the shed satisfied that she had done all she could for the night.

45
Saturday 4th January 2020

Billy was on the first of his four days off; he was sitting at the spare bedroom window where he whiles away most of his time. He had noted the visit to the shed by the women with a bucket and a carrier bag half an hour ago, Kate was out walking Buster, she said she would get rolls to make his breakfast when she got back. His stomach was grumbling with hunger, he decided he would start breakfast before she got back, he knew through experience there would be no movement at the shed until between 1 and 2 pm, but there was always a chance they would change their routine.

'I hope you are not in there Anna,' he said to himself.

When Kate got back the sausages and bacon were nearly ready, he put the kettle on and sat at the table.

'I know we have had this conversation, maybe we should go to the police now.'

'We could be made out to be fools Billy. We have been spying on our neighbours who could be totally innocent.'

'I think they would check that shed if we showed them the notebook with the movements in it.'

'As you said we had this conversation, we have

no proof that any crime has been committed apart from your dreams and don't get me wrong I totally believe in you and what you have been experiencing. I think we should stick to the plan and wait for January the twenty-fourth to come around then all will be revealed, I'm sure of it.'

'Ok, but if someone is in that shed they still have another twenty days to go, that is on us.'

'If there is then our neighbours will get found out, if not then we will feel silly, but we won't be in any kind of trouble for it.'

'I hear you,' Billy said as the kettle clicked off and he got up and made the coffee.

Jasmine had slept all through the night; Anna watched her chest rise and fall for the last hour or so thinking that she had been sleeping too long.

'Anna Anderson,' she said to a sleeping Jasmine.

Jasmine moaned like a tired school kid being woke in the morning to go to school.

'Jasmine I am trying to help your baby and you; I just want you to know that I won't give up until the bitter end.'

Jasmine woke with a start and glanced around the shed no find no one there.

What I am I doing I should have let her sleep, I know I can connect with her, I don't do it nearly enough, but I don't want her to think she is losing her mind stuck in this hell hole. There is one thing I need to tell her, it concerns the night they will be moving her, she won't know exactly when that is, she didn't even know it was Christmas until she was told and for some reason I don't think she has kept track of time since then. I need to tell her to try and keep the disk on her when the time comes. I know it's not part of my mission to get the monsters caught for what they did to me; however, I am sure going to try. If she has the name tag on her when she gets rescued it will be something for her to prove that I was here and if it gets left in that mattress it may never be found. I am sure her word will be enough for the police to search the place, but what if they believe her state of mind is effected by her ordeal, oh what do I know, it's not as if I am some sort of super sleuth. All I know is I want her to take it with her, I will try to make that possible.

Breakfast and lunch came and went; Anna followed Candice into the house when she brought a clean bucket with lunch. The house was getting barer and barer every day. Anna thought they were a touch premature with their packing, to them, especially Candice what was about to transpire was exciting, a new chapter, a fresh start, in a way a whole new life. Motherhood was her life's ambition; she was going to be prepared for it as much as she could. She had already stock piled things for the baby, clothes, nappies, bottles and a few toys; she wanted the transition from her old life to her new one to go as smoothly as possible. Anna stayed there all day and into the evening to hear if any of their plans had changed. Nothing they said gave the impression that their plans had been altered.

Billy was in the living room with a movie on and Kate was keeping watch at the window when Anna went to their house that night.

It's Saturday night at 9.05 pm, Billy and Kate should be out enjoying themselves. Instead I have them shackled to that window.

It felt as if Anna had been waiting half a life for Billy and Kate to turn in for the night. She tried to watch the movie with Billy, it was a war movie, Anna had no interest in it whatsoever, war films were far too depressing for her, anytime Tom would suggest one she would just give him a look as if to say no way. Maybe Kate felt the same way. Maybe that is why she opted for spending her night in that room staring into that garden instead of being snuggled up on the couch with her husband, or it might be her determination to get some dirt on her neighbours.

Anna worked on Billy for twenty minutes before she decided enough was enough for the night; she knew he already had all the messages he needed from her. She wanted to be as thorough as one of the robot vacuums that go around picking up every speck of dust and dirt, flicking particles out from the skirting boards and returning to suck it up, not stopping for a second until the job is done.

46
Thursday 9th January

Before work Tom put a new appeal on Social Media for any information on Anna, he saw the new one the police had put on the day before. There were many messages of support both from people who knew them and from strangers from his previous appeal. Even though everyone meant well none of the well wishing was doing anything to find Anna. He did appreciate all the trouble people were going to, taking time out of their day to send him their best, though all he wanted was a message saying that someone knew where Anna was. It had been eight weeks since she went missing without a trace and his patience were wearing thin; Sergeant Rooney had not been in touch with either him or Anna's parents for some time. They say no news is good news. Tom knew that did not apply this time. He had been to see George and Ruby last night and was going back there tonight for dinner; he saw the same frustration in them that he felt inside himself. He went to work and at breakfast time which was at 9.30 am this morning he phoned Rooney.

'Hello, Sergeant Rooney.'

'Hello sergeant this is Tom Ross, I know if you had anything new you would call. It's just my wife has been missing eight weeks now, I was just wondering if there is anything else I can do?' he asked, although he knew he was doing all he could.

'Ah Mr Ross, I was talking about you only a few moments ago,' Rooney said.

Tom suspected this to be a lie; in fact Rooney was being truthful. Tom said nothing so Rooney continued.

'I am not long off the phone to the local news station and they have agreed to do another piece on Anna, this time they would like to shoot it at her parents' house tomorrow at one o'clock. They want it to feature them, you and your dog if that is ok.'

'That sounds good, George and Ruby will not have a problem with that I wouldn't think; I will call them straight after this call and let them know. Do you know their address?'

'Yes, I have it, please let me know what they say, so I can call the news station back to tell them they have the go ahead.'

'Yes, of course sergeant.'

Tom hung up and called his in-laws right away.

'Hi George, I'm straight off the phone to Sergeant Rooney. Would you and Ruby be able to do a TV appeal tomorrow at one at your house, they want us all there including Rex?' Tom asked.

'Ruby is at work so I can't ask her, but yes we will do it. I will phone and tell her. She will be happy to hear that her daughter is not being forgotten about.'

'I wouldn't let that happen to her George.'

'I know, I better get a start on the housework so that Ruby doesn't fuss about it later, you know what she is like.'

'You bet, see you later.'

Tom told his boss Paul that he needed the day off tomorrow and Paul agreed at once. There was not much he could do to ease the worry of his employee, so if Tom needed time off Paul was more than happy to give him it.

Jasmine was in a foul mood today, Anna could see it in her face. She was doing a fair bit of crying. She had the name tag out, turning it over and over in her hand mumbling inaudibly, and then out of the blue she said something that sent shivers up Anna's spine.

'If you can hear me, the one that talks to me now and then when I am trying to sleep, talk to me more, tell me what is happening. Sometimes I hear you loud and clear as if we are sitting face to face and other times you are so faint I can hardly make you out. Is there any hope for me? They are going to kill me, aren't they? Are my parents searching for me? I have so many questions for you. You are the woman they killed right in front of my eyes aren't you? Why me? There are so many ways to have or get a baby nowadays, why are they doing it this way. They are evil; I guess you know all about that. Can you talk to me when I am awake? I suppose you can't or you would have done it by now.

'I wish I could Jasmine, nothing is ever easy on my side of reality, I will talk to you every time I see you asleep, I have an important message for you now anyway,' Anna said, they were wasted words, she knew she could not be heard.

This is breaking my heart. She is right about the Sutherlands being evil; I need to make them pay. What if they manage to slip through the net on the twenty-fourth? I have put all my eggs in that one basket. No the police will get them when Billy finally blows the whistle, they have ways and means to trace people, no one just disappears. People do disappear; I am living proof of that, well not living, but proof.

With plenty of time on her hands Anna decided to go for a walk, a very long one, she had been walking for nearly two hours when a morbid thought came to her. She closed her eyes and thought of her burial site, when she opened them she was standing in front of a fully built garage; the house that it belonged to was almost complete as well. The anger she felt was unparalleled, but at the same time she was a little in awe of the progress the builders had made.

Well there is no way anyone would know that my body is under there, that evil man Jack has made sure of that. How on earth can people be so heartless? I know why, because if he gets caught or should it be when he gets caught his life is over, or the life he has now is over. It will be straight to prison for him and his monster of a wife. As much as I want to be back in The Before, I really want to see them behind bars for their crimes, suffering and regretting their actions.

She hung around watching the workmen milling around the site for a while before returning to the shed. This was for sure the lowest ebb she had felt since she came back down here, watching the workmen was a wakeup call as to how much life goes on no matter what. If Frank was still here then she would have made a beeline for him, he would have pulled her out of the dumps, without him all she wanted to do was sleep so she took up her usual position and fell into a slumber easily.

When Anna woke four hours later she was feeling a lot better, the sleep seemed to restore her resolve with her mission.

That's it no more feeling sorry for myself, here is this poor girl going through hell. I'm not going to help her by weighing myself down with what I have been through, what is done is done I need to fixate only on getting that baby saved.

Jasmine was starting yet another book. It must have come with lunch Anna thought, although she was unsure of what time it was, she didn't need to wait long to roughly find out the time as Candice came into the shed with Jasmine's dinner which was a fish supper from a takeaway. Anna wished she could smell it. Not that she felt hungry in any way, that was a thing of the past for her, she needed to feel human. She knew she was what most people would call a ghost, but Anna wanted a small taste of what it was like to be alive. To smell something, to touch something or to even feel physical pain would be welcomed by her. Jasmine enjoyed her dinner tonight and washed it down with a cup of tea from the flask that was brought in with it, after that she tucked herself into the flimsy bed and got lost in her book.

Anna went into see the monsters. It didn't produce any new information so she went on the next part of her routine and went to see Billy. Billy had visitors, his son Aaron and his girlfriend Kirsty so Anna went back to the shed. She was hoping that Jasmine would be asleep so that she could start to plant the seed in her mind to have that damn name tag on her when it came time for her to be moved. She decided the best thing was to give her a code word which Anna would use the closer the move date came. That way Jasmine would know as well that the time was coming and to be ready to take any opportunity she could take to alert someone else of her predicament. Anna didn't think for one moment that the monsters would allow that to take place, but there was always an outside chance that a hiccup in their plan could happen.

Jasmine read her book for a long time before she surrendered to her tiredness, as soon as she was sound asleep Anna started planting the seed.

'Anna Anderson.'

Jasmine moved position.

'Jasmine the people who have you here are going to move you to a different location. This will occur on the twenty-fourth of January. I have someone watching for this that I can trust. What I need you to do is keep that name tag on you when the time comes. Three days before that date as I know you will not know when that is I will keep saying a word to you, when you hear it keep the name tag on you. This will not be easy because there are not many places for you to put it, but it is important. The word I will use is Rex. You have been through so much, I am doing all I can to bring this to an end, I truly pray that this ordeal will have a happy ending for you. I want you to understand all this so much; I need you to understand as it will make it easier to nail the evil pair for my murder, well I think it will.'

Anna spoke to Jasmine for the next hour or so, not about anything in particular and certainly not about The Before or anything that has happened to her since her death. She wanted to; although she knew that it is out of bounds.

Billy got his nightly visit from Anna with the usual words she had for him, she felt like a broken record, it had to be done, she was sure that Billy was up to speed. She was taking no chance in the last phase of her mission.

47
Friday 10th January

Sergeant Rooney turned up at the Andersons' house ten minutes before the TV station got there to check that everyone was in the right frame of mind to partake in the interview. They were all eager to get it done, anything to help find Anna. The same van that had visited Tom for his interview pulled up in front of the house. Jill and William both got out, Jill came up and knocked on the door while William went round to the back of the van to start unloading his gear.

'Mr Ross, do you remember me from your last interview?' Jill asked when Tom answered the door.

'Yes of course Jill,' he said holding the door open for her to enter.

Once all the introductions and the setting up of the equipment were complete they all settled down for the interview.

'Starting with you Mrs Anderson, I want you all to say what you want about Anna. You can say it as if you are talking to her or if you are appealing to the audience, whichever you want,' Jill said sympathetically.

Ruby said her piece as if she were talking one on one with her daughter, yes she cried, she just held it together long enough to finish. Both

George and Tom spoke to the audience, pleading for help in finding their loved one.

'That was good, we will get that on the news tonight if we can, if not it will be tomorrow evening,' Jill said.

William started to load the gear back in the van while Jill sat consoling Ruby until she was ready to go. Rooney had sat in his car when the interview was taking place. He saw Jill and William leave so went and knocked on the door. He was invited in by George; Ruby didn't ask anyone if they wanted coffee, she took it upon herself to make it for everyone anyway.

They sat in the kitchen at the table with a plate of chocolate biscuits sitting in the middle of their coffee cups.

'How do you feel it went?' Rooney asked.

'As well as it could have,' George answered.

'We need to get something positive from it, I feel as if this may be the last effort to find our girl,' Ruby sniffled.

'We will never give up, we will do all we can,' Rooney responded.

'Someone knows something,' George said as he had done before.

Rooney didn't know what to say to that, he knew that George was right so he nodded his head in agreement.

48
Saturday 18th January

The Sutherlands moving out most of their possessions did not go unnoticed by Kate who took buster out for a walk and hovered up and down in front of their house when she walked by. It took two hours or so for Jack and John to load up the rented removal van. This was one of two trips; the other would be tomorrow. The journey took nearly three and a half hours one way so doing it twice in one day is a bit of a push. Billy was working so she text him saying to call her as soon as he could. At 9.10 am when he was on his break he called her.

'Hey, what's up?'

'They are moving their furniture today, I just watched the man and his buddy load a van and drive away,' Kate told him impatiently.

'Well I was right to trust whatever it is that is giving me my information, that makes me feel better about doing all the spying.'

'We are on the right tracks Billy, we don't have long to wait. I wanted to follow him to see where he goes then thought more of it.'

'I'm glad you didn't, who knows what would have happened if they spotted you.'

'I will see you tonight darling, bye.'

Anna was in the Sutherlands while Jack and John were taking their belongings to the van.

Candice was supervising every move they made, it was clear Jack was getting irritated by her. Anna wanted them to argue, she wanted them to turn on each other. She didn't want harmony in their ranks. The more they were at each other's throats the more chance that Anna thought they would make a mistake, that Jasmine would be given an opportunity to escape, that some detail of their evil plan would be overlooked.

Unlike Kate, Anna had nothing to lose by going with Jack. When they had nearly done with putting the stuff in the van she thought herself into a space in the back. She knew by listening in to Jack and Candice's conversation that she was going to Inverness, she wanted to see it for herself.

At the destination she waited until the back door was put up before she thought herself out of the van. The old house that stood in front of her was stunning in her opinion. Yes the garden was a bit shabby; the house itself was not short on character. It was a brick dwelling; faded over the years, ivy climbed from the ground nearly all the way up to the eaves, the windows were sash. The front double door was wooden. It was the kind of place Anna would have been more than happy in. There were trees all around the sides and back giving anyone that lived here all the privacy they needed. Anna could not see any neighbouring houses. She felt a pang of rage that two evil people such as Jack and Candice could be so lucky in life.

It does not seem fair, the Sutherlands land a house like this, sure I know they didn't earn it, it was inherited, all the same, why is it that nothing is deserved in life?

Jack took an envelope out of his pocket and from it produced the keys to the house. Before they started emptying the van John came out of the van with a flask and some sandwiches, they went into the house. Anna followed. The inside of the house was a little more modern than Anna had been expecting. The floors in the entrance hall and living room looked like the original parquet, the skirting and facing had been changed to the best match possible as was the doors. The kitchen was modern with light grey vinyl click flooring, dark grey cupboards and light grey marble worktop, the only sign of any age in the kitchen was the stunning Belfast sink which Anna thought, although it was beautiful was out of place with the more modern surroundings. The house was by no means fully furnished, it did have some furniture scattered around, enough for people to live in it. A minimalist approach Anna thought.

Jack and Candice will have this place filled in no

time, they won't get a chance to live here if I have anything to do with it.

Anna had seen enough so closed her eyes and was back with Candice. The curtains and blinds had been left on the Sutherlands' windows. This made sense as they were still to live there another six days and Jack would be there for as long as it takes him to get rid of all the evidence. It was most of the bedroom furniture that was moved today, the living room furniture Anna thought would go tomorrow. It was all pushed up to the one side of the room stacked along with numerous boxes. The walls were bare; the only functioning things in the room were two garden chairs and a coffee table on which a small TV stood. Anna checked the bedrooms; Candice's room was devoid of furniture as was one other room. The smaller of the rooms was crammed with a double bed and a very small wardrobe. Suitcases and black bags full of what Anna presumed were clothes lined the rest of the wall space leaving hardly any space to move. They would not be very comfortable over the next week. Anna was happy about that, it was nothing compared to what they had put Jasmine through. Candice went out with a clean bucket and lunch for Jasmine. Anna went with her.

'We will be out after dinner to let you get

cleaned up and maybe get that hair washed, those sheets need a change as well it is starting to stink in here again,' Candice said to Jasmine.

'Are you going to move me somewhere else?' Jasmine asked.

'Where did you hear that?'

'Is it true? Are you?'

'I am going to ask you again. Where did you hear that?'

'I dreamt it. The dream seemed so real. It must be true or you wouldn't be so defensive. Then again I don't know you maybe you are like that all the time.'

'No lunch for you,' Candice threw a bottle of water on the bed and took the sandwiches with her when she stormed out back to the house.

Why did she ask Candice that? What did she think she was going to achieve by winding her up, the only thing it got her was no lunch. She knows that she is getting moved. At least she is hearing what I am telling her, although the last thing she should be doing is taunting Candice. I wish Frank was here. I miss him so much.

Tom was walking Rex when Anna closed her eyes and thought of him. He was in The Green, Rex was off the lead, Tom was just standing watching him sniff around a tree. It was obvious to Anna that Rex had made a full recovery, to see him no one would know that he had a recent injury and Anna was thrilled he looked so good. She walked around the park with her husband; they were just about to leave when she saw the soul with the black make that she and Frank had met. He was beckoning her to go to him; she paused for a moment contemplating what to do. She wanted someone to talk to more than anything, the colour of his make made her want to run in the opposite direction. Her mind was made up for her when she watched him disappear and reappear by her side.

'Hello again, do you remember me? You are Anna aren't you?'

'Yes and yes, I was with my friend Frank when we met you.'

'Who's the guy with the dog?' Gavin Peterson asked.

'My husband Tom, I was checking up on him,' Anna answered.

'I have not been to see any of my friends or family, to be honest they are better off without me.'

Anna didn't know what to say, he was probably right about that if the colour of his make was anything to go by.

'So where is your friend today?' Gavin continued.

'He has completed his mission successfully and is back in The Before.'

'Has he? So it is possible then, I feel as if I

am trying to do something that can't be done. I haven't found my power yet. It would have been easier if my guide had told me what it is, like your guide told you. I suppose when you have a make as dark as mine you are open to all sorts of punishment and who could blame them. I have done a lot of evil things; I am going to pay for each and every one just like I should.'

'You said you had ten years to complete your mission.'

'That's what Ravi told me.'

'Your guide is Ravi, that's who my guide is as well.'

'It's a small world after all. How is your mission going?'

'Good should be done in a week if all goes to plan,' Anna told him.

'Great, I would help you out, you know the rules; shades would be added to my make, as you can see I can't afford any more,' he said as he had before.

'I have help from the living; my power is I can connect with people.'

'Ah yes I remember, I wish I knew what mine was.'

'Don't you think Ravi will tell you what is it eventually, I mean after a period of time surely he would give you some sort of hint,' Anna said.

'I sure hope so; I really want to make amends. You could say I'm a changed man.'

'I need to go; it was nice speaking to you.'
'You know where to find me if you want to talk some more.'
'Thank you, I will keep it in mind.'
Anna walked away in the same direction Tom had gone.

I feel sorry for him; I know he must have done some bad things when he was alive to have a make that colour, without knowing what his power is, then I would say he is on mission impossible. I enjoyed having a conversation; I might speak to him again.

Anna walked as far as the Sutherlands' house and stopped outside. Gavin was on her mind. She wondered how hard her mission would have been if she didn't know what her power was.

'Ravi,' Anna said out loud and waited.

She liked standing in the rain now because it didn't affect her anymore, when she was alive she hated it, she hated the snow more not that they had seen much of that this year yet, Anna was definitely a summer person. The rain was not heavy; however, she knew that if she were alive she would be soaked through by now. The sky was dark grey. Anna knew that a heavier downpour was imminent; there was a little wind, enough for the rain to be blown about as if it were coming down in small waves.

By the time Ravi showed the sky was dark.

'Hello Anna,' he said startling her from behind.

'Oh hi Ravi, I'm so sorry to bother you, I have a question about another soul.'

'Don't ask me if it is Frank you have the question about. I am not at liberty to talk of a soul who has returned to The Before.'

'Are you disappointed that Frank and me helped each other out.'

'That is a matter to discuss when you return to us, which does not seem to be too far off; you are doing really well. I am delighted to tell you that you may be one of fastest to complete a mission if all goes well,' Ravi said, but did not show any sign of being delighted at all.

'I met Gavin Peterson in the park; I can tell by the colour of his make that he has done many bad things. He will never get his mission even started if he does not know what his power is. Is there any way that you could maybe give him a hint? He does want to make up for what he has done.'

'Since you have spoken up for him I will ask the powers that be if I can divulge that information to him, and if I can then he will have you to thank for it Anna, you are a kind soul. Now I am going to give you a hint, the last person you can connect with is an ex boyfriend.'

Anna never got the chance to say another word to him. He was gone.

Wow! That was a bombshell, on the one hand I don't think I need my last connection, on the other I don't have that many ex boyfriends, I could find out who that is in no time, maybe Ravi told me that for a reason, it is only right that I try to find the missing link. I will have a busy night tonight.

Jasmine had the name tag out again when Anna went to the shed; she was pleased to see that Jasmine was experimenting with places to hide it, not that there was many to choose from. Jasmine put it in her mouth, under her tongue, that made her gag so she took it out and tried it at the side of her mouth in her cheek, she could feel it from the outside which meant Jack or Candice would be able to tell she had something in her mouth. Jasmine checked herself up and down with the disc in her hand and a puzzled expression on her face. She pulled up her t-shirt and her jogging bottoms down at the side and put the name tag in the side of her pants; her pants were tight enough to hold it tightly between them and her hip. She took it back out shaking her head mumbling something that Anna could not interpret. Then her face exploded in excitement as if she had a light bulb moment. She took her hair down and wrapped it back up with the disc inside it, she shook her head, the name tag stayed put. She took it back out and put it back in the mattress with a smug look on her face.

Clever girl. Candice said earlier that her hair was to be washed tonight and that is not a regular occurrence so Jasmine knows that would be a great place to keep it undiscovered after tonight.

Jasmine had finished her latest book and was bored again; she spoke to her baby saying the same things over and over about how much she loved her, yes she was calling the baby a girl, maybe she had a feeling that only expectant mothers got Anna thought, maybe Jasmine was just wanting the baby to be a girl. Dinner was served to Jasmine without a word spoke by her or Candice. An hour later Jack and Candice were back with all the stuff they needed to change the bed and wash Jasmine's hair. Jack made another trip to the house and brought back a basin of hot water, a towel and a change of clothes for Jasmine. Once all that was complete the monsters returned to the house only to come back a half an hour later with a mop and a clean toilet. They did what they needed with only a few words of instruction to their prisoner. While Candice was doing the floor Jack made yet another trip to the house returning with a hot water bottle and a fresh book for Jasmine. She didn't show that she pleased with the book, although she started it as soon as the shed door was closed and locked.

The books she gets from them are the only thing in here that gives her any kind of pleasure. I wonder if she read many books before she was snatched and put in this place.

Anna knew Billy was up for work in the morning, she waited for as long as her patience would allow before she went to see him. She checked the time when she got there it was 9.35 pm; Billy was still at his post at the window. Kate was in the kitchen making some tea. She took a cup into the room for herself and Billy and sat on the bed while Billy kept his eyes peeled on the neighbours' garden.

'All this will be over one way or the other by this time next week, then we can get back to normal and book a holiday,' Kate commented.

'I know and believe me it can't come quick enough; I'm concerned that if someone is in that shed that we have waited so long to alert the authorities, but as you said we can't jump the gun. This is all such as mess.'

Billy had all the activities recorded for the night, after they finish their tea they went to bed. It didn't take long for Billy to fall asleep; as soon as he did Anna played her part in his torment. Afterwards she closed her eyes and thought of Paul Timpson, he was one of the ex boyfriends, she thought now was as good a time as any to get started on her visitations. Anna was unprepared for the scene that lay before her when she opened her eyes. She was standing in a small dirty room, bare floor boards, dirty curtains hanging from the windows, black leather couch with more holes in it than a golf course and a small coffee table with loads of drug paraphernalia. She was disgusted that anyone would want to live that way. There were two people in the room, a woman of undetermined age, very thin with long, greasy hair. Both her and her male companion lay on the couch out of it, a needle hanging out the male's arm which Anna realised was Paul.

'Anna Anderson.'

'Anna Anderson,' she said the words out loud several dozen times with no reaction from her ex so she closed her eyes and thought of Colin Murray. When she opened her eyes she was in a very different environment all together. Colin was leaning over a cot, ohhing and ahhing to a baby boy; she was pleased to see that some people were more responsible than others. She would need to try Colin later so she closed her eyes and thought of Graham McCartney. He was working; he was standing in a street outside a pub with a colleague. She thought he looked very handsome in his uniform; she would need to try him later as well, probably in the morning when he goes to sleep after his night shift. The only other person on her list was Gary

McCulloch, she had only dated him for five maybe six weeks. She thought he should be included in her list, he was in bed and asleep next to a blonde haired woman, a toddler lay between them taking up most of the bed. The blinds on the window were that thin she had enough light to make them out.

'Anna Anderson,' she repeated again and again. Realising she was not going to get any kind of recognition she went back to the shed. Jasmine was in dream land with the latest book from the gruesome twosome open on her chest.

'Anna Anderson,' Anna said.

Jasmine turned, the book fell on the floor next to the bed, but it did not wake her.

'Please don't say anything more to Candice. I should have mentioned before that what I am telling you needs to be on the down low, it only angered her today and it cost you your lunch, you need to keep your strength up for the baby, you should not be missing meals. I know you can't get any exercise and I know that it can't be good for you or the baby, try to keep Candice on side, she is nasty. Not just her, her husband as well you know. You saw what they did to me. What I am trying to say is be very careful, don't do anything to upset them; you will not be here long. You will be free soon if all goes without a hitch. One last thing, remember to listen for the code word I told you.'

Anna waited for what seemed like a couple of hours then returned to Colin Murray, he was out cold in bed, it was a double bed. He was in it on his own. Anna had a few thoughts where his wife or partner could be. She put that out her mind and got on with why she was here. Like in most of the bedrooms she visited, she had to let her eyes adjust to what little light she had.

'Anna Anderson.'

'Anna Anderson,' she continued with this line for ten minutes then gave up.

That means the only person on my list is Graham McCartney unless of course there is someone I have missed out. I can't think of anyone else. Is my mind going? It must be time for me to get back to the shed and shut my own eyes for a while before I revisit Graham in the morning.

49
Sunday 19th January

Jasmine was already awake and had her head in her book when Anna woke. She went straight to her own house and checked the time, it was 4.15 am. She went upstairs to find Tom and Rex on their bed, both of them sparked out. Anna lay down beside them, not to sleep, just to be near them, the three of them on the bed like they did when she was alive. It was too early to visit Graham so she lay there until Tom got up at 7.35 am, the whole time she lay there she thought of her life, of all the things she could have done differently, of all the people she should have helped and of all the people that she loved. She wished she had known Frank in life, she wished that Tom had not cheated, but she knew what had been done was done.

Graham was in bed when she went to him; a beautiful slim woman was getting out of the bed. The lamp at her side of the bed was on, not a bright light. It was enough to see properly.
'Anna Anderson,' she said, Graham groaned. The woman who had vacated the bed leaned over and kissed him on the forehead.
'Anna Anderson,' she said again. Graham shifted then turned over from his back to his side.
'Jack and Candice Sutherland live on Main Street in Hallington, they are evil Graham.

They are keeping Jasmine brown in their shed. They want her baby as their own. I don't know how much of this you will understand and I don't think I have much time left here, please if you can look into them, there is an Innocent to be saved.'

I don't know if this will do any good at this stage in the game, although I know now who my third connection is with.

It was a long day for Anna. She walked around the town in the rain, she could not feel the cold, she knew it was cold though with how wrapped up in hats and scarves everyone around her was. She spent most of her time in the shed watching Jasmine time after time tying the name tag into her hair in between reading her book. She visited Billy like she did every other night and spoke to Jasmine when she eventually went to sleep. Then she lay down herself and let sleep take her.

50
Monday 20th January

Anna knew that Candice had finished up her work on Friday. She thought that was the reason she had brought out Jasmine's breakfast and fresh toilet a little later than normal today. Anna had gone into the Sutherlands' house to check the time, it was 8.30 am and Candice still had her housecoat on then.

A long lie for this witch by the look of it.

The anticipation for Friday to arrive was eating away at Anna; the days seemed to be getting longer and longer. She tried hard to fill her time with walking as much as she could because time felt as if it were standing still when she was in the shed. A frost that had thinly covered the ground was disappearing. People hunched against the cold, there was no rain this morning which must have been welcomed by the people that were outdoors. She was walking past May's house and decided she would check up on her. It was the first time she had done so since Frank had gone and thought to herself that perhaps she should have done it before this. She thought herself into the house; she walked from the hall into the living room where she found May with Eloise. Anna noticed that May now had a coffee table which had two half empty cups and a Victoria Sandwich cake with two slices missing.

'Thank you for coming round Eloise, I do appreciate it.'

'You are family, of course I will come, and more often if I have anything to do with it.'

'When did you say the results of that unnecessary DNA test will be back?' May asked.

'Friday at the latest, but listen Richard already knows what they are going to say.'

'I know, I want him to see it in black and white. After fifty-plus years total confirmation will put my mind at rest as well.'

'Are you still coming for dinner tomorrow?'

'Yes, I wouldn't miss it.'

'I will pick you up at around 6.30 pm,' Eloise said.

'That would be great; I will make sure I am ready.'

This is great, they are being a family; I didn't think that they would go through with the DNA; I suppose Richard had to be sure, he has a family to think about. Frank had the privilege to know the truth from Fenza. He didn't need anyone to prove it to him, it would be great if Frank is able to look down and see the outcome of his mission.

Anna went back outside and continued on her walk, the old and weather beaten posters of her had been replaced with fresh ones. She knew that was the doing of her parents. She didn't stop at any of them, there was no point.

Graham McCartney got up at around 2.30 pm. He had no work for three days then he would be dayshift. He was certainly going to enjoy his days off; he hated nightshift with a passion. He stepped into the shower once it had heated up and stood under the fast and powerful flow. It was then that he felt that he had forgotten something. He finished his shower got dried and put on some clothes; it was too cold to walk about half dressed today. Graham sat on the bed and thought of Anna. He didn't know why she was on his mind today, she was though. It gave him a strange feeling, one that he could not understand. He was halfway through making his breakfast when a sudden thought of Jack Sutherland jumped into his mind.

'What is it with me today? Maybe I am just feeling a little sentimental over Anna. Sergeant Rooney said that Jack Sutherland had nothing to hide; I am not so sure, shaking a gut instinct is not easy even after you have been told there is nothing in it. The nightshift has taken my sanity; I'm even talking to myself.'

Anna walked into the precinct. It was fairly quiet, no Christmas shoppers milling around now. She went to her shop in Barnes Road and thought herself inside. Sam was at the counter talking to a young man in a suit as she went closer she heard that they were talking about dry cleaning, it was a complaint being made and Sam was as ever apologetic for the mix-up. The young man handed over a dry cleaning bag saying it was the wrong garment, Sam took it and opened it and yes the young man was clearly right as it was bridesmaid dress inside.

'I know who this belongs to Sir, let me go and check to see if I can find your suit,' Sam said walking into the back shop only to return a few moments later.

'Here we are, please accept my apology,' Sam said handing the garment over.

'No problem, we are all human,' the young man said then left the shop.

It was good to see Sam; Anna knew the business was in good hands, she missed his company. He always knew how to make her laugh and sometimes cry with laughing.

She left the shop and walked on; she thought about going to the Leisure Centre to see Rebecca Blacklaw, but didn't want to get angry so thought better of it. She started walking back to the shed, taking her time so that it took her longer.

Jasmine had three new books spread out in front of her on the bed.

I don't know if she has time to read three books between now and Friday, she is quite a fast reader, I'm sure she will give it her best shot.

Anna went into the Sutherlands; it was 4.20 pm when she peeked at the clock. Candice was reading a book of her own; she was lying on the bed in the cramped, small room. Anna stood staring at her in disgust for a while then left her to go walking again.

I wonder if Graham is nightshift tonight. What good am I doing going to connect with him now? If only Ravi had told me about my third connection a while ago. I will go to him anyway, never know it might come in handy. I wonder how Frank is doing in The Before, I wonder how mad Fenza was with him helping me with my mission, he would have the shades taken off his make for completing his mission, he will have the two added on for helping me, I will have them added as well, we knew the rules. We broke them so we need to pay the price.

Darkness had come down and brought with it the rain. Anna was wandering; she was walking up and down the same streets over and over with nowhere to go and going nowhere fast. She did this for a couple of hours before she realized she was doing it.

What is wrong with me? If I were alive I would say that my mind feels foggy, that I don't feel myself. Can a soul lose their mind? If they can then I guess that is what is happening to me.

'Anna, Anna,' she heard a voice call her and turned around to see Gavin approaching her.

'I have been looking for you, to tell you my good news,' he said.

'Good news?'

'Yes. Ravi told me what my power is.'

'I am pleased for you, really I am. Maybe you can start properly on your mission now.'

'Yes, I can, once I learn how to use it.'

'What exactly is your power?' Anna asked.

'I don't want to say. It seems pretty lame compared to yours.'

'Listen I don't know how many different powers they have got for us, I am sure they will give us the best power to get the job done, what is it?' Anna asked again.

'Well apparently I have the power to influence dogs.'

Anna thought about why he would be given a power like that. She soon realised that he should be able to get his mission done in no time with it.

'You don't seem pleased about it, it is so simple it will get you out of here in record time,' Anna said.

'I know what I need to get the dogs to do, I need them to dig up the site where that body is buried, but I tried to command a few today, they seem to be ignoring me.'

'Things are not that easy in death Gavin. It is hard going; you will need to master this power to get the benefit out of it.'

'You are right, I know that. I will not see many dogs in the park tonight. Tomorrow is another day.'

'That's the spirit. No pun intended,' Anna said with a laugh.

For the first time she saw Gavin smile, it changed his full face. He looked softer and humble, the kind of face that did not reflect the personality that goes along with the colour of make he was wearing.

'Please come by and see me in the park if you are at a loose end,' Gavin said.

'Count on it,' Anna replied then started walking towards the Sutherlands. She felt as if it was time for a nap.

Waking up in the shed was one of the worst places she had ever woken up, but Anna did not want to sleep anywhere else apart from with Jasmine.

Jasmine was flat out so Anna spoke to her. She said the same things as she had said before; she wanted to tell her something new. There was nothing Anna could think of. She had lost track of time. She didn't know if Jasmine had her dinner before she went back to the shed or if she had slept through one of the monsters bringing it into her. She went in to the Sutherlands' kitchen and saw it was 8.25 pm, she also gave the calendar a check that Candice crossed the dates off to make sure she was on the right day, she was, the sleep had not shaken off the foggy mind she had earlier and she wanted to make sure she had not missed a day. Her thoughts seemed to be a little scrambled; she did not know why she was feeling like this. She did not like it.

I knew I hadn't missed a day. The way I am feeling today I just couldn't be sure. I need to give myself a shake; I can't afford to miss anything. I will get more sleep tonight, with any luck I will be back to my usual self tomorrow.

Anna sat with the Sutherlands for a couple of hours then headed over to Billy's for her nightly chat to him. He was still up; both he and his wife were watching TV. She sat with them and watched the programme they were watching. Game of Thrones it was, although Anna had never watched it herself she knew that was what it was as some of her friends had spoken about it to her. After the episode finished Kate went to bed. Billy took Buster out for a walk, Anna went with him. When they got back Billy sat for a while in the kitchen with a cup of tea and a chocolate biscuit before turning in for the night. She didn't need to wait long for him to fall over; she repeated her usual speech to him and left for Graham's. Luck was on her side tonight. Graham was tucked up with the pretty woman lying in his arms. She parroted the one way conversation she had with him the last time she saw him then went back to the shed and had another sleep of her own

51
Wednesday 22nd January

Anna was back to her normal self with the fog in her brain lifted away, it was with her all day yesterday, but she managed to connect with her three people which was all she could have hoped for. She had way more than the recommended amount of sleep last night. Jasmine was sitting up with her back to the wall reading as usual. Eat, sleep and read that was Jasmine's full existence. Anna could not help but feel angry about it, it seemed such a waste. Jasmine could have been enjoying her pregnancy like most women, for her the only enjoyment she was getting was coming from the books. Candice came and went without a word to her captive. With nothing to do except watch Jasmine read Anna went outside for another of her walks.

Rooney sat at his desk. He was at a loose end so was re-reading all the notes on the two missing women; however, the only person on his mind was Katie Irvine, ever since he had met her at the vets he was smitten. He wondered if she was involved with anyone. There was only one way to find out, call and ask her out. He didn't allow himself any more time to think about it he lifted the phone and dialled the number he had memorised. The receptionist told him she would not be in until six o'clock for the nightshift; he thanked her and hung up. He had made up his mind he would go there in person later.

Graham McCartney was convinced he was going crazy, he was off work, all he could think about was Anna and the other missing woman; he decided to go to the gym to try to put it out of his mind.

When Anna came back from her walk she went into the Sutherlands to check the time it was 3.20 pm, no one was home so she went to the shed. Candice was in there with Jasmine, she was not there for any reason. She was talking to her as if she was her friend. She was talking about her family as if Jasmine knew them; Jasmine listened, although didn't take any part in the conversation. Halfway through a sentence Candice got up and left as if she had just remembered that she had something urgent to take care of.

That is one weird woman.

Rooney knocked on the door at the vets at 6.15 pm. There was no answer so he called the number for the vets. When the phone was answered he told Katie he was at the door. She hung up and went to let him in.
'Hello sergeant I hardly recognised you without your uniform. Is this about the two missing

people?'

'No and please call me Stephen. I am here on a personal issue and that would be to ask you to go for a drink with me please.'

Katie blushed and said. 'So you are asking me on a date?'

'If you are unattached of course,' Rooney said a redness crawling up his face.

'Yes and yes, how is this Saturday it is my weekend off.'

'Yes that would be great.'

'It's a date; do you have your phone?'

Rooney took his phone from his pocket a little puzzled. She took it from him and put her number in it.

'Give me a call on Saturday, we will arrange where and when,' Katie said with a wink.

Rooney left with a spring in his step and a smile on his face, he had a good feeling about her. A good policeman should always follow his gut.

Anna didn't go near Billy. She gave him the night off; she thought he deserved it with what was to come. She visited Graham again and spoke to Jasmine whenever she noticed that she was sleeping. She was trying to reassure her that everything was going to be alright. She didn't even know that herself. The only thing she knew for sure was that she was doing everything in her power to give this young lady a future with her baby.

52
Thursday 23r January

Graham McCartney was plagued by thoughts of Anna and Jasmine. He checked Jack Sutherland's address and van registration in his notebook, he had a feeling he was going to need them, a feeling that he could not explain.

Anna had a busy night tonight. She was going to torture her three connects until she was sure they had the message loud and clear. The problem for her was filling in the time until that time came. She went to May's and spent the full day with her, they watched a movie and some TV, and she even leaned over her shoulder while she did a crossword just like Frank did. At 6.40 pm Richard knocked on the door, Eloise and their son John was with him, they were invited in. Once they were in the living room Richard burst into tears and ran to hug May.
'What is going on? What's wrong,' May said hugging him tight.
'The results are back,' Eloise said holding out a sheet of paper.
'I don't need to see that I know what it says, something I already know in my heart.'
'Richard knew as much as you, he just needed to see it for himself. Come on Richard it is my turn for a cuddle,' Eloise said.
Richard peeled away wiping his eyes and nose

with the back of his hand, then took a tissue from a box on May's coffee table. 'It's official Mum.'

Anna stood mesmerised by the scene; the warmth she felt in the room lifted her spirits. Her elation only lasted as long as it took her to return to the shed. Jasmine was crying, not just crying. She was wailing so much so that Anna thought she was in severe pain. After a moment or two of listening to that gut wrenching cry it died down to a muffled sob. Jasmine lay down and pulled the duvet over her head. Anna had thought that maybe she had gone into labour and was glad that was not the case. Jasmine eventually came out from under the cover and started to read her book as if nothing had happened.

Hormones I take it.

What Anna had to do would be done later when her victims were asleep, she had a few hours on her hands so she went Hallington Park and didn't take long to find Gavin. Although it was dark the lights there did their job, she had no fear of going in there at night now, now she had nothing to be scared off. Gavin was pleased to see her and told her he was starting to get the hang of his power. He had been able to get two dogs to go come over to the burial site and do a little scraping. He assured her that he would be an expert in a few days and his mission would be done as well. She hoped he was right. She was starting to like him. She stayed and talked with him for a couple of hours, grateful for normal conversation, a two-way conversation.

It was 9.05 pm when she left Gavin and went to Billy's. He was already in bed and asleep, Kate and Buster were nowhere to be seen, out a walk Anna thought.

'Anna Anderson.' Billy stirred so she continued. 'Billy, I know I have annoyed you for a while now, I wish there could have been some other way to complete my mission, but you are my greatest hope. The Sutherlands will move the girl tomorrow, probably at night; I can't be sure about that, you need to be ready. The Innocent needs to be saved from the monsters. I have every faith in you and your wife. Take any measures you need to, please get the best result for The Innocent. You have done great up until now. I am so proud of you.'

Billy gave a slight snore and changed his position.

'ANNA ANDERSON,' Anna shouted as loud as possible and Billy jumped up from his bed and stumbled halfway across the room.

'Ok, Ok, I get it,' Billy spoke to an empty room.

Next was on her list of three was Graham McCartney, she had to wait for an hour to pounce on him with her words and didn't know if it was too late for this connection, she said what she had to say then left to go back to the shed.

When Jasmine finally closed her eyes and nodded off Anna started with her instruction.

'Anna Anderson.'

'Anna Anderson.'

Jasmine made no movement or sound; Anna knew she could hear her.

'It's me again. The time has come for you to be ready, take any chance you can get, you may not know what I am going on about, you will soon enough. Keep that name tag on you as soon as you wake up, keep it safe and be strong. Do you remember the code word? It is Rex; I am saying it now to alert you. Rex, Rex, Rex.

Her work was done all she could do now was wait. For the first time in as long as she could remember, she prayed.

53
Friday 24th January

The reason Billy was in bed so early was because Kate and him were taking his responsibility very seriously. Kate had come back from taking Buster his walk for the night before she took up sentry at the spare bedroom window. She woke Billy at four in the morning to take over from her, Jamie Mc Laughlan was coming over at eight, if he was needed before then he promised that he would be on call. Kate got up when Jamie came in to make breakfast and a lot of strong coffee. After breakfast she fed Buster then took him out. Between nine and half-past Billy and Jamie witnessed moderate comings and goings from the shed, a basin, a bucket, a carrier bag and what seemed like clothes wrapped over Candice's arm. Jamie was getting reeled into the scenario. After seeing the nearly full note pad with dates and times he was convinced that Billy and Kate were onto something big.

Anna was jumping from Billy's to the shed and the Sutherlands getting a full picture of what everyone was doing and when. She was pleased with everything she was seeing so far, she was nervous that an overlooked detail would scupper everything that she had worked so hard on. She wanted to say goodbye to her parents,

Tom, Rex, Clara and Jamez today at some point thinking that this could be the last day that she would spend down here among them. She made up her mind that she would do it now. Anna never for a moment thought that the Sutherlands would try to move Jasmine during daylight hours so with everything being taken care of by Billy she went to Clara.

Clara was in a quiet classroom, all her students had their heads down working hard, Clara was at her desk doing the same, marking homework by the look of it.
'I'm here Clara, I love you with all my heart, you were a great sister to me, I hope you cherish all our memories, take good care of my niece and Peter and always be true to yourself. I will miss you more than you know. I know one day, preferably a long time from now we will meet again. There are things that I want to say to you, but I know you can't hear me so I will save them for you until the time comes when we are reunited. I love you, bye for now,' Anna softly whispered the words through her tears and closed her eyes.

Jamez was at nursery. Her hands and half her face were covered in different colours of paint. Anna was not sure if she should say anything at all to her niece, there were no words to convey how much she loved this kid so she stood and watched her for a while, thinking of all the things in life she had to experience, the good and the bad. She knew that Jamez would be able to handle anything that life threw at her, her parents would see to that. Anna blew her niece a kiss and said, 'I love you sweetheart,' she didn't linger; she closed her eyes and went to her mother.

Her mother was in the kitchen doing the dishes in the sink, she was crying, tears were streaming down her face, she was making no sound, it ripped Anna's heart from her chest.
'Mum please, don't cry for me anymore, I am going to a better place where evil doings are nonexistent. I pray that my body is found and the people who killed me are punished so that you can put all this behind you and carry on with your life. I know that all this has taken a heavy toll on you and Dad and that you will never forget me, I know you will always love me and I you. All I ask is for you to be happy somehow.'
Anna walked towards her mother and put a hand on her shoulder, it went into her shoulder. Anna pulled away slowly, the feeling she got this time was of grief and melancholy, a feeling she did not like. She knew that this was the way her mother was feeling. She wanted to take all her mother's pain away; there was no possible

way to achieve it.
'Love you for an eternity Mum,' Anna said before leaving her and going to the living room.

Her dad sat in one of the armchairs reading a newspaper with Rex at his feet.
'Dad I need to go, take good care of Mum and Rex, Mum needs you more than ever. I love you and a piece of me will be forever with you. One more thing, I know that Tom will not be one of your favourite people at the moment because he cheated on me, but try to let bygones be bygones, he is in pain over this. I know that he regrets what he did, I have forgiven him and so should you.'
She bent down to Rex, the tears flooded her eyes, 'Where's my good boy? I love you Rex.'

Tom was last for her to say goodbye to, even though none of her loved ones knew she was there. It was important to her to see them one last time. Tom was working away plastering a room on his own, the radio was on and the volume was way down, not that it mattered he couldn't hear her anyway.
'Tom my darling, I need to leave now. I want you to know that I forgive you. I don't want you to be alone in life so please try to get over me and move on; you are a good catch, anyone would be lucky to have you. We will be reunited in a different place one day in the future

I hope, until then please be happy, that is all I want for you. I love you with all my heart and soul. I wish I was still with you so that we could have lived out the rest of our lives together, it wasn't to be.'

She stood and watched him for a few minutes with the tears blurring her vision.

'I love you,' she said again, closed her eyes, she was gone.

Kate, Billy and Jamie were in the spare room watching the Sutherlands' garden intently. At around two in the afternoon they started taking it in turns, two watching and one taking a break. Billy was first for a break as he had been on duty since early in the morning; he went straight to bed and got one and a half hours sleep. He took over from Jamie, who insisted that he didn't need a break so went and made them all some coffee and cut up the coconut sponge he had brought with him. They sat in the room having their refreshments until Billy spotted movement at his neighbours. It was Jack going to the shed with a carrier bag; he was in and out of the shed within minutes. It was recorded in the notebook.

'They are not doing anything until it gets dark, that's my bet, but we can't take the chance of moving away from this window. I'm sorry that I got you two into all this,' Billy said.

'We are all in this together now. I was a bit late to the game, now I'm committed to seeing it through, I only wish you had told me sooner,' Jamie replied.

'The only reason I didn't was I didn't want to sound silly, there are things I didn't tell you. I think now is the time in case you want to get out of this while the goings good.'

Billy shared everything, the name tag, the weird feeling and dreams He held nothing back.

'Wow, there are strange forces at work here.'

'That's what I said,' Kate agreed.

Anna chuckled listening to them talking about a strange force. She was the strange force. Her mission was in safe hands so she went in to hear what the monsters were saying.

Both Candice and Jack were at the kitchen table; Jack had a newspaper laid out in front of him, only looking up from it now and again to take a drink from whatever was in his cup. Candice was on her tablet, when Anna peered over her shoulder she saw that Candice was checking out baby clothes.

'Do you want to go over the plan for tonight one more time,' Jack took time out from reading to ask this wife.

'How many times do we need to cover it? I know what to do; we get her in the back of the van. You drive away, I follow you, you come back tomorrow and take care of that fucking shed, the house and anything else then you will join me next weekend with a bit of fucking luck.'

'Calm down Candice I only asked. We need to make sure nothing goes awry.'

'Nothing will.'

The plan remained the same since the last time Anna heard it. She was glad that there were no last minute changes. Everything was as it should be. She loitered in the Sutherlands' house; Jack went for a Chinese takeaway for dinner. While he was gone Candice prepared a flask of tea. When he got home she put Jasmine's dinner along with the tea and a bottle of water into a bag and took it to the shed leaving Jack to put their food out. After the Sutherland's ate their dinner and Candice had tidied up, she took the last of what she needed out to Jack's van where there was a large bean bag all prepared for Jasmine to sit on while they transported her to the house in Inverness. They had already decided to tie her hands and feet together in case she tried anything to escape. It would not be a comfortable journey for Jasmine.

Kate had ordered in pizza for dinner. The three of them ate it in the spare room afraid to take their eyes off the dimly lit garden. Kate went first for a nap then Jamie and then Billy. Billy could not finish his before he was woken up.

'Billy, Billy,' Kate said shaking him awake. 'It's happening. Something is happening over the fence.'

Billy only took a few seconds to digest this comment before he was up and in the spare room having a look. It was true, something was going down; Jack's van was reversed right up to the shed door. The view of the shed door was completely blocked from the watchers in the room. The three of them desperately tried to move position passing the binoculars from one to the other frantically searching for a peek of what was going on. Billy's adrenalin was pumping; all of what he had experienced all led to this moment.

'I can't see a thing; I'm taking Buster out to the garden, just a normal man taking his dog out.'

Anna was watching everything from everyone's position. It was a luxury that only she had. She flitted between the shed and the room to make sure that everything was being spotted. The van pulled out of the garden and stopped at the end of the driveway. Billy was at the corner of his house taking everything in. The woman came round from the back, took her keys out of her bag and walked to the pavement where her car was parked and got in. The van pulled out of the drive, the car followed it down the street. Billy rushed up the stairs with Buster behind him.

'Right come on, grab what tools you need Jamie, we are breaking into that shed.'

'I'm going with you,' Kate said. Billy knew that he would not change her mind so nodded his agreement.

It was 11.20 pm. There seemed to be no one else around, the rain came down lightly in tiny specs. None of the three had bothered to put a jacket on, that was the last thing on their minds. They raced to the shed. Both Billy and Jamie had torches and waited until they were in the Sutherlands' garden to switch them on, they didn't want to draw any unnecessary attention to themselves.

'This is it, no turning back; if we are wrong then I will take what consequences we get for breaking in here,' Billy said as they stood at the shed door.

Jamie did not hesitate he went into his bag and pulled out an axe.

'I'm doing this the quick way,' he said before lifting it above his head and bringing it down at the side of the bigger lock on the door.

He gave it four hard blows on either side of the lock, by the time this was done there was hardly anything left of this part of the door. If the door had opened in the way it would have been easier to kick it in from the point he was at, but nothing was ever easy. He took another few swings with the axe at the smaller lock; this one seemed to fall apart under the pressure. He firmly grasped the handle and pulled. The bigger of the locks still had a small hold, he smashed the axe on it another few times with rapid succession and the lock gave in. The door was half wrecked, it swung slightly open. Jamie's experience in being a locksmith never came into play. Sheer brute force got that door open. Cautiously they stepped inside, the lamp was still on. The small heater was switched off. The three of them stood there for a few minutes in silence, each of them trying hard to take in what was before them.

'I was right, someone had been kept here. I have a feeling it was Anna, why didn't I go the police awhile ago with this?' Billy asked.

'We are now, come on let's get out of here and alert them, these animals will be caught tonight,' Kate said as she turned and walked out the door with the other two behind her.

Billy called the number Rooney left for him. It went to voicemail, he left no message. He hung up and dialled again. He got voicemail again. He hung up and dialled again. This time a sleepy voice came on the line.

'Hello.'

'Is this Sergeant Rooney?' Billy asked.

'Yes and who is this?'

'Billy Barclay, you need to come quickly my

neighbours have been keeping someone in their shed. I wish I had called sooner, I needed to make sure. I think it may have been Anna Ross.'
Rooney was out of bed like a shot.
'Tell me everything,' Rooney commanded.
Billy told him nearly everything. He left out the name tag and the weird stuff, but told him they had a notebook with the comings and goings and even apologised for breaking into the shed.
'Stay where you are, do not go back near that shed we will be right there.'
Rooney's mind went from sleep mode to being as sharp as a tack. He called Inspector Halliday and explained what had happened. He told him to get a hold of PC Graham McCartney and PC Nicole McMillan and get them to Hallington Police Station as soon as possible they had their suspicions about Jack Sutherland, there was no way he was keeping the two young police officers out of this if this was really the breakthrough that they were looking for. He called Detective Inspector Norman Mathieson, filled him in and asked him also to go to the station. He threw on some clothes and headed out the door. When he got to the station he headed upstairs, he found PC McMillan at her desk. She had the car registration numbers of Jack and Candice Sutherland at the ready.
'Get an ANPR out on those right away. They must be found. Do what you need to find out if

they have any other properties and Nicole your and Graham's gut were right I'm sorry.'

Detective Mathieson arrived five minutes later. He made a few calls and got a team together to go to the Sutherlands' house including forensics and CID; he left to meet them there. PC McCartney was out of breath when he came through the door into the room where Rooney and PC McMillan were busy on the phone.

'Right, the Sutherlands have a place in Inverness that he inherited. It might be the only place that we need to concentrate on,' PC McMillan waited to say until Rooney came off the phone then handed him the address.

'Ok, Norman Mathieson will take care of the scene at their house and question the witnesses. Graham you and I are going for a drive. Nicole, Inspector Halliday is on his way, I want you to be here with him. You can keep everyone up to date with what is happening, I want everyone to be on the same page,' Rooney said before lifting his keys and nodding to Graham to follow him.

'The quickest route to Inverness is the A90 then onto the M9 at Perth. We will presume they have taken that route and go the same way,' Rooney announced when they got in his police car. He thought about taking his Ford Mondeo, but they needed the police radio for communication purposes.

'Do you think it is Anna?' Graham asked.
'We don't know. We should not jump to any conclusions, we will find out soon enough.'

Anna was in the back of the van with Jasmine. Jack was driving sensibly so that Jasmine would be as comfortable as possible, although that would be hard since her hands and feet were tied and they had put a gag in her mouth. Anna thought she looked terrible, as if she was in some pain. She still managed to lift her hands to her head and slip the disc from its hiding place in her hair. She gripped it in her fist as hard as she could.

That's right darling. You keep that safe. This will be over soon, I promise.

After a half-hour on the road, they heard that Candice's car was spotted going on to the M90 at Perth and that police were giving chase. It was the news that Rooney was hoping for, that the Sutherlands were going in the direction they thought they were going. Rooney put the foot down on the accelerator. He wanted to be there when they were caught. In all likelihood he would be too late for that. Information they received confirmed that Candice had stopped for the police after a five minute chase; the van was making a run for it. Jasmine was bouncing around in the back; Anna was deeply concerned for her and the baby. If Jasmine was not gagged Anna reckoned she would be screaming her head off. It didn't take long for Jack to admit defeat and pullover. The police swarmed the van, put Jack in cuffs and then opened the back door. A wave of total relief washed over Jasmine's face when she saw the police. A young female officer went into the van and took the gag away from her mouth.

'Oh, thank you, my name is Jasmine Brown, I have been held prisoner in a shed for months,' she uttered her first words to someone other than the monsters for months, it felt great.

'You are safe now miss, are you ok? My name is Liz.'

'I think I may have gone into labour.'

The officer untied her and nodded for the Ambulance crew to go in and get her. She was indeed in labour and was taken to the nearest hospital. Nicole called Graham on his mobile, once he had it on speaker phone she relayed everything that was happening; she wanted both Graham and Rooney to hear it from her.

'Jasmine is still alive. Nicole call Jasmine's parents, in fact send someone to take them to the hospital, they will want to see her as soon as possible. Let them know where she is, nothing else at this point, one woman found, one to find,' Rooney said.

When Rooney arrived at the hospital where Jasmine was taken, he spoke to a few of the officers who were on site when they found her. They showed him a plastic bag with a silver disc in it, on one side it said Rex and on the other it had a mobile number. He knew right away that it belonged to Anna Ross's dog and was now also hoping to have some good news about her. The young police officer who had been first in the van with Jasmine stepped forward.

'She told us that they murdered a woman in front of her in that shed, she said they hurt her dog as well. She has been in that shed for months. We are not too sure of her frame of mind.'

'What she said is probably true, this disc does belong to another missing woman, indeed her dog was hurt, that much we do know. How is she?'

'She is in labour, a hard one I was told, we don't know any more than that. The doctors are with her.'

'Thank you,' Rooney said and went to reception to ask to speak to a doctor.

He was asked to take a seat. With Graham at his side they waited.

'Sergeant Rooney?' a doctor in a white coat came to him 10 minutes later.

'Yes I am he. How is Jasmine?'

'As well as expected after what she has been through, she is in labour as you may know. She is having a difficult time and is asking for her parents.'

'They are on their way as we speak. When can we talk to her?'

'It won't be anytime soon, I wouldn't even want to hazard a guess. Now please excuse me I will go tell her that her parents are en route.'

An hour and a quarter later her parents walked into the hospital. Rooney spotted them at the reception desk and walked over to them.

'Sergeant Rooney, she has been found,' Sheila Brown said through her tears and came over to Rooney and hugged him.

'Yes she has,' was all Rooney had to offer.

The receptionist alerted the doctors that her parents were here and someone came and ushered them away.

'I pray that the kid is ok,' Graham said to Rooney.

'I'm sure they are in good hands. I want to know more about the woman they murdered; I have more than a feeling that is was Anna Ross.'

Graham let go of his tears, he knew her and liked her. He had a lump in his throat since he had seen that officer with the name tag.

Rooney put an arm around his shoulder, 'Better out than in.'

Anna stayed with Jasmine until her mother came into the room then left as she felt as if she was imposing. Sheila was extremely happy to see her daughter, after giving her a long embrace she concentrated on the job at hand, which was to help her daughter and the doctors to deliver her grandchild. Anna waited out in the corridor with Phil Brown who was pacing up and down anxiously.

Rooney and Graham went back to the car and called Nicole. She updated them on the search of the Sutherlands' shed and house. She told them there was no sign of Anna Ross. They sat in the car for two hours before returning to the hospital. A porter took them to where Phil was waiting in the corridor at Phil's request.

'Sergeant Rooney, I would like to thank you for bringing Jasmine back to us.'

'It is a member of the public you need to thank Sir, we got a call earlier and acted fast on it,' Rooney told him.

'Well she is back with us now, that is all that matters, and to that member of the public I am truly grateful, I hope to get the chance to thank him personally.'

'I am sure that can be arranged.'

It was a long drawn-out night; Phil was kept up to date now and then of Jasmine's condition. Graham and Rooney stayed there with him. Rooney wanted to speak to the patient, but knew that would not be possible any time soon. It was 9.30 am when Sheila came out of the room; her husband stood up and went to her just in time to catch her in his arms as she broke down.

'Anna,' she turned to see Ravi standing behind her, 'It is time to go.'

She wanted to know what state Jasmine and the baby were in; she had no time to appeal.

54

Anna woke up in what seemed like the same room as she had before with the white walls floor and black bed. The only difference was the colour of her make. It was lighter than before. She did not know how long she had been lying there, although she did feel refreshed. Anna barely had time to swing her legs over the side of the bed before Ravi came in the concealed door.

'Hello Anna, how do you feel?'

'I feel ok, what happened is Jasmine and the baby alright?'

Ravi did not answer; he went to the door, it opened by itself. Jasmine came into the room; Anna was confused for a moment until she noticed the make she was wearing.

'You didn't survive the birth,' Anna said with utter disappointment. 'I didn't succeed.'

Jasmine went to her and put her arms around her. Anna was surprised that two souls were able to hug normally.

'You did succeed Anna, my baby made it, you saved her. I told Mum to call her Anna not long after that I woke up here. Thank you.'

Tears rolled down Anna's face. She was happy that baby Anna made it, upset that Jasmine would not be part of her baby's life.

'Please do not cry Anna, I have accepted what

has happened, my baby will have a good life with my parents and her father. I need to go now. I am sure I will see you soon.'

Jasmine left the room only to be replaced by a face that Anna was glad to see, it was Frank.

Anna ran to him and gave him a long, warm embrace, she was still crying, they were turning into tears of joy.

'I have missed you so much.'

'And I you, my dearest Anna. Well done on your mission, I know you wanted to save them both; however, we don't always get what we want.'

Ravi gave them a few minutes to catch up then said, 'Frank it is time for you to go back out there, you can catch up with Anna when she also admitted to The Before.'

When Frank had left she turned to Ravi.

'Will the police find my body? Will those terrible people get what is coming to them?'

'Anna, Jack Sutherland came clean about everything, he has told the police where to find your body and yes I am sure they will get their punishment.'

'I have so many questions.'

'I will answer all your questions in time. First there is an important question I must ask you.'

'What is it?'

'The Supreme has requested that you take another mission, if you choose to accept it of course.'

Printed in Poland
by Amazon Fulfillment
Poland Sp. z o.o., Wrocław